Saying Yes
A Game of Seduction

Heather M. Miles

ISBN-13: 978-0997038705

ISBN-10: 0997038705

Dedication

This book is dedicated to my second mother and friend, Sandy. The
woman
who stands by me when I'm right, when I'm wrong and when I'm
somewhere in between.
Thank you for always believing in me.

CHAPTER ONE

One timid step forward on a stunning Prada pump and Eliza was engulfed in a new world, a forbidden world. She stood motionless as her eyes adjusted to the dimly lit room. The only thing grounding her was Nick's warm hand in hers. Her heart thumped painfully in her ribcage as everyone in the main room turned to glance at them. She felt the heat of dozens of eyes roaming over her like she was the newest delicacy on the menu. Since she'd never been here before, maybe she was.

Her breathing ramped up, pushing her breasts more tightly against her too-small dress. She wanted this…right? She'd pestered Nick to show her his world and here she was in the belly of a seductive beast. A world she sought entry into with the reluctance of a naïve child, but she was far from a child and far from naive. She'd had several lovers, but the experiences were limited – vanilla – plain and safe. She was here to broaden her understanding of the sexual world beyond her self-imposed boundaries. She was an expert in human sexuality, educated to know every facet of her degree and how it played out in the world around her. But a degree didn't tell the entire story of human nature. Nor did that knowledge translate into her own life. She'd been challenged to broaden her understanding and she wouldn't shy away.

The distinct smell of fresh cut lilies mixed with a subtle hint of vanilla wafted against her nose. She didn't know if it was the scent from the dozens of flickering candles that shimmered throughout the room, or the small vases of flowers that were centered at each table, but it was romantic nonetheless. She inhaled a calming breath and let it soothe the tension from her back and shoulders.

"Let's get you a drink, beautiful." Nick's breath was damp and warm against her neck, pulling her from the awe of her surroundings. He urged her forward with his warm palm centered in the small of her back. She nodded, straightened her spine, and walked more assuredly towards the unoccupied stool that was the farthest away from the growing crowd that lined the longest side of the bar. Eliza didn't know what the night held, and she wouldn't speculate, but alcohol was surely on the menu.

Nick held up his hand and a gorgeous bartender sauntered her way. Oddly she wished Nick wasn't standing behind her. He wasn't her boyfriend, not even her lover, but she'd never dare come alone. She needed the comfort of experiencing The Raven's Nest with someone she trusted. She felt the saliva trap in her throat, unmoving like a lodged gumball as she took in the view of the man before her. It was natural instinct to let her eyes wander lazily over the bartender's exquisite frame like a desperate teenager assessing him on superficiality alone…nothing about him was amiss from head to toe. Their eyes locked and he hit her with a knowing smile. She swallowed again and the bundle of spit unlogged, falling like a pool of heat right between her thighs.

"Champagne for the lady and vodka tonic with lime for me, please."

"Coming right up." He answered Nick, but never took his eyes from her.

Eliza set her clutch on the creamy wave of onyx that was lit from below. It was unlike any bar she'd ever seen. The sensual ambiance it created in the open space set an impressive tone. She tugged the hem of her obscenely short dress and slid onto the stool trying to position herself in the best light. She wanted to look sexy and had a great sense of style, but the dress was so minuscule she wondered if it could be classified a dress at all. Convinced by Nick that she needed to turn up the sex appeal, Eliza put on her favorite little black dress, only to be presented upon his arrival with the tiniest dress she'd ever seen. It had a designer label, but was more suited for a stripper. She obliged Nick like she had most of her life and pulled the tight sequined tube up her lean legs and body until she felt it was placed adequately enough not to show the lips of her labia or the pink of her nipples. She knew if she moved an inch too far in any one direction it would reveal everything. He'd been reluctant to let her into his private world, but now that she was going into that world, he was putting her on display. She'd never felt more self-conscious in her whole life.

The sex on legs bartender tossed a jet-black napkin with a gold raven insignia centered in the middle across the bar and set the vodka and tonic in front of Nick. He fingered the small black straw to the side and took a long pull from his drink. Eliza's mouth grew dry as she watched the display. A champagne flute was slid in front of her and she watched excitedly as he uncorked her favorite bottle of bubbly with a familiar pop. Her mouth pooled with anticipation. The effervescent fluid filled the glass, but never exceeded the rim. Eliza was impressed.

"Nicely done," she smiled, shyly, and wondered if she looked as out of place as she felt.

"Thank you." His green eyes danced over hers, then fell to her lips. She squeezed her thighs a little tighter and foolishly drew her bottom lip between her teeth. He sniggered. "Robert."

Apprehension settled in the middle of her gut and she wondered what to say. Was everyone forthcoming with their true identity? Or were alias' preferable? She decided not to worry about their protocol and answered honestly. "Eliza."

Eliza didn't know what the criteria was for obtaining a position as a bartender at a discreet, private sex club, but if they all looked like the god before her she imagined the benchmark was set somewhere between sexy and fuckable. He met the mark on every level.

Wanted – Bartender
Must be gorgeous, 10% body fat, gleaming white teeth set beneath pouty, kissable lips and six pack abs. Seduction and Charm a must!

He was a dream in a tailored black tuxedo, minus the jacket. His pants were snug against the bulge of his manhood and the curve of his ass. His crisp white shirt was unbuttoned at both wrists, with the cuffs folded up, loose around his forearms, just the way she liked. His hands looked callused from hard work, but were groomed and clean. Eliza wondered what it would be like to feel them caressing her wanton flesh. She felt the heat of a blush rise up her neck and took a sip of the cool champagne, hoping to calm her runaway thoughts. She was assessing him with the eyes of a lover and felt a little embarrassed. She'd never been one to ogle, but he was a rare specimen. His wavy brown hair hung just above his shoulders, caressing the collar of his shirt – all bad boy and sexy as hell. His verdant eyes spoke volumes above the curve of his lips.

"Eliza, if there's anything I can do for you..." He leaned across the bar, edging close enough for her to smell the mint in his mouth and the masculine cologne that caressed his skin – woody and warm. "And I do mean anything. Don't hesitate to ask." He winked and topped off the glass before stepping away to tend to the other patrons.

She imagined how nice it would be to feel his lips on her, his mouth suckling her tits and his thick fingers toying with her wet sex, but she'd never ask. She knew from looking at his hot ass that he would need to go on the list of guys she labeled "heartbreaker" and avoided at all cost. Hot, sexy, flirtatious, and fuckable equated trouble with a capital "T." Eliza had seen her share of men that fell into that category and wouldn't fall prey to Robert's overtone. She brought the sparkling liquid to her lips, without offering a retort to his comment, and prayed the effects of the alcohol were instant.

"I think you have an admirer." Nick chuckled under his breath and pressed a warm kiss to her shoulder. "I'll be back."

Eliza's heart thumped behind her ribs, nervous to be left alone. She turned and gazed into the piercing cobalt eyes of Nick Slade who was acting flirtier and more protective than usual. He was her best friend and confidant. Her go-to for just about everything and anything. They'd attempted dating as teenagers, but soon discovered it was a "no go" when their first kiss awkwardly fizzled and they moved on to greener pastures. He was always flirting with her incessantly, but he was really pouring it on tonight. She suspected it was hard for him to see her in such an unexpected environment – his world.

Nick was a manwhore. A bonafide lover of woman with an endless supply of pussy. Women were obnoxious when it came to Nick, throwing themselves at him mercilessly. He was as sharply dressed and as striking as the god behind the bar, nothing shy of pure sin. He caught the smile, eyes and petting paws of every woman in the room as he made his way across the space and out of Eliza's sight. She did a quick shake of her head. Every woman she knew was in some form of love and lust with Nick. But she knew what most women didn't. Nick wouldn't be tamed…couldn't be tamed. He was insatiable. Based on the premise of the anything-goes club, they probably didn't want to tame him. If anything, it was just the opposite. They wanted him reckless, willing to make their every fantasy come true and didn't hide their interest.

She smiled, this was the perfect setting for him.

Nick was the only person Eliza knew who had the sexual appetite and wealth to gain membership to a high-end sex club or even know of its existence. It took several attempts to coax him into bringing her. He had flat out told her "no" the first time she asked, and the second. When she purred in his ear at dinner the previous night and flirted with him endlessly, pawing his thigh and sucking on his earlobe like a sex starved vixen, he finally buckled. She didn't know if he was protecting his playground, or if he was afraid she'd be interested in participating. Either way, his membership at The Raven's Nest benefited her curiosity, professionally and personally. Not that Eliza wasn't aware that clubs of this kind existed, especially as a sex therapist, but this one was below radar and virtually in her backyard. Only the privileged gained access. She wanted to see, taste and touch everything, but the quicksand of her discomfort kept her locked to her chair.

The music that bellowed from the speaker's overhead were no less sexy than the club itself. The playlist was tailored to the environment, with a smattering of new artists and old. Adele, Sade, John Legend, Marvin Gaye and even a little Justin Timberlake. Eliza let the music take her where her mind wouldn't go, and with the sway of her shoulders and wave of her hips, she relaxed enough to look around. She wanted to look like she belonged. She was dressed to kill and tried to look like she was familiar with the protocol, but she was an obvious outsider. The veil of trepidation hung over her like a beacon for all to see. A blaring sign of her nativity and inexperience. She hoped the alcohol would camouflage it and took another sip of the liquid courage that danced and popped against her tongue like tiny pop rocks before settling in her anxious stomach.

The Raven's Nest was magnificent, richly appointed and sensual. Blood red velvet winged back chairs set around glass coffee tables, with vases of tightly gathered fragrant flower arrangements donned every table. The ceiling opened in the center of the room, allowing a bi-directional view. Eliza looked up and met the eyes of a couple staring down at her. She clutched a nervous hand around her glass, strangling it to her mouth, as her stomach wrenched like a vice behind her sequined dress. She didn't know whether to smile or turn away, instinct told her the later, but the champagne was making her bolder so she met their gaze head-on. She hoped to come across friendly, but non-committal. God, she was so out of her element.

The Raven's Nest was an interesting dichotomy of sex and sophistication. Well-known socialites, attorneys, and high-profile businessman were scattered across the room. Some she recognized, others she didn't. She tried to avoid too much direct eye contact but didn't want to come across as untouchable. She wasn't interested in throwaway sexual affairs, yet here she sat wondering if she could turn her mind off and let her body have free rein. The heated gaze of several men in the room bared down on her, warming her goose-pebbled flesh and causing the flutter of a million butterflies to invade her stomach. Two men across the bar raised their glasses her way in mock toasts. Eliza tipped her glass their way, then downed the last drop of brut.

Eliza scanned the dark room but couldn't locate her playboy chaperone. She let her mind run rampant and wondered if she'd been left in a dark, murky sea of shark infested water while he partook in a sexual tryst behind closed doors. Nick was experienced with this environment. She could bet that he'd be donning a crimson shade of lipstick on his return and it wouldn't be on his lips. She felt like waiting bait.

Robert, ever the proficient pour, strolled to her rescue all brawn and beauty, to top off her glass.

"Thank you."

"Anything you need, just ask." His tongue lingered lazily over his bottom lip, leaving a slick streak it its wake. Eliza's abdomen clenched as heat singed her insides. With a breathy sigh, she turned away. Was it hot in here? The temperature rose by ten degrees as he repeated the word, "Anything."

She looked up through thick lashes and offered a shy grin. She wondered if the bartender's words were meant as a statement or question. Was it an offer? What was the etiquette? Was he hitting on her? Or did he treat all the women with the same attentiveness he was showing her? She had a Ph.D. for crying out loud, but couldn't decipher the mere gesture of a hot man behind the bar. She sighed again and fidgeted with her shrinking dress. Maybe coming wasn't such a good idea. But she had begged Nick to bring her and now she'd play it out no matter what. Tonight she'd be the voyeur – observing the scenes and sights that had her mind antsy for knowledge. And next time, if she had the inclination and bravery to live outside of the cocoon of her accomplished persona, she'd be more.

She sat wide-eyed, taking it all in like an eager sponge. Maybe Eliza had read too many salacious books, or watched too many B-rated movies. She imagined The Raven's Nest a seedy hole in the wall, fraught with sexual deviants and sleazy dressed patrons. Not a posh, high-end club for the social elite. Everything she'd imagined demystified upon entering the lust laden heaven, dusted in wealth.

Eliza watched from her periphery as a leggy blonde in a black lace corset and tight leather skirt walked from one end of the room straight towards her. She eyed her like a tigress ready to pounce on fresh meat. She tried not to stare, but the woman was a sight to behold, extremely attractive with an aura that parted the panting, drooling male and female patrons like the Dead Sea. She was on a mission and Eliza quickly ascertained it was her. She closed the gap and moved so close that Eliza could feel the heat of her skin on her back and her warm breath against her ear. The smell of jasmine quickly invaded her nose.

"Vanilla," she whispered, tickling her ear and sending a chill down her spine. Oh fuck! What the hell did she mean by that? The silence between them seemed deafening. What was she supposed to say to that? Eliza felt more out of place than ever, but wouldn't concede as much.

"The scent you're wearing is laced with vanilla."

Eliza blew out a breath and felt a sense of relief wash over her tightly wound body. She looked over her shoulder at the stunning blonde who was even more beautiful up close. "Yes. Laura Mercier Vanilla Gourmand."

"Nice choice. Men are attracted to vanilla. It would appear it works on women as well." She winked and dazzled Eliza with a brilliant smile. "Eliza is it?"

She turned slightly and replied, "Correct."

"Wonderful," she purred. Her word was laced with rich honey, sweet and smooth, but the way she held her pouty lips in a firm line told Eliza differently. She was being sized up. "Since you are a guest here, you will need to sign this waiver. The privacy of this club and its members is vital."

Eliza glanced at the sheet of paper and then to the smiling Barbie doll who didn't know the boundaries of personal space and most likely didn't care. "It's dark in here. What does it say…exactly?"

"It says if I want to fuck you, you'll keep it our little secret and anything outside of here has nothing to do with what happens while you're within these walls." Her eyes narrowed into a teasing squint and she slowly rolled her wet tongue across her red full lips, leaving them glassy for Eliza's benefit. Her words were taunting and Eliza didn't doubt she did a lot of fucking with that mouth.

Eliza refused to act like the implication was a threat and turned her body, squaring off with the flirtatious blonde. "I understand, but maybe if you and I are going to fuck, I should know your name?"

The temptress brought her mouth within an inch of Eliza's and whispered, "Angel."

Eliza felt the tickle of a waiting giggle at the back of her throat, but pushed it away. *Total porn name…awesome!*

She took the pen from Angel's manicured French-tipped fingers and scribbled her name by the "x". Without thinking, she wrote her name as she did daily, Dr. Eliza Swift, clear as day in her perfect penmanship. Instantly, she wanted to scribble through it but didn't want to imply she had anything to hide.

Angel glared down at the loopy signature then back to Eliza. Her navy eyes lingered on her heatedly. The words grazed Eliza's ear. "Dr. Swift, the pleasure has been mine. Enjoy the night ahead." Every hair on her body rose like waking willows. She shivered and grew stiff as the words lingered like hot sex from the vixen's mouth.

Angel turned on a six-inch stiletto that she'd clearly mastered and sashayed out into the abyss of wealth, glamour, and raw energy. All eyes followed her as she moved back across the expansive space.

Eliza was not one to ponder long on the same sex other than the occasional admiration for someone's beauty. But had to admit the sheer sex appeal of Angel went straight from her parched mouth to the apex of her thighs. Embarrassed to feel so flushed with wetness, Eliza crossed her legs.

"I see you met Angel," Nick said from behind her.

She turned and looked into the persistent blue eyes of her best friend. He might be her buddy, but right then she wanted to push him to the floor and mount him like an animal in heat. Eliza likened Nick to a crack popsicle. He dripped with sensual heat, igniting a desire so intense that it was hard to break free. He left you jonzing for another lick right after the first taste, and before you knew what hit you, you were hooked like an addict to his lustful prowess and attention. She'd seen many woman claw through hell to get a chance with him, then crumble when that chance was nothing more than a one-night stand. She would never fall prey and refocused her attention to the buzz of sex and desire in the surrounding room.

"Yes. She's quite the concierge."

"Concierge," he grunted. His muscled chest vibrated under the small amused pleasure of her comment. "I assure you E, she's no concierge. She throws a lot of dominance around with other women, but she's submissive with men."

"I wonder how far she takes that role with women. She's very aggressive."

"Find out," he challenged. "That's what this is all about, right? Discovery? You've gained the attention of everyone in the club and could have anyone – male or female. Take your pick."

Stimulated by his words, curiosity won out over sensibility, and with a greedy smile, she stepped out on a limb and roamed the two floors to see what all the hoopla was about.

As she wound her way around the club, taking mental notes for her *research*, the intensity of a heated gaze pressed into her shoulder blades. The feeling was strong enough to make her knees go weak and her nipples harden beneath the fabric of her dress. Glancing back, she tried to see where that feeling had suddenly come from. But at the moment no one seemed to be looking her way.

Brow furrowed, she shook it off and took the first step up the stairs to get a peek into what went on in the club's private rooms.

Chapter Two

"Your four o'clock is here, Dr. Swift. Shall I bring him back?" asked Molly.

"Give me five minutes."

"He's an eleven," Molly whispered into the receiver.

"Let's keep it professional please," Eliza corrected her youthful receptionist.

Molly was charming and efficient, but childish and downright unprincipled at times. She'd been less than discreet on numerous occasions with her ridiculous rating system of some of the male patients. It drove Eliza crazy. But then again, an eleven...Eliza had to secretly admit she was intrigued.

Eliza slipped back into her heels. Having removed them between sessions was a nice reprieve for her toes. She liked expensive high heels, which weren't always practical, nor comfortable, but like many women, she was a slave to a beautiful shoe. These particular black pointed-toes Gucci's were gorgeous, but by day's end, it felt like the Chinese foot-binding ritual. Regardless, they made her legs look great, so she didn't complain. She just adjusted her toes accordingly.

She eased her chair back from the desk and walked over to the mirror, tightened her messy ponytail, and fingered a loose brown curl back in with the others. Her hands worked from waist to thigh smoothing out the creases that had formed on her favorite black swing dress. It hung comfortably against her lean frame, not too clingy and not too loose. Then with a twist and click from her lip gloss wand, she swiped the nude gloss across her lips.

She leaned over her desk to get the printed schedule. The four o'clock slot was booked to a new patient, Lake Mitchell. He didn't give much information about the reason for his appointment, but that wasn't uncommon in Eliza's line of work. Most of her patients rarely went into depth about their real issues until they breached her door.

As a clinical psychologist, Eliza had gained a reputation and notoriety in the field of human sexuality. She specialized in sexual behavior, the lack thereof, and a variety of other unusual behaviors. Homosexuals, heterosexuals, cheaters and liars. Those who don't prescribe to either sex or both. Those that were considered true sex addicts or the polar opposite - asexual. They filtered through her door daily. Some by choice and others by court order. She treated the cases that were deemed untreatable by other therapists, her referrals were vast and broad in breadth. No one was untreatable in her opinion and she had the heart to fight for every last one of her patients to see that they got the help they needed.

"Molly, please bring Mr. Mitchell back."

"Yes ma'am. Right away." Then with the breathiness of a prank caller, repeated into the receiver, "Eleven."

"I heard you the first time. I have a word for you if you don't stop it. It's "fired."

Eliza edged around her desk as the door opened and in walked the "eleven." Only he was clearly a "twelve" or better. Holy shit, Molly had her doing it now. Frustrated with the stupidity of her superficial judgement, she moved forward to greet him with an outstretched hand.

"Good afternoon, I'm Dr. Swift."

He extended his hand and enveloped hers with a firm squeeze. "Lake Mitchell. Thank you for agreeing to see me." A mischievous smile spread across his cheeks, and with an additional step he was in her personal space.

Her chest constricted and her breath caught in her throat. She tipped her head back and craned her neck to meet his eyes. She could tell he wielded his good-looks like a weapon. His breach was intentional and didn't go unnoticed. It would be the first thing she'd jot down in his file. In the first few seconds she surmised he was overt and arrogant. She couldn't deny, however, that he was captivating on first inspection. He could only be likened to kryptonite; easily debilitating to anyone in its path. He stared down at her, dominant and powerful, like a lion over prey.

She took a step back and released his hand. "Please, have a seat."

Eliza discovered early in her practice that a less formal atmosphere was more conducive in therapy. There was a deep, wax leather sofa on one side of the room and two plush down-stuffed chairs across from it, divided by a coffee table. The walls where a rich bronze with various pieces of art hung stylishly. It was an open space with tall windows on two sides. The sun beamed through the slats in the wood blinds and filtered late afternoon sun into the room. Her desk sat on the opposite side of the office, but she'd made it a practice never to sit at her desk for patient sessions. The towering superiority left patients cold and uncommunicative. She always waited to see where the patient sat, offering them first dibs, then usually found the chair that had the best visual and auditory vantage point. Eye contact was everything in assessing the validity of conversations held behind closed doors.

"Where are you sitting?"

"Wherever you'd like me to," she said, casually.

He walked over to the leather couch, unbuttoned his suit jacket, looking to her for approval. "May I?"

"Of course. Make yourself comfortable." She tried not to stare but lost the battle and watched as he disrobed the expensive coat, and tossed it over the arm of the sofa.

She guessed him to be about 6'3" in height, which dominated her tall stature of 5'9'. His smooth skin was perfect olive, with high set cheekbones and a strong, cleanly shaved prominent jawline. His suit was dark gray, clearly custom tailored to fit his toned physique with exact precision. His lavender shirt was pressed to exactness, with a muted silver tie that set the darkness of his suit off with expert style. Everything was clearly designer. He wore it as well as any runway model could. Lake Mitchell wasn't just hot...he was beautiful. That thought was quickly swept aside. He was a patient, not a conquest. It was time to find out just how fucked up he was. Everyone had secrets. She bet his were no less juicy and torrid as the rest…maybe even more.

His eyes were crystal blue with an iris malady. She'd caught a glimpse of it when he'd first walked in trying to over-power her with his dominance, but she didn't have enough time to narrow down what exactly the defect was. She wanted to say part of one iris was brown but needed to take a better look. She watched him carefully until he turned and beamed at her lingering stare.

"Ready," he said.

She put her jaw squarely back in place, unaffected, and reached over to her desk to get her notepad and pen. "May I get you something to drink?"

"Scotch and water would be great."

"I can accommodate fifty percent of your request."

"I'm betting it's not the Scotch." He chuckled.

Eliza offered a grin. "You'd be right. I have water, Coke, Diet Coke and Sprite. However, alcohol would certainly put a twist on my sessions. I wonder if my patients would be more forthcoming."

"It has been called the 'truth serum' for a reason. Since I have nothing to hide, I'll just have water."

"Interesting choice of words, Mr. Mitchell. I think everyone has something to hide, or at the very least something they'd prefer not be uncovered." She turned around to face him with a glass in one hand and a bottle in the other. "On ice or in the bottle?"

"On ice is great." He pointed to the glass. "You may be right, but I will do my best to answer your questions as honestly as I can."

"That's certainly preferable."

She filled the cup with ice and watched as each cube settled into the other. The thought of grabbing one and gliding it across her heated neck was appealing, but with the eyes of the man behind her watching her every move, she refrained. Eliza cracked the cap on the bottle and filled up the cup. She handed it to him and watched as his lips parted to take a sip. At his reaction of 'Ahhh…,' she turned and walked to the other couch.

She looked at her watch and wondered if she'd make it a whole hour under his intentional magnetism. She'd never felt so affected by a man in her life. She cleared her parched throat and took a seat, wondering why he was the only one with something cool and wet to drink. She looked up from her pad and paper to the simpering male who was working to test her will in her own office. But he wasn't the first man to try it, nor would he be the last.

"You look like you could use something to drink. Can I offer you a sip of my water?"

God, yes. "No thank you."

"If you change your mind." He tipped the glass from side to side. The ice clinked against the crystal causing her mouth to go from parched to spitting sand, but she still nodded no.

"If we can, let's get started. I'd like to get a little background information first, and then we'll go from there."

"Will I get a chance to ask you some questions as well?"

"Sure," she lied. There was no way she'd open herself up to any man within these walls. He was smug to think she'd offer him anything, but she'd play his games – at least for now. "By the way, interesting eye you have there."

"You like that?"

"I believe it's called heterochromia. If I remember correctly. It's a very rare malformation of the iris. Genetics gone awry…but rather cool."

"I don't know if I'm supposed to take that as a compliment or not, Dr. Swift." He cocked his head and smirked. "Are you implying that I'm genetically flawed?"

"That remains to be seen, but your eye certainly is."

"I'd be happy to let you get a better look sometime if you're interested." He took a sip of his drink and looked over the rim at her. His gaze was heavy with implication.

"Not necessary. I took the opportunity when you brazenly breached my space upon entering and again when I handed you your drink."

He laughed openly as she called him out on his initial inappropriate behavior but seemed genuinely thrilled at her perceptiveness. "Okay, Swift, what else?"

Eliza didn't miss that he'd dropped the "Doctor" in her name, but continued on with the preliminary questions.

"Age?"

"I'm 36."

"Profession?"

"Entrepreneur."

"Rather broad and vague, but that's fine. Drug dealers, pimps and prostitutes could claim the same." She knew he was neither, but wasn't letting him off the hook of honesty. She tilted her head and assessed what he'd make of her comment. Maybe he already had something to hide, as she had suggested earlier.

"Dr. Swift, if I rattled off every company I owned we'd be concentrating on my profession and my reason for coming is personal in nature. Let's just say I'm the CEO of a very large corporation, with national and international holdings."

She diverted her eyes from him to her pad of paper and felt the pride and happiness of a win. He'd taken the bait and answered her question with tangible facts. She was hopeful that he'd continue to be as forthcoming with the rest. At least she knew now that he was more than just a pretty face. He had business sense. And based on the quality of his attire, some form of wealth. The only word she scribbled under profession, was the one she'd fought to overcome, entrepreneur.

"Married? Single? Or, Divorced?"

"Single," Lake said, quickly, leaving no room for error. "I've met a lot of *right now's*, but no forever's. I guess that makes two of us."

She sat straighter in her chair and leaned forward with narrowed eyes and a look of true surprise. She looked down at her barren ring finger, then back to Mr. Mitchell. Wedding rings didn't always indicate whether someone was married or not. She knew this better than most. She counseled married cheaters daily. Educated guess?

"What makes you think I'm not married?"

"Are you?" He beamed from his seat like he'd scored a clear win. His eyes had her imprisoned as he waited for her response. One she'd probably do best to refrain from answering, but if this were a game of cat and mouse, she'd definitely wanted to be the cat.

"No," she growled, unable to mask the irritation in her voice. "I see you've done a little homework on me, so I guess there's no hiding that point. Yes, Mr. Mitchell, I've never been married."

"I am aware of your social position, Dr. Swift. It wasn't to be one of my questions but thank you for answering it."

It suddenly felt like the tide had turned, and now she was the one in the proverbial hot seat. She crossed her legs and settled back into her chair. What an asshole. Her muscles tensed and her jaw tightened. Did she know him? She didn't recall his name from a past encounter. He was so good-looking. She would surely have remembered meeting him before. She ignored his comment and continued on.

"Parents?"

"My mother is no longer alive. And let's just say, my father and I don't see eye-to-eye."

"Would you like to discuss the differences between you and father?"

"He's an asshole. Not much more to say."

"What would he say if I asked him the same question of you?"

He tapered his mesmerizing eyes and dialed in on her like a fighter pilot who'd just made his mark. "He'd probably use the same words I just did."

"Would he be right?" He was cocky for sure, but an asshole remained to be seen.

"I have my moments." His face eased as he delivered his answer, but his confidence never waned. "Don't we all?"

"Agreed," said Eliza. "Siblings?"

"None that I'm aware of, but not out of the question."

His father was not only an "asshole", but a suspected "player" as well. She hung onto the implication of his statement and noted it on the paper. *Dad – cheater?*

"Okay." She looked into his eyes, trying to assess the authenticity of his answers. "Children?"

"No," Lake said adamantly. Apparently trying to separate himself from the previous statement about his father.

He unfolded his crossed legs leaving them intentionally parted, then slid his palm slowly up his thigh. Eliza followed the move of his hand to the seam of his tailored dress slacks, resting her eyes on the sizeable bulge behind the rich material. He was being overt in his enticement, and she'd taken the bait. If she had to guess, she'd just been invited to try it out and wanted to roll her eyes, but refrained.

"Family questions…interesting," Lake said, drawing her attention back to his pert mouth.

"The people in our lives tend to mold us into what we are, or what we aren't, Mr. Mitchell. I'm interested in knowing what life you have beyond these walls, so I can better understand the things you say within them."

"Nicely said."

She made a small curtsey with her head. "Sometimes I say just the right thing."

"I'm counting on it."

More innuendo. She set her pad of paper down over her thigh, balancing it on her crossed leg, and looked at him raptly. Every response felt more and more leading. He was intentionally dishing out bread crumbs and she was ready for him to present the whole loaf. She'd let the flirtation go on long enough. "So what brings you in today?"

"I've had this…shall I say…obsession, or at the very least, fascination."

"Obsession is a powerful word, Mr. Mitchell. The need to possess something, with that kind of intensity, can be consuming for some people. Is your obsession with something or someone?"

"Someone." He ran his index finger and thumb along his prominent jaw, assessing her intensely. "She's completely unaware of my desire for her, but it's no less valid."

"It's not uncommon to want someone without their knowledge. Is she married, or taken?"

"My research tells me she's not married, but I don't doubt there aren't many men that desire her. She's intelligent and beautiful. I hope there's no one vying for her affection, but I can't be sure. Maybe it's what I want to believe so that she becomes more obtainable to me."

"Well-educated statements. Isn't it funny that we often want something we can't have? But you do believe she's obtainable so let's start with that."

"There are very few things I want that I can't have."

"As much as I'd like to counter that statement, I believe it's probably true." Lake grinned like Eliza just held up a score card declaring him the victor of the round. But Eliza wasn't ready to tap out quite yet. "However, when it comes to people, Mr. Mitchell, they must want to desire you in some form or fashion as well. Let's assume you're a smart businessman." He nodded with pride. She could see the expansion of his chest and bet his head grew. She imagined his cock did too. He was the smuggest, most conceited man who'd ever dawned her door. "You should know when it comes to mergers and acquisitions, even in matters of the heart, there's always a potential obstacle that can keep you from getting what you want."

"Obstacles are merely temporary road blocks. I believe I'm better suited to *claim* her as my own than any other man."

A flush of heat scaled her neck. She wondered herself what it might feel like to be claimed by Lake Mitchell. His desire seemed omnipotent if not a bit over-powering…cocky, to say the least. Her beating heart picked up pace in her chest and she could feel the moist heat settle in her clasped palms. She unlatched her fingers and toyed with a loose hair at the back of her neck, twirling it around her index finger with the nervousness of an old habit and quickly pulled her hand away. If she was honest, the idea of him wanting anything or anyone and not getting it, seemed foreign. Eliza knew a ton of good-looking people, even wealthy people with means and influence, that didn't get what they desired. They were alone and lonely, or worse, not alone and more lonely than when they were single.

"Claim?" she repeated for understanding.

"Yes, claim. I use it loosely, but when I go after something that I want it's because I intend to make it mine. Not temporarily, but permanently. I make sure everyone knows it belongs to me and me alone. I'm not the sharing type."

"No, I imagine you're not. But you're single, unwed and have no children. I don't imagine you're a virgin." This time Eliza smiled along with him, feeling braver as she regained her footing in their conversation. "If you went after every woman with the same fervor, don't you think that checklist would be completed by now? You are thirty-six."

"Touché, Eliza."

Lake reached over to the arm of the couch and pulled his suit jacket onto his lap. Eliza didn't know how to respond and didn't miss the use of her first name. They had twenty minutes left in his session, and the sight of him readying to leave unsettled her. She unfolded her knees, scooted to the edge of the chair and placed her pad and pen on the coffee table. She'd clearly done or said something that had displeased him and she wanted the chance to fix it. Eliza didn't know why it mattered so much to her, he was perverse in conversation and overt in his mannerisms, but for some reason it did. She didn't want him to think less of her. Innately she cared. She didn't let even the most fucked up patient leave upset if she could avoid it. "Are you leaving?"

"In a minute. Right now I'm just taking in the conversation and the scenery."

Eliza looked around the room confused when his words hit her squarely in the chest and she met his eyes curiously.

"I'm not referring to the office."

"Oh." She threaded her hot, moist palms over the bottom of her dress, smoothing it down her thighs. To counteract the awkwardness of her misunderstanding and dissuade him from further attempts to undermine her professionalism, she stood and offered her hand.

Lake paused, looked at Eliza's waiting hand like it was a work of art, then stood up and took it in his. The undercurrent of his eyes felt like electricity jolting her where she stood. He had her strangely befuddled. Every attempt to bring them back to the patient-physician relationship was thwarted by a look, a smirk or an insinuation.

"I'm sorry if I said something that offended you, Mr. Mitchell." His grip grew tighter over hers. She should have yanked her hand back but was mindlessly under an immoral trance and didn't. She was like a bug who veered too close to the blue light – death was imminent. Lake Mitchell wasn't an eleven, or even kryptonite. He was the devil in an Armani suit. She didn't know who he intended to claim but wished them luck, they'd need it. He was a formidable contender that clearly took no prisoners.

"On the contrary. This has been one of the most stimulating conversations I've had in some time. Your words were concise and well thought out. I admire your honesty and will take every word you said into consideration."

"If I can leave you with one last thing, Mr. Mitchell…"

He cut her off. "Please call me Lake."

She didn't. "People can't be owned. They can be enslaved, justly or unjustly. Your need to possess or "claim" if you will, the woman you're so enamored with, is a very powerful idea and something I think needs more discussion." She gave his hand a pumping squeeze and started to pull away, but his grip tightened over hers.

"That's where you're wrong, Dr. Swift. There's more than one way to be bound to another human being. Love for instance." Eliza fought the desire to look away. The palm of her hand warmed and grew clammy against his. "I look forward to exploring the argument of possession and claiming further." His face was serious, but there was a hint of eagerness and joviality behind the mask. If she didn't know better, she'd think he was talking about her. She pulled her hand away and brushed the back of it across her forehead. The uneasiness of their conversation had grown to new heights. Eliza cleared her throat and met his piercing gaze.

"Well...I. Look. Forward. To. It." Her words edged out staccato, bumpy and less confident than she'd have liked but her brain was frazzled and her mouth was parched. "If you want to discuss this further, feel free to make an appointment with Molly on the way out."

Eliza started for the door. She could feel her lungs seize, from the lack of oxygen. She didn't realize she'd been holding her breath. Her chest expanded and her eyes fluttered shut as she inhaled the much needed air. She turned around to face the dominant man who was hell bent on pushing the boundaries of her professionalism. He was watching her so intensely it sent chills down her spine. She met the flawed, but brilliant blue eyes of Lake Mitchell and wondered if he had this same effect on everyone. She suspected the answer was "yes."

"I'll do that."

She pulled the door back and watched as he put his jacket on, tugging his sleeves down at the cuffs and adjusting the collar of his shirt. One awkward lapel was flared at his neck and as much as Eliza wanted to fix it she knew touching him, even in the most benign way, was something she'd shouldn't do. He walked over and moved self-assuredly back into her personal space. His cologne wafted over her nose, drawing her in like fresh baked goods, just pulled from the hot oven. She inhaled him then realized his game and grew angry. With a huff, she took an obvious step backwards, opening the door farther so he'd take the hint.

"It would appear you have two issues, Mr. Mitchell."

"Lake," he reminded her. "What would that be, Dr. Swift?"

She pointed to his collar and he slid he hand around his lapel until he found the unruly culprit and righted it. "You could have merely fixed that."

"Yes, but I didn't," she said with an exasperated sigh.

He quickly feigned being heartbroken and pressed a finely groomed hand over his muscled peck. "You're killing me." He dropped his hand and folded both of his arms across his chest, challenging her for more. "What's my other issue, Eliza?"

"Now you have three."

He threw his head back and laughed heartily. The smooth baritone of his rumbling voice settled over her like triple distilled bourbon. Damn this was like a comedy of errors, hers and his. "You need to learn the boundaries of personal space and I'd prefer you not call me by my first name."

He shook his head and grinned. "I'll take both into consideration."

"Please do."

Lake Mitchell left her office and Eliza could swear he'd marked the room with his "claiming" scent. Or was it her that he'd marked? She stupidly lifted the top of her dress to her nose and realized it wasn't a dream. It was like she'd been encased in the aroma of woody patchouli and Irish Spring. She was glad he was gone.

"Holy fucking hell!" She shut the door and flung herself into the executive chair behind her desk. The casters spun and rolled a good two feet before she dug her heels into the carpet to keep it from traveling farther.

Who the hell was Lake Mitchell? She rolled back to her phone, picked up the receiver and called out to Molly.

"Go ahead and close up shop."

"Sure thing," Molly said. "Told you he was an eleven."

Eliza didn't even know if she could be pissed at the youthfulness of her comment and didn't chastise her. "We might want to consider adding a nine to the front of that. That was the most intense session I've ever had." She heard a faint giggle from Molly, as she hung up the phone.

She typed the name Lake Mitchell into the search engine of her computer. The first thing that popped up was tagged with a headline, "Billionaire Philanthropist…" Mr. Mitchell was the CEO and majority shareholder of Synergy Worldwide, a corporation based out of Kansas City, Missouri with global ties. He was on every important board in the metropolitan area and was considered the Midas of the twenty first century at a mere thirty-six-years old. Eliza didn't doubt it for a minute. Lake was a force of nature, an all-encompassing whirlwind of male sophistication, unwavering relentlessness and dominance she knew extended well beyond the boardroom.

She spent twenty minutes researching the man who'd walked into her office and professed to be obsessed with someone he intended to claim as his. *I'm not the sharing type…* The words hung in the air like low hanging fruit that begged to be plucked and devoured. She had to admit, if she was the one being claimed by him, she wouldn't want to share him either.

Chapter Three

Eliza walked out of her building and waiting at the curb, leaning against a coal black 911 Porsche Turbo, was Nick Slade. She didn't know why he was here, but was thankful to see a calming face. She rushed from the stairs and threw her hands around the neck of her best friend.

"Hey, Nicky-poo," she squealed into his ear.

He wrapped her into a warm hug and gave her an affectionate kiss on the side of her head. "What's up?"

"Nothing. It's just been a long day. I wasn't expecting you."

"Do I need a reason to see my best girl?"

"Of course not. I'm so glad you're here." She grabbed his hand and shook it with childish affection. "Let's detox with some wine."

Nick pulled Eliza's jiggling hand up and stilled it against his chest. When she was off kilter, he was her calm. It had been this way since she could remember. The strumming of his heart beneath her palm had the slow gentle rhythm of an acoustic guitar. They'd keep each other going during the good times and the bad, as children and now adults. Tonight he needed to soothe her ruffled feathers, even if the boundaries of confidentiality limited her ability to talk about her strange encounter with Lake Mitchell.

"What did you have in mind?"

"Maybe wine and an appetizer on The Plaza...Gram and Dun...outside?"

The Plaza was a beautiful area in the middle of Kansas City. It was famous for its luxury outdoor shopping, restaurants and swanky upscale bars. Every year hundreds of thousands of people lined the streets on Thanksgiving night as they lit the four block venue up with Christmas lights. The buildings twinkled and so did the people who considered it the start of the holiday season. It was a magical event.

Eliza's office was within walking distance, while Nick worked from a towering skyscraper downtown. It was the upscale place for the who's who and they found themselves there more evenings than not. It was no wonder she was single. She spent every waking moment with Nick. Having a man as a best friend put a damper on her personal life, because no one ever really knew the score.

"Sure…" He hesitated then cocked his index finger around hers. "But tomorrow we do what I want to do."

She wrinkled her nose and gave him a mischievous look. He was being vague, which was never a good sign. "Sure."

"I want to take you back to The Raven's Nest." The smile that broadened his face was reserved for goofy snapshots in one of those cheesy booths that gave you three seconds to pose and shot out a trio of black and whites you'd never show anyone. She wondered what was up with the childlike excitement.

She pulled her finger away and looked at Nick thoughtfully. She didn't know how far she was willing to go. It was one thing to watch and another to partake. "It's intimidating."

"You need to live a little. Take a risk." She felt like she was missing something. Like she should be reading through the lines, but the lines between them were always so concise. Or were they? She loved Nick, couldn't imagine a life without him in it, but this was flirting with danger. Surely he wasn't suggesting…them…together?

"I loved having you there. I was nervous about it at first, but the way you lit up…it was amazing. I don't think I've ever seen you blush like that. It was a turn on to see you so excited."

"Watching is one thing, but doing is something altogether different." Eliza hesitated. It was the moment of truth. Maybe she was reading too much into the offer of going back. "You're not suggesting…" She pointed to Nick and then at herself. "You and me?"

"Damn you can be such an ego killer." Nick ran his hand through his hair and looked at the sky frustrated. "Why can't we just have fun and see where it goes?"

Eliza bowed her head and contemplated what he was suggesting. It would never work, but she couldn't lose her friend – her best friend – her rock. The dreamy Adonis who indulged in her whims instead of slinging his dick around town. Well…he did that too, but damn he was her "everything" and she couldn't lose him. This day was growing more bizarre by the minute.

"I never know how to react to these little blips in our lives when you think you want us to be more."

Nick stepped forward to close the gap between them and Eliza stepped back. She hated herself for it but didn't know what else to do. It was an awful impasse. She gnawed the inside of her lower lip and stared forlornly into the eyes of the only man she cared about.

"E." The single letter was laced with sadness…a plea for understanding. But she couldn't imagine budging on something so monumental. He'd been fawning over her more than usual since that night and now the disjointed puzzle was finding its way back together. More calls and texts than usual, more affection, more protective…more possessive. It wasn't innocent flirting. He'd decided without telling her that he wanted more.

"What's up?" She needed to cut to the chase and nip this in the bud.

"I don't know." He stepped forward and she didn't retreat. "It's not about the club. E. It's about you and me. I wanted to explore some of your interests…together. Forget I said anything."

Eliza reached for Nick's hand and put it against her sternum like he'd done to her moments earlier. "Friends."

Nick rolled his eyes and pulled her into a jostling hug. "Infuriating." She didn't know if they'd fully reached an understanding, but for now it was enough.

"It's been a long day. I don't want to fight with you." He kissed her forehead and she softened in his grip. This was her Nick, her buddy. She'd fight to keep them close, but she wasn't his forever.

"I don't want to fight with you either," he said, accepting the small defeat.

"I could really use that wine now." Eliza stepped out of his embrace, not wanting to linger in his arms too long. She loved him, but didn't want to feed into his desires for intimacy when being friends was all she could offer.

"Wine sounds great. It's been a hellacious day for me. I have a business deal I'm trying to negotiate and it appears my competition has just been infused with some financial backing. I don't know who's stepped in at the tenth hour, but my people are working diligently to figure it out."

"Uh oh."

"Yeah, uh-oh's right. Lucky for me I don't lose." He bounced his finger on Eliza's nose. "Anything."

Nick's comment wasn't lost on Eliza. She was the one he didn't intend to lose. But she was glad for the diversion. Talking about his business deal took the attention off of *them*, and that's where she needed to keep it.

****

Lake was about to leave when Nick Slade pulled up to the curb outside Eliza's office and she emerged, descending the stairs of her office with style and grace. "Wait Sam," he yelled to his driver. He felt compelled to watch the scene before him, jealousy tightened his chest. She was so stunning it was all he could do not to leap from the car and scoop her up like a crazed caveman. He barely made it through their session. His ability to breathe normally was thwarted the minute he entered her office.

Her black swing dress hugged her firm breasts with precision then flared at the smooth curve of her hips. Her legs were long and lean. Every time she'd cross them or uncross them, Lake felt his body shudder with anticipation that would go unmet. He wanted to touch her…taste her mouth, feel her body pressed up against his. She wore very faint makeup, which made her flawless skin glow more brightly against the beam of the sun. Her hazel eyes were like rare gems. A kaleidoscope of green and brown that held him captive. And her lips…holy hell…her lips, they begged to be devoured, savored and taken with the passion of a man who was desperate to fulfil her every fantasy – and more. Her brunette waves were chicly pulled back into a ponytail, with a strand or two fighting for release. When she nervously twirled it between her fingers, he almost lost it. Her innocence was unexpected. Lake knew she was truly affected by him. He wanted to dominate her thoughts and eventually her body. It was all he could do to keep his cock from selling him out in her office. If she looked hard enough, she would know he failed.

Lake worked diligently to discover everything he could about the stunning woman who stumbled into his world. Stepping into hers was probably detrimental, but there was no other way. He had to see her. He had to be in her presence and wanted her in his. She was smart and witty, contemplative and thoughtful. Beauty and brains tied together in an amazing sensual body.

Contempt threaded Lake's nerves as he watched the playful interaction between her and Nick. Anger washed over him like a blanket of raw heat. He wanted to get out of the car and kick Nick's ass but sat idly and watched. He didn't know if their flirting was innocent or something more. A curl of his lip and a low knowing grin settled across his face when she pulled away from him. She was feisty indeed. Despite Lake's personal history with Nick, he knew Nick wasn't right for Eliza. He didn't know their history. He was only concerned with her future. She deserved better than the likes of Nick "fucking" Slade.

"Shall we leave or do you want to torture yourself some more?"

"Watch it, old man," said Lake, being pulled from his transitive state by his limo driver and confidant, Sam. "Take me back to the office."

The limo pulled away from the curb and the beautiful brunette was gone. Lake would have to wait until tomorrow. It killed him to think of walking away from her for even the briefest moment, but he had to concede for now. The thought of her had tantalized him ever since she'd shown up at his member's only club. He could recall every detail of her as she sat at the bar timidly taking in the surroundings. The chestnut waves of her long hair, the ridiculously small sequined dress that barely hid her perfect breasts and cute little ass. It made him crazy. He wanted to wrap his jacket around her and hide her from the peering eyes of everyone in the room. It was like watching prey being circled by predators.

He was glued to his seat, taking in every square inch of her. Watching her mannerisms, and reactions to the sensual scene playing out around her. She pounded back the champagne hoping for liquid courage he was happy never came, fidgeting with her hair, just as she had done today. She was sexy as hell. He'd never felt such an intense desire to possess someone in his life. When Nick came back and pawed on her possessively it made his stomach churn and his blood boil, so he left the club.

She was his obsession. She signed in that fateful night and he'd thought of nothing else since. Lake was used to getting what he wanted and that included Dr. Eliza Swift.

"Thanks, Sam," said Lake as the limo pulled up to the dark-mirrored skyscraper that housed his legacy, Synergy Worldwide.

Lake walked into the building and ascended skyward to the twenty-fifth floor. His secretary handed him several messages as he entered his office. "Hold my calls, please, Cindy."

"Certainly," she replied.

He walked over to the expansive wall of windows and looked out at the vast city landscape. With his arms confidently crossed over his chest and grin on his face he let the success of the day settle in. He'd finally met the beautiful doctor and had an appointment for tomorrow. He wanted to end the charade. He wasn't a patient – he was her future. If she wanted to discover her limits in his club, it wasn't going to be with anyone but him.

******

Eliza and Nick had just sat down at the table outside the restaurant when her phone chimed. Nick excused himself to make a call as she looked down at the screen. It was a text from Molly.

Mr. Mitchell made another appointment for tomorrow at 4:00.

Eliza swallowed hard at the idea of seeing him again. She didn't anticipate he'd reschedule so soon, or at all, after his early departure. He had a profound effect on her sensibilities. She'd never been so out of sorts around any man in her life. He needed to come with a warning label. "Caution: may be detrimental to flesh, eyes and speech." One touch and every hair stood on end. The sight of him alone made her want to liquefy and puddle at his feet. Talking? Forget about it. She barely managed to find her voice and when she did, it was a jumbled mess of randomness.

Thanks for the heads up.

11!

Grow up! He's clearly a 12. Now it was Eliza's turn to giggle.

13?

Unlucky number, and too high. He's cocky!

You like cocky. Wasn't that Nick I saw pull up when I was leaving? Hence...

Touché! See you tomorrow.

"Who are you texting?" Nick's voice startled her from her revere of thinking about Lake Mitchell. With the rattle of metal legs against the concrete patio, Eliza bounced in her seat. "I'm sorry, I didn't mean to scare you."

"I just wasn't paying attention." She put her phone in her purse and settled back into her seat. "It was Molly letting me know about a change in my schedule for tomorrow."

It donned on Eliza that Nick would probably know of Lake Mitchell. They were both high-profile businessman. But patient confidentiality kept her from asking. Nick was a relatively jealous guy even as a friend. Eliza didn't need to add to the stress of their situation. He was an open flame and she wouldn't throw gas on him.

The results could be catastrophic. She was already riding the edge of awkwardness between them, much more and she'd be the one to combust.

"Change in your schedule?"

"Yeah. No biggie. I had an add-on for the late afternoon."

"Oh-la-la, more sex talk for my girl," Nick chided.

"Despite what you think, not all my patients come in rattling on about sex. Frankly, it doesn't come up as much as you think. Because we tend to deal with the emotional issues that surround it."

"Bummer." Nick did a Popeye sweep of his arm and snapped his fingers.

"Oh, good Lord. Pull your head out of the gutter."

"Oh, I can think of somewhere else I'd like to have my head. Interested in knowing where?"

A flood of heat swept over Eliza's flesh like a tidal wave. Nick was never one to hold back verbally, but he was making her uncomfortable. She couldn't believe he was coming on so strong. She took a gulp of Chardonnay, grateful that she'd gone with the cool white wine instead of her usual evening red.

Eliza set her glass down and peered at the man who'd suddenly flipped the switch on the boundaries of their relationship. Nick could have the pick of the litter when it came to beautiful, successful women, and shy of an early mid-life crisis, she wondered where the hell his head was. Why her and why now? Nick's emerald eyes flickered sexily from across the table, and his mega-watt smile let her know it wasn't just innocent flirting. She acted unfazed and skipped coolly over his remark.

"Who called you?" It was a diversion, but she prayed it worked.

"My office," he said, easing back into his chair. "Apparently they've uncovered some details about my competition. I'll probably have to go back to the office unless you have something better in mind."

"Sure don't," Eliza joked. "But I will take you up on that date for tomorrow as long as you cut the shit. Dinner. My choice. Anything further will be at my discretion."

Nick leaned across the table and covered Eliza's hand with his. "Deal."

"Don't fuck up our lives, Nick." She needed him to get it through his dense skull. They weren't happening. She'd explore his private world, but her heart was off limits. She valued him above all others and wouldn't sacrifice twenty years of friendship just to see his gleaming eyes and slick tongue between her thighs.

"I won't but don't discount my love for you."

"I don't, but you need to keep your dick in your pants." With a snort and grunting laugh, she had her best boyfriend in the world choking on his wine. Eliza hoped it was the end of the discussion, but she knew better.

Chapter Four

The exhaustion of the day settled in after the first glass of wine like Nyquil on already spent muscles and nerves. She was never more thrilled to be home in the quiet confines of her condo. She nestled into the cool cotton sheets and tried to read, but after the third nod and second re-read of the same passage she quit fighting the inevitable and put the book down. The rich yellow glow of the lamp next to her bed cast shadows through the room. She pondered and replayed every moment of her encounter with Lake Mitchell. The thought of him coming back to her office tomorrow knotted her stomach. She couldn't decipher if she was anxious or nervous and figured it was a little bit of both.

She gazed across the room at the black wide-legged dress slacks that hugged her hips, the white French-cuffed shirt, and her red suede pumps. Classic and professional with a hint of playfulness. She'd rummaged through her closet for nearly an hour, which wasn't like her. She was usually pretty keen on what she wanted to wear and would rarely lay her clothes out the night before. She'd merely get ready and walk in and select whatever complimented her mood, and off she went. She had a great sense of style and a well-stocked wardrobe. Her choices were exceedingly good. Each piece was selected with one person in mind – Lake Mitchell – Billionaire Philanthropist. The man who purposefully called her by her first name and breached her personal space, throwing around bravado and sexual innuendo like a buffet to a starving woman. *Fuck him! She wasn't starving!*

Eliza flipped over with a grunt, bouncing on the mattress in a harsh tangle of sheets and punched her pillow three times like a prized fighter delivering the final blows to her competitor. The more she thought about how she'd gone to stupid lengths to impress that chauvinistic asshole the angrier she got. What did it matter? He was a patient for fucks sake and not the first to stroll in and hit on her.

He was no different than the other sexual deviants that dawned her door. He just used more sexually charged words: "Infatuation," "obsession" and let's not forget, "claiming."

Eliza turned off the light and with a drawn out sigh and drifted to sleep.

****

Eliza walked through the door of her office in high-spirits, renewed and confident. But was quickly deflated when the first person she saw wasn't Molly, but her mother - Yippee! Yesterday sucked...but this was worse.

Molly gave Eliza an apologetic gaze from behind her desk.

Sylvia Swift was a man-eater, never satisfied and always on the prowl. She'd never been the doting mother Eliza had wished for, not when she was a child and needed the tenderness of understand and compassion and it had grown worse as she'd grown into adulthood. The idea of hearing her blabber on about her newest conquest made the granola bar and coffee in Eliza's stomach feel like a floating turd in a slosh of acidic bile. Then she'd start in with the analysis of her life, or the lack there of. Where were her grandchildren? Was she ever going to settle down and get married? Who was she dating? Her mother's inquisition was like a game of Russian roulette, only you didn't wish for blanks, you prayed the bullet would come quickly and put you out of your misery. She wasn't a mother...she was a fucking assassin.

"Good morning, Mother," said Eliza with a fake smile she hoped would mask her disappointment. "I didn't realize you were coming."

"Oh, Eliza, no need for the charade dear, it isn't becoming. I am your mother and avoiding me just pisses me off. Besides, I haven't seen or heard from you since last Saturday."

Eliza had a standing date with her mother. They met at the same time and the same place every Saturday for what some considered mother-daughter bonding time, but it always felt like being strapped into an electric chair. You just didn't feel the force of the electrocution until she opened her mouth and embarrassed the shit out of you. "Are we not on for tomorrow?"

"We are." Her smile held a hint of sarcasm that Eliza didn't mistake. It was going to be a fun morning. "Can't a mother want to spend time with her only daughter?"

"Only child, mother," Eliza clarified. "I have my first patient at nine." She looked to Molly for confirmation.

Molly watched the interaction like a bystander at an awful accident. Eliza didn't know which of the two of them was more uncomfortable.

"That's right...nine o'clock. Her first appointment is at nine. Yep..."

Eliza sighed...*really*? Her receptionist couldn't have sounded any more staged if she were a puppet. A simple "yes ma'am", or nod of the head would have been sufficient. Clearly she wasn't the only one rattled by her mother's unwelcomed appearance.

"That's fine." Sylvia waved her manicured hand at Molly. "I won't be here long."

Eliza and her mother walked down the hall to her office. She flipped on the light and ambled over to her desk, while her mother busied herself turning each of the wooden slatted blinds so the early morning sun would filter into the room. What if Eliza didn't want the blinds open? She did want them open. She just didn't want her mother taking that liberty without asking her first. It wasn't a counseling session, though it might have been more appropriate. She opted for the sterility of her desk over the plush furnishings on the other side of the room.

"There," she exclaimed proudly.

She took a chair across from Eliza and smiled brightly, pleased with herself. She was dripping with every fine piece of jewelry she owned. Although the pieces were exquisite individually, the magnitude of seeing her draped in all of them was gaudy and overpowering – a total Sylvia Swift move. Her mother was stunning at fifty-five with short brown hair, blunt cut in a stylish bob, and the same hazel eyes she'd bestowed on Eliza. If she didn't know what a self-serving social climber she was, Eliza would almost like her. But that knowledge, combined with the fact that she sucked at parenting, left her cold in her mother's presence.

"So what's so pressing that it couldn't wait until tomorrow?"

"First let me say, you look beautiful today. If I didn't know better, I'd say you were glowing. What's going on in that pretty little head of yours? Something you'd like to share? Pray-tell it's a man."

Eliza hated being baited by her mom and sat idly contemplating her response. "I appreciate the compliment." She didn't know if she was glowing or not, but her confidence was high – she felt pretty. Her mother might be a royal bitch, but she had impeccable taste in clothes. It's one of the few things she'd imparted to Eliza. A sense of style...minus the necessity for overdone adornment.

"My practice is well and I'm well. Let's talk about you?"

"Let's do." Sylvia crossed her legs and strummed her manicured hand over the arm of the chair. Eliza could the see the bloom of excitement on her mother's face and heard the tone of her voice raise by an octave. "I've got a date tonight."

"Okaaaaay," she said, drawing out the "ay" and wondering why this was such big news. Her mother was always looking for the next best thing. What she never realized was the next best thing was her father, but that was long over, so now she was on a steady diet of wealthy older bachelors. Sadly, none of them ever stuck. Beautiful or not, Sylvia Swift was a handful. "Am I supposed to guess who, or do you plan to tell me?"

"Jonathan Mitchell, investment banker and widower, late sixties – never remarried. I met him at a fundraiser last week. We've talked several times, and he's invited me out to dinner tomorrow night."

"I'm thrilled for you," Eliza lied. "You'll have to let me know all about it."

"Why does it always feel like you're analyzing me, Eliza? Maybe I'm not going to win an award for motherhood, but I've always done the best I could. You've had a life of privilege – the best schooling, designer clothes and money. Your father was the bread winner but quit, entirely discrediting me. It would be nice to have an ounce of your approval for once."

Approval is earned; she thought, but replied, "I'm sorry if I've made you feel like I was discrediting you, mother. It wasn't my intention. It's taxing to hear about your dating endeavors. Settle down. Find solidarity and self-worth. You don't need a man to make you happy, I assure you. Happiness comes from within." Eliza almost felt sorry for her mother. It was odd to see her seeking Eliza's approval, when it was usually the other way around.

"These are different times, Eliza. I've always had someone caring for me. I don't want to spend the rest of my life alone. I could say the same to you. Find someone to love. For christ sake…get laid."

"Mother!" Eliza screeched. "I am not having this conversation with you. Thank you very much."

"You are a beautiful, well-educated woman. There's this thing called marriage. You know when two people fall in love and make a commitment to one another, then exchange vows and have kids."

"I'm aware of the term. Aren't you a shining example of why it doesn't always work?"

"That was a low blow and unwarranted. Your father and I loved each other dearly for almost thirty years. It fell apart. I wish it hadn't, but it did. And now he's with that twit who's only a year older than you. Don't use us as an example, Eliza. Marriage can be a wonderful thing."

Eliza's jaw almost hit the floor with her mother's admission. It was a rare moment when she dropped the veil of superiority and bitchiness to reveal she still had a beating heart.

"I'll keep it in mind. I appreciate the pep talk."

Eliza's mother waved the back of her hand to dismiss Eliza's comment. "How's Nicholas?"

"Why are you the only one who still calls him Nicholas? He goes by Nick, mother." She sighed and crossed her arms over her chest defiantly. "He's fine. We went to happy hour last night."

"I think he makes a much better Nicholas, than a Nick. Regardless, he's a good catch and comes from good stock. Don't discredit him as a viable life partner." Eliza pinched the bridge of her nose and shook her head in total disbelief. But Sylvia was on a roll. "As long as he's matured enough to keep his dick in his pants, or in yours." She winked for good measure "I'm good with it."

"Is that a joke?"

"No, it's not. He's got a good pedigree, and he's easy on the eyes. My grandchildren well be well cared for and good-looking. What more could a grandmother ask for?"

Eliza looked at the diamond encrusted face of her Rolex and prayed her mother's time was up. She didn't know how much more she could take.

Sylvia Swift was beautiful and well put together, dripping with wealth and class, but could be as crass as a two-bit street walker. Did anyone else have such conversations with their mother? Eliza wanted to throw herself on her desk and have a William Wallace moment…FREEDOM! But instead, she cast her eyes back at the woman who resembled her and addressed the Nick question.

"Nick and I are friends, mother. Just friends. Nothing more and nothing less." Eliza couldn't help feel a pang of doubt settle in her stomach. Her mother wasn't the only one shoving him down her throat. Nick himself was flirting with the idea that they should be more as well. "I'm not aware of his progression into a monogamous adulthood. He's always been somewhat of a 'player.' But that's neither here, nor there. It's not my place to judge him. He's my best friend, not my suitor."

"Then I suggest you quit spending every waking moment with him. It's hard to find a valid suitor when you're the arm candy for your best friend."

"I'll take that into consideration." Eliza stood from her desk and her mother followed suit. "The Classic Cup. Tomorrow at noon?"

"Of course."

"Lovely." Eliza walked her mother to the door. "Good luck with your date. What did you say his name was?"

"Johnathan Mitchell, debonair, business mogul," she replied with a broad, toothy smile, clearly hopeful.

"Any relation to Lake Mitchell?"

"Yes, dear. That's his son."

Stu-fucking-pendous. Eliza couldn't get Lake Mitchell off her mind and her mother was about to go on a date with his father. She had officially entered the Twilight Zone. "Good luck. Rumor has it, he's an asshole." *Or at least his son thinks so.*

"Being an asshole and wealth go hand-in-hand Eliza. Know it now." Her mother kissed her on the cheek, probably leaving behind a waxy red lip print and a wave of Channel No. 5 that blanketed the room. "I love you, Eliza. I'm not the enemy. I'm the only mother you've got. I just want what's best for you. It's all I've ever wanted."

"I love you too, mother." It's all Eliza could muster. She did love her mother, but her mother's love wasn't just stifling, it was crippling. "I'll see you tomorrow."

Eliza shut the door and walked back to her desk, stopping at the mirror to thumb off the uncomplimentary color of red that caressed her cheek like a bright flare against her olive skin. She studied her reflection, assessing herself against her mother's comments. The good, the bad and the ugly. Her mother had genetically gifted her with beautiful hazel eyes, multi-colored with flecks of green, gold and brown, yet there was an underlying sadness if she looked too close. Eliza sighed, unsettled by her mother today. Something was different. They'd almost had a rare genuine moment, yet Eliza wasn't going to fall for it. She steeled her shoulders. She'd spent too long building walls against Sylvia's personality flaws to let her in now.

Chapter Five

It was 3:45 when Eliza heard the faint, but self-assured baritone of Lake Mitchell's unmistakable voice from beyond her office door and sat straight up in her chair. Her stomach flipped with unwarranted anxiety. In a rare moment, Eliza grabbed an antacid from her desk drawer, chewed the chalky disc up and took a sip from her bottle of water. She was stupidly nervous and suddenly parched.

She could hear Molly giggling incessantly, high pitched and flirty. She knew the charmer was working his magic in the lobby.

Molly popped her head around the door, glowing like a lightening bug. "Mr. Mitchell is here." Molly's voice squeaked with excitement.

Eliza wasn't surprised that Lake Mitchell's allure extended beyond her. His charisma was like a tornado, taking down everything in its path. Molly was clearly in the whirlwind of his magnetism.

"You may bring him back." Eliza got up from her executive chair, walked to the mirror and did a once over on her appearance. She was reapplying her nude lipstick when she saw his reflection in the mirror.

"I hope that's for me." His smile was infectious; his words playful.

Eliza capped the wand and turned around nonchalantly. "No, Mr. Mitchell, it's for me." She walked over and proffered her hand. "I'm glad you decided to come back."

He quickly closed the gap with a step in her direction and accepted her hand. "Me too."

His touch sent jolts of electricity straight to her core – more charged than yesterday, if that was possible. His heat climbed over her hand and arm, leaving a path of pebbled skin in its wake. The woody scent of patchouli and a hint of soapy freshness tickled her nose. They stared at one another pensively…assessing one another, before Eliza pulled her hand away and invited him to take a seat.

"Where are you going to sit?" Lake asked, as he had the day before, and she replied with the same answer.

"Wherever you would like me to sit."

"Will you sit next to me on the couch?" He looked at her musingly, his eyes narrowed – waiting for her to comply or retreat from his suggestion of nearness.

"If that would make you more comfortable. Of course."

A wide, happy grin spread across his cheeks and she had to admit how nice it was to see the pride he took in the win. It more casual than she preferred with him in particular, but not uncommon. She often sat on the same couch with her female patients and a few of the longtime male patients as well. People blossomed in therapy when they felt like they were there under the guise of friendship and not assessment.

"May I get you something to drink?"

"Scotch and water minus the Scotch."

"Very funny." He was in a spirited mood and Eliza liked it. Intense or not, Lake Mitchell did have a less intimidating side. It was refreshing to see. "Sorry I can't accommodate the Scotch."

"The water's fine, Eliza."

And there went the air in the room, swiftly sucked out with a string of words and the use of her first name. She could feel her whole body stiffen and the air escape her lungs. She inhaled slowly and looked over her shoulder. "You like using my first name."

"I do. It's beautiful. I wish you would use mine."

He asked as much yesterday, but she hadn't complied with his request. He clearly didn't intend to comply with hers either. "I'll try to work on it."

Eliza turned back and poured his water over the ice, just as he liked it, when she felt the sensation of his proximity at her back. The heat and smell of him encased her like force field that was meant to keep her in, not close her out.

"How's your day been?" he asked. His tone was smooth like whipped butter – gentle and sincere.

She didn't turn to talk, but continued muddling around with the water that was already fixed. "It started like hell but has gotten a lot better." He could twist and bend those words however he wanted, it was the truth. Her mother's visit was unexpected, unwanted and just plain un-fucking-believable.

She turned around and he was so close she had to pull back, but it was too late and she spilled a tiny bit of his water on the front of his shirt. She started to reach for his shirt, but stopped dead of the mark. "I'm so sorry." She pulled her free hand back like it had just been burnt by hot embers and he started chuckling.

She shook her head and handed him the glass. "That's what you get for not knowing spatial boundaries, as we discussed yesterday."

"That was my fault?" His smile was infectious and exasperated or not, it was kind of funny. She put her hand over her mouth to stifle a giggle and looked into his mesmerizing sapphire eyes, honing in on his beautiful brown imperfection. It was a dangerous game and one she needed to avoid. He leaned down towards her face, and her breath caught. Surely he wasn't going to attempt anything so foolish as to try and kiss her in her office. But he stopped within inches of her mouth.

"Do I make you nervous?"

Eliza didn't have time to think through her answer, and answered honestly. "Yes."

"Why?"

"You're omnipresent."

You wouldn't have seen a brighter, more gleaming smile, if you were shooting a toothpaste commercial. His teeth were white and perfect like two rows of chicklets. He was devouring her words and in turn she felt like he was eating her too. She was the all-you-can-eat buffet of a starving man. She wanted to take a step around him, but his eyes had her locked in place.

"Nice word." His cheeks rose to meet the thick fan of lashes that feathered playfully with his delight of a liquid giggle.

"I'm glad you liked that." Eliza exhaled and edged around Lake, but he was so close it was hard not to brush against his arm as she made her way to the couch. Screw her pad and pen, she had a rock solid memory and needed to sit the hell down before she fell down. Her nipples were as hard as rigid peaks, brushing against her lace bra, and she knew without a doubt that the dampness in her panties wasn't urine. This was going from bad to worse.

She took her place at one edge of the couch and turned her body sideways with one foot planted on the floor and the other tucked behind her knee. Lake removed his suit jacket, took the opposite end, and positioned himself in the same fashion.

Eliza took a calming breath, but it did nothing to settle her nerves. She didn't know where to start. Was this even a good idea? Could she continue? Should she? She needed to refer him to someone else, but deep down she didn't want to. Why did he keep testing the boundaries of her professionalism? This was as fucked up as it got. She'd never been put in this situation and she dealt with some of the most deviant sexual predators around. Some masked in sheep's clothing and others cloaked in pure unabashed sin.

"Eliza." Lake started, his voice was laced with concern. The air felt thick and warm, the sexual tension ripe. "I'm sorry if I've made you uncomfortable. It was never my intention."

"Wasn't it? You call me by my first name, you have no personal boundaries, you're driving me insane with innuendo and you seem to have a way of turning my words into something personal."

"Your first name is as beautiful as you are. I understand about the personal space, but the allure I feel for you is compelling. The innuendo is honesty. I'd like to convey myself and my words more openly, but I'm trying to maintain some self-control. I turn your words into something more than what they are because I want them to be personal. I want this to be personal."

Her shoulders fell with her stomach and her hands balled together, threading her fingers together like a coil of snakes.

"Lake…" His name sounded out like the screech of a needle across a black vinyl record. Eliza couldn't believe her own ears. She had just given him the last pearl - his first name. It was like Christmas morning and she was Santa…with the big gift…and he was the giddy child that had just gotten what he wished for. He sighed happily. The curl of his mouth showed his delight. He collected the pearl and added it to the strand of giveaways she'd bestowed him in their short two-day encounter.

"Say it again."

"Say what again?" She knew she couldn't retract it, but didn't have to acknowledge it either.

"Eliza," Lake grumbled, leaning forward.

Eliza looked at him with faltering confidence. "Lake."

"Why was that so hard?"

"I need to refer you to someone else." She rubbed her temple in slow circles. "I don't think I can treat you."

"What? Why?" He put his glass down on the coffee table. The glass landed heavily and rang out loudly in the silence. "Are you attracted to me?"

"What?" She was so taken aback she jumped to her feet. "Ah…no…"

"Really…?" he sneered, clearly not happy with her answer. It was shit and it smelled like it.

"I'm so sorry. I'm supposed to be treating you, but I've breached a line here and I don't know how to recover."

Lake jumped up and growled. "You've breached nothing. You're the reason I'm here. You're my obsession. My infatuation. The person who's on my mind when I wake up and when I go to bed."

"Mr. Mitchell, you don't even know me."

"So now we're back to Mr. Mitchell." He threaded his fingers through his hair roughly.

"I'm so sorry." She turned away and started for her desk. So she could jot down the name of a colleague. The name of someone who could meet his needs. Help him obtain his desires.

"Eliza Swift, you better turn and listen to me right now." He wasn't yelling, but his voice was stern and commanding. Eliza had her arm around her waist. Her stomach rolled wildly like five class rapids, but she wasn't in the safety of a raft, she was in a kayak without a paddle. She didn't know whether to cry or throw up.

"Damn it, Eliza!" he yelled, halting her in her tracks. "You are not listening to what I'm saying. This isn't some bullshit joke, and I'm not your patient. Keep the money or give it to Molly. I don't care. I came here for you...*only* for you. Please..."

"I'm so sorry that I've made you feel like you have to salvage my feelings in some way. I've altered your position and reason for coming. This is terrible." Eliza was sure the blood had drained from her body, she felt like a ghost in her own skin. "I'm fine really. You should probably go."

"You're fine. That's what you're going with." He made his way across the room, tracing her steps. "You look like you're about to cry, and I'm not going to be able to keep from pulling you into my arms. I'm crazy about you. This is the most maddening experience of my entire life. I feel like I'm falling head-over-heels for someone I don't even know and you aren't giving me the opportunity to right this wrong."

"I feel so out of sorts," she admitted, reluctantly. "You don't know me because if you did, you'd know that I am a professional. I take this role as seriously as the one you have at Synergy."

He cocked his head and looked at her inquisitively. "You've been looking into me? I'm flattered."

"Now I've really crossed the line - from unprofessional to stalker...awesome!" Eliza needed Lake to leave.

"Yeah, well I know a lot about you too. But it's not enough. I want to know everything."

"Mr. Mitchell you really need to go."

Lake drove his hands into his pant pockets and stared at her, hurt, dejected and irritated. She didn't know what to say or do further to ease the tension between them. Eliza could see his frustration mounting but was powerless to change the outcome. She didn't want to let him leave distraught.

This was going to be one of the worst days of her life. First her mother, now Lake Mitchell, and to top the fucking evening off, she'd committed to dinner and The Raven's Nest with Nick, who'd decided to blur the lines of their friendship with sex. Fuck that! Nick didn't stand a chance and Lake was off-limits. Those grandkids were moving from *long-shot* to *when hell freezes over.*

She walked over to her desk, pushed the crease of her thighs onto the edge and sat with her arms crossed. She was in a haze of misunderstanding – his and hers, misrepresentation his and hers, and unprofessionalism – all hers!!! It only became worse when she no longer wished to fight her attraction and stared at him. He was a magnet and she couldn't fight the pull.

Lake was putting on his suit jacket and fixing his collar. God, how she wanted to do that for him. She wanted to touch him, breach his personal space…she wanted…to feel his lips on hers. She was taking the blame and pushing him away when all she wanted was for this to be something different…something more.

Then it hit her and her chest tightened. This was it. It was the last time she'd see him. Eliza didn't know if it was grief or anger at this situation that made her madder, but either way, it was over.

Lake made his way from the couch to her desk, and in true form, came as close to her as possible. His masculine smell and the warmth of his body was liquid heat over her flesh but she didn't move – she couldn't and wouldn't move. She'd already screwed this up so badly it couldn't be made right again. She was looking at his chest, not his face. If she could avoid his eyes, she'd be okay.

He lifted her chin with his index finger. The shock of his intimate touch made her shiver. "Look at me."

Lake's eyes were soft pools of sky blue – pleading for understanding. She gripped her desk tighter, hoping to steady her body and her breathing. "Tell me you want me as much as I want you? Tell me I'm not dreaming."

She could feel each word drip from his mouth like melting ice cream she couldn't lap quickly enough. She closed her eyes, unable to give him the words he wanted. It would end her career. How could she tell him that she wanted him? Did she want him? If she was honest, she'd say yes, but this was her office. This was her life, her career…her reputation. Maybe it was just physical? It was definitely physical, but it was more too. He intrigued her. His words held her captive like binding chains. She'd thought of nothing but him since he'd walked through her door. "I can't give you what you want."

Eliza's eyes were closed when Lake's hand cupped the nape of her neck and tugged her forward. His forehead dipped and rested against hers. She could almost taste the mint on his breath – wintergreen – sweet and inviting. "Yes, you can."

She opened her eyes. Her heart was thrashing behind her ribs. She needed to fight this. She needed to stop this now before it was too late. It was already too late. "I can't."

"You can't or you won't?"

"Does it matter? Both."

"I'm dying to make you mine. But as you've said, you have to want me too. I will never force myself on you, Eliza. I'm going to say this one last time. I came here for you, no one else. I want you and only you. Now you have to decide what you want."

Everything seemed so surreal. It was like a disjointed puzzle she couldn't put together. There wasn't an instance she remembered ever being in his presence, unless it was unwittingly, and she wasn't so delusional that she believed she was really his obsession.

He reached into his pocket and handed her a thick, expensive business card. On one side it had his professional information. He flipped it while still between her fingers. The other side had a free-hand written phone number in perfect penmanship. "It's my cell. Call me. Text me. Give me the words I'm desperate for. I came for you twice. I am officially no longer your patient. If you want me, you'll have to make the next move."

Eliza looked at the card and then to Lake who was adjusting himself in his pants. She quickly looked away, pulling her lip between her teeth. His lengthened cock was bulging from beneath his strained zipper.

Lake shook his head and groaned. "This is what you do to me. I'm a mess." He raked his hand through his perfectly groomed hair, leaving it tousled on his head. Her breath caught. It ramped his sexiness up tenfold. She wanted to reach over and touch him just to see if he was an aberration? She'd never encountered someone so spellbinding. Her palms were sweaty, her flesh hot – sticky.

"Please fix this," Lake pleaded.

"I don't know how to fix this." Eliza looked at the floor, dumbfounded. She didn't know how to handle the situation that was unfolding before her. "I'm sorry."

"Quit saying you're sorry. There's nothing to be sorry about. Come to dinner with me tonight?"

She looked up at him, with apologetic eyes. "I can't. I have a commitment."

Lake narrowed his eyes pensively. "Break it."

"I can't."

"You can, but you won't," he said pensively.

"You're right. I won't." She looked away.

"Will you call me later?"

"I'm not sure."

"Can I hug you?" Lake was already on her before she could reply. His strong arms enveloped her in warmth. She didn't put her arms around him, she couldn't fall prey to his desires. Everything was wrong…so very wrong. He kissed the top of her head, released her and walked out the door. She didn't feel lonely…she felt empty. Her time with Lake Mitchell was up.

Eliza felt bereft and conflicted. She couldn't even wrap her head around what just happened. She stayed glued to the edge of her desk, staring at the floor. The only thing breaking her trance was the chime of her phone. She put Lake's business card down and reached for it.

Excited! See you at 6:00

Perfect timing. The dagger she felt gutting her just took its final turn.

See you then.

Eliza turned to leave than walked back to her desk. She grabbed Lake's card. Using it wasn't an option, but she wanted to have it nonetheless. To send him a referral for another doctor, she told herself. She turned off the lights and walked out the door. The day from hell wasn't over.

Chapter Six

Eliza downed not one, but two glasses of pinot noir while getting ready for her date with Nick. She selected, then reselected her outfit, no less than a dozen times. In the end, she decided on a navy blue dress that hugged her body and draped off one shoulder. She paired it with some nude pumps and diamond studs – classic and chic. She didn't wear any other jewelry. Always mindful, not to over accessorize, like her mother who thought that donning every diamond encrusted possession made her look affluent, when it only made her look flashy and flagrant.

When the rap on the door came at 5:50 Eliza's stomach fluttered nervously with the wings of a million butterflies. She opened the door and there Nick stood looking as sexy as ever. Sadly, the sight of him did sparked nothing but profound admiration in her. There was no to hide the fact that she just didn't feel anything but friendship for the man who'd always been in some form of love with her.

"Hey, beautiful."

"Hey," she replied. "Come in."

Nick brushed past her, leaving her in the wake of musk and masculinity – classic Nick.

Eliza lived in a warehouse in the downtown business district of Kansas City. She always loved the idea of loft living in the city. When developers started the revitalization of the vacant downtown business to allow for loft living, she saved every penny after graduate school to buy one that overlooked the Missouri River. It was custom furnished to her exact specifications. Every detail handpicked for esthetic beauty, but with comfort and functionality in mind.

"Wow!" Nick turned and eyed her thoroughly, with obvious intent. "You look incredible. You ready to go."

"I am. Where we headed?"

"I was thinking Italian."

She didn't know why she asked. It didn't matter. The idea of eating made her stomach twist and roil. She nodded and finished her glass of wine.

Nick made reservations at a famous Italian restaurant just up the street from Eliza's condo, Garrazzo's. It was old school – classic mobster – in every way. The waiters were older, seasoned, and skilled in their craft. Most of them had been there since the inception, and all related in one way or another to the owner. The ambiance was "rat pack" cool with dim lighting and red linen tablecloths. Sinatra was playing overhead and Chianti was flowing like a raging red river. The smell of garlic was so strong Eliza could practically feel is seep into her pores when she first stepped through the door.

Nick ordered their best-known dish, chicken spidini, and Eliza stuck to the Caesar salad. Adding the anchovy as an extra barrier to ward off her unwanted suitor. He was pouring on the charm. It wasn't going to be easy.

Nick's phone rang incessantly and he finally excused himself to take the call. It was a nice reprieve for Eliza. She grabbed her phone, but it remained silent. Why she expected anything different, she wasn't sure, but she felt melancholy all the same. She wrapped her fingers around the stem of her wine glass and gulped the last drop. Two glasses at the restaurant, combined with the two glasses at home left her belly warm with the flush of tannins. She fanned her face with her hand and watched Nick cross the room with a look of frustration.

"I apologize, E." He massaged the back of his neck with his hand, smoothing the tightly corded muscles. "This whole business deal has become the bane of my existence."

"I'm sorry, Nicky. Want to talk about it?" He grinned at the use of one of the many pet names she used to refer to him. She didn't know any other way to act around him. It didn't dawn on her to change her behavior, but she didn't want to feed into his flirtation with wanting more from her than she could give. She was happy when he brushed over it.

"I think I'm in for a bitter fight over the Kansas City Star and its subsidiaries."

"The newspaper?" asked Eliza.

"The one and only. I don't know if you're aware of this, but at one time my father owned The Star. It's been struggling for the past several years, and with the onslaught of social media, the physical paper has become a dying breed."

"I can imagine. Everything's gone digital. I actually enjoy reading the paper. I didn't know it was in that much danger of becoming obsolete."

"We think we can save it, but someone else is making a play for it. They're coming hard and strong." Nick reached over and brushed his knuckles down her cheek. "I'll work it out. I don't want to ruin our night talking about business. What do you say we get out of here?"

"Sure, but we need to talk."

Nick sat back in his chair, sullen – dejected and she hadn't ushered the first word. "Does it have to be now?"

It couldn't wait. "I love you, Nick."

"I know you do. I love you too."

"But…"

He cut her off.

"It's okay, Eliza." He reached over and took her hand in his. "Say no more. I won't push. Let's just enjoy the night."

They both stood up and the effects of the wine settled over her. She wobbled in her heels and laced her arm through the crook of Nick's elbow. Nick, observant to her state of intoxication, used it to his advantage. He leaned over and pressed a warm kiss onto the side of her neck. She giggled and drew her shoulder up to her face as a shiver rolled down her spine.

"I like you a little drunk. I hope it works to my advantage."

She tipped her heat against his shoulder. "It won't."

With a groan from Nick's pert lips, they left the restaurant for The Raven's Nest.

It was Friday night. The place was packed with beautiful people, clad in finery and barely there attire. Nick held her hand as they made their way to the bar. The last thing Eliza needed was more liquor. But when the brilliant emerald eyes of the panty-melting god behind the bar grinned her way and held up the bottle of Veuve Clicquot, she beamed with welcome delight and nodded her acceptance. Fuck it! A couple more glasses of liquid courage and she'd lose her inhibition. She didn't need to go from relationship to relationship in search of the perfect mate like her mother. She could take her pleasures one day at a time and hope for the best. The idea of being blindfolded and fucked thoroughly was sounding better and better. The thought sent a sweet slow burn between her legs.

She laid her clutch on the bar and slid onto the familiar stool she'd previously occupied on her last visit. It gave her the best vantage point in the room. She could take in everything and everyone. She still felt apprehensive, but decided to play the evening out.

"The sight of your exposed clavicle is making my mouth water." Robert said with a wink. "You couldn't look more beautiful, Eliza."

She instinctively skimmed the protruding bone with the tips of her fingers and he groaned his approval.

She blushed. Robert was a charmer and a flirt. Oddly, tonight it put her more at ease.

"Thank you, Robert. You don't look so bad yourself." He pushed the leaded crystal glass across the lit bar and filled it with the liquid gold she loved. The effervescence tickled her nose as she took her first sip.

Eliza could feel Nick at her back and the pulse of John Legend's song "Tonight" in her ear. She settled into his familiarity and let the rhythm of the music take her where her mind wouldn't go.

"Do you want him?" Nick whispered. Eliza looked at Robert and shrugged with a tilted head. She didn't know what she wanted.

"Maybe."

"Then go get him, E." He pressed a tender kiss against her forehead. "There's not a man here that wouldn't jump at the chance to be with you. Take your pick."

She looked over her shoulder at the only man she'd ever really loved and felt a pang of sadness. He was freeing her and she could tell it hurt him to let her go. "You think?"

"I know." He whispered hotly in the shell of her ear. "I'll be back. I need to take care of something."

"Sure."

Eliza watched Nick make his way through the crowd until he was swallowed up in a sea of flesh and barely there dresses. She was once again left to take in the incredible view of sensual people, in the most sexually charged environment she'd ever encountered. The sex filled eyes of men slid over her. And for once Eliza wasn't shying away from their heated stares. She was out of her element but didn't care. The alcohol strengthened her backbone and fortified her courage. Tonight she'd play the sex goddess they imagined her to be, even if she were far from it.

She was about to finish her unneeded glass of champagne, when the brush of fingers swept her hair from her neck. She closed her eyes and leaned into the touch. She naturally assumed it was Nick until the smell of mint and jasmine invaded her nose and a feminine purr tickled her ear.

"You are too hot for your own good," Angel purred in Eliza's ear. "You've amassed quite a list of men who are interested in entertaining you; women for that matter."

Eliza looked over her shoulder and brazenly inquired. "Does that list include you, Angel?"

"It does. But tonight I'll relent to let you have a male's attention. Something tells me you aren't quite ready for the likes of me, beautiful. But don't doubt my desire for you."

Eliza squeezed her thighs together and a rush of heat tickled her spine. She couldn't help but turn around and face the temptress that was set on challenging her. Angel didn't move an inch to accommodate Eliza's face. They were a breath away from kissing. "You desire me?"

Angel moved so close that Eliza could smell a hint of cherry in her lip-gloss. She was surprised at how turned on she was by her. Maybe it was the erotic environment, maybe the music, but Eliza was so sexually amped up that if anyone touched her, including Angel, she'd melt. "I do. But tonight you're not mine. You've been requested in the "Sloth" room." Angel pointed to the upper level. "Black hall. First door on your left."

Without warning, Angel pressed her lips to Eliza's. "Don't do anything I wouldn't do…which is everything." With a giggle and a turn of her stilettos, the gorgeous glamazon walked out of sight. Eliza sat in her seat motionless. She should have been stunned by Angel's overt flirtation, but nothing surprised her. She turned around and Robert was leaning against the bar, looking at her with a shit-eating grin. "Looks like you have more than one admirer here tonight."

"It would appear so."

Eliza took a final sip from her glass then slid it across the bar. She had a lot to drink but her balance and wits were intact. Weaving through the crowd, she walked up the stairs in search of the room labeled "Sloth." Her heart pounding with each step upward. She was a jumbled mess of anxiousness and excitement. The word rattled around in her head. It was one of the seven deadly sins. Sloth was being emotionally and physically inactive. Maybe her illicit lover was trying to draw her out as a neophyte. She wondered if she had the balls to follow through. This was her chance to be more than she was before entering, her chance at discovery, and her chance to push the boundaries…no limits.

She had only been there one other time but knew the halls were color coated. The black hall was the first hall you came to when you ascended to the second floor. Seven sins on each hall of the four halls. The world narrowed down the dark hallway, pressing in around her with its line of doors. Most of the doors were closed, including the door she was instructed to find. Eliza was at her final destination.

She laced her hands together and brought them up to her mouth. She couldn't remember what lie beyond the door. Was it the suspended strappy leather swing that hung from the center of the room like a sexual amusement ride? Or the wall sized wooden "X" that had shearling padded cuffs to shackle your ankles and wrists. Eliza circled the soft skin below her hand with her fingers and licked her lips. Maybe giving up control was the answer. She wouldn't think, she'd just react to the pleasure she was given. A heated chill slid down her spine. Maybe it was the room with the sensual black lights and circular bed that could accommodate a crowd. Goosebumps settled over her flesh. If she only knew what she was walking into she'd breach the door with ease, but it was the unknown that made her nervous. Would he be a gentle lover or a dominant man hell bent on making her submissive? Was she submissive?

Slave to Love, by Bryan Ferry, echoed from the speakers. Eliza put her hand on the door handle but didn't turn it. Her pulse was galloping. She took a calming breathe, leaned her forehead against the cool wood and shut her eyes.

The graze of warm fingers against her back made her shudder. Every hair stood on end and her breath caught in her chest. The rich smell of cologne washed over her, but she didn't open her eyes. She wanted to let her sense of touch, sound and smell work for her, not her sight. She let her paramour run his fingers over the exposed flesh of her shoulder. She could feel the heat of his body edging closer and closer and knew instinctively that it wasn't Nick. Her pulse quickened and her mouth pooled with saliva. The brush of a nose and the feather of lips on her skin made her sigh as damp heat flooded her panties.

"Turn around." The unmistakable baritone of his voice resonated into the very depths of Eliza's soul. Her stomach fisted into a tight ball. She swallowed hard and took a shaky breath. Frozen, she didn't open her eyes and wouldn't turn to face him. If there was ever a time to wish for the power of invisibility, it was now. If it was a dream, she wanted to wake up. She knew it wasn't. It was him.

"You're not going in that room unless it's with me."

A tinge of anger replaced the anxiety she felt only moments earlier. Was this a set up? Had he orchestrated the whole thing? She lifted her head but angst kept her eyes forward. "Why are you here?"

"Because you're here."

She didn't need to turn her body to see him. He was a beacon in her periphery. She eased her head further around so she could take him in fully. The untouchable, "claimer of women" who was hell bent on testing her professional boundaries, was here to test her physical and mental boundaries as well. Since Lake Mitchell walked through the doors of her office, the "911" of dominance played a leading role in her every waking thought. He smelled distinctly of soft patchouli with a hint of vanilla, woody and sweet. She wondered what he tasted like…his mouth…his skin. He was so fucking divine she wanted to devour him whole. Her mouth continued to water as her eyes swept over his finely sculpted frame. He had on charcoal dress slacks that sat perfectly at his waist and skimmed his thighs, tapered at the ankles – very English, thought Eliza. His horse-bit Gucci shoes were polished to a high sheen and the top button of his starched light blue shirt was open, revealing a faint wisp of chest hair, sprinkled over perfect olive skin. She sucked her top lip with the tip of her warm wet tongue. She kept her eyes glued to the hollow of his throat, unable to meet the imperfection of two-toned eyes that awaited her.

"Why are you here?" she repeated. This time her tone was unmistakable. He'd gone too far

"Look at me, Eliza," Lake's husky voice drew her like a moth to a flame, just as it did every time he spoke. She followed the line over his Adams apple to his sensuous lips. Her breathing got shallower as she fought to control her heart rate. She finally made her way up to the pools of blue that were heated with intensity.

"What do you want, Mr. Mitchell?"

He groaned and grasped her chin with his thumb and index finger. "Cut it with the Mr. Mitchell shit. You know what I want."

She pulled her face back. "Actually, I don't. First my office and now here. How many lines do you intend to cross?"

"As many as it takes to make you mine."

"I'm here with someone else."

Lake crossed his arms over chest and stared her down with a smirk. "You might have come with Nick Slade, but you won't be leaving with him. He's down the hall in "Gluttony" sandwiched between three women."

Eliza sighed and looked away. It wasn't disappointment that had her in its grips, it was frustration. She wasn't mad at Nick. In fact, she was relieved. But she needed to leave. She wouldn't walk through the door labeled "Sloth" with Lake or anyone else and she couldn't just go back to the bar. It was an epic fail.

"What do you want, Eliza?" He closed the gap she created with one step. Her body ignited with the nearness, burning from the inside out with heated lust and irritation. They were walking a fine line. "Look at me, beautiful, and tell me what you want."

She gave into his demand but didn't give him the words she knew he wanted. She didn't know if what she felt for Lake was just fascination, infatuation or desire. She couldn't feign apathy and disinterest. She was affected by him and he knew it. He brought his hand up to caress her cheek. She didn't pull away from the intimacy of his touch. The alcohol was finally pulling her under, her defenses were slipping away and she was powerless to do any less than fold into the warmth of his hand like an affection starved animal. "I want to go home."

It was the only definitive want she could muster with one hundred percent surety.

"You need to stop fighting the inevitable." Lake leaned into her face, and she could feel the warmth of his lips next to hers. "This time I'm not going to ask."

Lake's mouth came down over hers, taking her breath away. His warm tongue slid smoothly over the seam of her lips and teased her tongue to play. Eliza no longer had the will to fight her desire of him. Wrong or not, at that moment, she wanted to give in. She needed his kiss. She had to know if what she felt for him was real.

His kiss was sensual and filled with unspoken meaning, unsaid words that lingered thickly in the air, hot and steamy…a balm of heady lust. It should have felt wrong, but it didn't. She should have pulled back, but she dove into his mouth with pent up anguish and unmatched need. She brought her hand up around his neck, tangling her fingers in the dark, thick hair at the back of his head. It was the invitation he needed. His body pressed into hers and the kiss deepened. She moaned into his mouth, unable to control the deep-rooted hunger… the yearning. It was the music, the environment and the hottest, most dominant man she'd ever met, pulling her under the abyss of lust.

Lake pulled his mouth from hers. "Sam's waiting in the garage with the limo. Go get in the car. I'll be there in a minute."

Eliza was apprehensive, but turned silently and walked back downstairs. Her mind was cloudy and her body felt boneless. Tonight she would pass on "Sloth" for something even more unknown – a ride home with the devil who was infiltrating her very soul. She couldn't be claimed, but her body sure could.

She gave Robert a half-hearted smile as she walked past the bar, and he reciprocated with a wink and wave of his hand. When she reached the elevator, she finally exhaled. It descended and the doors parted. Fifteen feet in front of her was an expansive black limo with an older gentleman leaning against the rear passenger door. He opened the door like he knew she was the intended recipient of his good graces. She drew her lip between her teeth nervously and walked forward.

"Good evening, Eliza. I'm Sam." He dipped his head and extended his hand. He knew her name. Normally that fact alone would have shocked her, but she was dealing with Lake Mitchell. Nothing surprised her anymore. She accepted his hand and refrained from repeating her name.

"Mr. Mitchell said that you'd take me home."

"Of course." His smile was soft and genuine. "Mr. Mitchell should be here shortly. Go ahead and get in. We'll be off soon."

Sam helped her into the car. The door shut and darkness engulfed the space. The tinted windows pushing out the light. Eliza slid all the way to the other side of the cool leather seat and rested her head against the glass. She was fighting to keep her eyes open. She finally let them close and the events of the day played back in her head like a Lifetime Movie – all drama and suspense. Tomorrow things would seem clearer. She might regret it in the morning, but kissing Lake was nothing shy of magic.

Chapter Seven

Lake watched Eliza walk through the sea of gawking men and felt the low thunder of edginess slide over him like itchy wool. He hated having anyone look at what he considered his. She didn't know it and hadn't succumbed to him, but he wouldn't stop until the statement was true. She waved to Robert, his bar manager and out the door she went. The two had apparently made some connection, but Lake thought nothing of the innocent flirtation. Robert made his money off his good looks and charm, and Eliza would be no less enamored of him than any other female. He was Lake's most loyal employee and the one that sent him the text regarding Eliza's presence at the club. He had left specific instructions with his staff that if Eliza showed up again, he was to be notified immediately.

Two words flashed on his screen – *"She's here."* Lake gripped his phone so tight he thought it would shatter in his hand. The business meeting he was in came to an abrupt end with his departure. He wanted to get to the club before she crossed the line into the seediness of exploration with someone other than himself. If she wanted those experiences, she'd get them but it would be with him and no one else.

Lake walked in calm and collected, but it was a façade. His blood was boiling and his hands were balled into fists. He prayed he wasn't too late. When he'd walked through the door, Robert pointed to the upper level – the halls – the rooms. He bolted through the crowded room, shrugging off the eyes of the members and took the stairs two-by-two to find her. Lake prayed that he would be able to stop her from making a mistake that would crush them both.

Now that Eliza was safely away from this particular room, Lake looked at the door labeled "Sloth" and stepped into the dimly lit space, itching to know who had requested her. Candles flickered like teasing licks of gold against the walls. Lake's stomach tightened and seized at the sight. Craig McKinnon was standing in the corner, patiently waiting for Eliza's arrival. He wasn't expecting Lake. He donned jet black leather pants, heavy biker boots, and no shirt. Chains were suspended from the ceiling and a table of paraphernalia for bondage and submission lined the wall. The thought of seeing Eliza whipped with a cat-o-nine tail or something worse made his heart ache painfully in his chest.

"You'll have to pick someone else, Sam. That one's mine."

"Of course. She looks tasty. I'm jealous."

"I've yet to find out, but she's off limits. Make it known." Lake hated to admit that he'd yet to conquer the beautiful brunette, but if anyone touched her, they were as good as dead.

Craig McKinnon, growled with disappointment and threw the silk scarf he'd intended for Eliza on the floor. Lake felt his fists tighten, but closed the door and let it go.

He walked through the crowd and allowed a few customary handshakes as he made his way towards the door. He reached across the bar and pressed a folded hundred dollar bill into Roberts's palm. "Thanks."

"She's a hot one."

"Don't forget your place, Rob," Lake barked.

Robert grinned and held up his palms in retreat. "Can't blame a man for looking."

"Yeah, well, just make sure it stays at that." Robert chuckled and handed his boss a shot. Lake threw it back and headed out the door in search of the woman who had him on the edge of his sanity.

When Lake got out of the elevator, Sam was waiting at the door of the car. He didn't speak to Lake but nodded in affirmation that Eliza was inside the car. For the first time in the last thirty minutes Lake sighed with relief.

Sam opened the door for Lake and Eliza lifted her head briefly from the window to look at him then leaned back into it. She was drunk. It pissed Lake off to see her like that. Why the fuck had Nick allowed her to drink that much? His contempt for Nick Slade was at an all-time high.

They exited the garage and the city lights filtered into the car. Lake reached over and put his hand over the top of hers. Mad or not, he wanted to be close to her, needed to touch her. She lifted her head and looked at him with sleepy hazel eyes. His anger softened with her gaze. It was a genuine look of admiration. Tonight he was her knight in shining armor. Tomorrow he hoped to be more.

"Thank you."

"You're welcome." Lake didn't know what she was appreciative of and didn't care. He was just happy she was safe and in the confines of his car.

Lake reached over and feathered her cheek with the back of his knuckles. She was so beautiful. It took his breath away. Her eyes fluttered shut and then opened – glassy and watery like she was on the verge of tears. His heart plummeted. She looked sad. The thought of her broken in any way made his heart ache. He slid closer and scooped her up into his arms, cradling her to his chest…hugging her…holding her. God, this beautiful, delicate, creature was going to be the death of him.

They pulled up to her condo in the warehouse district of downtown Kansas City. Lake knew where she lived, but he'd never been in the building. The information he'd obtained on her gave him the address. She lived in unit four hundred. Based on visual alone, it was four stories. He assumed it was on the fourth floor, but he'd have to wing it.

Sam came around the car and opened the door. He reached down to grab Eliza from Lake's lap, but he shook his head. He'd barely had her in his arms for less than ten minutes and wasn't ready to relinquish her yet. Even to his most trusted friend. With Eliza still cradled to his chest, he slid off the seat and told Sam to wait with the limo.

There were only four units on each floor of the massive building, which stunned him. The units had to be impressive in size.

"I can walk, Lake," Eliza whispered warmly in his ear. Her arms were locked around his neck and her cheek made purchase on his shoulder. Her tired, intoxicated eyes were heavy-lidded, but held no less magic for Lake.

"I'm sure you can, but I like carrying you. Where's your key?" She jiggled the small clutch and reached for her keys.

He bent down with her still holding on and opened the door. It was magnificent. He wanted to roam, but knew it would have to be another time. She needed sleep.

"Where's your bedroom?"

She pointed to the right. "Last door."

He stepped into the room, reached over and turned on the bedside lamp. The room filled with soft light, casting a spell of romance in the beautiful space. He walked her over to the bed and set her down on the edge.

"You look stunning tonight."

She had her bottom lip nervously tucked between her teeth, but managed a shy smile. Her innocence never ceased to amaze him. His gaze lowered to the shallow contractions of her chest as she worked to control her breathing in the charged air. He had to fight the increasing urge to kiss her again.

Instead he kneeled down and slipped the nude high-heeled pumps from her feet and watched as she wiggled her brightly painted toes. He licked his lips and sighed. He lifted her dainty feet to his thighs to massage them. Her face lit up with satisfaction, then with a devilish sigh, she flung her body back onto the bed with a bounce. Her arms flew to the sides and she settled lazily into the billowy comforter. It was an awkward vantage point. He could see up her dress. A glimmer of lace peeked from beneath the hem. His breath stalled and his cock thickened against his zipper. *Holy fuckin hell!* He released her feet and hopped up. It was a cruel test of self-control. Heat flowed over his flesh like slow lava as he stood over her. She was sexy, languid and soft. And completely unaware.

His mind ran rampant, a whirlwind of hot desire. Not touching her was proving to be more torturous than he anticipated. This needed to be a get in and get out mission, but was proving to be more of a "mission impossible." He wanted her conscious and aware of every touch, every kiss. He wouldn't have it any other way.

The fabric and fit of her dress did little to hide the leanness and definition of her fantastic body. Lake grabbed her hands and eased her up so she was standing.

"I know you're tired, sleepy head. Let's get you under the covers." He leaned around her and started unloading the plethora of pillows that lined her headboard. It was showroom perfect and expertly made in varying tones of white and cream. The plush, down-feathered duvet was soft and luxurious under his fingertips. He had the bed partially disassembled when Eliza threaded her fingers around his elbow and leaned her forehead onto his arm. His breath caught in his throat at the sight of her, the feel of her – her warmth and the smell of her perfume was making him crazy with lust. He dug his hands into the back of her hair and kissed the top of her head. "Almost there, baby."

She looked up and knocked him back with a wide grin. "You called me, baby?"

He lifted her head up, so he could see her face. "I did."

"I liked it."

"Me too." He turned to face her. "Dress or no dress?" He didn't want to be so forward to just start disrobing her.

Eliza cocked her head and assessed him with greedy eyes. Heat singed his insides like red hot embers. He went from semi-hard to rock hard with the bat of her dark lush eyelashes. Holy fuck this was brutal. She looked ethereal. Lake felt raw with carnal desire. He took a deep cathartic breath and waited for her answer.

"No dress." She lifted her arms like a child for him to take it off. Lake shook his head and grinned, barely able to swallow. He was so sexually hungry, he wanted to devour her whole. *Vixen!* He slid his fingers under the hem and pulled the soft dress up her thighs and hips, over her small waist and beautiful breasts, until it was off. The material was silky in the palm of his hand. The smell of her perfume was an intoxicating pull against his senses. He couldn't resist drawing the fabric to his nose. A myriad of scents mingled together to intoxicate him further.

Eliza dropped her forearms over the top of her head in the most seductive pose Lake had ever seen. His cock jerked in his pants. What the fuck! She was playing a daring game with a potent competitor, she just didn't know it.

She had on the skimpiest bra and panty set Lake thought he'd ever seen. He made a bold move and looked around her back at her perfect ass. If she wanted to be seen, he wouldn't deny her his eyes. The faint string of lace that caressed the slit of her ass gave new meaning to G-string and the tiny triangle that barely covered her sex was almost see-through. She was bare – pure, silky flesh. His pulse raced and his mouth pooled with saliva. Lake wondered absentmindedly if he was actually drooling. The matching strapless demi-cup bra hugged her small ribs and held her breasts up in teasing perfection, with her hardened pink areolas peeking from the top. The air was warm and dense between them, erotic and lustful. It was a wonder either of them could breathe. His heart raced in his chest. Their eyes never faltered from one another, every sense heightened. He was rock solid. She teased her lower lip with her glistening tongue and Lake quit breathing altogether. And she didn't think people could be claimed…she was throwing the net and he was letting her.

He reached over and pulled the covers down then stepped back over to the stunning vixen who was fucking with his head and body. He could smell her desire, her perfume, and her floral shampoo…all of her. Everything mingling together like pure heaven – his heaven. It was all he could do not to reach between her thighs and stroke his hand along the seam of her pussy. He knew he'd find her sopping wet.

He tipped her head back and looked into her eyes. "Get in bed."

"Maybe I don't want to sleep in this bra and panties either." She was fucking teasing him. Lake couldn't believe it. It had to be the alcohol. He didn't think she'd be so brazen if she were sober.

"Maybe, but I'm not helping you out of them because I'm still mad at you."

She brought her head to his chest and hugged him, falling back into the innocent more docile woman he'd come to know. "I'm sorry. I shouldn't have kissed you."

Lake felt his heart crack and surge with anger at the same time. How was it that she always seemed to misconstrue his words?

"Look at me Eliza," he demanded, trying to control his voice. It was late, she was sloshed, and he was so sexually amped-up he was about to come in his pants. He pulled her body in tightly as he spoke. "First and foremost, I kissed you. It was magical and it meant the world to me. So you acting regretful just pisses me off. I'm fucking crazy about you. I've never wanted a woman as much as I want you. While I'd love to take off your bra and that strand of lace you call panties, it's more than I can handle. I don't have the willpower to be next to you fully naked without wanting to touch you."

She stood on the tips of her toes and pressed a kiss into his neck. A low groan escaped his mouth. "God, you've got to stop. I'm hanging by the thinnest string ever. I'm hard as a rock, in fact I might be dying." She gave him a mischievous smile and pushed two fingers against his carotid artery – checking his pulse. He pulled her hand away and kissed the tips of her fingers. "Cut me some slack and get into bed." Lake moaned.

She shook her head. "You're not dying."

Little did she know. He chuckled under his breath and released her hand. Eliza brazenly brushed her palm up his thickened length. Lake came down over her in a rush of pent-up desire. Her lips were full and soft. He could taste the champagne on her tongue and lapped it with his own like it was the life-giving food for a starving man. He felt desperate for her in every possible way. He knew, holding her in his arms, that this was much more than infatuation. He didn't just want to claim her, he wanted her heart and soul as well. He reluctantly broke free from the earth-shattering kiss, wrapped his arm behind her knees and scooped her off her feet then turned and flopped her playfully onto the mattress. He pulled the covers over her and watched as she nestled into the sheets and comforter, wrapping herself up like a caterpillar in a cocoon.

"Sure you don't want to stay?" she asked.

"Actually, I'm not sure," Lake replied honestly. He didn't want to leave her in that state of intoxication. He turned off the lamp and watched her roll over onto her side. He knew she'd be out in minutes.

Lake went out to her living room and walked to the wall of windows that overlooked the bustling city skyline. He wasn't thrilled about finding her at The Raven's Nest – far from it. She was searching for something - experiences. He'd give them to her, but he needed to know what they were. What were her fantasies? He might be wrong, but he imagined that most of her experience were benign. She was testing her boundaries and testing his as well.

It just plain pissed him off that she was with Nick in any capacity. Tension coiled around his neck. He needed to know the connection. He prayed it was one of friendship and nothing more. The idea of him touching Eliza sexually made Lake's dick soften like butter. Nick's history with women was all-encompassing, a playboy of the worst kind. His lust knew no boundaries. Regardless, his time with Eliza was going to come to an end.

Lake was infusing his father's corporation with the financial backing to purchase the Kansas City Star. It wasn't something he was initially interested in, but when he found out that Nick's company was making a play for it, he readily put up the additional funds his father lacked. Lake had been at odds with his father most of his life. They were like oil and water, but keeping something out of Nick Slade's reach was more appealing than even the anger he had bottled up for his philandering father.

Lake sent Sam a text letting him know that he'd decided to stay.

Too drunk for me to leave. I'll call you in the morning to come get me.

She's stunning close up.
Amen. I'm screwed.
Funny!
Lake laughed. *The truth!*

Lake watched Sam pull away from the curb. The red taillights glowed brightly in the inky night sky. He turned from the windows and took in Eliza's home. He was impressed with every minute detail of the beautiful space. It was an incredible contrast of wood and steel, brick and concrete, with plush, luxurious furnishings. It was immaculate, and everything was meticulously placed. It was open, with a partial wall jetting out to divide the dining room from the kitchen.

Lake walked to the refrigerator and checked its contents. Fully stocked with fresh fruit, meat, cheese, and beer. He wasn't that hungry despite leaving dinner early, but grabbed a strand of grapes from the crisper and a Boulevard Pale Ale. He took it over to the couch and plopped down. He toed off his shoes and rolled up his sleeves, then laughed heartily at the audacity of his situation. Lake couldn't remember the last time he'd slept on a couch. He found the remotes on the coffee table and took his luck pushing different buttons. The room came to life. The surround sound echoed out overhead from every direction. She had an incredible sound system. That combined with the big screen T.V. that was suspended in the center of the brick wall, made him a happy man. Lake was impressed. He settled into the plush, white linen sectional that dominated the living room and took a long pull from his beer. He grabbed the fuzzy fleece throw from the back of the sofa and draped it across his legs. It was going to be a long night.

It was almost twelve-thirty before Lake shut the television off and fell into a restless sleep. The soft padding of bare feet woke him. Without moving, he opened his eyes and watched Eliza walk groggily into the kitchen. She grabbed a bottle of water and chugged the bulk of its contents. She slid the back of her hand across her mouth and sighed, then laid her cheek on the granite countertop seeking its coolness. He wanted to be mad at her for drinking so much alcohol, but what was done, was done.

She lifted her head and started back towards the bedroom when she spotted him on the couch. She was so sexy he couldn't take his eyes off her. A curl of a smile lifted the apples of her cheeks. She was happy he stayed. An unfamiliar warmth tugged inside his chest. Seeing her light up like the sun in a dark room made sleeping on the couch worth the price of admission.

Either she wasn't modest or no longer cared. Her body was pure sin. He swallowed hard and let his eyes roam her freely. The scant lace that covered her breasts and pussy left Lake fighting for breath like a fish out of water. She sauntered over and stood above him, an angel sent from above.

"You stayed." He voice was raspy and low. It rolled across his ear like warm honey.

"I did," he replied. "I didn't want to leave you in that state. How do you feel?"

She crouched down next to his face and whispered hotly over his lips. "Lonely."

"That's not what I meant," Lake countered.

"I heard the question. I just chose to respond differently than you expected. Knowing you're out here will make it hard for me to sleep. How's it working for you to know that I'm right down that hall?"

"It's tough, but I'm trying be a gentleman."

"Chivalry is dead," she joked.

Lake reached around her back to her slim waist, and pulled her onto the sofa. He wrapped her up in the blanket to warm her cold flesh. He loved the little lace ensemble, but it didn't do shit to cover her skin. She moaned happily and nestled into his side, wedging her foot between his calves to absorb every ounce of his body heat. He was less than thrilled to be fully clothed next to her, but knew that barrier was all that kept him from seizing the moment. The smell of her perfumed body lotion and shampoo was about to push him off the cliff of his resolve.

"Better?" Lake asked.

"Much." She caressed his cheek and his heart surged in his chest. She turned his face to hers. "I really like that eye."

"The one that's flawed." He teased her with her initial word of analysis for his genetic malformation.

"Yeah, that one." Her grin was infectious, her lips supple. He was captivated by her. Lake cupped her face gently with his hand and ran his thumb over her bottom lip. She purred out, "Please kiss me."

Her voice was etched with longing. It was crazy how spellbound he was by her. She was like a present…a gift he was eager to unwrap. He pressed his lips gently to hers, pecking – testing. But she was hungry for more. She teased him with the sweep of her tongue and he lost it. He closed his mouth over hers, stealing her breath with a kiss he knew would seal her fate and bind her to him forever. It was sensuous and potent, generous and consuming at the same time. He tasted her tongue as it slid smoothly over his in an erotic waltz. The moan that escaped her luscious mouth sent Lake reeling. He rolled her beneath him and kissed the line of her jaw, down to her neck and then came back to her succulent mouth.

He clasped his hands to hers and pulled her arms over her head locking them in place. He had this sensuous creature captive. He couldn't believe she was surrendering to her desires, letting him in…giving over a small piece of her control. His heart was racing. He'd take it without question.

"What is this Lake?" She shivered and sucked her lower lip between her pearly white teeth. She was giving in, but questioning the validity of her situation. Lake didn't want her questioning anything. This was what he wanted – what she wanted – what he'd been hoping for, pleading for.

"This is two people giving into their desire for one another." He circled his nose around hers and pecked her pert mouth. "It's you letting go."

"Why were you there tonight…at the club?" She drew her lip between her perfect, white teeth, nibbling it nervously. She was a juxtaposition of confidence and insecurity. It was refreshing to see both sides. She was more reachable than she even knew. The façade of not wanting him was slipping away. She could play coy, but her body and eyes didn't lie. She was as affected by him as he was her.

"I own that club, Eliza. I told you when I came to your office that I intended to claim you, you just didn't believe me. You submitting your body and mind to anyone else isn't an option."

He could see the surprise on her face. She tilted her head and looked at him contemplatively, assessing the weight of his statement.

"You own a sex club filled with beautiful women who'd probably slit my throat to get to you and you want me?"

"I don't want anyone but you." He kissed the side of her mouth. "And you want me too. He kissed the other side of her mouth, her lips parted, eager for more. "Give in to that need, baby."

Lake kissed a trail down her neck and chest until he was hovering over her erect nipple protruding from the lace that barely covered the swells of her breasts. He teased it with the tip of his tongue, eliciting a low rumbling moan from her throat. Breathing rapidly, she arched farther into his mouth and he met her need with sucking pulls over both breasts with a moan of his own. He was losing himself in the taste and feel of her body against his. Every inch of her flesh was sweet and warm. He released her hands and roamed her thoroughly.

His body was molten like a threatening volcano. One kiss or touch away from explosion. "I have to touch you."

Lake wasn't the kind of lover that asked – he acted, but Eliza was a whole new ballgame. Her wholesomeness wasn't an act. She was sexy and sensual – no virgin, but not quite prepared to submit to all the things he wanted to do to her.

With half-lidded, lust filled eyes, she nodded her acceptance and whispered. "I want you to touch me."

Lake's flesh prickled with charged sensual heat. His dick was pained to be released and his heart was about to climb out of his chest. She was giving him her consent. Without hesitation, he moved his palm over her lace covered flesh, which was damp against his hand. "God," she moaned out. She was grinding on his hand in slow desperation. Lake couldn't take it. He slid his finger under the top of her panties, over her baby-soft flesh, and into her waiting need. The creamy, warmth of her essence set him on fire.

"You're so wet." She turned her head shyly to escape his words, but he brought her eyes back. "Don't hide from your desire, Eliza. I love that you want me as much as I want you." He massaged his fingers over her G-spot and she bucked into his hand. "Own it."

Eliza was writhing beneath him as he continued his measured touch in the depths of her sensitive flesh. His dick was solid and straining for release against the zipper of his pants. He wanted to replace his hand with his cock, but it wouldn't be like this. He wouldn't settle for a quick fuck on her couch like two eager teenagers. When he took her for the first time it would be in his bed, she'd be completely sober and he'd make that claim for her real.

The small mewls and moans escaping her mouth were like drops of honey from her perfect lips. He might not fuck her, but he'd deliver a night she would never forget.

Her hips moved with a hypnotic rhythm as she answered each trust of his penetrating fingers. Her eyes were liquid. She was riding the edge of her orgasm and he wanted it – had to have it.

She threaded her fingers into his hair and tugged him desperately to her mouth. Lake could feel her chest constrict with every labored breath. He circled her tight swollen clit with the soft pads of his warm, wet fingers and her body started its slow pulsing climb to release. He drove back into her silky flesh until he could feel her sex sucking on his fingers, pulling, taking what it needed to go over the edge. His entire body was clenched up tight, yearning for release. Yet he held back. If this is what he got from fingering her, he couldn't wait to have his cock buried inside her.

"Yes, oh God, Lake." He plunged deeper, filling her with two thick fingers, milking her G-spot and watching as she came undone in his palm. It was sexy as fuck.

His heart was pounding in tandem with hers – fast and furious in the throes of unrestrained passion. She panted heavily against his lips and he swallowed her moan with a penetrating kiss.

Eliza let her arms splay out like dead weight at her sides, sated and content. "Ahhhh….,"

He looked at the stunning beauty and wondered when she had her last orgasm. She was replete, which made him want to give her more. He wanted her rung out and limp with satisfaction. Tonight it was all about her. "Better?" He was breathing as heavily as she was.

"Much." She nodded her approval with a sheepish grin.

"You're so beautiful."

"Your words are like candy and your hands are magical. I'll take both." She took his bottom lip friskily between her teeth, nibbling her way into his mouth.

He obliged her with a kiss and she giggled playfully. He wrapped his hands above her hipbones and she almost threw him off the couch with her hips, bucking to break free. She was ticklish. "Whoa!"

"I'm sensitive there," she said, trying peel his hands from her tender flesh. "Oh, god…please stop."

Lake didn't release her, he just grabbed her a little tighter and she went wild trying to break his grasp. He moved down her wiggling body until he was staring at saturated lace. The smell of her arousal was like low hanging fruit to a starving man. He wanted to taste her, had to taste her. He kissed the top of her drenched panties and she stilled – frozen. His well-played diversion had the desired effect and when he released his hands from her sides she settled down.

"Jesus," she bellowed, gasping for air.

"I'll remember that little pearl when you get out of line. Now I know how to get your compliance."

"Doubtful."

"Yeah. Too good to be true." He grabbed the flimsy strands of lace around her hips. "Lift." She lifted up and Lake worked them down her legs and feet. When they were finally off, he lifted them on his index finger. They were little more than dental floss. "These tiny things could hardly be considered panties. For what little they cover, you might as well go without."

Amusement crinkled her eyes. "For the price I paid for them, I assure you they're panties. They cover what's necessary." She pulled up to her elbows so she could look at him. "Why am I almost naked and you're in a pair of dress slacks and a shirt?"

"Because this is all about you beautiful." Lake stuffed her panties in his pocket and she looked at him incredulously.

"Do you intend to return those?"

"No." Lake grabbed her under her thighs and gently tugged her body down closer to him. "Now that I've unwrapped the prize, let me see what I've won."

"Oh my God!" Eliza shrieked, throwing her arms up and folding them across her eyes in embarrassment.

He couldn't believe how modest she was. Her body was incredible – flawless. It was a shame she had to wear clothes at all. She was centerfold material. "Quit hiding from me."

It took a few seconds, but Eliza uncrossed her arms and gave him back her dazzling eyes. "I want to take in every inch of you. It's not an inspection, its discovery. I want to know how you react to every touch. Let me give your body what it needs. I can fulfil all your fantasies…if you let me."

"All my fantasies?" Her voice was faint…a low whisper. Would she tell him what they were? She needed to get over her inhibitions.

He'd talk her through every experience, but he wanted to hear her say the nasty, sexy words. He never loved to hear a woman curse, but when it came to the bed – the raunchier the better. He wanted her begging to be fucked.

He knew his words were intense and powerful, but that was the only way he knew how to operate, unfiltered and honest. "Every single one."

He ran the tips of his fingers up her creamy, soft thighs and she shuddered and let out a squeaky sigh. Lake pushed her legs farther apart so he could smell and see the beautiful flesh at the apex of her thighs. Even in the dim light her barren flesh made his mouth water. She was musky and sweet. Her clit was still engorged from her orgasm and her essence glistened in a pool at the opening of her succulent pussy. His already hard cock jerked painfully. It wouldn't take much for him to cum. If she even breathed near his dick – he was done for, caput…over. He'd never exhibited as much restraint with a woman and didn't know why he was handling her with such kid gloves. She was giving herself to him, but he wanted more. It had to be earthshattering. There was no room for error.

"Bare." He ran his finger tip from her bellybutton down her abdomen to the stop of her slit, teasing he sensitive flesh. "I love it."

"Brazilian," Eliza responded proudly.

"Really?" He was growing more excited by the minute. "That's ass too?"

"Yep."

Lake wanted to turn on all the lights so he could see her, all of her. "Come with me." Maybe this was an inspection after all. He got off the couch and lifted her into his arms.

"Where are we headed?"

"To your bed."

Her face brightened, but Lake wouldn't give in to his vow of waiting to make love to her, despite the temptation. And god was she a temptation of the strongest kind. His dick was weeping to cum.

"You're always carrying me."

"I like having you in my arms."

Lake took the last several steps into her room and set her on the bed. She got up on her knees and put her hands on her hips. She stared at him inquisitively. What was next? What now? He took a step back and gazed longingly at her. She was amazingly unaware of her effect on him. Every muscle in his body was stretched tight like rubber bands pulled taut against his bones, threatening to snap with his willpower at any moment. His stomach was knotted with unmet anticipation.

Her eyes dipped to the bulging mass and he swallowed hard. His erection was tortured to hide behind his dress slacks. The depth of need between them was thick in the air like dense fog. He couldn't keep his eyes from roaming over her. It felt predatory, even to Lake, but he wasn't good at hiding his desires and wouldn't start now.

It seemed like a sin that the remaining material keeping him from seeing her fully was a tiny push-up bra that was half covering one nipple and hiding the other. Eliza must have sensed his thoughts because as he was thinking it, she reached around her back and unclasped it. She tossed it aside and covered her breasts with her hands.

"Modesty suits you. But since I've already had them in my mouth, it's probably not necessary to cover them."

Her hands slid slowly back down to her hips. "They're perfect."

She smiled and crooked at finger at him, calling him in. His heart fluttered eagerly in his chest. Eliza drew him in by the collar of his shirt and pulled his face to hers. "I'm really glad you stayed."

"Me too." He buried his hand in the back of her hair and pulled her head back so he had access to her mouth. The intensity in her eyes clawed at his soul. They couldn't hide her emotions. Lake knew they'd always tell him what he wanted, even if the words were never given. "I want you, Eliza."

"From the way you said that, I don't think you mean sexually."

"Make no mistake, I want you sexually. I'll have you sexually, but I won't make love to you. Not tonight…not here. How do you think I want you?"

"Based on our recent conversation, I'm going with the word 'claiming'. I didn't believe you when you said it was me that you wanted. I thought I had altered your reason for coming because of my attraction to you. I've never crossed the line of professionalism with any patient. No one's ever had that effect on me before."

"Claiming is just part of it. I want *everything*."

"What if I don't have *everything* to give?"

"You do. I just have to prove I'm worth it. Which is what I intend to do."

"Why won't you make love to me? I don't get it. I'm completely exposed – open. I'm saying yes."

He smiled.

"Because when I take you, and I will take you…" He licked the seam of her mouth. "All of you." His warm tongue dipped between her sugary lips. "It will be in my bed and you will be making a conscious decision to be mine. I intend to fuck you so thoroughly you'll be ruined for all other men." He felt her breath catch and her chest contract. He had her melting in his hands. He was feeding her mind…drawing her out with anticipation. "When was the last time someone made you so crazy with lust you begged for release? Or had an orgasm so powerful it brought you to tears?" He kissed the shock right off her mouth.

"But right now I want to taste you."

She blushed at the realization of his words and practically crawled up his chest to steal his mouth. "You're making me crazy."

"On your stomach, legs off the bed. Let me see my prize."

"Where's my prize?" She skimmed his thighs with her hands and cupped his cock. Lake groaned. "You're not going to make this easy on me, are you?"

She shook her head playfully and kissed his jaw.

"Your prize is right in front of you. You just have to take it." Lake grazed his lips across hers as he leaned into her ear. "Now…on your stomach." He gave her a loving push and she fell to the mattress. She rolled timidly onto her stomach and moved to the edge of the bed. He knew he was already testing her boundaries. Exposing her like a flower to the sun.

Lake went down onto his knees and rolled his sleeves up. He wanted free use of his arms as he touched her, tasted her…licked and sucked her. Every inch of her sugar perfect in his mouth and on his tongue.

She wiggled her naked, soft body back to the edge of the mattress. Lake couldn't have imagined a more incredible sight. He moved his full body over hers, letting her absorb his warmth. "Don't be scared. I'll make it good. Do you trust me?"

"I do." He didn't know how far that trust went, but for now he'd accept the gift of her submission.

Lake kissed a trail down the ridge of Eliza's spine. The remnants of perfumed body lotion tickled his nose as he made his way down her warm, smooth flesh. She purred beneath him and softened into the mattress. He ran his index finger gently down the seam of her heart-shaped ass. When he palmed the globes of flesh, spreading her open for his perusal, she shivered.

She was pink and succulent, her tiny clit dangled between the soft fold of her labia like a weeping rose. The sweet smell of her essence made Lake's mouth water. Just the sight of her sprawled out on the bed before him with her needy pussy in his face was like being front row in the best dream of his life.

He circled the tip of his tongue over the tight knot of her ass and she squirmed. Lake smiled. He knew no one had probably ever touched that tiny bundle of nerves and it pleased him.

"Have you ever had anal intercourse?"

"No." Eliza eked in a quick huff then buried her face in the comforter. Her silly embarrassment was getting the better of her.

"Is it something you want to try?" Lake asked, hopeful. The thought of taking her tight little ass made his chest warm with excitement. "Will you let me fuck you here?" He put his thumb over the puckered rosette and he felt her body tense.

"Relax, Eliza." Lake moved his finger from her virgin opening and watched her muscles untangle themselves. "It's something we would have to work at. I have to admit the thought of taking you there has my cock as hard as a steel rod."

"Lake…," she mewled into the plush, billowy down comforter.

How in the hell was she going to make it at The Raven's nest? Her modesty was off the charts. There was no way she'd agree willingly to let others watch her be fucked thoroughly by him or any other man. She didn't even know what was intended for her behind "Sloth." Lake wondered if she would have had the guts to follow through, or if she would have back out gracefully. Craig McKinnon was a gentle Dom, but the thought of her being whipped by him, even sexually for pleasure, made his stomach flip and roil.

He'd fulfill her yearning for new sexual experiences, but for now he'd appreciate her body until she lost her modesty in his presence. He wanted her naked and ready for him…always ready…always wet and dripping with desire for him.

Lake spread her labia then licked her hooded clit, circling his tongue around it and lavishing it with his mouth.

"Hmmm…," she hummed.

Her pussy seeped with approval. He licked the full length of her, gathering her essence and smoothing it up her tight ass.

"Oh my God!" Her words were muffled, but he knew every move was drawing her closer to the explosion he longed for. Every taste and touch made him more feral. Eliza was a heady mix of heaven and hell – sweet and feisty. She was his biggest challenge and he wanted to conquer her in every way, physically and mentally.

When he dipped his tongue into her heated sex, he felt the tiny pulses of her amping core preparing for release. He reached around and grabbed her thighs, holding her tight against him, so he could continue fucking her with his mouth. She squirmed and writhed, but he didn't stop. Lake wanted to take her to the edge. When he felt her body start its slow roll into orgasm, he quickly pulled his mouth away, replacing it with the warmth of his palm tightly covering her sex. He wouldn't let her come – not yet. He wanted to *edge* her out.

"No! Don't stop…please," she cried out. He hands were fisted over the cotton duvet and her body was shaking wildly on the mattress.

"Control your breathing, sweet girl. It'll be better if you can hold out. It's edging. Learn to control your body, your breathing and your orgasms will be stronger – better."

"You're the devil, Lake Mitchell." She looked back at him with a pleading grin. He could feel her pussy drooling against his hand. She was right where he wanted her. "My stomach is in knots, my pussy is throbbing and my clit feels so engorged it probably resembles a small penis and you want me to breathe through it?"

Lake laughed. He couldn't help it. Seeing her flustered warmed his heart. "You just need to build up your sexual stamina," he joked. It wasn't much of a joke though. In reality, he needed her better equipped to handle his desires. He wanted to fuck her all night long, over and over, until they were spent and sated.

"Can we work on that another time?" She giggled.

He moved his hand and could see the pool of her yearning. She was ready and so was he. The brush of his wet, warm tongue over her crease made her crazy with desire. She fucked his mouth, rocking gently into his face as she moaned out. She was close. He seized her clit between his lips, then slid his fingers into her hot core.

"Oh god…Lake…" He pulled her orgasm forward with his mouth and fingers, working in tandem to drive her over the edge. Her back arched and her stomach came off the bed. His strokes were long and deep. He felt her pussy clamp down on his fingers as she screamed out his name. "Lake!"

It didn't get any better. Hearing her yell his name was like melted chocolate over a sweet tooth – dreamy and sweet.

Lake climbed her back, kissing his way up her warm flesh and molded his body over hers. She was breathless and spent…right where he wanted her. He brushed the loose waves of chestnut hair off her damp neck and pressed a kiss at the side of her panting mouth. "Good?"

Eliza reached back with both hands and brought his arms under her, then laid her head against his forearm. "I don't think I like the edging." She wasn't grinning, but he was.

"No?" Lake pulled her earlobe into his mouth, gave it a sucking tug and released it with a pop. "Sorry, baby."

"Stay with me." Her words were only a hush…a soft pleading whisper. He melted a little more.

"I'm here."

"No. I mean, stay in here, in my bed. Sleep with me. I promise not to take advantage of you while you sleep." She kissed the top of his hand, then turned it over so she could cradle her face in his palm. Every move she made tugged at his heart. He was going to fall quick and hard for this exquisite woman. "I just want you next to me. Just tonight…I…

Lake cut her off. "Just tonight?"

"I don't know what tomorrow holds for us Lake, but right now you feel like mine."

His heart picked up pace against his ribs – threatening to catapult from his chest into her delicate hands. Did she just say he was hers? Little did she know, he was hers from the moment she walked through the darkened door of his club. He'd been consumed with wanting her. He kissed the back of her head and smoothed his cheek over hers in a tender display of affection.

"We will talk about the future of our 'tomorrows' in the morning. Get under the covers. I'll sleep with you."

"You will?" She lifted her head and turned her shoulder so she could see his face. She seemed surprised that she'd gotten her way.

It made Lake's stomach drop. He didn't want her doubting his sincerity when it came to her. He was all in.

"Of course I will. I'm crazy about you." Eliza started to roll from underneath him, and when she moved onto her back he took one last opportunity to let her know how much being here with her meant. He pulled her back into his chest. "I'm not going anywhere."

It was already 3:15 in the morning. Lake knew he'd be tired as hell tomorrow, but he didn't regret staying.

Eliza leapt from the bed and went into the bathroom. Lake eased from the bed and started disrobing. He knew it was going to be treacherous to get in her bed, but he sure as hell wasn't sleeping in his pants and shirt all night. The couch was one thing, but the bed was entirely different. He slipped his slacks off and laid them on the chair in the corner of her room. He turned around, and there she stood leaning against the bathroom door frame, watching him. Her stunning feminine form was calling out to him. It was all he could do not to rush her and take her down like a lion over prey.

"I tried not to stare at you, but you make it hard," said Eliza

"I make it hard?" Lake continued to unbutton his dress shirt, but slowed the pace and met her stare head-on.

"You are incredibly hot and dripping in sexuality. Pheromones are bouncing off you in every direction like pixie dust. It's pretty powerful stuff. I imagine women have a hard time being around you."

He slid his shirt off, and her heated gaze traveled up and down his body. She was being obvious, and he loved her attempt at overtness. He was slowly drawing her out of her shell.

Lake crossed the room with only his tight designer briefs left to hide his erect cock from the beautiful brunette who'd consumed him from the moment he first laid eyes on her. He stood over her and looked down into her enchanting hazel eyes. He could still feel her sweet honey on his fingers and taste her on his tongue.

"Hot, I like. I'm not quite sure about the pixie dust part and I don't care how other women perceive me. The only person I want to capture with my pheromones is you. I'm glad it's working."

Eliza went up on her toes and stole his breath with a kiss. "It is."

He swept her into his arms, pulling her into his chest and capturing her chin with his fingers.

"I'm going to make you fall in love with me."

She could no longer hold his stare and tried to look away, but Lake wasn't going to let her escape. Not this time. She'd hear him out.

"You're intense." Eliza looked into his eyes and he puddled at her feet.

"Yes, I am. I say what I mean, and mean what I say." He circled his nose around hers and kissed her gently. "What about falling in love with me would be so bad?"

"It's a pretty lofty statement for two people who just discovered one another."

"I guess only time will tell." He looked back at the clock. It was now 3:35. "We'll talk more about this tomorrow. Let's go to bed." He scooped her up, put her in the bed and slid in behind her. He reached back and turned off the lights, then curled into her. She pulled his arm over her waist and pulled his hand up to her face. She was a perfect fit. Lake was content just holding her as the both fell asleep.

Chapter Eight

Eliza woke groggily. The night's events came blaring back like a freight train, screeching to a halt in front of her. She felt the warmth of Lakes body spooned against her back. Their legs were tangled beneath the warmth of her plush down comforter. His breathing was slow and methodical, not a hint of a snore. She probably wouldn't have known anyway because by the time they finally fell asleep, she was out like the dead. Lake Mitchell was in her bed. Holy shit! This was bad, bad, bad. What the fuck was she thinking? But god he was so amazing…so gorgeous…so sexual and hot as hell. Could she do this? She didn't know him. How did a billionaire, well-known businessman, philanthropist end up owning a sex club?

"It smells like burning metal," Lake whispered in her ear.

"I don't smell it."

"It was a joke." He tugged her tighter into his stomach and chest. "I can practically smell the cogs of your brain working overtime from here. What's going on in that beautiful head?"

"Nothing," she lied. Then she was honest. "Everything."

"Let's talk about it."

"Can we do it while we eat something? I'm starving."

He kissed the back of her head. "Me too. I was summoned from my dinner meeting to come rescue a damsel about to make a grievous mistake."

Eliza couldn't deny that maybe he was right but she'd never admit it. She wanted to test the waters of her sexuality. Going to The Raven's Nest was wading into the shallow water, but she wanted to swim in the deep end. Maybe she'd take that leap with Lake. Maybe she already had…here he was, looking delicious in her bed.

She rolled out from under Lake's arm and was about to get out of bed, when her bashfulness came back. He'd had his mouth on every inch of her body, his tongue in the recesses of her pussy and he'd finger fucked her into the most incredible orgasm ever. Acting shy now seemed foolish even for her, yet she was frozen to the mattress – naked. It was ridiculous.

Pissed at her self-awareness, Eliza got up and walked around the bed with the confidence of a Victoria Secret model. The heated eyes of the sexiest man alive covered her skin like an electric blanket.

"I'm going to take a quick shower," she yelled out from the bathroom where she found refuge. She turned on the hot water in her large walk-in shower and turned to look at herself in the mirror when she saw Lake's reflection behind her. God he was phenomenal. Her breath left as their eyes met.

He was cut like a body builder, but lean like a runner. Every striated muscle was defined and toned. His waist was small, his chest was broad, and his washboard abs were rippling down into the scant line of hair that dipped below his tight navy underwear. The bulge of his thickened cock was strained against the cotton. She drew her bottom lip between her teeth timidly – she'd never felt more exposed.

"Don't ever get out of bed and not kiss me," Lake said as he walked up behind her, leaned into her back and rested his chin on her shoulder. They were talking to each other through the mirror. "It will be the last thing you do every night and the first thing you do every morning."

The air was getting thick and steamy warm around them…dense and hot. She reached back and cupped his cheek. "I'm sorry. I was feeling stupidly self-conscious."

"Stupidly is right. You have nothing to be self-conscious about. You're perfect."

She turned so they were facing one another and put her hands on both of his cheeks, so he was solely focused on her words as if he hadn't been since the moment they met. But this time she needed to remove any misconceived notions about herself. "I'm a lot of things, but don't think I'm perfect because those are hard expectations to live up to. I'd like to think I'm a work in progress, but I'm flawed in many ways. Please don't set me up to fail with you this early."

Lake grabbed her with one hand behind the nape of her neck, taking control of the conversation. "I know you're not perfect, but I'm not so sure you're flawed either. You won't fail because I won't let you."

He angled his head to capture her lips as he kissed her hard in the most hedonistic way. Her heart was nervously full, but she remained anxious about their future. She'd been let down enough not to count on the words of any man. And unlike her mother, Eliza had molded herself into the model of self-sufficiency. It would take more than words to change that. He pulled away from her mouth, and she sighed. His kisses were nothing shy of pure magic. She'd just been jolted back to life.

"Good morning," Lake said, pulling her out of her love-drunk stupor.

"Good morning."

Eliza walked into the shower and let the hot water cascade down her head and back, freeing her mind to process everything. She reached through the cloud of steam to get the shampoo, when the brush of cold air from the open door hugged her skin. Goosebumps pebbled her flesh. He stood before her, a sculpture of muscles and smooth olive flesh – naked. The final piece of material that kept the most intimate part of his body cloaked was finally gone. She looked at his solid form and massive cock, both mouth-watering. Her stomach drew tight. "Holy fuck!"

"Eliza!" Lake yelled.

"How the fuck to do expect me to not fucking touch you when you're fucking naked in my shower." Now she was the one looking at the ceiling, raking her hands through her wet tangled hair.

"You're too pretty to use such a word. Save it for the bedroom, beautiful. Use another word, like fudge or crap or…I don't know…anything other than fuck."

She had her hand clasped over her mouth. Her chest rumbled with laughter. "Fudge? Really?"

"The only time I want to hear that word from those luscious lips is when I have you so crazy with lust that you're begging me to fuck you."

"I don't beg."

His lips came down hard on hers, and in a sexy low baritone, he whispered, "You will. I guarantee it."

Her stomach knotted like a pretzel and the air flew from her lungs. "You're so cocky."

"It's a promise I can keep."

Hell, truth be known, the sight of him before her made her feel a little beggy, but she'd play his waiting game and see who broke down first. He smiled at her mischievously like a cat that had just caught the canary and she shook her head at his little game of intrigue. Tit for tat, right? She pushed him playfully back against the steamy glass wall.

"What?" he asked inquisitively, holding her gaze with his dazzling sapphire eyes.

"You're kidding, right? I've been half-dressed or naked all night. Now it's time for me to see my prize."

Lake let out a hearty chuckle. "Touché."

He dropped his hands to his sides confidently and urged her forward. Eliza's gaze roamed over his perfect olive flesh. Despite his dark head of thick brunette hair, he wasn't very hairy. A smattering on his firm chest and a small trail down his abdomen to the mess of curls that hugged his cock. He was flaccid, long and thick – big…really, really big. No wonder it had been fighting all night to break free from its constraints. It had to be a strain every day, just to tuck it in and keep it in. She wondered if it would even fit inside her.

"Shall I turn, or is the sight of my cock enough to hold your attention?"

She licked her lips tauntingly then backed into the water and shut her eyes like she was completely unaffected. Lake rushed her and grabbed her at the sensitive top of her hipbones, causing her to giggle out in the tight space and buck wildly under his menacing fingers.

"You little shit. How dare you look at me like a starving woman over a buffet then act unfazed? You don't fool me, Eliza Swift. I ought to stick my dick in that dirty mouth of yours." He nipped her nose and released her hips.

She found her composure, cupped both of his cheeks with her hands, framing his face and whispered hotly over his mouth, "I relish the idea." She ran her tongue slowly across the seam of his mouth then winked.

"You're a tease."

"I'm a tease? You're the one who won't have sex with me. Not the other way around." She went to grab the shampoo, but he pulled it back from her reach.

"Maybe you're not ready to have sex with me?"

"You're probably right. Based on the size of your penis, I may never be ready."

Lake closed the gap between them and whispered so low and soft into her ear that the wings of a million butterflies invaded her belly. "I assure you it will fit perfectly."

Eliza felt her heart jump in her chest. He was a sexual deviant of the worst kind – a tease, sent by Satan to torment her. He was tantalizing, beautiful. He was sex incarnate and he was holding out.

He squeezed the shampoo into his palm and smoothed his hands over her wet hair, massaging her scalp. Her eyes closed and her head rolled lazily with his enticing hands. His wet kiss over her slick lips pulled her from the revere of his caress. She was liquid, turned on, gooey in his hands like warm butter. Every touch was perfectly placed. When his soapy hands smoothed across her neck and down her chest she hummed out a soft moan of approval. Her breasts were heavy and her nipples were hard peaks. The silkiness of his bubbly hands gliding over her sensitive flesh was like a sexual *Bachata*…the dance of lovers. He pushed her back into the water and then sucked each breast with tender compassion before his hands found their way to the seam of her vagina. It was all she could do to not come undone. The slow throb of her sex was a dragging pull in her abdomen.

"You're dripping, baby."

"You're making me crazy."

Lake's mouth came down over hers, stealing the last of her breath. Eliza wrapped her arms around his neck and kissed him back with the same fervor. She was already losing herself in him and this holdout to have sex with her was making her panicky. She was a ticking-time-bomb of lust that was about to explode. Lake said she would beg, and she said it wouldn't happen, but here she was on the cusp of imploring him to take her, pleading for more. She wanted him…desperately.

He was kissing her mouth, her chin, her neck. She needed to touch him. He was a brick of flesh when she did – thick and hard. She wanted to impale herself onto him. His will was stronger than hers.

"Fuuuuccckkk," she said in the most unbelievable sigh-screech-pleading voice. She realized her mistake when he groaned and quickly spit out something less offensive. "Fudge." Eliza could feel his smile against her lips and knew he approved of the juvenile expression.

"Good girl."

Lake parted her ravenous sex and thrust his fingers into her. She was sexually paralyzed by the assault. Her mind couldn't process the yearning…the longing and desire…the passion. It was raw sexual need.

He lifted her up and pushed her back against the wall. They were face to face and eye to eye. Her pulse was surging and her heart was racing. She wanted him, really wanted him…his cock filling her, stretching her. She needed to feel him. Screw his

Mexican standoff. She'd submitted – it was Lake's turn. She could feel his hard length at her crack. They were both panting desperately. The hunger was thicker than the dense hot cloud in the confines of the small space. He was an inch away from being buried in her. She knew he was riding the edge of his resolve.

"What do you want, Eliza?"

He wanted her to beg and damn it she wanted him…more than anything she wanted this incredible lover, this beautiful specimen of manhood and sexiness to take her all the way. She wouldn't beg – not yet anyway.

"What do you want?" Eliza repeated his words.

"I want you to ask for it. I need to know you want me."

"Is this the begging part?"

"No, baby, this would just be asking. I've been giving you what you need, so you haven't had to feel the desperation of not getting my touch…my attention. One small lift and its over…you're mine for good."

Her body felt as shaky as her emotions. His words were powerful. If they took the final step, she'd be fully "claimed" by him. Lake was the master of profound words. Did she dare take it? What did being *his* mean?

The heat, the water, his hands and the mastery of his touch had all come together in an intense moment of lust. She wanted the sex, but she knew it would seal her fate and bind them. Maybe not the way Lake said, but no less profound.

"Your body is betraying you. What are you going to do about it?"

His eyes were narrowed and he had a smug look on his face. It was a test of will. Would he finally give in if she asked? Would she have the balls to be so brazen? She wanted him so bad it hurt in the pit of her gut. But in the end, the hype of his words had her nervous. She was afraid to give him that one last thing. Sex was never casual, and someone always got a piece of her heart in the process. This time she knew all his words would come to fruition and she'd never be able to turn back.

She unclasped her feet from around his waist, and he eased her legs to the tile floor. "I'll wait."

Lake groaned, but kissed her with life giving force. "You're going to be the death of me…as sure as I'm standing."

"Maybe…"

****

Eliza emerged from the bedroom in search of the new dangling carrot in her life. She needed to figure out what she was going to do about Lake. What did she want from him? What did he expect from her? She was stone cold sober and there were a million unanswered questions rolling through her head.

She found Lake in the kitchen drinking a cup of something that resembled coffee, or maybe it was milk. She couldn't be sure. The aroma lingered over her and her mouth watered in anticipation. Lake handed her a mug of the inky fluid then laced his fingers in hers.

"Black. Just the way I like it." She sipped from the steamy cup.

"Spend the day with me. I have lunch meeting, but after that we can hang out," Lake asked.

"I can't. I have plans."

"What kind of plans?" He inquired, possessively.

"I meet my mother every Saturday for lunch." She watched his shoulder's relax. "It's a standing date that feels like being thrown into the electric chair, but she's my mother. I'm obliged to go."

"Dinner tonight. Sam will pick you up at 7:00."

She hadn't even agreed, when he kissed her on the cheek and put his cup in the sink. He was leaving. In a panic to get more details she blurted out, "You own The Raven's Nest."

"I do."

Eliza felt a little stunned by his omission. Piece by piece things started to connect. He said that he never intended to be a patient and she believed him. It was his only access to her, unless she made her way back into his club and he wasn't taking that chance. The infatuation, obsession and wanting someone – was her.

"You own an exclusive sex club," she clarified. It wasn't a question as much as it was a statement.

"I do."

"That's how you first saw me?"

"It was. I still remember that ridiculously small sequined dress you had on. You were stunningly beautiful, like a rare gem in a room of rocks. I was mesmerized. I wasn't supposed to be there that night, but when I spotted you at the bar, I was paralyzed with trying to find out who you were."

"The dress was ridiculously short, but I didn't pick it out. My friend Nick gave it to me."

"So you're going with 'friend' when you refer to Nick Slade?" Lake asked sarcastically.

"Nick's been many things to me, friend is just one of them," Eliza answered defensively. She didn't feel the need to explain her relationship with Nick. Hell, she didn't know if she could – it was sketchy…undefined.

"A friend that you fuck."

Eliza felt a jolt of anger prick her like a pin. "You're crass and out of line. Don't be an asshole." Eliza walked around Lake and put her cup in the sink, but he was on her in seconds flat. He wrapped his arms around her and put his face between her shoulder blades like a mournful child.

"I'm sorry. That was a shitty thing to say. I was acting jealous, which is unlike me." Lake grabbed her sensitive hip bones, playfully teasing a smile from her mouth.

"Stop it, Lake!" She tugged at his wrists, and he whipped her around by the waist. She might be smiling because he tickled her, but she was pissed. He wrapped his hand around the nape of her neck and kissed her chastely on the mouth. "I won't share you, Eliza. Once you're mine, that's it."

"You're the one who owns a sex club, Lake. Maybe I should ask the same of you?"

"First of all, you will never have to share me. I'm yours *if* you want me. Secondly, it's not just a sex club. It's a place where people can have consensual fun, discreetly or openly, and know they're safe. People pay a lot of money for that luxury. Thirdly, it's a business, not my personal playground. Why were you there?"

"I was challenged by one of my patients that maybe what I deemed deviant, wasn't deviant at all. Admittedly, maybe he was right. I'm no virgin, but some of the things my patients talk about are things I'm knowledgeable of, but are foreign to me personally. I guess I was curious. I went but didn't have the balls to do anything more than watch."

"I know."

"How do you know? Maybe I used that sex swing you had suspended from the ceiling."

"You didn't." He smirked. "But if it's something you want to experience I'd be happy to oblige you."

Eliza's stomach twisted. "I'm curious, but I'm not sure if I have the power to follow through. Sex means something to me. I don't take it lightly."

"Yet you accepted the invitation of a stranger. When I saw you at that door, my heart hit the floor. You didn't belong to me, but there was no way I was letting you go in there with anyone but me. Oddly, I already felt like you were mine. That's why I questioned you about Nick. He was not acting like your friend. He was acting like a lover."

"Nick's not my lover, Lake," she confessed. "He was a little more touchy-feely than usual when we were there." She didn't follow through with the fact that Nick wanted to explore expanding their relationship, but wanted to set the record straight.

"I'm not a big Nick Slade fan. For more reasons than just you." Lake got within an inch of Eliza's face, his breath was hot against her lips. "Nick can't have you."

"He doesn't have me," she replied. "I'm holding out for someone who's worthy of my love."

"As you should." Lake nestled his cheek against hers then found her mouth and pressed a gentle kiss against her lips.

Eliza finally gave in to his demanding tongue and deepened the kiss. He was breaking down all of her barriers, the walls she hid behind to protect her head and heart.

"I'll see you at 7:00."

"Sure."

Eliza watched Lake leave. After the door closed behind him she wondered how he was getting home. She ran across the living room and out onto the balcony. A black stretch limo and his chauffeur, Sam, stood at the ready. She saw Lake exit the building and get into the car. Sam shut the door, looked up at her and tipped his hat, then waved. Eliza reciprocated with a shake of her hand and a smile. She didn't know what role he played in Lake's life, but she knew he was important.

She heard the chime of her phone and went to see who'd sent a text. She had a new contact – Lake Mitchell. Three phone numbers, two addresses and a selfie.

I miss you.

Chapter Nine

Eliza arrived at the Classic Cup, to a fully made-up Sylvia Swift sitting on the patio. Her mother was stunning, despite her ostentatiousness.

"Good afternoon, Mother." She bent down to kiss her cheek. "I thought we were having a glass of wine, not the bottle."

"You may drink as much or as little as you'd like, but don't dictate my limits." She sipped her wine and threw a manicured hand into the air for the waiter. "Love, could you be so kind as to get my daughter a glass of wine?"

"Mother," she said with irritation, "the bottle's right there. I could have poured it myself."

"It's what he does, Eliza. Let him do it for christ sake."

"Thanks, Chris." Eliza gave him an uncomfortable grin and exhaled. He was their favorite server and met her mother's demands with the finesse of a saint. However, there were times her mother pushed the boundaries of snobbishness and alcohol exacerbated it. The saving grace was a well-earned tip at the end of the torture. Her mother always took care of Chris, dropping a hundred dollar bill into his hand or pocket like she was paying for more than his attentiveness.

"Shall we order?" Eliza asked.

"Sure. I'll have the smoked salmon. You get the cheese plate. We'll share."

"Fine." Eliza took a big swallow of her wine, then nervously opened the door on her mother's dating life. "So how was your date with Mr. Mitchell?"

"He rescheduled for tonight. He's got some business deal he's working on with his son."

Eliza knew she was referring to Lake. It surprised her that they were brokering a deal together. Lake thought his dad was a cheater and an asshole, but clearly had business dealings with him. Eliza looked across the table at the mother who drove her insane and understood perfectly the fine line between love and hate.

"I'm sure he'll make it up to you when you see him. Where is the big date taking place?" Eliza mocked. She didn't care but played at being interested.

"The big date is at Plaza III," she countered and knew it was a jab Eliza wouldn't overlook.

"Daddy's favorite restaurant. How apropos."

Her mother laughed and tapped her empty wine glass. The strumming rap of her mother's diamond ring against the crystal made Eliza want to reach across the table and slap the smug grin from her face. Chris, attentive as always, walked over and filled her glass with the chilled Chardonnay.

"Why are you always protecting your father? He's moved on, maybe you should too."

"I'm not protecting him. I just know you well enough to know that it's no coincidence that you'd choose to eat dinner in the one place he frequents most. I don't know if it's malicious or if you're trying to make him jealous."

"Neither. Despite what you think, I don't give your father that much thought."

Eliza knew better. Her insides grew warm from the wine and the disregard. "Funny. I bet he's all you think about."

Her mother took a long drowning sip of her wine and stared her down. She couldn't refute the facts. She was still hung up on her father. She was fooling no one. Eliza was grateful when their food arrived. It was a cease-fire of words. They ate and drank in silence – a quiet reprieve.

Eliza was daydreaming when she looked up to a wide-eyed Sylvia across the table.

"What's wrong?"

She reached down and quickly fished out her lipstick, reapplying the burnt red to her plump lips and smoothing out her dress. She was getting dolled up for someone. Eliza was so intrigued by her mother's behavior she started to turn her head to see who'd caught her attention, when Sylvia spoke under her breath. "Don't turn around, but Jonathan Mitchell's son just walked into the restaurant. I'm sure he doesn't know me, but I certainly want to make the best impression if he does."

Eliza's heart dropped to her feet. She held her breath and turned to see if Lake was really here. She never mentioned where she was going to lunch and wondered if it was just a coincidence. Lake Mitchell had low-jacked her life. She found herself in an odd predicament. Did she go in and say "hi" or go about her business? She chose the latter.

"Did he see you?" She hoped they'd flown under radar. The last thing she needed was to answer to her mother about Lake Mitchell. Her mother would have them married by the end of lunch and impregnated by dessert.

"I don't think so." She sighed, then with a full toothy smile interjected, "Damn he's hot."

Eliza smiled and felt her heart bounce excitedly behind her ribcage. She couldn't agree more. "Cool your jets, cougar. It's his father you want, not him."

"Maybe so, but you're a different story. He's probably the most eligible bachelor in this city, Eliza. You're twenty-nine, with a birthday in four weeks. I'd love to see you married with children before I die."

"Eligible or not, I don't know if Lake Mitchell's the marrying type, and I'm in no rush to get to the altar. You've had a failed marriage and a not-so-successful dating run. So quit pushing."

Eliza finished her glass of wine and waived for the check. Today she'd leave the hundred. Chris deserved it. She stood to leave and kissed her mother on the cheek. "I love you. Call me and let me know how the date goes with Mr. Mitchell and go somewhere else besides Plaza III."

Her mother rolled her eyes. Eliza knew her suggestion had fallen on deaf ears, but she let it go. She was happy to leave unscathed.

Eliza walked through the restaurant to leave and felt nervous. This was her regular Saturday haunt, but she suddenly felt like a stalker. She peered over the bustling room and didn't see him. She was almost to the door when she spotted Lake from the corner of her eye. His back was to her, but she could place him anywhere. Her heart bloomed in her chest until the site of his lunch date came into view. He was with a woman – not just any woman, but *her*. She looked different, softer, but she was unmistakable. It was Angel, the temptress from the club. Their eyes met and Eliza stood frozen, staring. Her heart plummeted fast. Then, as if she were watching a bad movie play out before her eyes, Angel threw a gleaming smile at Lake, tipped her head and giggled then pushed her hand beneath his. She looked away. Her stomach tossed and turned like an acidic, gurgling pool of angst.

Eliza turned so quickly she almost took down a server in the process. "I'm so sorry." She put her hands in the air and backed out the door. She couldn't pull the air back in her lungs quick enough. She was going to throw up the cheese, salmon, and the wine in a kaleidoscope right on the sidewalk.

Didn't he just ask her to spend the day with him? She guessed when she was too busy, he'd found a replacement. Eliza was sure there was no lack of women who would gladly oblige him. Her own mother would probably throw her under the bus to get to Lake. Hell, he owned a sex club – he probably had women on speed dial.

Angel worked for him? Maybe it was a business meeting? He didn't belong to Eliza and she was surprised to be feeling so out of sorts over him. But he'd just confessed that he felt like she belonged to him. Oddly; she felt the same. Regardless, the bitter singe of betrayal soured her mouth.

She was planning on shopping for a new dress to wear over to his house, but with the wind out of her proverbial sails, it didn't seem important. Eliza drove home confused and down. All the happiness of the morning, gone. She had a Ph.D. in psychology and knew better than to jump to conclusions, and read into something before asking questions, but that logic was reserved for her patients. It never seemed to flow the other way. She'd let the doubt creep in and it would all be over before it even started.

She heard the chime of her phone from her purse and reached in to grab it…Lake.

I wish you were here.

I was there asshole – you just didn't know it. Eliza didn't respond. She tossed her phone in her purse and drove home. She was exhausted from the long night and the afternoon wasn't panning out any better. Sam was supposed to pick her up at seven, but she didn't know if she'd consent to go. She decided to take a nap to clear her head. When she woke up three hours later, she still felt unsure.

She grabbed her phone to call Nick when she found a series of texts from the previous night. Each one answered. Lake had responded to every single one.

Where are you?

Lake's response – *Home. I had to leave.*

We need to talk, E. I want to explore "us" further. I don't like the idea of you being with someone else.

Too late jerk. Lake was clearly getting mad, and the texts reflected it.

Jerk? Don't be cold. I'm IN love with you.

Fuck off! The heavy blow to Nick's heartfelt comment was the last text of the night.

Eliza needed to call Nick and give him an explanation. One he'd probably hate, but she needed to clear the air. They were best friends. She would never tell him to *fuck off* after he'd just told her he was in love with her. They'd never be more than friends, but she'd never consent to hurt him.

"Hey." Nick's voice held little to no emotion.

"I just wanted to apologize for last night. I shouldn't have just left the club without telling you. I'm sorry."

"I was worried to death. How did you get home?"

"I…" Eliza stalled. "Uh…Lake Mitchell had his driver take me home."

"Lake Mitchell?" he growled into the receiver. "Eliza Swift this better be a fucking joke."

"Quit talking to me like that you prick!"

"I'm a jerk. I'm a prick. Which is it?" Eliza felt bad, but she had had it. Lake and Nick could both go fuck themselves.

"I'm sorry I called." She was about to push end when she heard him yelling her name.

"Eliza! E…!"

"What, Nick?"

"You're going to tell me to *fuck off* and then go out with Lake-Fucking-Mitchell. I'm about to lose my god damn mind. Did he take you home, or did his limo take you home?"

"First of all, I didn't tell you to fuck off," Lake did. Secondly…" Nick cut her off.

"Fuck secondly, I just got my answer. Where were you when he was answering my text messages?"

"Sucking his big cock, of course," Eliza spat. "Is that what you wanted to hear? You're a jerk." Eliza slammed her thumb hard against the screen of her phone and hung up on her best friend. No longer able to fight the bubbling emotions, she rolled onto her stomach and cried. Nick called no less than ten more times and then finally resorted to texting.

You can't see him. I forbid it.

You are in no position to dictate who I see or don't see. You didn't seem to worry too much about me when you were fucking two other women last night.

I didn't fuck anyone last night. What are you talking about?

Lake was the one acting jealous last night. He believed there was more between Nick and Eliza than there really was and seeing the text messages with Nick professing his love didn't help. What a screw job! She was in the middle of a cock fight between two dominant assholes hell bent on staking their claim over her.

I don't want you with Lake. Even if you can't be mine. You're ripping my heart out.

I love you too, just not the way you want me to. I need you to be my friend – now, more than ever.

This is the second worst night of my life. Last night was the worst. I told you I wanted you and you pushed me away. Lake may have been the one to tell me to fuck off, but your denial cut just as deep.

I'm sorry, Nick.

Me too.

How the hell had going to one club, caused so much havoc for her? She was fine. She and Nick were fine. Lake was probably more than fine. Hell, maybe she preferred *vanilla* after all.

It was five-fifty. Eliza had a decision to make. Did she go with Lake or stay home? In the end Eliza decided that staying in was better than the ulcerous night she'd undergo in Lake's presence. She would probably never mention her sighting, and in the end, they would both suffer for it.

Her shower bordered on scorching. Her olive skin emerged pink, but she was so thankful to have washed the day's stress away. She smoothed her favorite perfumed lotion over her freshly shaved skin and used her blow dryer haphazardly on her long brown waves. She skipped the makeup and threw on her favorite sweats and tank top.

She walked into the kitchen feeling happy and refreshed. She reached in the wine fridge and plucked a chilled chardonnay. She considered the less sophisticated idea of chugging it straight from the bottle, but refrained. Her mouth watered as the dark yellow liquid poured coolly into her glass. She tipped the wine to her waiting lips and let it roll smoothly across her tongue, assessing it, savoring it, and letting the magic of the first sip calm her.

Eliza kept a fully stocked kitchen. Cooking was therapeutic – she preferred it to going out. She assessed the food situation and laid out all the things she needed to make pasta. She needed comfort food. Nothing more calming than a carbohydrate coma of linguine. The wine and dinner, she hoped would right her troubled soul.

She turned on the stereo and the surround sound kicked in. "He Won't Go," crooned into the air and Eliza felt an instant sense of joy. Her shoulders eased. The sultry rhythm of the music captured her mind and body. She swayed slowly across the room to the patio and walked out onto the balcony to a fabulous spring sunset. She sipped her wine and watched as the last remaining orange fell slowly beneath the water, descending into the Missouri River.

The knock on the door was faint and barely heard over the music. She hustled in, wine in tow, and peered out the peephole. It was Lake's driver, Sam.

He stood about six feet tall. Eliza guessed him to be in his mid-to-late sixties, with salt and pepper hair, broad shoulders, and an unassuming face. He had soft, kind eyes – fatherly. Maybe that was his role in Lake's life.

She opened the door and faced the first of her night's hurdles. "Good evening, Sam?" It came out more like a question. It wasn't their first official meeting, but in her eyes, the drunkenness of last night didn't count.

"Miss Eliza, I'm here to pick you up."

She looked at his gentle smile and outstretched hand and took it willingly. It was warm. He gave her a gentle squeeze then encased it with the other. It was a very endearing move. She didn't know him, but liked him instantly.

Eliza felt bad, like she was letting him down personally. "I'm sorry, Sam, but that's not going to be possible. Tell Mr. Mitchell, I appreciate the invitation, but I can't make it."

"Miss Eliza, please come with me. Mr. Mitchell asked me to retrieve you, and I've promised to deliver you."

"I'm sorry you've made promises you won't be able to keep. It's been the most unbelievable day and as much as I hate letting you down in your quest to retrieve me. I'm just not up for a night with Mr. Mitchell."

He looked at her inquisitively. "Mr. Mitchell will be sadly disappointed. He was very excited about the prospects of spending an evening in your company."

"I'm sorry, Sam." She felt like a heel, but closed the door and walked back to the kitchen to refill her wine glass. Seconds later her phone was ringing. She reached over and looked at the lit screen. Lake's name and picture were blaring at her. He was beautiful. Her heart plummeted. Eliza let it roll to voicemail. She wasn't surprised when the first text came through.

What is going on? I have been going nuts thinking about you all day. I can't wait to see you.

Eliza didn't respond.

I have your favorite champagne on ice and a lovely dinner planned. Get in the car!

She still didn't respond. How did he know what her favorite champagne was? It just pissed her off that he presumed to know her so well. All the internet searches didn't amount to shit. It was all superficial stuff. He'd never know her because she wasn't willing to put herself out there – again.

Please!

Eliza finally gave in and sent her first message. *Maybe you should have started with that!*

What is going on? Call me right now!

No! Why did you text Nick last night like you were me?

I was unsure of your relationship with him. He said he was in love with you. It made me jealous. You said you two were friends.

We are friends. You're in no position to dictate who I see and don't see.

What does that mean? I'm on my way over!

No, please don't come over. I just need some time to think about all this.

Bullshit! Something's wrong. If this is about Nick, I'm sorry, but I won't share you. I want you for myself...only for me. Why are we texting? Call me.

She looked at her phone, head tilted with a heavy heart. But she was supposed to share him? She sighed. *I don't need any more stress in my life.*

I'm crazy about you, Eliza! I miss you! Sam will knock again, and you will get in the car. See you soon.

No!

Confused, Eliza set the phone down and started her trek back to the patio when the knock came again. She turned and stood, unmoving. She knew who it was and felt bad for Sam. Hell, she felt bad for herself. She really, really liked Lake. This morning she was floating on a cloud of romance, lust and hope then everything seemed to crash and burn. She understood jealousy. It was a vicious emotion. She wasn't even all that pissed about Lake's texts to Nick. It was wrong, but she understood how he must have felt seeing them. He didn't understand their relationship. Truth be known, Eliza didn't know if she understood her and Nick's relationship. He was trying to change it, blurring the lines. If the shoe were on the other foot and she were at Lake's house and he got a text message from a woman telling him she was in love with him, she'd probably feel just as jealous and hurt. Hell, she was sick with angst over his lunch date. She walked to the door and just as expected, there stood a pleading Sam with his hands in his pockets and a weary grin.

"Please come with me. Mr. Mitchell is adamant that I get you in the car, even if I have to pick you up and carry you. Please don't make me do that."

"Where is he commandeering me to?"

"His estate. He's planned a lovely dinner."

She stood staring at this seemingly calm creature at her door. He was to retrieve her or take her by force. Eliza wondered if he had the balls to follow through.

"I'm not dressed for dinner," said Eliza, clinging onto her resolve. "Especially at someone's estate."

"It's a home like any other. And if you don't mind me saying, you couldn't look more beautiful just the way you are." Eliza looked down at her brightly painted toes, loose sweat and tank. She was the model of "bum chic."

"You are making this very hard for me, Sam. I had resigned myself to staying home, but I'm feeling conflicted." She opened the door fully, took a step back. "Where are my manners? Would you like to come in?"

"Will you be accompanying me?" Sam asked. "If not, maybe I should stay out here and do some calisthenics in preparation for carrying you." The grin that crept up his cheeks made her giggle.

She covered her mouth and stepped out of the way. "You can come in. I'll go."

Sam stepped in the foyer of her condo and she shut the door behind him. Eliza led him into the open space over her living room, but he pointed to the patio. She nodded her approval.

"Can I get you anything to drink?"

"No, thank you," Sam said, taking in the surroundings. "This is the biggest condo I've ever seen. It's lovely."

"Thank you." Eliza gazed around the room happily. It was an incredible space. She felt the warmth of pride kindle her face. "I'll be right back."

She walked to her master bedroom to slip on tennis shoes, and decided at the last second to change. If she were going to go, she'd make him drool. She slipped on a loose black halter dress and some strappy sandals. A brush of blush, a swipe of mascara and nude lip gloss made her sparkle. She stared at herself in the mirror. She didn't know if giving into Lake's demands was the right thing to do or not, but she knew if she didn't explore her feelings further, she'd regret it. She needed answers.

Eliza walked through the living room when Sam walked back through the patio door and smiled wickedly at her.

"What?" Eliza mused. "I'm a girl for goodness sake. I don't want to look like a complete troll."

"Miss Eliza, if you didn't shower for a week and rolled in mud, you still wouldn't look like a troll. Mr. Mitchell's going to lose his mind. You look gorgeous."

Eliza lit up like a Christmas tree under his well-placed words. She needed a boost of confidence and appreciated the compliments. Lake was demanding, but his driver was as smooth as fresh spun silk…a charmer.

"Oh, I get it. Good cop, bad cop." She playfully nudged his shoulder. "Mr. Mitchell's clearly the bad cop."

He didn't answer. He just shook his head at her like she was a silly child. She felt insane for agreeing to go to Lake's home. It was like walking into the lion's den. She should have turned around, but didn't.

Chapter Ten

Lake's gorgeous brunette was feisty. He knew he'd never get away with her not knowing about the texting to Nick, but something felt off. Lake didn't get it. They'd spent an incredible night and morning together. She was opening up to the idea of him and he couldn't want her more. He admired her independence, but wanted her devotion. He didn't want to worry about Nick or any other man for that matter. There was so much to learn about Eliza. Lake suspected that beyond the spirited, confident persona, she was as fragile and guarded as any woman he'd ever known. If he thought he'd win her easily, he probably wouldn't want her as much. Now that she was in reach, he didn't want to let her go.

Lake looked at his phone, pacing the floor like an eager adolescent. She had better have gotten in the car or he was headed to her house to find out what the hell was going on.

On the way.

Sam came through. A sense of relief washed over Lake. He took a deep breath and sent a response.

Perfect. Don't text and drive.

As expected, there was no return text. With Eliza in the car, Lake would take no chances.

It was almost eight when the car pulled through the iron gates. He watched the limo make its way up the circle drive through the security camera in his office. Eliza had finally arrived. His heart jumped excitedly in his chest and his breathing quickened. He was still mad that she had tried to back out at the last minute, but she was here. It was a win.

Lake walked casually to the front door to welcome her.

She stepped out of the car and the air rushed from his lungs. She looked amazing. The black halter dress hung loosely around her neck and dipped low between her breasts. It clung tightly to her hips and ended mid-thigh. Her incredible lean, muscled legs were edible and the strappy heels looked perfect against her brightly painted toes. "Stunning," Lake mumbled under his breath as she made her way from the car. He could already feel his body react to the sight of her. He shifted his pants to make room for his expanding cock. It was going to be a long night.

He watched as she took in the magnitude of the house, staring at every nuance that made it so unique. Lake felt the same way when he first saw it as a naïve child of five. That's when his uncle owned it, but now it was his. It still held the same appeal. It was magnificent by any standards.

Sam held out his arm and Eliza laced her arm through his elbow. They'd apparently developed a sense of trust and it warmed Lake's heart to see her smile.

Lake stood confidently in the entry hall, waiting, hoping for a smile of his own. Frustrated with her behavior or not, he was excited to have her in his home.

"Welcome." He gave her a warm grin, but remained glued to the wall with his arms crossed. She needed to make her way to him. He wouldn't bend on this. She had already stubbornly refused to come at his request and despite the fact that she had decided to come, he wanted her to make the first move.

"I can't believe this is your home. It's one of the best on Ward Parkway. It's breathtaking." She walked up to him with her lip drawn between her teeth. She was acting timid. He immediately sensed a hint of liquid courage on her.

"I'm glad you like it," Lake stated matter-of-factly. "Thanks for honoring me with your presence. I would suggest in the future if you make a commitment to me, you keep it. Or at least have the courtesy to call and cancel. I am not accustomed to begging." It was a real statement, but the minute the words left his mouth, he knew it was a mistake.

Her smile fell and anger took its place.

"I'm sure you're not, asshole." She turned her back on him and started for the door. "I've made a terrible mistake."

Lake circled his fingers around her delicate arm and pulled her back. "Don't walk away from me Eliza. I didn't mean to hurt your feelings. I'm sorry. I'm just mad and confused."

"Quit trying to hurt me," she said sadly. He was more confused than ever. Wasn't she the one standing him up?

"Hurt you? I could say the same thing," he replied, bewildered. "Why don't you tell me what's *really* going on here?"

"It's me…I'm just…" She reached for her hair and twirled a strand between her fingers. The move he'd seen on three occasions. The club, her office and here. Clearly a habit developed from nervousness. Like gnawing her beautiful lip away like a piece of bubble gum.

"Quit fidgeting, Eliza." Lake gently pulled her hand from her hair and laced his fingers through it, using it to pull her closer. Reluctantly, she moved towards him.

"I feel scared…of this…of you." She looked down, unable to hold his gaze.

Lake lifted her head with his finger under her chin. "What's happening between me and you is incredible. Quit fighting it…quit fighting me…this. I couldn't want you more."

Eliza looked delicate, unsure – fragile. He didn't get it. How had they come so far only to be back here? His heart fluttered in his chest when she touched his cheek with her hand. He pushed his face further into her palm and sighed. He told her she was going to be the death of him and he believed it was true. He was already dying just trying to fight to keep her and he'd barely gotten a chance to be with her.

He could hear the door close behind them. Sam had relinquished her to him, like a father would a daughter, watching to see the initial interaction and deciding it was okay. Sam was like that, protective and brawn on one hand, and authentically kind and caring on the other.

"Come on," Lake said, pulling her by the hand outside onto the patio. The champagne still sat corked, chilled and waiting. Lake already had a glass of scotch, waiting on her to arrive, but wanted to uncork the tempered bottle anyway.

"You still up for a glass of your favorite Brut." Lake lifted the bottle in the air and waved it in her direction. Eliza nodded and with a *pop* the cork went sailing into the air.

"Veuve Clicquot. It's my favorite," she chided. "But you already knew that because you know me so well."

"Better than you think," Lake countered with a smirk.

"So tell me, Mr. Mitchell. What do you think you know about me?"

He handed her a glass of the canary liquid and tipped his glass to hers. "Cheers."

"Cheers."

His eyes settled over her and she met his steady gaze.

"Well, let's see," Lake started, with a wide shit-eating grin. "You went to Kansas State for your undergraduate and masters degree, then Kansas University for your Ph.D. You're an only child, and your parents are divorced. Your father is an extremely prominent Kansas City attorney and is remarried to a woman almost half his age. Your mother is a socialite and has never remarried, but not from lack of trying. You drive a white Toyota Camry and own a warehouse condo in the City Market District of Downtown, Kansas City. Which is incredible by the way. I'm guessing you make $80,000 to $90,000 a year, which is far less than you probably deserve. You've had your own practice for a little over two years now. You've never been married and have no children…that I'm aware of. You're ambitious, hardworking, smart, witty, *beautiful* and incredibly sexy."

"Wow! I don't know if I should be flattered or freaked out." Eliza crossed her arms over her stomach and clutched her sides. If this was his way of easing her anxiety, he sucked.

"You didn't think I'd come for you if I didn't know exactly what I was getting. I'm not successful and wealthy because I'm careless and stupid. I know exactly what I want and I'm not afraid to go after it. That includes you, Dr. Swift." Lake took a cautious step towards her, trying to close the gap that was quickly becoming a crevasse. "It's a resume, nothing else. Anyone can find that information without too much effort. Only you can tell who you are and what you want out of life."

"Why me? You're successful, wealthy and handsome." Lake narrowed his eyes and assessed her, brows furrowed. Did she not have a clue of how others saw her? How everyone lit up at the sight of her. She was captivating. It was going to be his Achilles heel, the bane of his existence to watch men fawn over her. Nick was already trying to pull her back into his lair. They might be friends, but Lake wasn't stupid. Could a man be a true friend to this beautiful stimulating creature without wanting more? Doubtful. "I'm sure you can have your pick of women." Eliza's face fell and a slow catching sigh slid from her lips. His heart ached.

"Look at me, Eliza." Lake took a final step forward, put his hands on her shoulders, and stared at her intensely. "You're amazing in every sense of the word. I'm totally enamored when I'm in your presence. I've literally made myself crazy trying to find a way to meet you, to see you. I wanted the chance to make you mine."

"I can't just be another girl, Lake. I don't have it in me to wait on the sidelines for someone to think I'm enough."

He looked at her mystified, she looked like she was about to cry. Her chest contracted heavily and he could see the tears pool in her eyes. She gently pulled her shoulders back, seeking release, but he wouldn't give in until he figured out what was going on. Lake was baffled.

"What are you talking about? Why would you ever wait on the sidelines for anything or anyone? You aren't another girl, Eliza. You're the *only* girl." Lake caressed her cheek, and she shut her eyes. "What is going on?"

"How was the Classic Cup?"

"What? Lunch?" He shook his head, bewildered. "It was fine. Why?"

"It didn't look like a business lunch to me. You and Angel seemed rather cozy. Or, do you hold hands with all your female business associates?" She shrugged out of his grip and took a step back.

"You were at the Classic Cup… today…for lunch? Why didn't you come talk to me?" The puzzle pieces were starting to come together.

"You seemed engrossed. I didn't want to disturb you."

"Engrossed? Angel works for me. I assure you, I didn't hold her hand," Lake took a step forward to close the breach of space between them, but Eliza held up her palms to warn him off. She'd already convicted him without the benefit of a trial. What the hell?

"Please don't." Her eyes looked as heavy as his heart. Fuck her hands! Fuck her stupid retreat! He didn't stop his approach. He'd fix this or die trying.

"Quit running away from me and listen. I don't know what you saw, or think you saw, but Angel is an employee. Nothing more and nothing less. She manages The Raven's Nest. Why would I invite you to spend the day with me if I was meeting someone I was romantically interested in? I would never compromise my relationship with you."

"Relationship?"

Lake wrapped her in a bear hug and picked her up off the patio floor. He buried his nose into her silky, floral hair. Her feet were dangling like limp tentacles. Lake was happy she'd lost her will to fight him.

"Yes, relationship." He pressed a kiss into the corner of her mouth and groaned. "You silly, complicated woman. The relationship I'm desperately trying to build with you. I'm not perfect, Eliza, but I'll never betray you. I'm a lot of things, which you will soon discover, but I don't lie about anything."

"She saw me, Lake." Her voice was laced with sadness. "She giggled and flirted with you so I'd think it was more than business."

She wrapped her arms around his neck and buried her head on his shoulder. Lake prayed the tension and misunderstanding was fading. He never wanted her to doubt his affection. She clasped her hands at the nape of his neck and he sighed with relief. He might not be out of the woods, but she was softening. "That's better."

"I'm probably getting heavy. For some reason you always feel the need to carry me around like a child. I thought I'd take some of the strain off."

"If you want to ease the strain, wrap your legs around my waist." Lake grinned devilishly down at her. Eliza sighed breathily and he stole her lips with a kiss. She was enchanting, even angry.

"Nice try, but I'm mad at you." Lake squeezed her tighter when she attempted to wiggle from his grip.

"I see that. I promise that I won't hold any business meetings with Angel outside of the office."

"She manages a sex club. If you meeting her there is supposed to make me feel better, it doesn't."

Lake shook his head and chuckled under his breath. "I meant my corporate office. Synergy, not the club," he reprimanded.

"I'm being foolish. You can hold business meetings wherever you see fit. I just didn't expect to see the same hand that had touched me so intimately hours earlier in another woman's hand at lunch."

Her soft breath played warmly at his neck and her beautiful hazel eyes were heavy. Lake had to fix this…quickly. He wanted her affection, not her distress. No wonder she tried to back out, she felt betrayed. This wasn't about Nick. This was about Angel.

"You're not being foolish, Eliza. I'd be furious and hurt too, if I thought I'd seen the same."

Lake buried his fingers into the silk of her chestnut waves and tilted her head back so he could see her telling eyes. He dissected every minute of his limited time with Angel at the restaurant. It was brief, but he knew what Eliza was talking about. The same flagrant touch by Angel pissed him off and he scolded her for it, but it didn't matter. Eliza only saw the breach of trust and let it settle into her mind as authentic acceptance of her advances.

"I know what you're referring to now. She did try to put her hand over mine. If you had watched a second longer, you would have seen me pull my hand away. Angel's a flirt. Her advances are unwarranted and unwanted."

"Yes, she is." Eliza knew firsthand the validity of that statement. She had been the recipient of her flirtation as well, but it didn't change the facts. It hurt. "I fucking hated it. It hurt. I was high on you and then I was shattered," she admitted. "It sucked."

Lake grinned at her adoringly. His heart came back to life with her words. She was giving him pearls. Her admission that he had an effect on her heart and head was like music to his ears. She liked him…he wanted more than like, but it was a start. "I like you jealous, Dr. Swift." He loved that she was acting invested. "I love that you care. I'm sorry that you felt hurt. I will make sure that it never happens again."

"You can't protect my heart, Lake." Her words were so curt and matter-of-fact it was like a knife penetrating his stomach. He might not be able to protect her heart from what others did, but he would do everything in his power to make sure he never hurt her or betrayed her trust in the future.

"I sure as hell aim to try. You can't hold onto shit like this. You of all people should know this. We have to communicate," he pled. "Lies and secrets will kill us, Eliza. If I do something that hurts you or makes you mad, say so. I want *everything* with you. Your devotion, your honesty, your love and affection. I want to share your dreams and have you share in mine. Everything means *everything*…all in."

"What if *everything* is more than I have to give?"

Lake wanted to kiss away her fear of the unknown. She was like forbidden fruit in his arms, and he was tempted to commit an eternal sin if it meant he could have her forever. "Then I'll take what I can get." He brushed the hair off her soft, supple neck and inhaled her beautiful scent. She smelled like sweet vanilla and gardenia mixed with fragrant soap; pure Eliza. She was like a drug and he was jonzing for another hit.

"Excuse me. I'm sorry to interrupt, Mr. Mitchell, but shall I serve dinner?" They both turned their heads and looked to the open door.

"Are you hungry?"

She smiled up at me then looked shyly over at Katherine, my all-around go to for almost everything and for all intents and purposes - mother. "She cooked?"

"You didn't think I would bring you here and not feed you?" I grinned, clutching her closer.

"I don't know what to think. Honestly, I feel a little overwhelmed. You are the single-most dominant, aggressive and forward male I've ever encountered. You'd overpower the most confident woman, or break her down to a mere shell of herself."

Lake looked into her eyes. He wouldn't break her...no matter what.

"And what kind of woman are you?" Lake asked.

"I *was* all the accolades that you just praised upon me earlier, but you're like kryptonite. I'm powerless against your charm."

She hugged him tighter. "I'd love some dinner."

"That would be lovely, Katherine," said Lake. He turned his focus back to the gorgeous brunette who was taking his heart with tender words of regard perfectly placed around his heart like rose petals. Lake looked at her affectionately. Tonight he'd gained a little more of her trust. Eliza was giving up a little more of her control and so was he. Lake couldn't remember ever wanting anything more than her approval, her commitment...her love.

Chapter Eleven

It was a beautiful spring night. Lake's house was majestic. His enormous pool was ethereal. It shimmered against the darkness like a disco ball, lit from the bottom. Water splashed serenely against the boulders that circled the hot tub. A roaring fire snapped and crackled in the middle of the patio, warming the cool air. She didn't know how much time he spent out here, but if it was her house, she'd live outside. She didn't know what the rest of the house looked like, but if it was as magnificent as the backyard she was in for a real treat.

Eliza watched Katherine lay out an incredible display of food. The table was set with expert detail. From the beautiful white linen tablecloth to the cream and pewter trimmed china, sterling silverware that shimmered and crystal that danced with the light of the fire, nothing was overlooked. Eliza looked down at the plate of pasta, decorated with eight jumbo shrimp, wafting in garlic butter, rich and pungent. Eliza laughed.

"What's so funny?"

She pointed to the plate. It looks like I'll be able to keep your tantalizing mouth at bay with all the garlic."

"Doubtful. I love garlic and can't resist your mouth." He lifted his champagne glass to hers, and she reciprocated with a gentle tap. "Here's to scampi."

Lake went to refill her glass, but she put her hand over the top. "I've had enough."

"You can have another glass of champagne."

"Well thanks, Lake." She sat back in her chair and looked at him sarcastically. "I appreciate you allowing that, but I probably need to keep my wits about me. I never know what you're going to hit me with next."

"I'm going to hit that sweet ass with the palm of my hand in a minute. Sarcasm doesn't suit you, beautiful. I was merely pointing out that you aren't driving. In fact, you don't have to leave…at all…ever."

"Ever? That's very ambitious."

"Nothing is out of the question. It's a matter of saying yes."

Eliza couldn't take her eyes off Lake. It wasn't just his beauty that drew her in like a moth to a flame, but the entire aura of him. He was confident and decisive. He never wavered and stared her down until she surrendered to him.

"Sound's delightful, but sadly I can't. I need to go to my office for a while tomorrow. After you left yesterday, I was admittedly worthless."

"Well, you didn't leave with a hard-on, so you fared better than me."

Eliza covered her mouth with her napkin to stifle her laugh. "All things considered, I guess you're right."

"I'm sure your darling receptionist thought I was crazy. I practically walked out with my back to her. It was rude. I felt stupid." Lake was fighting the grin that threatened to creep slowly up his face. Despite his best efforts, he couldn't curtail it.

Eliza didn't imagine he was often embarrassed. He was the model of composure. But to see him a little out of sorts was refreshing.

"Stop laughing," Lake chided. "I sat in my car for ten minutes like some silly teenager. It was ridiculous."

"I'm sorry."

"No, you're not. But you can make it up to me by not working tomorrow. Spend the day with me."

"What would we do?"

"That's a loaded question." He sat up taller in his chair and she felt a pang of nervousness creep over her pebbled flesh. "How shall I answer?" He flashed a mischievous grin and Eliza shook her head.

"Reel it in, sexy," she teased. His laughter danced through the air, settling over her like rich warm chocolate, coating her from the inside out.

"Whatever you want?"

"Whatever I want. Funny, I don't see you relinquishing control so quickly. What if I wanted to go bowling?"

"We'd go and I'd kick your ass."

"What if I wanted to go bike riding, or hiking or horseback riding?"

"I'd say I have a bike, I can hike and I own horses – all doable. What else?" Lake challenged.

"What about just hanging out and watching movies all day? Cooking and baking and endless wine?"

"Throw in the sex and I'd say it's a winner."

"You said you didn't think I was ready." Eliza turned the tables and challenged Lake back. She set her fork down and moved her empty glass towards the bottle of champagne he'd offered moments ago.

Lake's mouth curled happily. "Change your mind?"

She was sure he was talking about the alcohol, but strangely it felt like he was referring to the sex as well. "I did." She watched him fill her glass and waited until it was full before pulling it back.

"I did say you weren't ready. I stand behind that statement. Maybe I wasn't ready either. I had a moment of pure, gut-wrenching weakness when we were in your shower. I wanted to fuck the shit out of you."

Eliza crossed her legs beneath the table to curtail the flood that was pooling between her legs. Heat rose up her neck and settled warmly over her face. She was sure she was three shades of pink.

Lake leaned across the table, trying to draw her in, but it was futile, she'd been glued to his lips since the word *sex* fell from his mouth. "I want it to be here, in my home, in my bed, where I can give your body the attention it deserves. I want to touch, taste and feel every single inch of your sweet, succulent flesh. I want to steal your heart while I steal your orgasms."

Fucking hell…was she even breathing? She fanned herself with her hand. Her mouth was parched. There was no saliva to swallow.

She looked down at her glass of champagne and realized she'd unknowingly slammed half the glass during Lake's little speech, which wasn't little at all. In fact, she was spellbound by every word – he loved to render her speechless. Prided himself on shocking her. He stared at her like a lion ready to pounce. Was he drooling? She would be if only there were something left to drool – every ounce of wetness had slipped from her mouth to her weeping pussy.

"What are you thinking?"

"You make me nervous."

"Nervous." She felt the rumble of his laugh from across the table. "What about talking about sex makes you nervous? It's what you do for a living for goodness sake."

"I don't think it's the talking that makes me nervous. I think it's *you* that makes me nervous. Your words and mannerisms are predatory and intense."

"I must admit having you here is more overpowering than I had anticipated. I won't deny how much I desire you. I'm exercising extreme self-control."

Eliza set her glass down and leaned into the table. Lake's blue eyes were heavy with lust as he watched her subtle advance for his attention. He had her riding the edge of his words. Her body was already reacting to the memory of his touch, the feel of his hands…his mouth.

"What do you want from me Lake?" she asked more brazenly than she felt. She reached up and grabbed a strand of hair, twirling it around her finger while she waited for his answer.

"Ah…the hair twirl." Lake smirked. "What do you think I want?"

"If this is about sex, maybe we should just get on with it. You make me extremely…" She looked at his mouth, then up to his imperfection. "Excited and scared all at the same time." She grabbed her remaining glass of yellow brut and wiped it out in one big gulp.

Lake stood up, walked around the table and turned her chair to face him. The scraping sound of metal on concrete echoed in the shimmery night. He straddled her body with his arms, leaning over her with a devious smile. His clean, musky smell feathered her nose. She was in over her head.

"You'd offer to have sex with me right now because you're *excited* and *scared?*" He brought his thumb up to her mouth and slid it across her lower lip. She pulled it between her lips, sucking it thoughtfully, teasingly. He dipped down to the shell of her ear. "Okay, let's go."

He held his hand out and she eased her clammy warm hand into his palm, but remained glued to her chair. Lake knew he'd stunned her by calling her bluff.

"Ahhh…not as brave as you thought." He pulled her up and tugged her to his chest. He cupped her ass with one hand and eased the other around the nape of her neck. "Listen and listen well my sweet, sexy girl. If this were just about sex, I would have already had you." They were so close Eliza could taste the garlic on his tongue. "I appreciate the offer, but when I take you," his voice dropped an octave and vibrated against her chest. "And I do intend to take *all* of you, it won't be because you're scared."

Her heart dropped to her stomach. "Please don't break me."

Lake's eyes widened and he shook his head. He could play coy, but he had it in his power to destroy her. Eliza was sure many had fallen prey before her. When his mouth found hers it wasn't with hunger, it was with compassion and understanding. He kissed her like she was as necessary as the air he breathed. No kiss had ever tasted so good. It woke every one of her senses. She gave him back the same passion. She was ready to be captured, consumed, and taken by Lake Mitchell.

"I could say the same for you."

"You could never be broken."

"Don't be so sure, Eliza," His words sliced through her like a streak of lightning. The fact that he'd admit as much blew her away. Their chests strained against one another, competing for each labored breath. His heart beat wildly over hers and his solid length pushed into her abdomen like a threatening storm. She'd claw her way into the eye if she thought she'd survive him. He was going to steal her heart…he'd said as much and she believed him.

"I'm asking for *everything*. I won't settle for less." He placed his hands on the sides of her face, framing it in the most seductive way. The way every woman alive wanted a man to hold her. Like there was nothing else, no one else…only her. Lake found the crease of her lips with his tongue and sliced through her resolve like a warm knife cutting butter. She melted into his unfiltered lust. She yearned to be taken – dominated by him. She just didn't want to see it coming. His forwardness stripped her flesh, held her bare and consumed her whole. He was raw…untamed. Her instinct to run from him was overshadowed by her need to see him live up to his words. She wanted a man to take her in the most erotic ways. She didn't want to think, she just wanted to act. Lake didn't release her mouth until he was entirely quenched and she was left a ragged sexual mess.

"Are you still scared?"

"Your kisses are powerful. I'd be lying if I said anything other than yes."

"That's why the sex will be so intense. You need to be a little vulnerable…uninhibited. The kind of lust and passion I'm going to pull from your body and mind will alter your perception. You want to test your boundaries and I want to test them too. I'll never hurt you, but I'll push your limits. It's about trust. Will you let me take you to that edge?"

He stared steadfast into her eyes as she panted out the only word she had left. "Yes." She wanted to rip his clothes off and pull him down over her, she wanted to feel him inside her. She was ready to beg…she no longer cared. "Lake…"

As if on cue, with imperfect timing, her new *pseudo father*, Sam, stood peering at them from the wall of windows that looked out at the backyard. Eliza giggled and buried her head in his neck. Lake groaned out like a maimed animal. "Tell me this is a joke.

Good god. Do you have a curfew?" That just made her laugh more. Her belly shook and she bounced against his chest. She hugged him tighter and let the levity take hold. Lake looked over his shoulder and shook his head, scolding his confidant without words. If looks could kill, Eliza knew Sam would be dead.

"Guess my time is up."

"The fuck it is," Lake growled. "Last time I checked he worked for me, not the other way around."

"Don't be mad. It's sweet. He's protecting my virtue."

"Fuck your virtue."

His mouth crashed down over hers with such hunger she was sure there would be nothing left of her. The liquid pulsing began slow and picked up speed between her thighs. If she didn't leave now, she'd never leave. He'd get everything, right here and now.

He pulled her hips hard into his erection. "Feel that? It's yours. Stay with me tonight."

"I can't." His heated breath lingered over her mouth as he sighed in pent up frustration. He was a solid rock of hard virility and she was dripping between her thighs. "I'm no less desperate for you than you are me." She palmed his erection and he panted breathlessly in her ear. "Stop, or I'll rip that dress off and take what's mine."

She reached up and ran her fingers through the thick bed of dark hair and teased his mouth. "I'm so wet…"

"That's it." Lake went to scoop her up, but she ran. When he finally caught her she was a giggly mess.

"Shall I come back, Miss Eliza?" Sam called out. They both answered in unison.

"No."

"Yes."

She flipped around and kissed Lake chastely. "Thank you for a sexually frustrating night," she teased.

"It doesn't have to be frustrating. Let me take care of it."

"Gotta work tomorrow." Eliza grabbed her purse and rushed out the door.

Eliza knew she had left Lake a panting mess as she slid into the back of the car. Sam shut the door and she exhaled the breath she didn't even realize she was holding. She was dying inside. Her body was shaky and her pussy trembled, wet with need. She knew just a simple well-placed touch on her desperate clit would push her headfirst into an orgasm. She didn't even know if she could fight the urge not to masturbate on the way home. He begged her to stay and god did she want to. The amount of will it took not to just let him slide his fingers inside her was torture. She looked out through the darkened glass to the front of his exquisite house. The front door opened and his beautiful silhouette shaded the light from within. Her stomach tightened at the sight of him. He was shaking his head and rubbing the back of his neck. Her lungs seized. She waited to see what came next.

He mouthed something she couldn't decipher in the dark of the night, then he was running towards the car. She lit up like a firecracker, exploding with happiness. The smile that pushed at her cheeks claimed her whole face. Eliza bet this guy never had to chase anyone. She had to admit how much she liked that he was going out of his way to get her.

He got to the limo and threw back the door in a huff. "Please get out. I won't ask you to stay, but I need to feel you in my arms. I have to know before you leave that you're mine."

Eliza stared into his incredible eyes and took in his plea. No one had ever captured her heart like this beautiful man. She didn't leap to his request but lifted her finger in a pulling gesture towards the interior of the car. "Come here and find out."

He lunged in and was over Eliza in seconds in a tangle of hands and lips. This time he didn't ask for permission to touch her, kiss her or feel her. He didn't have to – she was as desperate to prove her desire as he was to take it. He was kissing her and trying to talk at the same time. "I don't…" he kissed her mouth, "want you…" and then her cheek, "to leave…" He kissed her neck and she moaned into his ear. Her body sizzled, her breathing was tormented. She wanted him. He claimed her mouth with reckless abandon, trying to seal their night with a kiss that would cage her heart and hold her captive. It worked.

"I have a dinner meeting tomorrow night. I would like for you to be there. I'll call you in the morning." Lake brushed her soft, flush cheek with the back of his knuckles and she melted a little more. They turned their heads when they heard the privacy screen being lowered.

"Miss Eliza, will you be staying?"

Lake quickly covered her mouth. "Yes, she's staying."

She nipped at his fingers and licked his palm. He pulled his hand away and sighed. "No, Sam. Mr. Mitchell was just getting out."

"Mr. Mitchell, my ass." He tackled her neck with his mouth and she giggled and writhed beneath him like a snake trying to escape. "I miss you already and you haven't even left." With his head hung low and his dick straining against his pants, Eliza watched Lake climb from the car, a gorgeous mess of manhood.

Chapter Twelve

Lake walked into the house with his cock at full mass beneath his pants, his stomach in knots. Relief was nowhere in sight for the second night in a row. He walked back out onto the patio to help Katherine clean up.

"She's beautiful."

"She is."

"She left." Katherine seemed pleased with his plight. "I like her."

"She's a good girl, and much stronger-willed than me," Lake said as he gathered the plates. The clinking of china was harsh in the stillness that surrounded them.

"She's not stronger-willed than you, Lake. Not many are. But she has a sense of self-worth, and for that, I admire her. It takes a strong woman not to succumb to your advances. In the end, she'll be better for it and so will you. Maybe she's *the one*."

"*The one*? Pretty ambitious words even for you," Lake chided and kissed her on the cheek. She was like a second mother to him. His own mother had been gone for thirteen years, but Katherine had taken care of him for as long as he could remember. He was protective of his life, of his family, but he had to admit Eliza was different.

They walked into the house, with Lake on her tail. He was about to dive into the dish water and help, when his phone rang. He grabbed it in a rush. He thought it would be Eliza, prayed she'd changed her mind, but it wasn't. Instead he found the one name on his screen he'd never have anticipated…Nick Slade.

He contemplated not answering it, but maybe it was a conversation that needed to be had once and for all. He left the room.

"Good evening," said Lake, his tone calm and relaxed. "To what do I owe the honor?"

"Cut the fucking shit!" Nick's voice was slow from alcohol and thick with contempt. "You can't have her!"

"Surely, you didn't call me to dictate my personal life. I know you're not so foolish to believe that you have that kind of power over her or me."

"Eliza's been mine since…forever, you prick."

"She isn't yours, Nick. She's your friend and if I had it my way, she wouldn't even be that. Don't push your luck."

"She's not Angel. She won't bend the moral compass for you. She's never submitted to any man and I assure you she won't buckle to your will. She's too good for you. You may get her body, but you'll never have her heart. I took it at six and I've had it ever since."

Those words hit Lake square in the chest, but he wouldn't believe them. He knew the woman he was falling in love with had no interest in her childhood friend. Nick was mistaken and delusional. He was the one on shaky ground, not the other way around.

"No, she's not Angel. But Angel hasn't been my business for years. The last I remember she was still hanging onto your every word."

"You know what you are?" Nick asked, but Lake didn't offer an answer. "You're a poacher. Since when do you have to follow behind me to get a girl?"

"That's rich coming from you, Nick," Lake rebuked. "There was a time I could have said the same."

"I'm not with Angel anymore. She's a fucking man-eater."

"Interesting. I was told that you were found in the hands of that man-eater just last night."

"You're mistaken. What the fuck are you telling her…," Nick growled, guilty as charged. "God damn it! I fucking hate you!" Nick's words spewed like acid through the receiver.

Lake wasn't mistaken. He paced the floor, gritting his teeth. His flesh was on fire and his mind was reeling. "How can you text Eliza at eleven, professing to want more from your relationship with her after fucking another woman. I wonder what she'd think about that, you prick? Maybe you need to rethink your own moral compass."

"Go ahead and tell her, asshole. She would hate you for it. You can try and hurt me, but I mean something to her. We have history, which is more than I can say for you. She would run for the hills if she thought you'd hurt me to have her. Play your cards and see where it gets you. She may not be mine, but she loves me and I love her." It was like nails down a chalk board. Lake drove his hands through his hair and kneaded his neck, shaking mad. "She won't tolerate any shit from you. She's so out of your league it's not even funny."

"I will agree with you on one thing, she's not yours. Is there anything else you wish to discuss? If not this conversation is over."

"I know you were the one who sent those texts last night. She told me when we talked this afternoon." Lake didn't care about the revelation of his texts but hated the idea that Eliza tried to smooth his wrinkled feelings.

"Save the 'I'm in love with you,' for someone else, asshole, and you won't get any more texts from me. Keep it up and you'll get a hell of a lot more than some benign texts. Eliza's mine. You'd be wise to remember it."

Nick groaned. Then Lake heard the sound of glass shattering in the background. He didn't know if it was by accident or if Nick had thrown something at the wall, but it thrilled Lake to see him coming undone. He wasn't one to play all his cards, but wanted to gut Nick like a bottom-dwelling catfish. "So how's the deal going with Star, Incorporated?"

"What?" Nick's voice was riddled with surprise. Lake had just clipped his nuts.

"I heard you were making a play to buy The Kansas City Newspaper Conglomerate. I just wondered how that deal was going for you."

"What do you give a shit? It's great." Nick wouldn't give anything.

"You'll need much steeper pockets if you intend to obtain it."

"Fuck off!" Nick hung up, and Lake slammed his phone down on the counter. Still in the kitchen, he had to meet the eyes of Katherine. He didn't want to listen to her scold him, but had too much respect to turn away. "What?"

"I don't know what that was about and I don't expect you to explain it. As your friend and one of your closest allies, I'm telling you right now, if you screw this up with that beautiful woman, you'll never get her back. Some things only come your way once, Lake."

He uncrossed his arms and made his way across the kitchen then kissed the top of Katherine's head. She smelled like Youth Dew and garlic. "I won't screw it up. Promise."

Lake walked into his master bedroom. His dick was flaccid and his anger palpable. He threw himself on the lonely, spacious bed. The rich velvet duvet felt soft against his cheek. For the first time in a long time, Lake felt alone. Even though, he'd been single most of his life, with only a few women capturing a glimmer of his heart, he knew it was nothing compared to how he felt right now. It sucked to watch Eliza leave, but the call from Nick, was the icing on the cake.

Lake never intended to purchase the newspaper conglomerate, it was his Dad's deal. When he found out that Slade Industries was his father's direct competition, he agreed to put up the additional money to keep it out of their hands. It was still in negotiations and there were rumors that Nick's company was about to counter again. Lake didn't care how much they offered. He had deeper pockets than his father and Slade Industries combined. He didn't want or need to be a shareholder in the failing dinosaur, but he'd do whatever it took to keep it out of Nick's hands. Even if that included getting in bed with his father in another business deal.

Katherine was right, Lake was on a slippery slope with this one. Funding his father in the joint endeavor came weeks before Lake laid eyes on Eliza, but he knew if he kept that business deal from her it would cost him her trust and respect. He would never pit her between Nick and himself. Nick might be her friend, but he wanted her future. She needed to understand it had nothing to do with her. He couldn't deny that his disdain for Nick was a driving force now, but it didn't start that way.

Lake wondered if Nick discussed business with Eliza. Even if he did, Nick himself didn't know it was Lake's money keeping him from his deal. Or at least he didn't until Lake just hinted at as much. The idea of seeing Nick squirm thrilled him. Fuck Nick Slade and fuck Slade Industries.

Chapter Thirteen

Eliza woke up less refreshed than she hoped. She didn't sleep worth a shit. Sexual frustration threaded her abdomen all night. She almost broke down and grabbed her vibrator, but decided against it. He wanted her riding the edge of need and she was. She was a rubber band about to snap in half from the strain. Her pussy was as ripe as a melon, ready to be juiced. Eliza didn't know how much more she could take. Dinner tonight was going to pose some issues if she didn't work off some of the tension.

She didn't normally workout on Sunday's but needed the endorphins to push her through the day. She quickly threw on some nylon compression tights, a sports bra and tank, and her running shoes. It was dark outside when she emerged, but she had her route and could maneuver it effortlessly. The cool, damp early morning dew caressed her skin like a mist, as the pounding of pavement settled her mind. It was just her and her thoughts, her and the open road – and Lake Mitchell. Nothing could push him out of her brain.

He was a sexual titan, with big words and even bigger promises. She'd never been so turned on by any man. His tongue was liquid sugar, slick and sweet, dripping with perfectly placed words like a trail of candy left for a child. She'd never felt as shy, nor as bold. She wanted to take the gift he was offering, but didn't really know what it entailed. Boundaries and limits were one thing, but complete trust was another. Every time she downplayed him in her head, he came back larger than life. She didn't know what everything meant, but she was ready to give into his demand to find out.

Eliza turned the corner onto her street and slowed her pace to a walk. A sleek candy apple red Ferrari hugged the curb in front of her building, shiny and bright like a siren. A slow smile spread over her cheeks and excitement warmed her belly. She glanced down at her watch…surely not. It was six-fifty-two in the morning. With a new found pep in her step she advanced the exotic sports car. She bent down to look inside, pristine and empty. No signs of its driver. She drew in her bottom lip and circled around the back of the car. She slapped her hand over her mouth and grinned with the anticipation of a child in front of an overabundance of birthday presents…each one bigger than the next: SYNRGY4. She jumped back excitedly – he was here. Hell if this was four, what did one through three look like?

Eliza didn't walk – she ran into the building. Her thumb was a machine gun against the elevator button. The polished metal doors split and she rushed in, a whirlwind of loose wet curls and sweat covered flesh – she was sticky and stinky, but didn't care. She just needed to see him. The electronic chime as she ascended each floor was like the draw of a harp string, strumming away in her chest and ears – ding, ding, ding. She stepped out into the hall on dense legs and there he stood in all his glory leaning against her door, waiting…for her. He was melt-worthy. Her heart and pulse were competing somewhere between heart attack and stroke. She hoped neither won before she got her morning kiss.

Cerulean blue eyes warmed her from the inside out as he held her enslaved under his bright, sexy smile. Saliva pooled in her mouth and coated her thick tongue. She couldn't fight the blooming contentment his presence held for her.

He had on dark denim jeans, Jack Purcell tennis shoes, and a white button-down polo. She couldn't fake her roaming eyes. His ego was about to take flight under her heavy gaze, but she didn't care. Every inch of toned olive flesh was more perfect than the next. He was genetically flawless, except for his eye, and even that was perfect in its own right. It made him special – unique. He had an incredible sense of style. It wasn't represented in his wealth, though she was sure his wardrobe was more custom than most, but it was more with how comfortable he was in his own skin. She knew he would look just as put together in thrift store hand-me-downs. She licked her lips anxiously. Her hot body grew hotter – wetter, as she moved into his gravitational pull.

"Purcell's. I like it." Eliza pointed to his shoes.

"They're comfy." Lake curled his finger back methodically slow, over and over, calling her closer. "Come here."

Eliza's heart sprung to life and crashed enthusiastically into her ribs. "Kinda early?"

"Is it?" Lake beamed brighter than a mega-watt light bulb, blinding her with his ultra-white smile and perfect teeth. "I'm an early riser and I couldn't sleep. I see you've already been out for a run, so it's not that early."

"Yeah, I couldn't sleep either." The heat between them was stifling as innuendo hung heavy in the air.

"Good," he chuckled.

She practically skipped the remaining distance to him with a smile so wide it hurt. Lake's clean, spicy scent hit her like a wall, musk and fresh soap. She wanted to lick his skin to see if his taste matched his smell. She inhaled him into her lungs and gazed into his imperfect eyes. She wanted to throw her arms around his neck, but she was smelly and more self-conscious in his presence than when she'd first discovered he was here.

Lake folded her into a warm bear hug and bestowed her with a gentle kiss. Eliza didn't pull away, she couldn't…wouldn't, but looked at Lake like she'd discovered the presence of a third eye. "I'm going to get you all sweaty."

"I don't give a shit. If I don't touch you, I'll combust." Eliza sighed dreamily. "I've thought of nothing else but you since you walked out the door last night."

"Ditto!" She went up on her tip-toes to kiss his chin, but Lake quickly stole her breath with a panty-melting kiss. She laced her fingers though his hand and pulled him through the door. She was never so grateful that she'd at least brushed her teeth. "Come in."

They walked through the foyer to the kitchen. The smell of coffee filled the air. It was preset to start at seven and had just finished the brewing process. The sputtering, gurgle of the remaining press of dark liquid into the pot hissed loudly in the open space. "Coffee?"

"Absolutely."

She poured two mugs and watched as Lake came around her, went to her refrigerator and grabbed the creamer. She'd forgotten his familiarity with her space but liked that he was comfortable enough to maneuver around her with ease. She watched him dump the creamer into the mug, then spoon an equal amount of sugar behind it. His coffee went from pitch black to pale tan instantly. She chuckled under her breath and took a drink of the pure black dopamine in her cup. "You're cute."

"I like coffee, but can't drink it black."

"Either can my mom, but that's Blue Mountain coffee. I promise you, if you had taken a sip of it before the pound of sugar and cup of cream, it would have changed your opinion. It's the finest, rarest coffee in the world."

Lake tipped his mug to Eliza's then took his first sip of the cream and sugar with a hint of coffee. "I'll take your word for it."

"I'm going to turn on some music and jump in the shower. I'll be right back." She hit the Pandora button on her phone, and smooth 70's music filtered gently into the space. Perfect Sunday music – the music of her youth. "What kind of music do you like?"

"All kinds – blues, jazz, rap, classical, Top 40…you name it, and I probably like it. James Taylor is a favorite of mine, so leave it here."

"Me too. I'm kind of a 70's junky. It's what my dad enjoyed and what I grew up on."

She walked back over to the gorgeous man whose intense eyes held her captive, and without thought ran her fingers over his forehead and through his hair. He shut his eyes and moved into her hand. She really, really…liked when he did that. He'd follow her touch, no matter how sexual or benign, like he needed it.

"I need a shower. You going to be okay for a few minutes without me?"

"No." He was teasing, but she liked it all the same.

"The sun's coming up over the river. Take your coffee out on the patio."

She walked down the hall to her bedroom, kicked off her shoes and socks, fleshed off the second skin of damp clothes and stood soggy in her sports bra and panties. She walked into the bathroom and turned on the shower only to walk back in and find her gorgeous paramour waiting for her leaning lazily against the doorframe while sipping his mug of cream. Amazingly, she wasn't self-conscious. He'd already seen almost every inch of her. There was very little left to hide, but it didn't keep her body from tingling beneath his stare.

His eyes were glassy and full of life. His prominent brown defect was front and center against the blue lagoons that made up his beautiful eyes. He had a prominent jaw line, thick eyelashes, and smooth, flawless sun-kissed, olive skin. His features seemed softer today, less intense, but Eliza knew the dragon still loomed. He radiated sensuality. She'd kiss the flame but never let the fire claim her – she knew it was a matter of time before that changed and she was fully engulfed. The splendor of a half-cocked smile came to life against his brilliant white teeth and kissable lips.

"So you came to torture me with your good looks."

"There's no way in hell I'm going to be on the balcony, watching the sunrise, while you're naked and wet in the shower."

"I can see where that might be hard." She teased, enjoying the playfulness of his banter, while taking in the mouth-watering sight of him. "What would you think if I told you I thought you were pretty?"

"Pretty?" Lake smirked.

"Yes, pretty. Your features are prominent, yet soft, defined and flawless. It's hard not to stare…you're stunning." She could see his face pink-up with the curl of his smile. "Are you blushing, Mr. Mitchell?

"I don't know Dr. Swift, am I?"

"I believe you are."

"I like that you think I'm pretty and stunning. I want you to desire me, to want me. I want you crazy with lust…with love. Be greedy about me, beautiful. I'm sure feeling greedy about you."

"Greedy?" Eliza laughed, passing straight over the word *love*. "I like it."

She pulled her sports bra over her head and shrugged out of it. Lake's sigh echoed through the room. "Do you want me to take my panties off in the bathroom, so you don't pass out on me?"

"No. I can handle it."

She shimmed the damp lace down her legs seductively, teasingly slow and kicked them into the pile of sweaty clothes on the floor. Without a sound, Lake was on her, moving with the swiftness of a leopard going for the kill. He scooped her into his arms and kissed her salty neck. Eliza's belly and chest rumbled with laughter. "Guess, I couldn't handle it," he teased.

He opened the shower door and gently set her feet onto the smooth tiled floor. The steam was billowing around them, but it wasn't the thickness of the dense heat that left her breathless, it was the pure sensuality of Lake Mitchell. A sexual awareness was stirring deep inside her that she had never before known.

"Hurry up," he demanded.

"You're so pushy." She shoved him out the door, then shifted back into the cool water. Her need to simmer down was greater than her need for comfort.

Lake took a seat on her toilet and watched her intently. Having him there was distracting to her routine. She washed and conditioned her hair, loofah'd to polished perfection and shaved her body to within an inch of her life. She shaved every day, but wondered what Lake would think of the gesture. Would he think she was anticipating his touch? If he did, he'd be right.

Eliza turned off the water and swung the glass door open. Lake was waiting with her towel outstretched in his arms. He encased her body and started drying her like a parent would a child. It was complete body worship – it warmed her heart. He was breaking down all her defenses with tender touches, tender kisses and tender words.

"I hope all that extra body attention was for me."

"It was." She finished drying off under his heated gaze. The air thickened with unspoken words. He looked pensive, reserved.

"What's up?"

"Nick called me last night after you left." Her stomach grew tight with angst.

"Why?" She could guess but didn't want to.

"Why do you think?" Lake harrumphed, then sat back down on the commode and stared at her. "You – obviously."

"We had a pretty heated discussion yesterday." Eliza admonished and looked at Lake through the mirror instead of facing him. This conversation was one she didn't want to entertain, but knew she couldn't get out of.

"He didn't like what I had to say either. You say he's your friend, Eliza, but I need to know that's where it ends. No man wants to hear another man tell him that he's in love with the same girl he's falling in love with."

Her heart jolted. Lake's words were so twisted around each other that it was hard to untangle. Did he just say he was falling in love with her? She pressed her back against the cool wall so she wouldn't fall on her ass from the shock. She swallowed hard, focused and more alert than ever as she finally gave him her eyes.

Lake didn't seem to notice the effect he'd had on her as he went on, "I don't know if it was better or worse than him telling me you loved him too. I know Nick's important…"

Startled again, Eliza cut Lake off. "I don't love, Nick." She shrugged, looked away and then sighed. It wasn't what Lake thought, but she didn't really want to explain the depth of her relationship with Nick to him. They had history – she and Lake didn't. "At least not the way he wants me to. We've been friends since childhood. We practically grew up together. I don't know what's gotten into him."

"I know what's gotten into him," said Lake, lowering his head. "You're beautiful and he's jealous. I won't share you." His voice was small, almost as though he was convincing himself, rather than her.

Something indefinable shifted inside Eliza, pushing into all the careful boundaries she'd set around her heart. She walked over and cupped Lake's jaw, tugging his head up to look at her. The hope swimming in his eyes nearly took her breath away. She plunged a chaste kiss to his supple lips. "You don't have to share me – I'm here – with you – only with you."

Lake stood up, pulled her into his warm, muscled chest and kissed every inch of her face. Finally landing on her lips, gently seizing her mouth in claiming fashion. The smooth silk of his tongue against hers was sensual and sweet, and she craved every deep stroke. It was heavy with emotion and desire, settling over Eliza like a warm blanket. He was covering her in adoration, making love to her with his mouth. She couldn't fight the moan that threaded her lips. Lake swallowed it and demanded more. She was beginning to think that his demand to have her *everything* wasn't that far away. She was powerless to stop it her growing feelings and didn't want to.

"I promised you would fall in love with me. It starts with that kiss. Don't doubt it, baby. Kisses can change lives." Lake teased with a wicked grin. He circled her nose with his, playfully, then licked the tip with the quickness of a snake.

She didn't doubt it. "Your kisses are enchanting and I *do* love them."

"I'm glad you approve. I intend to kiss you like that every day. I guess I'll have to work a little harder to get your heart."

Once again she felt the shift in her boundaries and her stomach clenched, not knowing whether to shore them up or let them come crashing down. Heavy or not, Lake never backed down from his words. It was one of the things she admired most, but it scared the hell out of her at the same time.

Lake slapped her playfully on the ass and she pushed away. She was hot and bothered. It was an ongoing theme, a sexual storm always brewing between them. A drop of steam rolled down her spine through the crack of her ass, finding its way to the pool of wetness that caressed the opening of her sex. She probably needed to re-shower, but with him in her house and always touching her, she'd stay wet. It was futile to think differently.

She walked into the bedroom with Lake hot on her heels and flung her towel on the bed, eliciting a grumble from the sexual deviant in the room. She grabbed a bra, clasping it behind her back as he watched, tucking and pulling at her breasts until they sat perfectly in the lace cups. She reached into the drawer and fingered through her panties, but Lake stopped her by pushing the drawer shut. "No panties."

"Lake," she grumbled, hanging from a sexual cliff with no relief in sight. She needed some form of cover or else she'd no doubt leave a trail of wetness in her wake. The least she could do was curtail the slick spill with a strip of lace.

He leaned into her ear. "I know you're already wet. Let me touch you and help you out."

Eliza wanted to lunge onto his thick fingers but it wasn't going to be enough. She wanted him inside her, she needed him. But he was a hold out – a tease of the worst kind. He had the power to give her an orgasm, but she wanted him and wouldn't settle for a few digits. His cock was behind glass with one of those silly lines etched on it. "Break glass in the event of an emergency." It was probably an emergency now, but she'd never admit to it. She leaned into his ear and threw his hot words back. "I'm incredibly wet, slick and juicy with desire for you, but unless you're fucking, I'm holding out."

Lake's eyes were saucers when she finally rounded his face. Her words had the desired effect.

He grabbed her by the nape of her neck and pulled her face to his. "I'm absolutely fucking you. Frankly, I don't think I can touch you without wanting more."

"I want the night you promised – the begging and the crying because you've taken me to the edge of reason. So I'll suffer through the deep throbbing that's pulling at my seeping pussy." She didn't even know where the words were coming from. She had never been so brazen but liked seeing him distraught. Two could play that game.

"Holy-fucking-hell! I'm losing my mind." He swooped into her face. "I should have impaled you with my cock in the shower yesterday. I should have tied you to the bed last night and had my way with you. Now I'm saying yes, and you're saying no. Someone shoot me and put me out of my misery."

"Breathe through it…" She teased him with his own words. "Your orgasms will be better if you can control your breathing."

He shook his head in disbelief, slack-jawed. "You vixen. You'll pay for that. I'm going to edge you out so bad, that when I finally get you in my bed you'll be begging for my cock." He kissed her quickly on the lips and walked to the other side of her bedroom, raking his hands through his hair like a mad man. He clearly needed the distance. Having the intoxicating scent of his cologne out from under her nose was a relief for her as well. She chuckled under her breath and took pride in the fact that she had the power to frazzle his calm composure.

"Put no less than three pairs of panties on, and show me around this incredible condo. And I don't mean those flossy strands you call underwear, which will catch every amazing drop of your tasty wetness. I mean – bloomers, big, full-coverage – granny panties."

Eliza shook her head at his silliness, then reached over, grabbed her towel and wiped the wetness from between her legs. Lake grunted so loud she froze with the towel still between her thighs. Apparently she'd just committed a carnal sin against humanity. "Oh, stop it. I can't walk around dripping all over the place."

"Yes, you absolutely can. That was mine and you just wiped it away."

"Lake!" He was being juvenile and silly. She tried distracting him with a different topic. "I thought you might have taken a look around the other night."

"I did, a little bit," he admitted. "But I want to see it through your eyes."

"Sure." A sense of pride surged beneath her skin. This condo was her pride and joy.

Dressed in a t-shirt and sweatpants, with forbidden G-strings on, Eliza approached Lake with the tameness of a docile animal. She knew she'd poked the bear, pushing him beyond his limits. She didn't know his breaking point and hoped she'd never have to find out. He clutched her chin with his thumb and index finger, shaking his head with a vicious smirk pushing at his cheeks.

"I've had my fill of the bedroom and bathroom. Let's see the rest of the place."

Eliza had to admire his wit and playfulness. He was the most dominant, serious and forward man she'd ever encountered, but when his guard was down, he was the most easy-going, sweet, and lighthearted guy she'd ever encountered. She folded her hand into his and led him from her bedroom. "Come on."

She walked him through the entire place, showing him the stark contrast of dense concrete and aged wood, heavy steel beams, and exposed brick walls. Eliza had hand-picked the building based on the architecture alone. She measured and studied the space prior to buying it, and handpicked the biggest unit on the top floor. It offered the least amount of interior noises and the most majestic views of the Missouri River which was the backdrop outside her patio door.

"It's industrial but warm, open yet cozy. I brought in plush furnishings and heavy, big pieces to offset the sharp lines. I think it works."

Lake was watching her with adoring eyes that stunted her breath and made her heart swell three sizes bigger in her chest. "Do you like it?"

"I do." He closed in and curled a loose hair behind her ear. "It's amazing, just like you."

A bright smile spread across her cheeks. She was gooey with emotions like a melted marshmallow. His approval meant a lot to her. His appreciation for *her* meant even more.

"It's no mansion on Ward Parkway, but it's kind of cool."

"Stop!" Lake scolded. "I inherited that place from my uncle. It might not have been my first choice, but it's mine nonetheless."

"Might not have been your first choice? Are you crazy?" Eliza's mouth fell open as she looked at him, flabbergasted. "That's one of my favorite houses ever. Like ever, ever! I remember my mom and dad driving me through the Plaza, up Ward Parkway, and through Mission Hills as a kid. That house – your home, it's always been my favorite. It reminds me of the Louvre in France. It's an architectural masterpiece. Majestic in every way."

"Wow!" Lake grinned, his head tilted. "I've never once considered that house much more than a mausoleum that I was bequeathed. It's a monstrosity that requires a lot of money and effort to maintain. But I can't give it up because it holds more sentimental value than monetary value. Hearing you talk about it with such appreciation makes me feel proud. Next time you'll get a tour and a chance to roam if you'd like."

"I'd love that."

Eliza took his hand and walked him towards the kitchen, pulling out a barstool at the granite island that centered the space. "Sit." He took a seat. She couldn't help but want to thoroughly examine every hot inch of him. She loved that he was here. That he'd come without asking. Cupping his cheek, she turned his head to meet her eyes. "Let me see that eye."

"Damn! I thought you were about to kiss me."

"I was. The eye was just a ploy to get closer."

Suddenly she was off her feet and on his lap. "Don't tease me, Eliza."

"I wasn't teasing." She pulled his bottom lip in between her teeth, gently drawing him down and hoping he'd give her back the breath he'd stolen. Her heart was crashing against her sternum with nervous excitement. The feel of his lips were tender as they fell over hers, teasing her tongue and smoothly drawing her into his body. She could feel his kiss reignite a profound and unmistakable need within her. She looked into his lustful eyes as he released her mouth. "You feel dangerous."

"Dangerous?"

"I'm serious. Every time I touch you, I feel like I'm in danger of losing a piece of myself."

"Why don't you quit fighting it and let it happen?"

"What will you do with all the pieces?"

"Make them better than when I found them. You'll be whole when you come out on the other side." Lake's face lit up like he was Santa bestowing her with a present. Not just any present, but the only one that mattered.

"How many *right now's* are we talking about?" She knew she just threw chum in the water, but she was curious how this devilishly handsome man was still single. They were the words he used in her office to describe the reason he wasn't married.

"Are you seriously asking how many women I've been with?" He pulled his head back and narrowed his eyes. Her stomach dropped to her feet. Maybe she didn't want to know. Would she get the truth? Did he know? "Does it matter? Will you tell me the same?"

She sat up to get a better vantage point to his eyes, wanting to measure the validity of his answer. "Sure."

"Okay, Dr. Swift. Lay it on me. How many?"

She contemplated a lie but spit it out honestly. "Six. I've had six lovers. No forever's."

Lake looked at her intensely, assessing her answer. Her stomach was bubbling with anxiety. Was that a lot? She didn't know if he was judging her to be a prude or a slut. She wondered what he was thinking, but was too afraid to ask.

"For me it's up there."

"Up there?" Eliza sat a little taller on his lap. She licked her bottom lip nervously. "How far up there?"

"Up there..." He repeated, his voice an octave lower. She didn't know what *up there* meant but the sound of it made her belly gurgle. "Twenty. Thirty. Maybe more. I haven't kept count."

Her eyes fell to his lips and her muscles grew tense. She wasn't breathing. Twenty or thirty, maybe more was a lot of *right now's*. As a therapist, who dealt with human sexuality, she'd say at thirty-six years old, Lake Mitchell had made the rounds.

"Okay." She only offered him a single word. What else was there to say?

"You asked. Did you want me to lie?" She could see his body tense and heard his voice strain.

"Absolutely not!" She jumped from his lap and rounded the counter. "You're unbelievably hot. I can see it," she said, without the benefit of looking in his direction.

"There was a time when I was stupid and youthful. Sex was all I wanted." Lake was pleading for his life in the juror's box. Did Eliza put him there or did he? She could feel him staring at her profile. "I'm not very proud of the way I've handled myself with some women. I was self-serving and only focused on me and my needs. I took what I wanted and closed myself off emotionally. In my early thirties I finally figured out that my dick wasn't the way to my heart. I am extremely successful professionally, but not so successful personally. I've only loved one woman in my life...my mother. Everyone else has lacked authenticity. Their motivations for dating me were blaring. I had a serious girlfriend for a year or so, but she was a user. It was a sham. She wanted the fame and glory that went with my wealth and position. It was fake and so was she. I never loved her. She works for me now and we've both moved on."

"It must be a little awkward working with her?" A band tightened around her chest. He gets to hang out with his ex-girlfriend at work…lovely.

"She doesn't work at my office, Eliza. And it's not awkward because there's nothing there."

"Oh." She tucked her lip between her teeth. The confession, the numbers, all worked against him in her mind. If she was honest, she felt a little jealous and a whole lot sick.

Eliza turned away from Lake's piercing eyes and opened the refrigerator. She didn't know which emotion her face projected, but she was sure if he stayed focused on her long enough he'd discover it wasn't good. She felt the heat of him at her back then the gentle caress of his hands around her waist. When his head fell between her shoulder blades, she inhaled deeply and shut her eyes.

"Turn around and look at me, Eliza." She hated herself for judging him. She turned around in his arms, but didn't reciprocate the affection and left her hands at her sides.

"There's no one else and nowhere else I want to be. I'm not a saint, Eliza. I can't take back the past. I've waited a long time to find someone to complete me and I don't intend to back down now."

"That's awesome!" Her tone was laced with sadness and sarcasm. He could take his pick.

"Are you being sarcastic? Are you pissed? Or, are you jealous? I'm trying to decipher which emotion to hone in on. Maybe you shouldn't ask questions you're unprepared to get the answers to."

She hung her head in shame. She knew better than to make him feel bad for a past he couldn't change, but she couldn't suppress the bubbling emotions that brewed deep in the pit of her stomach, like black inky crude. "Maybe you're right. Or maybe my timing is shit. I don't think I was prepared to be kissing you one minute then think of your dick buried in a million plus woman the next. That combined with the fact that an ex-girlfriend works for you, killed it for me."

Lake sighed then brushed his knuckles down her cheek. "I'm sorry. I didn't intend to hurt you. But you have to be honest with me, Eliza. If I hurt your feelings, or you're mad, say so. I don't want to guess at what emotional state your in. While I enjoy chasing you like a love-sick puppy, it won't be to get the words I deserve. I'm nervous to be analyzed by you for my shortcomings and faults, but I have to be true to who I am. If you ask me a question, be prepared for the answer and don't shy away from the truth."

"I'm not analyzing you, Lake." Or at least she didn't mean to. "Your world is just so different from mine. I feel like a little girl when I'm with you. It's odd to feel small in someone's presence. I don't know if it's good or bad."

"How could you ever be small in my presence?" Lake groaned, shaking his head. "I've never worked harder to impress someone in my life. I hang on your every word, yearn for your touch, and watch for any sign that you feel the same way about me as I do you. I want your approval. I have been consumed by the thought of you from the moment you stepped into that club. If anyone feels small, it's me, Dr. Swift."

Eliza's heart climbed from the pit of her stomach and found its way back into her chest. His speech was genuine, heartfelt and sincere. She wrapped her arms around his neck and brushed her cheek tenderly against his. "Sometimes the things you say make me feel like my heart is going to burst from my chest. Do you always speak so passionately?"

"Never. I'm surprising myself." Lake feathered a gentle kiss over her lips and stared at her with profound realness in his eyes. "I don't know if I've ever felt like this before. I'm sure most people think I'm just an asshole."

Eliza laughed into his mouth. She didn't doubt he was probably right. He was like a powerful tornado taking down anything and everything that stood in his path. He was reserved and prideful, powerful and unwavering…a true force of nature. She didn't imagine he opened up to many people or showed his emotions. Yet he was opening up to her. He was a book, a mystery of unveiled words, emotions and profound claims about unmet futures and yearning desires. Eliza wanted to devour every page. She was getting the best of Lake Mitchell – the unmasked version others never saw. "I like you."

"I like you too." He backed her up against the stainless steel door of the refrigerator and stared her down. It was a predatory move but she didn't waver. Unlike the previous times, Eliza didn't fear his intensity – she welcomed it.

"You like me?" He smiled.

"I do…a lot."

She ran her tongue across the seam of his mouth, seeking entry. Once he conceded to her advances, he took over and covered her in a wealth of heady desire. The kiss was soul branding, unlike anything she'd ever felt. He was trying to access her heart through her mouth and his kisses were powerful enough to capture it. They'd taken an honest leap forward in revealing pieces of the past. Eliza could feel the power of Lake settle in her bones.

She wrapped her fingers around his waist and pulled him impossibly close. Her nipples hurt beneath her bra, ached to be touched. Her body was warming against his. Every muscle in her stomach quivered with anticipation. The familiar throb between the crest of her thighs was deep-seated and gaining momentum.

Lake's had slid over the thick cotton of her sweats and rubbed over her wanton sex. He didn't even have to touch her skin. She was riding the edge of her orgasm. "Let me touch you."

Her breath caught and her pussy clenched when his hand found her sensitive flesh. Her breathing was no more than a shallow pant as he negotiated his fingers between her slick folds into her velvety entrance. Eliza's head tipped back into the metal door and her eyes fell shut. "Oh, yes!"

"Is all this for me?" Lake asked in a thick, sexy baritone. "Look at me, baby."

Eliza didn't know how she was managing to stay upright, let alone speak. Her thighs were shaky vines, barely holding her up. She clutched Lake's shoulders and brought her forehead to his. His thick finger rolled over her tight bundle of nerves and she felt her pussy begin its aching climb for release.

"Watch my eyes, beautiful. Stay with me the whole time."

Eliza was already close to falling off the cliff of her orgasm. She could barely concentrate on breathing and didn't know if she could meet the demand of holding his gaze. He drove two fingers into her and circled the spongy pad of her G-spot over and over, milking her, demanding her submission – her soul with each stroke. She was grinding into his palm like a sex-starved slave that relied on his physical touch to live…to be freed. With one last claiming plunge into her core, she came undone.

"That's it, E. All the way…" His breath was hot embers over her lips. She rushed his face and lips in emotional desperation. This time she was doing the *claiming.*

He had called her, E. It was how her father and close friends referred to her. She loved that he'd chosen it for himself without the benefit of hearing someone else use it. The glow that settled on her face and sheathed her body wasn't just from the orgasm, but the sheer joy she felt in Lake's arms.

Chapter Fourteen

Lake could feel himself grow harder, straining against the fabric of his jeans with each languid stroke of her hand. She was going to push him beyond his threshold then kill him with another, *no*. He fucked himself with the holdout and she was making him pay the ultimate price by teasing the shit out of him. He watched Eliza take her pleasure in touching him and pushed the bulge of his thickened length farther into her palm.

Eliza swallowed his breathy moan with a kiss that made him feel liquid. "I need to feel you...touch you."

"You are touching me," he groaned.

"Stop teasing me." Her voice became childlike, pulling at his heart, shaky and pleading. "If you need me to beg, I will."

Her words shattered his heart like broken shards of ruby glass. Lake shook his head and caressed her cheek, dragging his thumb over her lower lip. "You don't have to beg me for anything. Everything I have is yours."

"Is it?"

"Everything," Lake repeated.

He couldn't remember every wanting to turn his life over to a woman. He was methodical, controlled and a step ahead of everything and everyone, but Eliza wasn't like anyone Lake had ever come across. Something about her was ethereal, rare and exceptional. Her hair was still damp from her shower and she didn't have on a stitch of makeup, but she couldn't have been more beautiful.

Lake would never concede to let her go. He'd prove his worth and earn her love. He wanted to laugh at the audacity of his situation. She had him by the balls figuratively and literally. He'd come into this with more money than he could spend in a lifetime, the power to wield an entire town, and a reputation that made him formidable, but she had all the control.

She reached down and unclasped the top button of his pants. His breath took flight as he sighed over her lips. The heat in his groin matched the heat in his belly. The sound of metal teeth parting resonated quietly between them as she drew his zipper down, slow, methodically. Lake watched her cool delicate hand slip below the band of his underwear and a chill rolled bumpy down his knotted spine. Her soft fingers captured his thick, straining erection. She urged it out of its cotton confinement and thumbed the weeping slit, rolling the pre-cum over the sensitive head.

He looked into her eyes and watched as satisfaction flamed brightly over her face. The sheer joy of his relinquished control and the ability to touch him freely looked good on her.

"That feels so good, E." His voice was a low labored whisper.

"I like it when you call me E."

"What about *baby*? Can I call you that?"

"Yep."

"Can I call you *mine*?

"You can."

Eliza's words settled over his heart and head like a warm blanket, soothing his need to possess her. He melted into her body and kissed her neck.

She reached below the base of his length and gently caressed his balls. His forehead dropped to hers as she worked both of her hands in unison over every tight inch of his sensitive cock. He ached with need, throbbing heavily with each stroke.

"I love this…touching you." she whispered, each syllable was a ripe cherry falling from her lips.

"Me too." His eyes closed. Inhaling deeply, he willed himself to calm, but all he could think about was being buried inside her. The fucking Mexican standoff was becoming a looming monster between them. He wanted to make love to her, fuck her and brand her with his hot cum.

His heart beat urgently against his ribs like a drum. His breathing was a shallow pant into her face and neck. He was losing control of himself and pumped his hips into her fist needing more and more of her perfect strokes.

Her hair smelled like fresh cut flowers, her skin clean. The scent of her pussy, sweet and musky, lingered between them. It was a heady mix, pushing him over the edge. As crazed as his body was, he couldn't cum in her hand. He wouldn't waste the first drop his life-giving sperm on her hand. He cupped both her cheeks, caging her beauty and taking her mouth in unrestrained desperation. His kiss was urgent, ravaging. She slowed her strokes and fell into the soft, languid caress of his tongue. Relief washed over him like a wave of cool water, tempering his body and mind. It was fucking stupid, but he wanted all of her and wouldn't settle for a hand job in the kitchen.

Eliza pulled away from Lake's kiss and slid down his chest. Her hard nipples jutted from beneath her flimsy tee-shirt like two thick eraser heads slicing his body as she made her way down onto her knees. *Oh fuck! Oh fuck! Oh fuck!*

The mere heat from her breath would make him come – her tongue even more. If she touched his cock in any way with her mouth, he was done for…over. He'd come so hard into her mouth she'd be drinking him down for days.

"Impressive." Eliza grinned up at him. His breath caught as he stared into her sparkling green eyes, the fleck of gold stood out brightly beneath the brown. The three colors that would pull him under. She was captivating.

"I'm glad you approve." There wasn't a man alive that didn't want a woman to look at his cock with complete adoration. He watched the tip of her tongue slowly glide across the opening at his belled head lapping up the seeping pre-cum. He knew it was all over. It was futile to hold out any longer, he'd give her this. There was no way in the world he'd stop it. It wasn't ideal, but she was. In the end he needed her touch as much as she needed his.

The minute her fluid mouth went over the crest of his thick, sensitive head, and her warm tongue slid along the underbelly of his cock, Lake let lust take over. "Oh fuck...baby."

His stomach tightened with each pull from her mouth. He dug his hand into the damp waves of silky chestnut hair and watched her suck him off like a fucking pro. She was everywhere – hands, tongue, mouth and lips – just the way he loved. He had to fight every urge not to fuck her mouth with abandon. His head fell and his eyes fluttered shut as she completely devoured him. She gripped the back of his thighs, holding him in place as she sucked him deeper. "Stop, baby. I'm about to come."

He didn't know if she'd swallow him. If she didn't stop – he'd find out. Lake moaned out as his balls drew up and legs tensed. It was now or never. "I'm going to come in that sweet mouth if you don't stop."

She pulled him all the way down her throat and swallowed. He'd never felt anything like it. The constriction over the head of his cock sent him reeling. Lake couldn't fight it. She wanted it and he'd let her have it...all of it. He plunged deeper, thrusting between her lips until she took his creamy cum like the sex starved kitten he knew she was.

"Eliza! Oh...fuck yes. Jesus...yes, yes, yes." Lake looked into her dazzling eyes and watched her suckle his cock like a champ. One more layer of her peeled back before his eyes. "Holy hell! You're so fucking hot!"

He eased from her mouth and dropped down onto his knees to meet her. She smiled mischievously and brushed the crease of her mouth with her thumb. Lake felt his cock jerk at the sight of her satisfaction. He grabbed her and tugged her into his chest, pulling them both to the floor. "I'm never letting you go."

"Because I swallowed your delicious cum?" Eliza teased, pulling her silly lip between her teeth. Lake sighed at the sight of her folding in on herself. She was a beautiful, sexual contrast, masked one minute and then revealed the next. Only to go back into hiding again. He'd break her of the shyness if it was the last thing he did. He wanted her open, honest, and unafraid.

"No, because you swallowed my delicious cum, and you said you belonged to me."

"Does that mean you belong to me?"

Lake stroked his fingers along the pulse in her neck then pulled her closer to answer her with a kiss, loving her mouth like he knew he'd one-day love her…fully. The sensual dance spoke volumes over his words, but he gave them to her freely. "Abso-fucking-lutely,"

Eliza rolled off Lake and offered her hand, pulling his half-clad body from the cold concrete floor. She straightened her haphazard clothes, and watched as he stuffed his semi-erect dick back into the confinement of his pants. She was grinning from ear-to-ear. His heart beat warmly in his chest as she looked at him affectionately. She was aglow with satisfaction and happiness; beautiful.

"I need to go to work."

Frustration slide over his warm flesh like a cold breeze. She was elusive, always slipping away. "Come with me," Lake pleaded. "Don't go in today. It's Sunday. I have an appointment to look at a building off the Plaza. I'm considering buying it and want your opinion."

"Off the Plaza? Anywhere near my office?"

Lake hated to be vague but didn't know what she'd think of him buying her building. If she came there would be no hiding it, but if she didn't, he'd gift it to her later. It was a bold move for Lake. She was strong willed. It would go good, or he'd crash and burn in a ball of flames. He wanted her to be able to collect the lease income from the other occupants. Plus, she'd no longer have to pay for her own space. I was a win-win in his book. "Why don't you come see it?"

She grabbed him by the belt loops and tugged him playfully into her chest and wrapped her arms around his neck. She was feisty and he loved it. Lake wrapped her up in affection and wanted to beg her to come, but she was stubborn. She'd stay faithful to her commitment to go to work, and he wouldn't push her. "You're not coming with me, are you?"

"You are very persuasive and hard to deny, but it will suck tomorrow if I don't finish those charts today."

He kissed the top of her head. He didn't want to let her go, but did have his own appointments to keep. "Don't forget about dinner tonight. Capital Grille at 7:00."

"Are you sure you want me there? Didn't you say it was a business dinner?"

"I do want you there. Business is an everyday occurrence for me, Eliza. I want you involved in my life, which means you need to be involved in what I do. My father has asked me to infuse some financing for a company he's trying to buy. We're meeting to discuss it tonight over dinner and drinks."

"I'm going to get to meet your father?"

"You are." Lake pushed his hands through his hair. The tension and disdain he felt for his dad was already threading its way into his mood. He knew having the distraction of Eliza would be a pleasant surprise for both of them. "Don't get too excited. We're not exactly close, but we do have a lot of business dealings with one another. I have to talk to him, even if I'd rather not."

"I'm won't pry but if you want me in your life, at some point I'd like you to tell me the history of what caused you two to be at such odds with one another." Lake kissed her on the cheek and grabbed his keys from the kitchen counter.

"Someday we'll talk about it, but not today." She'd done enough analyzing of his life for one day. The whole debacle with her inquiring into his sexual history was a colossal fuck up. Lake had never wanted to diminish certain parts of his past so badly, but would never lie about it either. Seeing her look so dejected crushed him. He certainly didn't need to add his dad's issues to the mix.

"Sure." Her eyes cast down and she started to turn away.

Lake felt like a dick. He knew he could trust her with his secrets, his worries – his history. He didn't want her to think any differently. He pulled her back into his arms and looked into her eyes. "Don't worry about me and my father. You'll probably love him. He's quite the charmer." It's one of the things that Lake hated most, because he brandished it like a sword, taking down women of all ages. Lake couldn't deny him the accolade – good or bad.

He walked towards the door, then turned back. "No panties and no bra tonight."

"A little tacky for a business dinner don't you think?" Eliza crossed her arms and looked at him like he'd asked her to go naked.

"Be creative." Lake smirked. "If I want to touch you I don't want to fight that strand of lace you call underwear."

"Maybe I'll go to Hall's." She lit up like a kid in a candy story. It was his favorite place to shop too. "It'll give me a reason to buy something new."

"Put it on my account."

"I have my own account. It's not necessary," Eliza countered.

"Don't be difficult, Eliza. Just put it on my account." She was so damn stubborn.

"Don't you be difficult. I have my own account." She put her hands on her hips and groaned loud enough for him to hear. "I don't need your money, Lake."

"Get over here!" Lake stood his ground and waited for her to cross the floor to him, but she didn't budge. The heat of anger threaded through his chest. This woman was going to be the death of him. She was non-compliant. He loved the challenge. "Eliza!"

"No!"

"You know what you need?"

"What?" she snapped back.

"A spanking." Lake rushed across the room like a cheetah taking down a young spring buck. She ran, but not quick enough. He tackled her waist, lifted her over his shoulder and made good on his words, spanking her three times. She was so cheeky, like a misbehaved child. She stiffened with each blow.

"Ouch!" She squirmed to get free but he didn't let her go. He held on tighter, locking her thighs to his chest. "Put me down you Neanderthal!"

"No!" Lake chuckled under his breath, walking back towards the door. "You are so insolent. When I say come here, I mean come here."

"I'm not your employee. Don't expect to snap your fingers and I'll come running."

Lake set her down and she cocked her hip out defiantly. He couldn't help but laugh, which only fueled her anger. "No, you're not one of my employees, but you will probably one day be my wife and the mother of my five children – you pain in the ass. I expect you to be compliant to some degree."

"You've lost your mind, Lake Mitchell." She shook her head wildly and rolled her eyes. He could feel his chest contract. He wanted to spank her again, but knew he'd be in for the fight of his life and thought better of it.

"I will call Hall's the minute I leave here and add you to my account. If there aren't charges on there for the things that you buy today, I'll be mad. I don't think it would be wise to make me angry."

Eliza pushed past him and opened the door. "Out!"

Lake walked to the open door and grabbed her chin. "Have a fun day shopping. I'll see you tonight. Be ready by 6:45."

"Yeah, yeah," she chided, then shooed him away with her hand.

Lake went into a full belly laugh. "Don't make me spank you again."

"Goodbye, Lake."

Lake grabbed her by the waist and gave her a chaste kiss. It was a scene right from a movie. A love story – the beginning of their love story…he hoped. "Bye, Beautiful."

Chapter Fifteen

Eliza went to her office to finish up the charts that she'd neglected to complete. She had been off her A-game since being overawed by the presence of Lake Mitchell. She could remember every second with him, then and now. The entire time she worked, she couldn't quit smiling. Lake was a complete juxtaposition – dominant and demanding then docile and accepting. She was completely taken by him, mesmerized and captivated. This started with his obsession. Tonight she'd make him realize it was warranted.

She walked into her favorite department store and stopped by customer service to make a payment against her balance. She didn't know what she owed, but turning up the heat meant turning up the money.

"Miss Swift your balance is zero." The young girl offered Eliza a smile. "Is there anything else I can do for you?"

A week ago she bought a pair of seven hundred dollar shoes, some dresses for work and a really nice pair of earrings. It wasn't possible that her account balance was zero. "Are you sure?"

The girl looked back at the screen. "Absolutely. Someone paid off the balance just today. $1872.54."

"Do you know who paid it off?" Eliza didn't know why she bothered asking. She already knew the answer.

"It doesn't say, but it appears your account is linked to Mr. Lake Mitchell's."

"Interesting."

Eliza thanked the clerk and made her way into the shoe department. If he wanted her to buy something, she would oblige him. She intended to slam his account with the finest pair of shoes she could find, a dress that would knock his socks off, and jewelry that would have him questioning his desire to pay for everything.

She sent him a taunting text. *Hope you like Gucci.*

I do indeed. Buy several pairs.

Interesting. Somehow our accounts are suddenly linked to one another's. Any idea on how that might have happened?

That is interesting. Bye, beautiful!

I don't need your money you incorrigible man!

Just say thank you and move on to the lingerie department. I'm sure you're in need of more strings. Just don't wear them tonight!

Thank you.

Better, my love. Your welcome.

The warmth of his well-placed word settled over her heart like melted butter, coating and caressing it until is glistened.

******

Eliza waited anxiously for seven o'clock to roll around. She'd perfected her look and had to admit the results were pretty amazing. After years of her mother forcing her into the pageant scene as a child and in her teens, Eliza was over the "dolling up" phase of her life. Her true measure was internal, not external. However, the reflection staring back at her was nothing shy of glamorous. She only hoped that Lake would think the same.

The black halter dress she bought hugged her neck and clung to her chest and hips, revealing the bare flesh of her shoulders and arms as well as most of her back. It hung mid-thigh and showed the perfect amount of leg. The rich fabric was thick and hid all the shameless nudity Lake requested for the night. But no amount of fabric could hide her nipples at full mast. She'd have to avoid Lake's touch, or they'd be on full display like daggers under a black cape.

It was 6:42 when she heard the knock on the door. Her heart seized and heat rushed into her stomach. Anticipation hit her hard. It was the moment of truth. She edged the door open to the wide, soft smile of Lake's driver and her new friend Sam.

"Good evening, Miss Eliza. I'm here to pick you up." He brought his hand to his chin, rubbing it thoughtfully as he gave her the once over. "You look absolutely stunning."

Happiness tugged her lips into a smile. His approval and response to the edge off her nerves. "Thank you."

"Mr. Mitchell's going to lose his mind." He offered her his arm, as he always did, in a fatherly gesture and they exited the building. The limo was standing at the ready by the curb. Her heart picked up pace in her chest.

"Tell me he's inside." She looked at Sam as he reached for the door.

"I'm afraid not, Miss Eliza. He's already there. Regrettably, they upped the time and he didn't want to make demands of you after he'd already told you seven o'clock. Please don't be upset. I assure you it was an unavoidable situation."

"Either you love him dearly or he pays you oodles of money to smooth over his mistakes. Which is it?" She looked into his gentle eyes trying to read the answer before his steady lips gave way. She knew he was more than a dedicated employee. He was a father figure, meticulously taking care of Lake like a son.

"I'd have to go with both."

A pang of true appreciation threaded her heart. It made her happy to know Lake had an ally he could trust. One that had his back, no matter what. Sam opened the car door and on the seat was a single red rose lying across a small envelope with her name written on the front. She picked up the delicate flower, put it to her nose and inhaled deeply. She pulled the card from the off-white linen envelope and admired the quality of his personalized stationery, heavy and rich to the touch. She slid her finger over the embossed cursive monogram LMC emblazoned on the top. The unknown "C" represented his middle name. Eliza would have to find out what it stood for. She unfolded the card and read the words he'd written in the most exquisite penmanship she'd ever seen.

Beautiful Eliza,

I'm sorry I wasn't the one who greeted you at your door.

They moved the meeting up to 6:30. An unavoidable change.

I can't wait to see you.

Lake

She clutched the card to her chest like a teenager who'd just gotten her first love letter. It was a simple note, but the fact that he'd even thought to write it spoke volumes. She tucked into her clutch and watched the city pass by as they made their way from downtown to the bustling Plaza scene. It was one of the most recognizable tourist attractions in all of Kansas City, lined with some of the finest stores and restaurants in an open air venue. Three blocks of high end luxury. At Thanksgiving the buildings came to life in wealth of Christmas lights that dazzled until the day after New Year's. It was magical.

They pulled up to the Capital Grill and the valet went to step towards the door, but Sam jumped immediately from the driver's seat and halted him in his step. He wasn't just protective of Lake, but of his possessions as well. It was a little overwhelming to be coveted in such fashion, but for now she'd concede.

He held out his hand and she emerged from the car with grace and poise. She stepped forward with nervous anticipation. Her stomach was a tangle of knots and her heart raced rapidly beneath her ribs. She took a calming breath and walked through the polished brass and glass door.

"The hostess will accompany you back. I'll be outside if you and Mr. Mitchell need anything." Sam urged her forward with his hand on her back.

"You won't walk me?" She felt like an idiot, but the comforting presence of Sam took away her fear of the unknown.

"You'll do great." Sam bestowed her with a genuine smile that eased her anxiousness. "Put it this way, you couldn't look any better. Go with that."

Eliza nodded her head and watched Sam leave. She turned back and the stunning hostess greeted her by name. "Dr. Swift?" she said pensively.

"Yes."

"Mr. Mitchell and the rest of his party are waiting your arrival. May I show you back?"

Oh, bloody hell. Who was the rest of the party? She looked back to the door and saw Sam pulling from the curb. She was left with no recourse.

"Thank you. That would be great."

She followed the hostess through the bar and the weight of a thousand eyes blanketed her as she walked through the room. Heat climbed her chest and settled on her neck. She was nervous but moved forward with as much confidence as she could muster.

"Here we are," the hostess beamed eagerly, waving her hand at the private dining room. Eliza held her breath as the door was pushed open and hearty laughs and baritone exchanges came to a screeching halt. Her confidence was a trembling earthquake and her heart fluttered in rapid succession with it. She was on full display. Five men, all sitting at a large elegantly set table, stood instantly as she entered the space. Lake's eyes danced over her with adoration. The tingle of awareness pebbled her flesh and brought a smile to her face. She focused on him but nodded to the others as they beamed brightly at her in the romantically dim light of the room. She moved forward and heard the clap of the wood door closing behind her. With nowhere to run, she faked coolness and pressed forward.

"Hey, you." Lake grabbed her hand and pressed a gentle kiss to the top of it. "You look absolutely stunning, Eliza. I'm so happy you're here."

"Thank you." His words warmed her flesh and reignited her self-confidence.

"Come have a seat." He laced his fingers in hers and walked her to the table. "Gentleman, this is Dr. Eliza Swift my…" He looked at her with a hint of mischief and curiosity behind his eyes. He didn't know how to address their relationship. What were they? She waited curiously as he decided which label to use. "Girlfriend," Lake finished.

A blush warmed Eliza's face and a smile curled her cheeks. Lake gave her hand a meaningful pump and winked his approval. More at ease, she curtsied her head and greeted them as a whole. "Good evening, gentleman. I apologize for my tardiness."

"It's us that should be apologizing to you." Lake's father rounded the table. He was unmistakable. Just as gorgeous as his son, despite their difference in age, with amazing crystal blue eyes that reminded her of shallow lagoons. "You have your mother's eyes, Eliza."

"Yes, I do," she admonished honestly, uncomfortable with any comparison to her mother. "It would appear that Lake was blessed with yours as well, minus his beautiful brown flaw."

"It's not his only flaw," he teased, eyeing Lake with spirited censure. "But his choice in you, my dear, couldn't be any better. He always had impeccable taste. It would appear he's picked a flawless diamond. You're stunning." Jonathan Mitchell was pouring on the charm, just as Lake had predicted. Eliza didn't know what stood between these giants of business and wealth, but she had to admit on the surface she liked his dad.

"Alright," Lake chimed in, his voice bristly with annoyance. "Have a seat and quit flirting with my girlfriend."

Johnathan Mitchell shook his head and smirked at his son before takin his place at the table. The rest followed. A team of servers walked through the door and began the process of refilling drink orders. Eliza was about to order when the server stepped around her and pulled a bottle of champagne from a sterling silver ice bucket. Lake gave her an affectionate wink and a knowing smile.

Eliza was admittedly giddy with delight that he'd taken the liberty to order her favorite drink.

The conversation resumed with everyone interjecting but her. Millions of dollar were on the line for the purchase of a conglomerate and they were in a bidding war. It was Mr. Mitchell bid to win, but Lake's funding that was going to get him there. She was proud of Lake. Despite the struggles between him and his father, he was an alliance when needed.

"So Eliza, what do you think?" asked Mr. Mitchell, pulling her from her revere. She tilted her head and looked at him curiously. Think about what? Surely he wasn't asking her opinion on a multi-million dollar deal she'd just found out about. Despite his beliefs about her and Lake's relationship, this was her first time within the inner circle of his professional endeavors.

"Lake doesn't usually involve his companions in his business dealings. He's the most guarded, private man I know. He doesn't take anything or anyone lightly. The trust he's shown by bringing you here speaks volumes for how much he respects and cares about you."

She didn't know if her lungs could get any fuller. She was gulping in the pearls of insight like candy. The knowledge she'd just been bestowed settled like tea leaves at the bottom of the cup. Lake was really letting her in, giving her access to his life – all aspects. This time Lake didn't scold his father for his comments. He looked at Eliza with profound esteem and respect.

God, she liked him…really, really liked him.

"We're trying to negotiate a contract for the purchase of Star, Incorporated. The Kansas City newspaper conglomerate. I just wondered if you had any insight or opinion on the matter."

The Kansas City Star…surely not one in the same. It felt like she was running on the beach, frolicking happily one minute, then speared by a poisonous dart the next, tumbling into darkness. Was this the deal that had plagued Nick for the last several weeks? She couldn't be sure, but something felt off. This was Nick's deal…

Johnathan Mitchell's deal, and Lake was financing the whole thing. The air suddenly grew thick, the room closing in. Her stomach soured with the idea that maybe she was being used to hurt Nick. It was small, but it felt like a hairline break in her heart.

She was on the spot…with Lake, his father and the three other men who were waiting on bated breath to hear her opinion. Eliza had listened intently and knew enough about the newspapers struggles from all the media outlets to address the question. Lake was looking at her, but she didn't have the courage to grant him her eyes. If this was a game she'd beat him with confidence and wittiness and never let him see how much the realization hurt.

"Well, it's only my opinion, but it's appears to be a matter of money now. They've lost their position in the market due to the digital age and profit margin is slim at best. They've been floundering for some time, as has all hard media. They can either accept a buyout, change, or continue the downward spiral. However, their recent acquisitions into other print formats, such as the social magazines, make them worthy of consideration. I, myself, am somewhat of a dinosaur, and still enjoy the feel of reading a real paper. I think with the right people in place, a fresh look at what's working and what's not, as well as bumping up a presence digitally it's a win-win situation. Let's face it, people still want the news – we crave it. It's how you get it that's changed. Cable news is thriving while the newspapers fizzle and die. Revitalize it and you've still got a winner. I would reconsider the asking price. They want more for it than it's worth in my opinion. Of course it's only my opinion. I've got a PhD in human sexuality, not an M.B.A from Harvard."

Holy shit! Was she even breathing? Eliza took a sip of her champagne and prayed it would clear the cotton from her mouth. They were all staring at her, mouths agape and eyes wide with surprise. Except for Lake who seemed aglow with overwhelming pride. It was a false sense of confidence that Eliza wanted to run from.

Jonathan Mitchell looked across the table and hit her with sharp eyes and a guttural chuckle that she felt reverberate down to her bones. "Hell, maybe I need therapy. If you're that invested in knowing that much about Lake's business endeavors, I can only imagine how great you are in your own profession. Bravo!" He lifted his glass into the air and so did the others. She obliged them and offered the same. She wanted to throw Lake under the bus to his father and colleagues.

"There's a lot of work involved if I do purchase it. My son says it's too much work, but supported me anyway. I'm not so sure he wasn't right. It's become a bitter war with Nick Slade and his father. Maybe I should sit back and see if they can breathe life back into it."

Eliza's heart sank a little farther into her stomach with the confirmation.

"I couldn't agree more. Let the Slade's have it," said Lake. "It's not worth the asking price and not worth the fight."

"How long have you been in these negotiations?" Eliza asked Mr. Mitchell, but watched Lake closely. She could read his body language from a mile away. Just the mere mention of Nick's name probably had him as nervous as she was sick.

"It's been a rough six weeks, Eliza. Offer – Counter offer. Offer – Counter offer. I need to decide what I want to do. They're driving the price up beyond what it's worth."

Relief washed over her like a cool wave. She didn't know if Lake saw her sigh, but it was a cathartic breath. The negotiations started weeks before he'd even laid eyes on her. She'd jumped to conclusions and felt bad about doubting his integrity. She'd never wanted a man more, but was scared shitless to be overpowered by him and his life.

Without warning, Lake reached over and grabbed the bottom of her chair, pulling her across the floor until she was flush with him. The heat emanating from his body felt like warm water caressing every inch of her flesh. She was hyperaware of everything about him. His spicy, sweet smell that hinted at patchouli, but was softer like sandalwood. The way his eyes held her captive with such intensity she had to look away for fear of melting. The way words fell from his mouth like a trail of Reese's Pieces…leading her, calling to her like a desperate child that can't fulfill a sugar tooth. Lake Mitchell was going to be her downfall. His kisses and his cock all worked in tandem to pull her heart under his spell. Could she survive him?

"Hearing you talk business like that made me hard. You're the hottest fucking woman I've ever met, Dr. Swift" he whispered hotly into her ear. A shiver rolled down her spine. She wanted to kiss him but knew it wasn't the time or place. She needed to know that they were okay. That this thing, this growing thing between them was real.

"I love the dress by the way."

"Thank you." She knew the dress was everything she wanted it to be. She'd complied with his no panty and bra policy and hoped the absence wasn't obvious to the other men at the table

Lake's warm hand slid over her bare thigh and she brazenly uncrossed her leg. She'd never been so daring, but her desire for him riddled her body like a disease. He was the cure. He feathered his fingers along her inner thigh, teasingly close. She had to bite down on her lip to suppress the squeak that threatened to climb from her throat. She tried to focus on the conversation, but her composure was waning. He was toying with her growing libido.

A mischievous grin played across Lake's face. He knew the effect of his ministrations and loved watching her squirm. He leaned into her ear and brushed the back of his fingers over the top of her sex. She shuddered in her seat and quickly took a sip of her champagne. "Tonight, you're mine."

Eliza swallowed the last remaining air from her small lungs and turned to meet his lustful gaze. The heated swell of need between her legs heightened with the promise of more. She was a tightly threaded ball of untamed desire. With more confidence than she'd ever known before, she leaned over and whispered hotly into his ear. "I'm counting on it."

"If you gentleman will excuse us for a moment, Dr. Swift and I have something to discuss." He scooted his chair back, and Eliza followed his lead. He walked her through the room and bar, into the hall that housed the restrooms. He knocked on the men's door and when no one answered he opened the door and pulled her in. "I've never encountered anything or anyone who's made me as uncontrolled as you. I've got to taste you, or touch you, or something. God, Eliza, I'm dying here, but you look so beautiful. I absolutely don't want to mess up how stunning you look. May I kiss you?"

"Please..." Lake pushed her against the door and moved his body against hers in a slow teasing grind, his length already thick against her stomach "Are you teasing me again?"

"I assure you if we were anywhere else, you'd know I wasn't teasing you." He wrapped his hands around her hips and took her mouth fully. The sweeping push and pull of their tongues simulated the need they both felt and hungered for. He reached under her dress and slid his fingers between the slit of her thighs. He quickly discovered what she already knew...she was saturated with desire. Every look, word, and touch had affected her. "I want you so badly."

He plunged inside her and circled his fingers over the spot that sent her overboard. Her moan echoed in the space and he swallowed it with a deep languid kiss. "E," he panted over her lips. The damp heat of his breath, the sweet taste of bourbon on his tongue and his desperate touch made her feel like a roasted marshmallow – toasty and velvety soft. He eased his fingers out of her slick wanton cunt and plunged them into his mouth, sucking and licking them clean, like the last meal of starving man.

Eliza gasped at the boldness. "Oh my God, Lake."

"Tell me you aren't embarrassed by that?" He leaned into her and ran his tongue along the crease of her lips, sharing her. "How can you be so sexual and innocent at the same time? It's such a dichotomy and never ceases to blow my mind."

"Sometimes you say and do things that shock me. I used to think you did it to get a rise out of me, but I know that's not the case. You're uninhibited. I counsel people all day long that talk about the most personal and sexually explicit aspects of their lives, but no one as feral as you. Your self-awareness and confidence are stifling."

"I'm only responding to how you make me feel, Eliza. I've never wanted anything more than I want you."

She wanted to believe him. She wanted that desire, but she was scared of it too. Maybe it was the holdout for sex that was turning this into something bigger. Maybe she was reading more into his statement than he meant. She was a woman. It was natural for her to get lost in her desire for him. She wasn't oblivious to the power he was already starting to have over her, but didn't want to get too caught up in his words. She gave him an awkward kiss on the cheek and turned away from his penetrating eyes.

Lake cupped her cheek and forced her to look at him. "What the hell was that?"

"A kiss on the cheek?" she said dismissively.

"I know what it was Eliza." His voice was laced with frustration. "It was an evasive move to my words."

"No, it wasn't." She knew it was a lie, but wasn't prepared to lay out her feelings. It had already been a tumultuous night of discoveries.

"Yes it was." He wasn't letting it go. "Talk to me."

A knock on the door sounded behind them and Eliza felt the vines of nervousness unwind from around her stomach. She sighed, grateful for the diversion. She'd just escaped a heart-to-heart she wasn't prepared to have. She turned to move from the door, but Lake held her face resolutely. "You're off the hook now, but we need to talk about this. Me saying how much I want to be with you shouldn't amount to a peck on the cheek. That's shit, and you know it."

He framed her face with his hands and brushed the words back over her mouth in slow succession. "I…want…you."

She nodded her head up and down, nervous to concede and too afraid not to. "I…want…you…too."

His devilish smile reappeared. "Better."

They exited the restroom and Eliza pulled Lake back around. If he was demanding answers, she was going to as well. "Why did you want me to sit in on this business dinner tonight?"

"Because I genuinely want you in my life. The shit my dad said about me is true. I'm very private and my circle of trust is very small. Your trust and confidence in me are paramount. The only way I'll ever win your heart is if you believe I'm worth giving it to. There can't be any secrets between us, Eliza. I wanted you to know about this deal because it involves Nick and his father. Our relationship has no bearing on it. It's strictly business."

"It is business, but your need to win may be clouded by your desire for me."

"It's my father's contract to get, not mine, but I won't lie to you. Keeping it out of Nick's reach is very appealing." He ran the back of his fingers down her cheek and her breathing stalled. "As for my desire for you…" His eyes sparked under the dim light like rare blue diamonds, putting Eliza in a mesmerizing trance. "My desire for you will probably cloud my judgement for as long as I live."

His lips never made the move to claim hers like his words had. She was speechless, suspended between the reality and the promise. Eliza didn't expect anything less deep from Lake. He never backed down and never filtered his conversations or actions, always remaining true to himself and his desires. It was an admirable quality, potent and honest. She brushed her lips over his and kissed the crease of his mouth, but he wouldn't let it be enough…it was never enough for either of them. "Kiss me like you mean it, baby. Show me how you feel."

Eliza complied without thought. She hungered for Lake's kisses. The ones that held her heart imprisoned and locked to him. The ones that melted her into a pool of wanton lust – raw and weak with need. Eliza gave him the kind of kiss she knew would say more than words and he accepted the gift with a greedy hunger that shook her to the core. She was losing herself in him, one kiss at a time.

"That's better," said Lake, circling his nose over hers and pecking her lips one final time with a moan. "Let's get this dinner over with, so we can get out of here."

She spent the rest of dinner listening to the conversations around her, but the one in the bathroom still lingered heavily in her mind. Lake said he'd never wanted anyone more and it wasn't the first time he'd made that statement. What if he did want her? *Really* want her? Dating him and loving him were two separate things altogether.

Eliza Swift, sex therapist, in a relationship with Lake Mitchell, the billionaire philanthropist who not only owned a vast array of corporate entities, but secretly owned a private sex club. One she had the courage to go to, but never the bravery to do more. She'd either be revered as the most knowledgeable, well-rounded psychologist in her field or a laughing stock amongst her peers. It might be a private member's only club for the most elite, but nothing that tantilizing ever remained secret long.

She watched him as he spoke, commanding the room and everyone in it. Lake sensed her ogling gaze and threw her a seductive smile. He was as brilliant as the sun – blinding and beautiful. Her body tingled with excitement…anticipation. She knew in that very moment, with a hundred percent surety, that he'd take her heart, even if she was too scared to let it go. He mouthed silently, "I want you."

"I want you too."

Chapter Sixteen

Dinner finished with customary handshakes and acknowledgments. It didn't take long to understand the magnitude of Lake's influence in the business world and the relevancy of what his partnership meant to his contemporaries. He didn't just inherit a couple of companies, he inherited a conglomerate that was global and far-reaching. Everyone hung on to his every word, and she couldn't deny she had as well. It was incredible to see him in a different light. He handled his professional life, just as he did his personal life – relentless and unwavering.

"Eliza, the pleasure has been all mine this evening." Mr. Mitchell took her hand and pressed a gentle kiss to the back of it. "Beauty and brains, it's refreshing. I can certainly see how you were Miss Kansas, you're absolutely stunning."

"That was many moons ago." A rush of heat wrapped around her neck. "I'm surprised you even know about that." Lake stood wide-eyed with disbelief behind his father, obviously caught off-guard by the fact that his father held a pearl of knowledge he didn't know. She gave him a sheepish grin and a shrug of her shoulders.

"My pageant days have been over for some time now, Mr. Mitchell, but I appreciate the compliment."

"Make sure to give your mother my best."

"Ah…that's right. I'd almost forgotten. How was the *big* date?"

"Date?" Lake questioned. Eliza looked at Lake and mouthed the word – "sorry."

"Sylvia Swift is quite the charmer." A genuine heartfelt smile claimed his face.

"My mother is a lot of things Mr. Mitchell, charming isn't one of them."

He chortled out loud and put his hands on his hips, posturing friskily. "She is a bit of a spitfire, but no less charming."

"Agreed." Eliza conceded then reached over to give him an earnest squeeze on the shoulder, but he quickly pulled her in for a hug. It was fatherly and unpretentious.

Lake sighed loudly behind them and Eliza rolled her eyes. He was being ridiculous – all male and jealous.

"Enough already. Don't you need to get going?" Lake growled at his father.

"Jealousy doesn't suit you, son." Mr. Mitchell released Eliza and shook his head at the audacity of his son's behavior.

"I'm not jealous," Lake demanded. "Watching you paw her to death is pissing me off."

Johnathan Mitchell looked at his son and chuckled under his breath. "It's called J.E.A.L.O.U.S.Y and I'm not pawing her to death."

Eliza walked around Mr. Mitchell to her stunning, intense man and grabbed him by the hand. He groaned and gave her a kiss on the cheek.

******

Eliza slid across the smooth black leather seat of the limo and looked out the window. Dancing stars peppered the black sky. Lake spoke briefly to Sam, then eased in next to her. He held his hand open and Eliza seized it with hers. The intimacy of handholding was never lost on her. She was electrified by his warmth.

"I'm sorry I wasn't the one who picked you up this evening. I hate that anyone, including Sam, got a first look at you. You look ravishing Miss Kansas." Lake smirked. "How did I not know this little tidbit?"

"I guess your Google search didn't produce the results you were looking for." She wrinkled her nose and sighed. "I probably would have never mentioned it, but my mother brings it up occasionally.

I'm sure that's how your father found out. I'm sorry I didn't mention their date. It seemed so insignificant to me, but I should have told you."

"Sounds like they're perfect for one another. They can be *charming* together." Lake made double air quotes with his fingers.

"You father *is* actually charming, but my mother is a bitch, and I'm her lifelong project." Eliza looked away. She didn't want to peel back the onion on her relationship with Sylvia Swift.

"Look at me." Lake tightened his grip on her hand and slid closer to her. "Your no one's project, baby. My heart swells every time I look at you. You're beautiful, intelligent, witty and funny. You never cease to amaze me. I feel like the luckiest man in the world when I'm with you."

Eliza could taste his words as they dripped from his mouth like honey. "Lake..."

"It's true." He pressed a kiss to her exposed shoulder and her stomach tingled with anticipation.

"So where are we headed?"

"I have to run to The Raven's Nest really quickly and then we're headed to my house. Katherine made carrot cake. It's my favorite dessert in the whole wide world. I've already shared too much of you with everyone else. The rest of the night is mine."

The slow creep of excitement scaled her spine. The promises...the expectancy...the holdout, all a heady mix. They were going to the club and then he was taking her home. She didn't know which one to be more anxious about.

"Sounds great." Eliza unconsciously reached for her hair and twirled it between her fingers.

"You're nervous?"

She'd love to lie, but it just wasn't in her repertoire to be dishonest, and she wouldn't start today. "A little."

"Why?"

She sighed. Was he kidding? She didn't buy for a minute that there wasn't a little bit of nervousness on his part. They'd been tip-toeing around intercourse for days. "Really?"

"Yes. Really?"

He turned his body to get a better view of her and it made her thoughts feel loud. She dipped her head and turned it slightly, wondering if he was just screwing with her or if he was serious. Did she really have to tell him why she'd be nervous? Maybe he should have taken his session in her office more serious.

"Sex has become the elephant in the room for us. You've made such a big deal about the begging, and crying, and how mind-blowing it's going to be. I'm nervous that I won't live up to your expectations or better yet, you won't live up to mine."

His chest buckled as a terse laugh spilled out into the tight space. His whole body vibrated next to hers. Her palm grew damp in his. Lake untangled his fingers from hers and loomed into her like a waiting lion about to seize fresh kill. Her heart jumped wildly as a predatory grin spread over his face. "I'm absolutely going to live up to your expectations and there's no doubt you will live up to mine. This is about discovery and openness. Learning and giving. I want to show you everything I know about pleasuring you and I'm open to letting you do the same. I'm not nervous. I'm excited. The taste of you, the sight of you, and the way you smell like vanilla and gardenia are intoxicating. The feel of your soft warm skin and the magic of your kisses turn me inside out. When I said, 'I want you' it wasn't just words. I really, really want you. I'm trying my hardest not to overpower you, but the desire I feel for you is palpable. I want to possess every inch of you."

His lips brushed against hers and she melted into him. The throb of each and every word settled into the recesses of her pussy like a magnet, pulling her to the edge of sanity. She was more nervous than ever after his little speech. No man had ever spoken so bluntly about what he wanted or expected, physically, emotionally or mentally. It was a powerful aphrodisiac. The kind of stuff movies were made of. She was in the middle of the most dramatic love story ever. It was downright daunting. *Breathe! Breathe! Breathe!*

They were both lost in the moment, when the car came to a stop. They were in the garage of the downtown building that housed The Raven's Nest. She didn't know how she felt about being here with Lake. If she showed signs of nervousness before, she probably looked like she was going to snap. Her insides were on fire and she was wet with desire.

"I want you, Lake." It came out as a desperate plea and for once she didn't care.

"I know you do. Let's hurry up and get out of here so I can get you home and show you how much I want you to."

It was Sunday night and oddly the place was alit with beautiful wealth and desire. Lake had her clutched tightly by the hand as they made their way through the room. Everyone acknowledged Lake with a nod and eyed Eliza.

They stepped to the bar and Robert lifted a bottle of champagne in the air like a dangling carrot. "Champagne?"

"That would be lovely." Eliza loved Robert and considered him her only real ally in the eccentric environment.

"Scotch and water for me Robert," said Lake.

"Eliza, I didn't think it was possible for you to look any more beautiful, but tonight you look extraordinary."

Robert was as hot as any man in the room, excluding Lake, and his flattery was always welcome. "Thank you. You're sweet."

"Yeah, and a big flirt," said Lake. "Do yourself a favor and don't flirt with her in front of me. Better yet, don't flirt with her at all."

Lake claimed not to be a jealous man, but his actions and mannerisms said otherwise. He was fiercely protective of her and she couldn't deny she loved it.

"Yes sir, Mr. Mitchell." Eliza winked at Robert and he winked back.

Drinks in hand, Lake led Eliza across the room to an expansive circular booth. The seat was covered in rich black velvet with a round glass coffee table perfectly centered in the middle. He ushered her into the center so she'd have the best vantage point, but she was the one that was on display. Clearly being here with Lake was making some sort of statement. The cold effervescence of the champagne tickled her tongue then settled into her warm belly. Lake bent down and lapped at the crease of her mouth. Her lips parted easily and she devoured a powerful, claiming kiss. By the time he released her, she was in a hazy fog of lust.

"That should keep the sharks at bay," Lake breathed hotly over Eliza's mouth. He ran his finger across her forehead and tucked a loose wave of hair behind her ear. "I'll be back in a few minutes and we'll leave." He turned to leave, then turned back. "Come with me?"

"I'll be good." Eliza shook her head at him and sighed.

He was bordering on overkill with the protectiveness. "Hurry up. I'm ready for you to show me all the ways you intend to pleasure me."

He stepped back into the booth and pulled her to her feet, but even with the exceptionally tall heels, he still dominated her. "I'm going to fuck you so good, you'll be breathless and in love with me before it's all said and done." He kissed the tip of her nose and released her to wallow in his words. She was already breathless. She'd never been fucked into "love," but if anyone had the power to make it happen, she didn't doubt it was Lake Mitchell.

Eliza practically fell back onto the booth, limp with desire. Heat pooled at the apex of her thighs. She sipped her champagne and waited for her gorgeous paramour to return. People were mingling and flirting with one another under the romantic glow of candle light and the rhythmic sound of Wicked Games by Chris Isaak filtered into the room like a sexual fog. She looked up to the second floor and watched as doors opened and closed – private and open play. She remained intrigued.

Eliza was lost in the scene around her when she heard the unmistakable purr of Angel. "I'd ask if you were here for me, but I saw Lake looking ever so possessive of you, so I take it you're here with him."

"I am." After being played by Angel in the restaurant yesterday she wouldn't mince words with the flirtatious maven of pleasure.

"Nick Slade, now Lake…you must truly be something, Dr. Swift."

Eliza didn't miss the fact that Angel added doctor to her name. She didn't offer a reply. It wasn't as much a question as it was a statement. She didn't need to explain her relationship to either man, but wondered the extent of Angel's connection to both. She worked for Lake, but Nick was another story.

Angel sauntered into the booth and stood in front of Eliza, towering in her silver glitter pumps and red sheath dress that hugged her frame like a second skin. Eliza admired her confidence. She was a siren for sure, but Eliza wondered how much of her was show. Under her aggressive, sexual persona, Eliza imagined she was as fragile as any woman.

"Would you like to have a seat? I'd relish a conversation." It was mostly a lie, but Eliza knew there was more to the club's dominatrix than met the eye.

"I'm not really interested in talking, but if you need a warm up I'm game." She dipped forward letting her breasts spill over the top of her dress before angling her legs down to take a seat. Her signature scent of jasmine splashed over Eliza's nose like a crashing wave. She was already so turned on from Lake that Angel's flirtations were actually making her hotter. Her stomach was tight and her mouth felt dry.

"You're very aggressive." Eliza observed her as a patient. She couldn't help it. "Is it a power thing or a woman thing?"

Angel slid closer and her tongue jetted out to wet her ruby lips. Eliza couldn't draw her attention from Angel's mouth, which she suspected was the desire effect. "You need to give yourself more credit. Maybe it's a *you* thing. Why would you think Nick and Lake would desire you, and others would not?"

All the alcohol had ironed out Eliza's self-consciousness. She took another sip and called her bluff. "So what did you have in mind?" She didn't know if she had the courage to follow through, but it was probably better to be dominated by an experienced lover, than fumble around with a woman as unproven as herself. Wasn't this about discovery, new experiences and trust? Was it all pussy licking, tit sucking and finger fucking? It seemed to Eliza that if you needed to strap-on a dildo, you might as well be fucking a man.

"She doesn't have anything in mind." Lake rounded the corner like a man on fire. Eliza stiffened and Angel let out a low frustrated sigh and rolled her eyes. Eliza wanted to giggle but thought better of it and bit her lip instead.

"There goes our fun." Angel glared at Lake and gave him a snarky half-grin then turned to Eliza and blew her a kiss. "Maybe next time, beautiful."

Lake's voice shuddered like thunder in Eliza's chest. "There won't be a next time."

Angel stood, unrushed. Her sparkly pumps gave her a fair advantage and she met Lake eye-to-eye. "Since when did you become so greedy over a woman?"

Lake crossed his arms over his chest and stood rock solid. "You have a job to do. I suggest you go do it."

Angel turned and stormed away. "Asshole…"

"Don't push your luck, Angel."

Lake looked at Eliza and shook his head. "How many people will I have to fight to make you mine?"

Eliza stood up and slid both arms around Lake's neck. "Done?"

He wrapped his arms tightly around her waist and tugged her into his chest – sealing them together. The groan of frustration rose from his belly and vibrated between them. "You're acting ridiculous. Isn't this your club? I'm not sure what her title is, but I'm pretty sure she was doing her job."

"Not with you, she's not." Lake's mouth crashed down onto hers. His kiss drained her of all thought. The desperation and yearning was like a slow deep burn in her core. "Who do you belong to, E?"

"You." She loved it when he dropped her name to a mere letter. She dipped her tongue back into the slip of his mouth wanting to taste him again, needing it to sustain her like food and water. She craved everything about him. "Just you." He moaned and captured her tongue with his. "Take me home."

They made it out with Lake tugging her along like a misbehaved child. She thought she'd smoothed his feathers, but clearly not. His behavior baffled her. *Enough!* She brought her Gucci's to a halt and pulled her hand away. "What are you so mad about?"

"I'm not mad." Lake ran his hand through his hair, leaving it perfectly tousled. It was his go-to move when he was angry or frustrated.

"Lake, it's a sex club. It's not the first time she's hit on me. It was innocent flirting."

"It wasn't innocent, I assure you. I don't want her flirting with you. I don't want anyone flirting with you. It's making me crazy. I've never felt like this about anyone. I feel like a child with a special toy, and every fucking kid alive wants to take it from me. I won't share you with anyone, and that includes that slutty man-eater. I'm sorry if I got angry. I just didn't plan on coming out of my office to see her drooling over you and you being so receptive. Is that an experience you want to have?"

"I'd never really considered it before, but she's super aggressive. I let her flirt with me and I toyed with her a little bit like she was toying with me. You told me to be open to anything. I'm just trying to live up to those words."

Lake sighed and looked up into the air like the answers were going to fall from the sky. He seemed conflicted. She had unknowingly landed in his world and he didn't know how to let her maneuver through it. She wondered how she became the one woman, out of all the others that had changed him so drastically. He brought his forehead to hers. "I'm sorry."

"Don't be sorry Lake, be honest. If it bothered you, it bothered you. You own this place. I'm trying to figure out how it plays into your life. But it doesn't change how I feel about you. I'm just trying to feel my way around you."

"I own it, but it's a business, not my life. I don't come here all that often and don't bring anyone with me when I do. It's not my playground, Eliza."

"Well, that certainly explains why every set of eyes was on us."

"If I ever bring you again you'll be tethered to me."

"Like a kid on a leash." she grinned.

"No, like a kid in one of those baby holding contraptions you strap to your chest."

They both started laughing. "You're so silly." Eliza practically jumped into Lake's arms. His lips swept over her jawline then moved down her neck. "You promised me carrot cake."

"I promised you a lot more than carrot cake," he whispered.

"Yes, you did." She grinned, anticipation teased her stomach. "Time to make good on that promise." Suddenly her feet were out from underneath her, and she was curled against the hard plane of Lake's muscular chest. Eliza brushed her lips over his ear. "I'm not nervous anymore."

She looked over Lake's back and saw a familiar face walking towards them – Nick. Oh, bloody hell. Their eyes met and he halted in his tracks. Within seconds, he was racing across the pavement to close the gap. His gait was heavy and his irritation palpable. This wasn't going to be good. The last time they spoke it ended with both of them shouting at one another and Eliza hanging up on him. Lake's nerves were already frazzled and the sight of Nick was probably going to drive him to the edge of sanity. This was a complication of the worst kind. She didn't want to sacrifice one man for the other.

"Eliza we need to talk!" Nick's voice echoed loudly in the parking garage.

Lake turned towards Nick with her still nestled in his arms. "No, you don't!"

Eliza could feel Lake's arms tighten beneath her. "Call me tomorrow, Nick."

"Now would be better." He came to a screeching halt in front of them, his arms over his chest.

"She said tomorrow, Nick. I'd say never, but that's not for me to decide."

"She can speak for herself, asshole!"

"Nick!" Eliza yelled, trying to diffuse the situation. "I'll call you tomorrow."

Lake smirked like he'd just taken down his rival in a heavyweight bout by TKO. He turned and walked Eliza to the open door of the limo. Eliza looked over his should at a very pissed off Nick Slade. She wondered what history had brought these men to this point. They were vicious adversaries and it was more than business. She felt badly for Nick. He looked dejected – sad. Strife never lasted this long between them and she didn't know if this was fixable. She was falling in love with his enemy.

Lake set her down on the leather seat and kissed her cheek. "I'll be right back."

"Please don't be mean, Lake." He groaned, but nodded then shut the door purposefully.

The windows were dark, but she could see him approach Nick. The strain and resentment could be cut with a knife. Their discussion was getting heated, pointing and palms waving, shaking heads and spitting words. Eliza wanted to believe she wasn't the topic of conversation but knew better. Lake came back to the car and Nick started for the door of the club. He might be furious with her, but it didn't keep him from enjoying a night of sexcapades with the woman of his choice. Eliza shook her head and sighed. Nick never failed to live up to his reputation.

"Home," Lake told Sam as he entered the car.

"You want to tell me what's going on with you and Nick?"

"I think he's an asshole and a womanizer. He's admittedly in love with you and even if you say that's not reciprocated, he's still a part of your life."

She crawled across the seat and straddled his lap, cupping his cheeks with her hands. "Look at me, baby." He bestowed her the gift of his beautiful blue eyes. "I want you."

He wrapped his arms around her waist and pulled her closer. "You just called me baby."

Her heart warmed with his smile. "I did." She kissed him tenderly and felt the tension slide from his face with a gentle sigh. "I want you and only you."

"Say it again."

Eliza tipped her forehead to meet his and feathered the words across his lips. "I want you and only you."

He buried his hands in the back of her hair and kissed her with the hunger she knew waited for her. "I want you too."

Chapter Seventeen

The car pulled up to the grandeur that was Lake's house. Eliza stepped from the car and looked up at the mansion in awe. It was truly a sight to behold. Magnificent and regal in every conceivable way.

They entered the foyer and Sam drove away. "I assume when I want to go home, you'll be driving me?"

"You aren't going home. You're staying with me." Lake said, matter-of-factly, like it was assumed.

"It's Sunday night. I have to work tomorrow and I don't have any clothes here."

"Yes you do. In fact, you have a closet full of clothes." Eliza jaw went slack. She tilted her head and looked at Lake in confusion. "I want you here…with me. So I asked Katherine to set you up with everything she thought you'd need to have more permanency in my home. I didn't have time to rummage through the vast amount of clothes and shoes that are lined up in the closet, but I assure you, you're covered for work and play…maybe more. The drawers are stuffed full of things.

Eliza brought her hand to her mouth in shocked bewilderment. He'd made preparations for her to stay. Like *really* stay. She didn't know how to feel about it. On one hand, she was flattered, on the other it was one more way she was overwhelmed by him.

He looked at her questioningly. "Are you upset?"

"I don't know. I guess I'm a little shocked." She tried not to act unappreciative, but it was a forward and presumptuous move. "You just never cease to amaze me."

"Come here, beautiful." Lake's voice was soft and sexy. Like a moth drawn to light, she moved into him. "I hope I never quit amazing you. You deserve to be amazed."

She took in a calming breath and pulled his head down to hers. "Thank you."

"You're welcome." He kissed her on the forehead and grabbed her by the hand. "Let's go eat my cake."

Excitement spread across his face. They walked into the dimly lit kitchen. It was remarkably modern, considering the age of the house. A row of modern bronze pendent lamps lit the large granite island that dominated the sprawling room. In the center, under a beautiful crystal domed cake plate was the holy grail of desserts. Lake's favorite – carrot cake. The smell of the cream cheese frosting filled the air like a cloud of cotton candy.

He pulled out a stool and tapped the seat with his hand for her to sit. She watched as he maneuvered around the kitchen, gathering up what he'd need to dig in. He pulled the heavy glass across the counter and plucked a post-it note from the top. He let out an exasperated sigh and handed the note to Eliza. *"Moderation."* She giggled...this was some serious shit. Lake ran a long silver knife through the cake, cutting the biggest slice and pulling it out onto his plate. It was no less than a fifth of the whole cake. The note made perfect sense. His beloved Katherine knew him well.

"Holly shit!" she chuckled. "You weren't kidding. You're going to be sick if you eat all that. Not to mention all the calories."

"It's my favorite, and you're going to eat half." A mischievous grin spread across his cheeks. "I'm not too worried about the calories. I intend to work them off."

Eliza blushed. "I bet."

Lake cut a huge hunk of cake with his fork and held it up in front of her mouth. "No. It's the first bite. You take it."

"I already know how good it is. I want you to have the first bite."

She looked back at the heaping mound and held her hand up. "You aren't serious? It's too big."

"Oh, I think your mouth can handle it." Lake winked and fire ignited in her belly. She rolled her eyes and opened her mouth as he eased it in. She could barely close her mouth around the succulent dessert and had to use her hand to mask the fact that she was going to have to chew part of it with her mouth open. She giggled around the cake. "Mmmmm..."

Lake nodded in acknowledgement then cut a small bite for himself. Eliza's gave an exasperated moan of disbelief. She looked like a chipmunk with stuffed cheeks and he was taking a child's bite. She couldn't talk because she was still eating, but playfully slapped him on the shoulder. He laughed and continued devouring the decadent dessert.

She finally managed to swallow the last of what was in her mouth. "You jerk!" She pointed her finger at him and playfully circled it in his face. "I can't believe you did that. It was like a bad wedding video. You get the dainty sliver of cake and I get slammed in the mouth with the top layer."

"I'll never do that at our wedding. I promise."

Her heart jolted. Wedding?

"Guess your house is a different story?" She felt a little awkward for the wedding analogy, but it was too late to take it back. Lake played right into it. Suddenly he had another enormous bite dangling at the tip of her lips. She leaned back and held her hand up. "No way. You eat it."

"Open up," he demanded.

"No."

"Please, baby." His voice was laced with sugary sweetness and gentility, but she wouldn't be baited. "I promise I'll just put part of it in your mouth, and I'll eat the rest."

"I'm not falling for your tricks, Lake Mitchell." She turned her cheek to the side and kept moving back as the fork kept advancing.

"Would I trick you?" His smile was so wide she could see the full display of his perfect white teeth.

"Yes, you would." She gently pushed his arm away from her face. "N.O. – no!"

"Did I tell you how I hate the word *no*?" Lake set the plate on the counter and fingered an enormous dollop of the creamy white frosting, and with bewildering quickness, slammed it across her mouth. She couldn't move quickly enough to avoid it and sat wide-eyed looking at her playful paramour. He was between her legs smearing it like an oil painter over canvas. She palmed his chest and pushed him back with both hands, but he was a boulder of hard muscles. It was no use.

"Oh, you're in for it now," she breathed through the sugary goodness that masked her face. Eliza hated to do it, but jumped up and reached over to the remainder of the icing on his slice, scooped up as much as possible with her hand and smeared it over his mouth and chin. He tried to retreat, but she held his neck so he couldn't get away. "Take that you little shit!"

They were both laughing uncontrollably, a mess in fine clothes and she couldn't have felt more content. This was the best of him. The guy she loved. The one who was stealing her heart. The laughter settled when he grabbed both of her wrists, thrust his chest against hers and pushed her into the counter. His blue eyes were soft but determined. He was the picture of untamed desire and raw sexuality.

"You're going to pay for that young lady." His words slid across her sticky lips.

"Your ass I will. You reap what you sow." Eliza tried to weasel out of his hand, but Lake tightened his hold. He dipped into her face and started lapping up the icing like a bear over a cub. His attentive behavior ignited emotions deep within her heart. The air was charged between them…electric with lust. He released her hands and kissed her with yearning need. It was a knowing dance – the one she wanted to keep dancing over and over. Her body spiked with a fevered rush of heat. It was now or never with this magnanimous man. No more hold outs. No more waiting.

Eliza gently swept her thumb over a dollop of missed icing on Lake's face and he pulled the digit into the warmth of his sensuous mouth. Wetness pooled between her legs and the air left her lungs in a heated rush. "Lake…"

She reached down and smoothed her palm over the hard length that was straining against his slacks. His breathing grew more erratic with each methodical stroke. She pulled her thumb from his mouth and replaced it with the deep sweep of her tongue. He took over the kiss, devouring her – tasting her. The sweet slow burn of lust-filled the air around them. It was like nothing she had ever experienced. His kisses were an act of sex in themselves…powerful and explosive…charged. A low throb pulled at her core. Eliza knew it wouldn't take much to spill over into an explosive climax.

Anticipation nearly buckled her knees. They were in his house. Everything she'd been waiting for was finally about to happen.

Lake's liquid eyes washed over hers as he reached around and unbuttoned the three pearls that held up the top of her dress. Her nipples tightened. The bodice fell to her waist, dragging across her tight buds, and exposing the heavy swells of her breasts. Her heart felt like it was too big in her chest and she couldn't find her voice. She was covered in goosebumps and each tiny hair that peppered her heated flesh was standing on end. She shivered hard when his mouth came fully over her tight areola. Her limbs turned to liquid. The mere act of standing was difficult. His hands slid down her waist and the rest of her dress pooled at the floor. Standing naked before him, completely exposed while he was fully dressed made her tingle with sensuality and passion. The muscles of her stomach were quivering with expectancy. There was nothing left to get but her beautiful Gucci stilettos and her heart. She knew he'd take both.

Her heart was pounding a mile a minute, ready to explode out of her chest and into his hands.

Lake took a step back and drew his eyes wistfully over her frame, stopping at her exquisite pumps. She clicked the heels. "There's no place like home…There's no place like home." She quoted The Wizard of Oz for levity.

Lake chuckled, "You are home, Dorothy."

She drew her bottom lip between her teeth and feigned confidence. It was hard to be on display in front of the flawless man before her. God, what was he waiting for? She wanted his hands on her. Eliza stepped over her dress and wrapped herself up in his warmth. His hands threaded her waist and slid down to cup the globes of her ass.

"Let me worship you." His whisper was soft but sure against her ear. "Let me have you."

Her breasts ached. Her entire body was vibrating. Eliza was in such a sexual fog she would have agreed to anything…everything. She cupped his cheek and he leaned into the comfort of her caress. Her emotions were all over the place, loose and pliable like her body. Easily manipulated to his will. He pulled at her bottom lip with his teeth so she'd release it and then ran his tongue over the part that she chewed, smoothing it… soothing it. A surge of wetness pooled at her opening… She groaned in torment. Her heart was racing like a thoroughbred, wildly trying to win the race. She needed to reach the finish line. It was maddening. "Lake," she moaned in desperation.

"You're shaking."

She nodded, unable to form words. She was strung so tight her stomach hurt, she was dripping down her inner thigh and her pussy was throbbing for release. Lake grabbed her hips and lifted up onto the cold granite counter then with a warm palm between her yearning breasts, he eased her back. The cold shock against her heated flesh caused her to arch her back as she fought the stark contrast against her charged skin. She drew her knees up and crossed her ankles. Lake reached beneath her and lifted her hips until she was at the edge. She put her heels on the counter to steady her body and then his hands split her knees and spread her wide for his perusal. If she felt like she was on display earlier, she surely was now. It was the most erotic thing she'd ever experienced.

"Beautiful," said Lake, happily taking in the full view of her weeping sex. "You are mine."

It was a statement she wasn't in any position to disagree with. Even if she were, she wouldn't. She liked the idea of being *his*. He pressed his warm palm down onto her abdomen trying to center her trembling body.

"Steady your breathing, baby. I'm going to give your body the orgasm it's begging for."

The tip of his finger rolled softly over her clit and she cried out. "God…god…oh…god." She put the back of her hand over her mouth to muffle the sounds his teasing ministrations tore from her throat.

He smoothed his thumb over her wet heat spreading it over her sensitive sex. She was dying, wilting in his hand. He still held her down only now it was both hands pressing her into the granite. The warm pad of his tongue lapped at her pussy in long strokes and her legs went impossibly wide. Her breathing was ragged and shallow. It was just a matter of time before the pulsing in her abdomen settled between the cleft of her trembling legs and her orgasm climbed free. Lake's expert tongue worked its way around her clit and opening, licking and sucking her into complete ecstasy. Her hips undulated uncontrollably against his mouth. Just when the tension peaked, Lake stood up and slid his ring and middle finger deep inside her silky core, tugging at her G-spot while pressing against his buried hand over the top of her sex. It was like nothing she'd ever felt before. Her body was crazed…her pussy was the udder of each quick pull. Her head rolled from side to side. He was fucking milking her for all she was worth and her body was reacting. "Holy fuck…Lake…"

He didn't relent – it was quicker – more rapid. Her back arched into his pumping fingers and her head came off the granite. Before she knew what was happening, the most powerful orgasm split her open and wet cum shot out her vagina. Her body wasn't her own. He continued the drive and it happened again. She could feel him pressing kisses to her abdomen, her thighs, her labia…her clit, while still continuing the onslaught of pulls. It happened again and again – orgasm after orgasm – spilling cum. She was coming completely undone – scared shitless. What had happened? Her knees flew up to her chest. She didn't even know what she was saying at that point. Her mind went blank, white light followed by murky darkness. Eliza's whole body trembled against the hard surface like she'd been thrown into an ice bath then doused with fire. She didn't even understand what she was murmuring. She was slack-jawed…a mess. "Uh! Oh! Oah…oahh…no!"

"Shhhh…shhh…" Lake's palm splayed over her stomach like a gravitational pull to settle her. Her heart was still racing and her breathing was erratic. "Shhhh…" The pressure of his hand and his voice brought her back into the moment. Overwhelmed, she clasped her hand over her mouth as wet hot tears spilled down temples, spilling coolly into her ear. Her body was shaking so hard she felt like she was going to throw up. She couldn't speak and didn't want him to see her eyes. She closed her weak, shaky legs against his arm and rolled onto her side as he eased his hand from her wet, throbbing core.

"Eliza." Lake's voice was soft, but commanding. He reached over to her arm and attempted to move her upper body to the edge of the countertop, where he could see her face. But her body was sweaty and wouldn't maneuver being pulled across the surface of the granite. He put his hands underneath her and lifted her limp body into his chest. Her hands were still covering her mouth, and she kept her eyes closed, but it wouldn't take a rocket scientist to know she was crying. "Don't cry. I wanted that to happen. It was perfect. You're perfect. Please look at me."

Somehow she forced her heavy eyes open, but didn't have the strength to remove her hand from her mouth. The tears were coming fast. She couldn't help it. She felt distraught and foolish.

"Please don't cry. I should have told you what I wanted to try before I did it. Your body's so responsive to just the slightest touch. I knew if I did it right I could give you a very powerful shooting orgasm. It's true female ejaculation. It was the most incredible thing I've ever seen. I loved it."

Eliza buried her head into his chest too scared to meet his eyes. She'd never felt as overwhelmed in her life as she did in that moment. Her body, her mind and her emotions were colliding together in one catastrophic explosion leaving her a limp noodle in his arms.

"You are the most incredible creature I have ever encountered. You don't even know the power you have over me. Let me make love to you."

She was trying to work out what happened, what he just said. Her desire for him was no less profound than before he tore the most powerful climax from her body. She needed him now, more than ever. She craved the closeness. "Yes."

Chapter Eighteen

Lake carried her through the house, down a long corridor. Paintings and pictures lined the walls. She wasn't able to adequately assess the paintings because she couldn't disentangle herself from the beautiful sight holding her. He was going to break her, she knew it. The power that he had already taken from her was enormous. She was scared she'd get lost in him and didn't know how she'd manage her heart. Tonight, in his arms, with that orgasm, and with his words. She gave him a piece of *her*…her heart and soul. He didn't have to ask for it. She gave it willingly.

They walked into what could only be the master bedroom. It was plush, masculine and luxurious in every way. The floors were wood, but a thick, shaggy, light tan rug dominated the middle of the room. There was an enormous fireplace on the far wall, with a rich, waxy dark chocolate leather sofa facing it. A massive four post bed centered the middle of the wall. The wood was so rich and intricate it was a masterpiece in itself. Tall decorative lamps cast a warm glow over the bed on matching nightstands at each side. The thick, lofty duvet was dusky brown velvet with gold embellishments. An enormous array of pillows in varying hues of gilded orange and brown lined the headboard. Lake had an extreme eye for design or had paid a professional oodles of money for the expert detailing of his luxurious home. Either way, it was gorgeous like its owner.

He smoothed his cheek across hers lovingly and then gently rolled his tongue over the crease of her lips, kissing the corner or her mouth. If she were a dog, she'd have taken the gesture as an apology, but she didn't need him to apologize anymore. The orgasms were intense, but euphoric. The contractions still fluttered deep in her abdomen. Lake said he would give her an orgasm that would make her cry and he lived up to his words.

"Your body is trembling. Can you stand?"

"Yes."

He braced her back and let her legs and feet drop to the floor. She felt wobbly in her heels. Lake dropped to his knees and tapped her ankle for her to step out of her shoe. She braced herself on his shoulder while he removed both. "Gucci. I like it. Did I buy these?"

"You did. I'm glad you like them."

He set her shoes at the end of the bed and stood up. When she saw the mess of wetness on the front of Lake's shirt she gasped. "Look what I did to your shirt." Eliza ran her fingers over the damp stain she caused. The idea of her ejaculating like a man was bewildering.

"I know. I'm framing this shirt." Eliza's eyes went wide – horrified. She didn't want anyone to know that her body reacted so poorly, let alone see the reminder. Lake pulled her forward by the neck and kissed her forehead then turned to walk away. Eliza reached out for his arm.

"Don't leave me." Her voice was hurried, desperate. She sounded needy, even to her, but she didn't care. She wanted him…right here…right now.

"I don't intend to leave you…ever."

She knew he was using big words. He was the king of forwardness and leading lines. She didn't want to ponder them to death or analyze them. The time for talking was over. She closed the distance between them and while looking into the intensity of his determined eyes, she started unbuttoning his tainted shirt. It would make the dry cleaners, if not the trash, but she was sure it wasn't something off the rack. It was probably custom tailored like the rest of his wardrobe. She eased it over his shoulders and tossed it on the chair next to his bed.

Lake watched her adoringly as she continued slowly undressing him. He was allowing her the freedom of learning the smooth dips and lines of his warm, olive flesh. He was hard and soft in all the right places, wide shoulders and a lean waist. She dropped to her knees and she saw his face light up. He knew what happened when she dropped to her knees and took delight in seeing her there. She tapped his ankle so she could remove his shoes. Then proceeded with removing his socks. He had great feet, which was no surprise. There was nothing about his body that wasn't etched with perfection. She gazed up at his lust filled eyes. "Nice feet."

"Thank you."

He reached down and slid his thumb across her lower lip and she pulled his thumb into her mouth. Sucking it slowly, teasingly. He moaned out, bent down, and replaced his thumb with his tongue, kissing her forcefully, urgently. Digging his hand into her hair, he pulled her head back to get more of her mouth. His need was growing and so was his cock.

"Eliza…"

"I know…" She unbuckled his crocodile belt, which she guessed to be real and expensive then unbuttoned his pants and let the claws of the zipper unfurrow. Eliza shimmied them down his muscular thighs and Lake stepped out. She tossed them onto the chair with the rest of his clothes. The thick length of his cock was tight behind his gray cotton boxer briefs. She wanted to touch him everywhere, but wanted to see his manhood first. She ran her fingers under the Armani monogrammed band and watched his stomach draw tight with her touch. Every knotted muscle in his defined abdomen rippled to the surface. Eliza smiled appreciatively. He was fucking hot. She knew the effort it took to obtain that kind of physique. It wasn't lost on her that this man worked hard for his body.

"Happy?"

"It feels like Christmas." She couldn't fight the giggle of excitement. "You've denied me long enough."

"Agreed."

She pulled the band over his hard erection and pulled them down his legs. When he stepped out and kicked them to the side she sat back on her haunches to take in the splendor of his sizeable beauty. "It's an amazing gift. Thank you, Santa." She covered her mouth with her hand to hide her full smile. "Tell me that thing has been enhanced in some way?"

Lake laughed heartily. His penis shook with his stomach and chest.

She had touched it and sucked it, seen it in the shower and behind the constriction of fabric, but having him in plain view and able to really touch and look at him fully left her awestruck. He was big…really big.

"It's not enhanced in any way, but it's yours for the taking."

She moved her hand from her mouth and let him see her contentment. "I accept."

Lake dropped to his knees and met her on the floor. Her stomach flipped and she licked her lips in nervous anticipation. He was virile and raw before her, ready to make good on his promises. There was only one way to ease her anxiety, she had to become the aggressor. She went up onto her knees and clasped her hand around the thick cords of his neck and pulled him into her. He wrapped his hand around her waist and moaned into her mouth. She reached down to stroke his fantastic cock, thick and hard against her stomach. Her fingers gently grazed the veined underbelly and circled the head. She didn't think there was any room for growth, but it was undeniable, he was growing in her hand.

"Lay on your back, baby." He complied and moved back onto his heels and then down on the rich, wooly rug that resembled sheep skin. It was so plush it was like being swept up in a cloud. Lake reached up for her, coaxing her closer. She kissed his palm and set her face in his hand. "Don't move."

She moved between his legs, prowling over him like a cat in heat. His skin was smooth and smelled distinctly Lake – clean soap, remnants of faint woody cologne and musky virility. Her fingers trailed his flesh. She wanted to know every crease, every indention. Where he had hair and where there was none. Did he have any scars or a birthmark? Or was he pure of any injuries or issues beyond the beautiful brown defect of his baby blues.

She gently stroked his full heavy sack, stimulating a low rumbling sigh as she fondled and massaged him. "Hmmm…"

"You like that?"

"Yes," Lake whispered. He was fighting to stay still. She could see his composure slipping. He looked like a caged beast, dying to be freed. She understood the torment. He had been putting her through the test for days. Now it was her turn to do a little toying of her own.

She ran the tip of her tongue across the pre-cum that sat at his opening. "God, yes. I love it."

She looked at his erect cock in her hand, measuring it with her grip. He surely belonged in porn. But she was glad to know right now he belonged to her. She lapped his balls, straight up his erection to the tip of his hard cock, then circled the tight belled head drawing him into the recesses of her mouth. His hand found the top of her head, needing to capture any part of her. He weaved his fingers over her scalp, threading her hair as he took a front row view of her lavishing mouth. She stroked him to the base, pulling the tip of his head taut and sucking it down fully with her mouth, gently grazing his sensitive skin with her teeth.

"Oh yeah…fuck, baby. If you don't stop, I'm going to come in your beautiful mouth again."

"That's the desired outcome." She breathed damply over his cock.

"Not this time beautiful." Lake leaned up, grabbed her under the armpits and pulled her up his chest, flipping her onto her back and settling his body into hers. He was like a missing puzzle piece, covering her body perfectly with his weighted, warm flesh. The air between them was dense with desire. She could feel his heart beat in rhythm with hers, fast and steady. His erection lingered at her slick core. "I have to be inside you. I can't hold back any longer."

"Take me." Her body felt electric – he was the current charging her.

Lake's mouth swept over hers as he pushed gently into her liquid hot center. Everything inside her stiffened. She fought the scream that threatened to escape her throat as he stretched her beyond belief. The air rushed from her lungs and she bit down on her lip as her body surrendered to his size.

"Breathe...E." He lifted up onto his hands and stared down longingly into her yes. She exhaled and he drove his cock to the base. Eliza knew his erection was lodged somewhere in her throat, every millimeter of her now claimed. He relaxed his hips against hers and let her settle into the fullness of him. Her hands were a death grip over the long strands of fur in the rug and her eyes were somewhere in the back of her head. Slowly, she inhaled the life giving air her body craved and her muscles relaxed.

Lake bent down and pressed a light kiss over her lips "Open your eyes baby. Let me see you."

Eliza's eyes fluttered open to the brilliance of Lake, looking at her like the world had melted away. Their bodies were intimately joined and her heart wasn't far behind. Emotions filled the air like unspoken secrets, binding them together like a knotted rope that couldn't be unwound. She desperately wanted to say something, anything substantial, but none of the words that lingered in her brain felt appropriate. She couldn't profess to love him because she didn't. But she did love the feel of his claim over her body, the way he always said what he meant and the way she felt coveted by him. "It feels like your dick is in my heart. I've never encountered anything like you in my life."

"I know. I feel it too."

She latched her hands over his shoulders and moved her hips into his pelvis, inviting him to take her.

"I don't want to hurt you. Let me make it good, baby." He pushed the hair off her forehead and she followed his hand like an affection starved cat. She loved every touch...she craved his fingers, his mouth, his words, and now his cock.

"You're not hurting me. I need you to fuck me, Lake." She ran her palms down the sides of his waist and captured his hips. "If you need me to beg I will. Keep me edging or squirting or whatever. I don't care. I want this connection. I need to feel every inch of you inside me."

"Surely you're a figment of my imagination."

Eliza reached up and pulled his face down to hers with both hands against his cheeks. "I'm as real as it gets." It was as real of a statement as any one she'd spoken since the day she met Lake. She didn't know what kind of women he dated in the past, and wouldn't speculate, but she knew very few women as authentic as her.

"I want you so bad, Eliza. All of you."

"Show me." He moaned into her neck and kissed a trail down to her breasts. His hips started a pressured roll into her warmth. The pace was slow – methodical – intentional. Her tight pussy adjusted to the feel of him. The sweet depth of him rocking into her and feeding her soul inch by delightful inch.

"Don't deprive me of your beautiful eyes." His eyes warmed over hers, pleading for attention. The inky black of his dilated pupils threatened to wash the sea of blue away. "I want to see your orgasm as I feel it."

She was hyperaware of everything about him. His smell, the taste of him on her lips and in her mouth. The way his muscular legs pushed his cock into her with calculated drives. He was sex and sin and sweet sensuality packaged up in a dominant male form. She couldn't get enough. Her heart and head were full, tingling with awareness.

"You're so tight. I'm not going to last long." His heavy, thick cock burned through her like fire. It was all she could do to stay in time and space. It was better than good, better than expected. He threaded his hands into hers and secured her arms over her head, taking her in with excitement and raw desire. When his mouth found hers, her body melted into the affection and adoration of his kiss. The moan that came out was a cry of love, not of pain. He was making love to her heart, sealing it up with tender kisses as he took her body with it. The deep familiar pulse at her abdomen tugged at her in her cunt and she knew it was over. "Please don't stop...please." She begged for her orgasm.

"I feel you...pulsing around me. You ready?" Lake's hot sugary breath caressed her face. She was overawed, emotionally and physically. She clung tightly to his heated flesh and watched as he pulled her climax forward. She loved each labored moan that laced his lips. Craved his cum, like she craved him.

"That's it...right there. Oh yes...right there." He was so deep it was a mix of delivered pain and exquisite pleasure. Just when she felt the rush of nerves loosen in her core, his hips slowed and settled over hers. "God...no!" She unknotted her hands from his and drove them into the back of his damp hair. She couldn't fucking believe it. She tugged his head away from her neck and bit his lip.

"Shit..." Lake yelled. His mouth rushed to take hers and the tinge of cooper filtered over her tongue. She was done fucking around with the master of hold outs. He was stealing her orgasm and holding onto it until he was ready for his own or ready to give into her need. It made her crazy, but she was learning that he wouldn't let her come until he was ready.

"Not yet," he breathed. His hips were a tight circle of undulation, crackling low, but keeping the fire alive. It didn't matter, she was too close. Even the slow rock couldn't take her release away.

"I can't hold on."

"Let me have it. Come with me." His tongue plunged into her mouth and his cock slammed into her pussy with forceful precision. Her body exploded.

"Lake..." Eliza couldn't stop the tide of her release. Her orgasm threaded the muscles of her thighs like charlie-horses, making her legs go rigid. Her sex was a pulsing renegade of desire. She arched into the weight of his warm body, grinding her clit against his pelvis and she came hard against his erection.

"Oh my God! Eliza, look at me." His words were nothing more than a pant above her, a brush of heat against her lips. "Baby, please let me see you." She could barely see through half-lidded eyes, but found the perfect brown flaw. Lake's legs grew stiff above her and with a deep thrust, his hot seed spilled into the slice of heaven between her silky thighs. His heart was a bass drum over hers. She captured his cheeks with her hands and feathered tiny kisses over his whole face. He closed his eyes and gave into her mothering assault. She wanted to eat the emotions between them. Hold them like they were tangible. A solid mass of something real and good. It was nothing shy of magic.

His body stiffened against her. Her body was too pliable to show concern, but her mind was aware that something was wrong. She ran her fingers through his hair tenderly and looked at him questioningly. This was so right. What could be wrong? "What?"

His eyes showed concern and his brows furrowed across his forehead. "No condom. I'm sorry, baby. Contraception isn't something we've discussed. I'm an asshole."

It was a shit thing to discuss when she was full of his sperm, but they were both adults. She'd been on the pill since she was sixteen. She suffered from cramps that left her bed-bound and nearly bleeding to death. It was the only way out of her monthly hell. She knew she should have asked him to wear a condom, but she didn't. Birth control was everyone's responsibility. She couldn't help but fuck with him a little bit. "What if I'm not?"

"Well, I hope it's a girl and she looks just like you."

"Lake Mitchell!" She pushed at his chest with both hands. "I'm on the pill. I was toying with you. There's no way I'd consciously have unprotected sex with you if I weren't on birth control."

His face fell…deflated with her words. The strong viral man turned quiet and moved his face into her neck. He was hiding.

Eliza felt the weight of unspoken words in the air like a thick dense cloud. She didn't know what he was thinking or feeling and he wasn't telling her either. Everything with Lake held deeper meaning. She brought her legs over his ass, locking her ankles together and rocking his semi-rigid cock farther into her milky core. "Look at me." It was her turn to figure out what just happened. "What was that?"

"Nothing." He kissed her neck and brought his face to hers.

"Happiness is me being on the pill, right?"

"Yeah." He shrugged and pushed against her legs so she would release him. He got up. She couldn't believe the turn of events. Her heart plummeted into her nervous stomach. "Wait here."

She knew he was acting emotional, instead of logical and let it go. She rolled over onto her side. She couldn't quit examining her relationship with Lake. She had to dissect it, chop it into a million pieces and analyze it to death. She was lost in thought, when the warmth of his bare skin nestled up against her back.

"Rollover." His warm words tickled her ear and goose bumps spread over her naked moist flesh. She turned onto her back and looked into his eyes, trying to read him, but he wasn't giving anything away. "Open your legs."

The warm heat of a washcloth was cupped to her tender sex. He was taking care of her body with the finesse of a caring lover. It was the most intimate thing she'd ever encountered. Lake Mitchell was a baffling man.

"What are you thinking about?" he asked.

"You." She leaned in and captured his lips with hers.

"What about me?"

"You're very complex."

"Care to elaborate." Lake pulled her body into his, molding them together, chest to chest with his legs vined over hers.

"So, Dr. Swift, how am I complex?"

"I'm trying to figure it out myself. When you walked into my office, I was taken by the power of the man behind the words. You're very aggressive. You were mysterious, for good reason. Your desire and wanting something with the sole determination to have it moved me. You were overly confident, but it's not unwarranted. You've amassed a lot of success. Then when I came to your house, you shocked me by blurting out what you knew about my life. I was freaked out, but I understood your desire to own that knowledge. Scared or not, something about you excites me. Then at my house, you showed me a different side, by opening up and being honest about your past. You say you're not typically jealous, but your actions speak otherwise. You're sweet and gentle with me, despite your desire to possess me. You're an incredible lover, but I wonder if I'm enough to satisfy you. You were upset that there was a potential that you could have gotten me pregnant by not wearing a condom, but acted hurt when I told you I was on the pill. You own a sex club and I'm sure you could have your pick of the litter. Yet, you picked a somewhat reserved, sexually inexperienced sex therapist to go after. I guess I'm just trying to learn what motivates you and what you want. You're a very eligible bachelor, but you've never been married and you haven't secured a legacy by having children. What gives Mr. Mitchell?"

"Do I get a chance to answer to any of that?"

"Please do." Eliza watched Lake's mouth and eyes intently.

"I am naturally aggressive by nature. Maybe a little over-confident at times, but I am used to getting what I want. Not everything is always attainable, but I love a good challenge, and never back down." He smirked and Eliza took it that he was referring to her as the challenge. "I was wrong to reveal how much homework I'd done on you. I'm sorry that scared you. However, it was a simple resume and not the things that interest me most. I cherish the pearls you bestow me about your life and your desires. I'm desperate to make you mine. I would never have come to your office under the guise of anything other than myself if I thought there was any other way. You asked me how many women I've slept with, and I gave you the answer. I wish I could change it. I didn't really give them any of me. I just took what I wanted. It was a shitty thing to do, but I grew up and realized that if I ever wanted to have a meaningful relationship with someone I'd have to make some changes. I've never been married because I haven't found the woman I want to give my *everything* to. I need someone who challenges me, but knows when to give in. Someone who's open to new experiences, but has dreams of her own. I want to genuinely share in someone's life and for her to fully experience mine. I'm not naturally jealous because my confidence gets in the way of my reality. I won't lie about wanting to possess you. I'm crazy about you. You're not like any woman I've ever met and that excites me. As for the club, it's a business. Maybe one I need to consider selling. It's not what I want my kids to say when they're asked what their dad does for a living."

He smiled. He brought the tip of his nose to hers and playfully wiggled it back and forth, then kissed her softly. The Eskimo kiss was his signature move and she relished when his nose circled hers. These were the moments that she loved the most, when he was stripped bare and open.

"As for the birth control episode," he continued. "I'm never careless when it comes to sex. I always use protection and we should have had that discussion beforehand. When you jokingly said you weren't on the pill, it didn't dawn on me to be mad because the thought of getting you pregnant excited me. Then when you pulled the rug out from under me and said that it was a good thing that you were on the pill, it felt like you were saying the thought of having my child was the last thing you could imagine. It hurt my ego. Normally I'd be sighing with relief, but in reality, I'd love see you pregnant with my child. So how do you feel about that, Dr. Swift?"

"As usual, completely in awe." She rolled Lake onto his back and climbed over his body, tucking her feet under his calves and resting her head against his chest. "Don't sell the club unless you want to. You told me that it didn't make you who you are and I believe that. I have to admit, dating you and someone finding out about it bothered me at first because I'll always want to protect my reputation, but I trust you. You're a titan in the business world and fare okay owning it. In the end, I might be better for having known you, than the other way around. I like you a lot."

He wrapped his arms around her back and squeezed her tight. "You *like* me?"

"Yes, I do." She smirked. More than she cared to admit.

"You want to have all my children…admit it?" His frisky smile widened.

"That might be putting the cart before the horse, don't you think?"

"Let's find out how potent I am. I'm going to fill that sweet pussy of yours with my best swimmers and I bet at least one can get beyond the birth control barrier."

"You're crazy, but if it means I get to experience more of your sexual prowess, I am up for the challenge."

Lake sat up with her straddling his lap. "Stay right where you are." He reached between her legs and she quickly buried her face in his neck. Now she was hiding. She'd never been so turned on by anyone and was sure she was dripping with desire. Every time he opened his mouth she wanted to climax. "Sweet…sweet, Eliza."

"I know. I'm completely affected by everything you say and do." Her words steamed the shell of his ear.

"It's wonderful, baby. I love it." He reached his hands into her long brown hair and pulled her head back so he could see her eyes. "You need to quit being embarrassed by these things. Embrace it, don't hide from it."

He smeared her nectar over her labia and pussy and brushed soft slow strokes over her clit. "You're really wet. I want you to slide onto me. It's going to be deep, but I'll let you control it. When you're comfortable I'm going to fuck you until you're screaming my name and begging for more."

She shivered. Even though she was already tender, she couldn't get enough of him.

She held his gaze as she slid inch by inch down his length, stopping half-way and praying her body wasn't going to just divide up the center to accommodate him. He was right about the depth and she wondered if she could make it down to the base without it lodging in her chest. He kissed her neck and didn't touch her until she worked her body fully over him. She panted her first breath into his waiting mouth. It was like his dick had sucked the air from her lungs from the inside. Shit he was big.

"Breathe, baby. You've got to breathe."

"It's difficult. Your dick stole my breath."

Lake's belly and hers jiggled against one another's as laughter trickled from their lips. He grabbed her hips to lock her in place. With every vibration from her chest she was sliding farther and farther off his hard length. "Quit laughing, you're pushing off me with your vaginal muscles." It was all she could do not to laugh more. She could feel the walls of her vagina seize his dick in a mock tug of war. "Stop E."

She put her hand over her mouth to suppress the laughter that was looming and made her way back down onto him.

"That's why having sex with you is so incredible and why I had to know if you were a squirter or not. I watched and felt you contract over my tongue and fingers, pulling in and expelling with the same energy, like a heart flushing blood. The way it grips my cock as you climax is magical. You have to relax though or I'll end up hurting you. Wet or not, you're really tight."

She nodded and buried her head into his neck. The faint smell of his cologne and the residual scent of his lingering soap was intoxicating. Her brain and heart were being powered by everything about him. As if he sensed her thoughts, he pulled her from her reverie.

"Look at me, Eliza" He lifted her face back to his and he gently cupped both of her cheeks, framing her face. "I need you to be mine."

Eliza tipped her forehead to his and threaded her hands under his arms and round the back of his shoulders. She couldn't get close enough and when he kissed her with unfiltered need, she melted over him. She could feel the emotion seep from his flesh as he started the steady roll of his body into hers. This time they left it all on the table.

Eliza didn't think her body could be so thoroughly used, but making love to Lake was different. It wasn't just taking and giving. It was more. It was an emotional ride that took everything. His eyes held her captive and his body held her accountable. He wanted to see and feel every orgasm as it came. He was a powerful aphrodisiac.

Eliza was half asleep when Lake lifted her against his chest and walked her into the billowing steam of his shower. She was a noodle in his arms, sexually spent, mentally exhausted and emotionally high. He washed every inch of her body and shampooed her hair. She basked in the sun of his affection and adoration, blooming under the tenderness with which he cared for her. She took the same loving care with him. Every touch seemed to gain her more of his heart…his trust…his love. They moved comfortably with each other. Eliza felt it in her home and even more in his

The heat of the water put her already used body into utter relaxation. She sat naked on the side of the tub, drying off as Lake did the same. She wondered if staying the night was the right thing to do, but the thought of leaving made her stomach ache and her heart feel heavy. She quickly dismissed the idea. The only person that would feel cheapened by her actions was her. She ruffled the towel over her long wet hair, sponging up the dampness when she noticed Lake staring at her in the mirror. A shy smile caressed her cheeks. He walked over and crouched down to meet her at face level. "I'm so glad you're here."

"Me too." She touched his cheek with her fingers and he kissed the center of her palm. "Lake…" she whispered. It was just his name but the way it fell sugary from her lips made it feel like she'd just admitted to her growing feelings. He laced his fingers into her hair and kissed her with such intense passion she was sure her soul had left her body and was floating somewhere above them. There was no way she was going to leave. He wanted forever and she couldn't make that guarantee, but tonight she belonged to him.

They walked back into the dimness of his bedroom and over to the side of the bed. He pulled the covers back and she slid into the smooth contrast of heated flesh under cool cotton sheets. The mattress was a plush cloud cradling her body and the pillow was the perfect firmness against her head. Lake cupped her cheek and kissed her goodnight. "I'm glad you gave me a chance to prove I'm worthy of you."

"Have I cured your obsession with me?"

"No." He shook his head and grinned eagerly. "It's going to take a lot more than a couple of dates and really great sex to cure my obsession. My want may have changed to need." He bopped her on the nose with the tip of his finger. "Bedtime."

The mattress dipped on the other side of the bed and she felt the warmth of his body fold around hers. His hand slid over her waist and circled her flat abdomen. "It's a girl."

Eliza sighed and rolled her eyes, grateful he couldn't see her gesture. He had a pension for spankings and she didn't particularly like them. She didn't entertain his absurdity, and said nothing.

Chapter Nineteen

Eliza reached out to seek the heated flesh of her lover, but only felt the coolness of soft cotton against her hand. She lifted her head off the warm pillow, digging fists into her sleepy eyes, trying to focus on the red beacon of light glaring in the darkness – 5:45. An early riser, she woke naturally in the dark. It seemed Lake was no different. She stretched her limbs fully, like a cat. The tight used muscles throughout her body expanded then retracted back to life. Her body was deliciously sore, but the mere thought of Lake being near had her clamoring for the tenderness of a morning kiss.

She pulled back the cocoon of spun cotton and turned on the lamp next to the bed, illuminating the beautiful space. Lake's bedroom was impressive. Like The Raven's Nest, every detail was exacting and complementary, masculine and feminine all at the same time.

She looked around for something to put on and remembered she'd been gifted a wardrobe by her…Eliza flopped back on the bed and put her hands over her mouth, hiding the threatening smile. Did she dare say boyfriend? He'd introduced her as his girlfriend the previous night and she wondered if saying it out loud made it real. She warmed to the idea of belonging to someone again. It had been a long time since she felt the security of having a *someone* in her life. Lake Mitchell wasn't just someone. He was everything and everyone wrapped up in wealth and dominance. She had to admit to herself how affected she was by him.

Eliza knew Lake had sent Katherine to task on setting her up, but she didn't know where to look. It felt nosey to invade drawers and closets, but walking around naked wasn't going to work either. Her dress never made it back from the kitchen floor, so she was stuck with invading Lake's personal space in search of clothes. She pulled back the heavy double doors on the wall across the room and light filled the vast space. This wasn't a closet it was another whole house. The size and breadth was incredible. Row upon row of beautiful high-polished shoes and custom suits and shirts lined the hangers and shelves. It was like being in a high-end retail store – divided by color and style, grouped and in precise alignment. She was anal, but this was a whole other level. She stood unmoving, amazed and awkwardly nervous to advance into the space. Her hands were still threaded tightly over the door handles, the hardwood floor beneath her feet cool and her in naked glory. It was silly. It was stuff – albeit exquisite stuff, but she wasn't plucked from obscurity – she knew a measure of wealth herself. Nothing as impressive as the man and the mystery before her, but family money.

She teased the carpeted room with her toes and then walked the rest of the way in, running her hands along the jackets and shirts as she made her way to the perfectly squared center island that dominated the space. She skimmed the cool stone with the tip of her finger and stopped at a hand-crafted wood and glass watch case. The unbelievable display could only be likened to a high-end jewelry retailer. These weren't just watches; it was a collection. Rolex, Patek Philippe, Cartier, Panerai, Richard Mille, Audemars Piguet and more. Gold, platinum, stainless steel, even rose gold. Some with diamond bezels and some without. All heavy and dripping with masculinity and affluence. Her father had a love for timepieces and a small collection of his own. Eliza knew what she was looking at was special, and probably worth well over a million dollars. Lake Mitchell wasn't the man you wanted to buy gifts for.

She turned the corner and there before her was a full row of women's clothes, tags still on, hanging with the same perfection and precision as his own wardrobe. A smile pressed her cheeks to her eyes as she walked into the space Katherine marked as hers. One-by-one she slid the hangers across the rod to take in each beautiful piece, lace, velvet, cotton and silk. Dresses and skirts, blouses and pants, casual clothes and a couple of formal dresses lined the wall. All in size six. She would have found it odd, but he was linked to her account at Hall's. Sizing her for clothes and shoes wouldn't have been hard to uncover. She crouched down and fingered the impressive row of shoes. Each shoe was more exquisite than the next. Eliza thought she was going to teach him a lesson by purchasing the Gucci heels on his account, *their account*, but what lay before her was nothing shy of thousands of dollars of shoes. Not hundreds of pairs, but the most expensive shoes on the market. She plopped down onto her butt and grabbed the black satin Prada's and slipped them lovingly onto her feet, turning her toe's and heels this way and that way to see how they looked. She was Cindrella in a real life fairtale. Goosebumps tickled her naked flesh and she knew it was time to find clothes. She put the pumps back in the kaleidoscopic of shoes and moved on. There was not doubt Katherine put Lake's wallet to the test, nothing was amiss. It was a bit much to take in, but she didn't want to seem ungrateful and let the curl of her lips define the moment.

She just wanted the comfort of sweats and a simple t-shirt; something easy. She bravely walked to the chest of drawers and opened them individually. Nothing but men's underwear in the top, men's socks in the second, tee shirts in the third and workout attire in the fourth and fifth. She moved to the other side of the island and stared perusing nosily, each drawer a new discovery – a new delight. With the pull of the handle she was graced with lace and satin, panties and bras lined the drawer. Each piece sexier than the next. She didn't imagine Katherine donned the same lingerie and wondered if these things were specific to Lake's request. The theme was unmistakable, sexy and on display.

She continued on until she found athletic wear. She didn't know if it was implied intention or cleverly purchased. She knew Lake worked out for that body, just as she did hers. It wasn't obtained by delving into heaping slices of carrot cake with succulent cream cheese frosting. She grabbed the pieces she needed and went to the bathroom to do a once over.

Eliza was surprised when she glanced at the woman whose reflection looked a lot like her, only better – fulfilled. It had been a long time since she was aglow with an inner joy that filtered out like rich warm heat, making her eyes sparkle and her skin shine. She pulled her curls into a messy ponytail on the top of her head and used the new toothbrush Lake gave her the previous night.

The house was eerily silent, as Eliza put on her clothes. Still no sign of the master of the mansion. The magnitude of the space was keeping her from hearing anything beyond the master suite. She threw on the running tights, sports bra and tank and padded down the hall barefoot in search of Lake.

Like a voyeur in the midst of secrets she eyed the various paintings that hung from the wall that led out of the master bedroom, studying the images with a keen eye. Some were exquisite pieces of art – others, clearly works detailing the Mitchell legacy. Jonathan Mitchell, Lake's father unmistakable in several. One dominant oil portrait centered the wall. Eliza knew it had to be Lake's uncle. The man who'd bestowed Lake his legacy and exquisite home. He resembled Lake's father, but with softer features and a richer smile. He had the same dominant blue eyes that ran in the Mitchell men, but the portrait captured a sparkle of genuineness – an unmistakable display of pride for a life well-lived. From what Eliza could tell, superficially, it was.

The next painting nearly took her breath away it was so alive. It imprisoned her mind and called to her soul like a deep rooted story begging to be told. Drawn to the sight before her, Eliza dared finger the work of art. The beauty of the woman on the canvas was ethereal. Light cast a glow across her face. Her smile, radiant even behind the smear of expertly detailed paint. Her long russet hair was swept up upon her head with falling tendrils that curled against her neck like jeweled adornments. The way her hand circled the chest of the young boy in front of her was like seeing love flourish on the delicate canvas. There was no doubt it was Lake. Even young he was extraordinary in every way. The painting was like nothing she'd ever scene. The detail was remarkable…lifelike. It was no mystery how Lake looked like an Adonis in perfect olive skin and regal features. He was genetically blessed by not one, but both parents.

"My mother." Eliza jumped back and clutched her chest with her betraying hand. She felt flagrant to be caught not only ogling the priceless painting, but for him to see her touch the face of the boy who was a man before her. The son, the nephew, the mogul and the only man that mattered. "Sorry," said Lake, walking up next to her and staring at the beautiful work of art. "She was amazing wasn't she?" He stared at the woman who gave him life. Eliza took his hand and leaned her head to his shoulder.

"She was stunning, Lake."

He pressed a gentle kiss to the top of her head. "She was."

"How long have you been up?" He looked well-caffeinated, or creamed – for Lake.

"Not too long. I couldn't sleep and staring at you made me feel like a creep." The deep chuckle that filtered the hall settle over her and she gripped his hand a little tighter. "I was afraid you would wake up and run for the hills. I couldn't chance it, so I got up."

"I probably would have found it a little creepy, but I'm new to you and new to your bed."

Lake tilted his head. His eyebrows furrowed in consternation. She wondered if she'd once again said something that was read wrong or worse, read correctly. Lake let go of her hand and put his hands against her cheeks, locking their eyes to one another. "No one gets to come here, Eliza. I don't make a habit of bringing woman into my home, or into the inner sanctum of my private world. Just you…only you."

What did she say to that? "Okay…stare at me all you want."

He smirked playfully, groaned over her mouth and kissed her chastely. "You ready."

"Ready for what?"

"I run on Mondays Wednesdays and Fridays."

"Does that mean run to a chair or couch?" She didn't want to run with him. He towered over her. It was going to be an impossible feat to meet his stride.

"I thought we could run down to the plaza and get breakfast."

"You're kidding?" Eliza started calculating the distance in her head based on the proximity from Lake's house. It wasn't a leisurely jog. It was a good three or four miles one way. "Don't let the workout clothes fool you." She tugged at his shirt and wrapped her arms around his slim waist.

"As a matter of fact they don't fool me. I made sure that Katherine bought you workout clothes. You are appropriately dressed, excluding your running shoes, which I'm sure are in the closet."

"Speaking of the closet. It's pretty impressive. Thank you."

"Is everything correct?" A sense of pleasure glowed brightly from the brilliance of his knowing wide smile. "Is everything to your satisfaction?"

"Everything is correct and to my satisfaction. It's all quite exquisite and too much. I have a wardrobe."

"Now you have two," he corrected. "I want you here. It makes sense to have appropriate clothes for all occasions. It makes me happy to walk in my closet and see your things lining the wall. Don't steal my thunder. Besides, I know the sizes are right because I own your Hall's account now."

"I'm not your wife, Lake. You are not obligated to any of my debts." Eliza kissed his jaw and ruffled her fingers through his sleepy hair. "I have a job. One that I have to go to this morning, in fact."

"At some point, maybe we can remedy the first part of your speech. As for work, what time do I have to release you to your patients?"

She brushed right over his marriage innuendo and quickly continued with the detail of her morning schedule. "Oddly my first appointment isn't until ten today. I had a patient move his regular Monday appointment around which freed up my nine o'clock slot."

"Great. You have time for breakfast and a run with me. If we hit it now," he looked down at his watch. "We can be back around eight-thirty or nine, take showers and I'll take you to work. I have a noon meeting, so it'll work out perfect."

Running was a part of Eliza's daily routine, but lazing about in the comfort of Lake's arms sounded better. "I will give you the greatest blowjob of your life *if* you don't make me run."

"I look forward to it." He pulled her into his chest and cupped the cheeks of her ass with a teasing claim. "But you will run with me. I know you run. I've witnessed your sweat laden body after one of the early morning runs just yesterday. Besides, I'll give you another full body orgasm *if* you run."

"Will I ejaculate on you?"

Lake's chest and stomach bounced against Eliza's, igniting a warm flame deep in her stomach. "I'd love it if you did. Watching you cum is the single greatest pleasure I've had in a long time."

"Like carrot cake?"

"Don't push your luck." Lake nipped at her bottom lip and she tackled his mouth with an earth-shattering kiss. The deep moan she provoked made her heart shudder against her ribs. She knew she wouldn't get out of running, but was happy to know she had the power to *wow* him.

"Good try." He gave her a hearty whack to her backside, spun her around and gave her a little push. "Go get your running shoes on."

Eliza went back to the closet, grabbed the Asics from the row of new shoes and laced them up. They fit perfectly. Eliza prayed they'd be kind to her feet. New shoes were a bitch to break in. When she emerged from the bedroom, Lake had her cell phone in his hands. He saw her advance and handed it over. She wanted felt anxious about his need to be omnipresent in her life, but knew it was futile and she didn't have anything to hide.

"Phones stay here." Lake set his cellphone on the foyer and Eliza followed suit. "Nick texted and called at least four times since last night. I didn't respond because I'm trying to respect your privacy. But when I heard your phone ring at five-thirty this morning it was all I could do not to answer it and give him a piece of my mind. I don't know why he would take such liberties to call that early, but it's inappropriate. If you feel like you need to call him, go ahead."

Lake crossed his arms defensively and looked away. Nick could wait, but her jealous lover couldn't. She set her phone down next to his and held her hand open for him to accept. She could see the muscles in his shoulders unbunch as the thin line of his lip curled at the edges, clearly pleased with her decision to brush Nick off.

The morning sun was breaking on the horizon, casting a shimmery glow as night started to turn to day. They both spent a good ten minutes stretching before Lake fiddled with his sports watch and gave her a thumbs up. "Ready?"

"As I'm ever going to be." Without delay they took off. Lake ran with the fluidness of a gazelle, his stride perfectly timed with his breathing. Eliza was a practiced runner, but found herself pushing her limits to keep Lake's pace. He carried the air effortlessly, while she struggled to stay in step with his long limbs. She was never more pleased to see the restaurant ahead of them as they slowed to a walk ten feet from the door. Leaning over to brace herself on her knees, Eliza fought to reclaim her breath. She panted like she'd just crossed the finish line of a marathon. "How-far-was-that?" Her voice was clipped and jerky like stones skipping water.

Lake rubbed circles over her back, barely labored. "Four miles. You did great."

"It felt like ten." She stood up and used her shoulder to wipe a trailing line of sweat from the side of her face. "How do you feel about piggy-back rides?"

"I think I'm too heavy for you to carry, but we can try it." His infectious chuckle came barreling forward, jarring and warm. Eliza couldn't quit staring at his mouth like it was the Holy Grail and held all the answers to her dreams. She joined in his amusement.

"Ha, ha!" She pushed him playfully, but like a rock it did nothing to move him. "I meant me on your back, silly."

Lake wrapped his arm around her and kissed the top of her head. "You're a great runner. We just need to work on the pacing."

"Or, I just need to run in a different pack," she chided.

He tugged her playfully like she needed reminding. "I am your pack. I'll slow down and you'll speed up – perfect synergy."

She sighed and let her head nestle into the soft fabric of his shirt. Partner running was going to be her new thing. It didn't look like she was getting out of it. She was grateful when their discussion ended and they finally made their way into the restaurant. She eased her overworked hamstrings onto the padded cushion of the dining room chair and let her tight muscles unwind. Lake ordered them egg white omelets stuffed with a garden of fresh vegetables, fresh fruit and bran muffins. She felt ravenous by the time the food arrived and ate with the vigor of a homeless woman who didn't know when her next meal would come.

"I enjoyed meeting your father." She broached the topic with a toe tap into the deep end of the pool and wondered if he'd open up about their relationship. Lake eyed her inquisitively.

"I could see that," he replied. "I wonder how your mother fared on their date."

"My mother's not an easy woman to please. She's a social climber with lofty goals. Your father is right up her alley."

"Not really my concern." His voice lost its luster and greyed out like smoke. He'd mentioned the fact that he thought his dad was an *asshole* in her office, but wasn't offering more. She wanted to understand, so she baited him for more.

"Asshole, right?"

"Yeah, something like that. Just make sure your mother isn't interested in marriage. He's not husband material."

"Oh, she's interested in marriage alright. She's been on the hunt since my father divorced her." It was a bone of contention between her and her mother.

"She's barking up the wrong tree, so to speak." He took the last sip of his orange juice and leaned across the table. Eager to hear what he was about to say had her ears perking up and she scooted forward in her seat. "Everything I own is a direct result of my uncle Edgar, my father's brother. He was the one that took care of my mother and me while my father was out fucking everything in sight. I hated him for being a shitty dad and an even worse husband. My mother was riddled with breast cancer and fading fast when I got back from graduate school. My father made a last ditch effort to play the role of husband to her, but it was too little and too late. Six months later she was dead. I turned my back on him after that. I spent the next two years being groomed by my uncle to take over his legacy, when he had a massive heart attack and died. He had no children of his own and left me everything. His estate and his corporation. My father and uncle had joint ownership in several ventures, which makes him my partner. I have to deal with him on occasion but prefer to keep my distance. I've never forgiven him for breaking my mother's heart. To watch the most important woman of your life die – fragile and in pain – a mere shell of who she once was, right before my eyes, was horrific. And the man who should have been at her side was too busy worrying about his social status and his empire to even give a shit. It was deplorable."

Lake's nose flared and he pushed back into his chair – the rope of contempt strangling his neck as he told his story. How and why he'd become the man before her. Eliza ached for the boy who didn't have the father he wanted, or deserved, and ached for the man who had to watch the only important parent in his life slip away into the darkness of a terrible, unforgiving disease. "I'm sorry about your mother."

"Me too. She would have liked you." He grabbed her hand and rolled his thumb over the top. The intensity of his stare made her heart flutter. She knew the gift of his words weren't easy. It was just a snippet of his life, but she was grateful that he thought enough of her to share his history. Eliza knew these moments were probably fleeting. His was the façade of perfection, never rattled. But everyone had their secrets, their heartaches and imperfections. He was better at hiding his than most. He looked at his watch then back at her. "It's time to go."

Like a punctured balloon she fizzled and deflated. She wanted to fling her body to the floor in protest, but didn't. It was inevitable, she was running back. Only this time it was going to be ten times worse. It was a gradual climb uphill, all the way home. She looked at her sole "pack" member who was rested and raring to go. "We're not walking back are we?"

"No. I've got other plans."

She felt her shoulders drop and jutted her lower lip forward, but she knew it wouldn't work. Lake was as determined as they came. "Should I be nervous?

"I think you'll be pleased." He got up, walked around the table and extended his hand. "Up you go, beautiful. No more stalling."

Eliza accepted the proffered hand and eased off her chair. She was fairly tall at five-nine, but felt small in Lake's presence. He dominated everything around him. He was the sun and everyone seemed to orbit around him. He was gorgeous and tall with an aura that drew everything in like gravity. She followed the line of his neck, over his protruding Adam's apple until she found his mouth and unconsciously licked her lips. The visual wasn't lost on Lake.

"See something you like?" His breath was hot against her lips and the citrus of his juice tickled her nose.

"You're so full of yourself."

"Am I?" He took a step forward where there was no step to take. Her erect nipples fought the binding of spandex against her chest to reach for him.

"You know how much attention you garner from women, so don't play at reticence." She gave him a sappy eye-roll and a pressured sigh like she was unaffected, but her body always betrayed her where he was concerned. "You love that women swoon over you. Even Molly, my secretary, called you an *eleven*."

"The only woman I want swooning is you." He wrapped her up tight in muscled limbs and tucked her under his chin. She could feel the heated eyes of every woman in the room glaze over like a fresh donut at the sight of him. She felt lucky to be the one in his arms. "Kiss me."

Despite the overt display in the middle of the restaurant, Eliza didn't hesitate. She pushed up onto the tip of her toes and captured his waiting lips like they were the air her lung needed to live. She let him linger in the recesses, claiming her tongue, as she swallowed the affection he poured into her mouth. Every kiss between them was more meaningful and magical than the last. He released her mouth and she sighed out heavily then rolled her head to the left in an overplayed swoon.

"That's more like it."

They pushed through the door and the warmth of the sun settled against Eliza's face. Lake's grin made her stomach bounce nervously. He moved from her line of sight to reveal Sam with an open door to the limo. Without thought, she jumped into his arms, threading her legs around his waist and locking her arms around his neck. She strung tender kisses over every square inch of his face like she'd been without his love for too long. With his hands wrapped tightly around her, imprisoning her love, Lake walked to the car.

"I guess not making her run back was a good idea." Sam chuckled.

"I guess so."

He bent down and lowered her to the seat. She moved over enough to let him in, then curled under his arm. "Thank you."

"You're welcome."

She smoothed her hand over the bulge of his muscled peck and rested it over the soft thump of his working heart. He covered her hand with his. The warmth was fueled by genuine happiness…the kind no one could steal, no matter what. It shot up her arm and set her soul on fire. "No, I mean, thank you." His gaze was tender and deliberate, like the world around them had faded out. "Trusting me with your family history and telling me why your relationship with your father is strained, probably wasn't easy. I'm glad you think enough of me to share your life. I need to know your past, or I'll never be able to fit into your future."

"It's not something I enjoy talking about, but I'm trying to open up and give you what you need, because I want that future...I want it with you."

When they pulled up to the house, Sam came around and opened the door. Eliza wrapped her arms around him and gave him a grateful hug. The fact that she'd ridden home in luxury instead of running the four miles back was another win in her book. "I don't know how he did it, but thank you, Sam."

"He sent a text earlier with a time. I'm happy to oblige." His soft, full cheeks rose with the tip of his lips. She didn't imagine Lake gave Sam many hugs, but the appreciation she felt for him was immense. He'd become a protector, a confidant and a friend.

Lake picked up his phone and handed Eliza hers, but not before glancing at the screen. The impressive roar that filtered from his chest and the look of frustration told her all she needed to know. Three missed calls from Nick. He loomed over her, eyebrows knitted tight, waiting for her to speak. Eliza didn't know what to say. She mussed the hair on the top of his head and sighed. "Stop it. I don't care if he calls a hundred times."

"I fucking do!" He gave her a chaste kiss and groaned his disapproval.

She needed to get ready for work so she headed for the shower and Lake headed towards the kitchen. She was in the bedroom when her phone rang out. When Nick's face flashed on the screen she raced to pick it up. She didn't need any more drama.

"What the hell, E! I've called you like a hundred times."

"I know you have, but I'm not going to get in some screaming match with you so you need to lower your voice, or you'll be calling a hundred more times." Eliza leaned against the wall and started massaging her temple with the pads of her fingers. She knew this conversation wasn't going to be one she wanted to have.

"I'm sorry," said Nick, groaning into the receiver. "Why aren't you answering your phone? You said you'd call me and I've yet to hear from you."

"Yes, I did, but I didn't know there was a time limit. What in the hell is going on with you?"

"I don't want you to see Lake anymore." He spit it out like he'd just taken a bite of something that was too hot for his mouth. It pissed her off that he felt he could take such liberties with her life.

"So you've said, but you aren't in any position to make that demand. What's the deal with you two anyway?"

"There is no deal." Nick voice was laced with contempt. "I just don't like him. He's not the right man for you."

"Who's right for me Nick? You? Are you right for me?" She hated that her emotions were getting the best of her, but Nick was out of line.

"I hate seeing you with him. Based on that little display last night it's clear you're fucking him."

"Nick!" She bounced on her feet and started pacing the floor.

"I can't help it. I know he's going to hurt you and I just can't let it happen. He eats women and spits them out when he's done."

"Look at the pot, calling the kettle black. I'm surprised you two aren't best friends then." She stopped dead in her tracks. "How was the club last night, Nick?" He was the master of telling her what she could and couldn't do, but it didn't keep him from fucking anyone he wanted.

"Great!" he yelled. "I fucked someone else and all I could think about was you."

"I fucking hate you!" Eliza spat out, then pulled the phone from her face and looked at it like it was the culprit of her attack.

Disbelief and anger had her trembling like a leaf. "You've got some fucking nerve."

"I know Lake – well. He'll rip your heart out. I don't want to see you get hurt. Taking you to that club was the worst decision of my life. I don't want anyone else to have you." There was a dramatic pause, neither of them spoke. "I love you."

"I know you love me, but the kind of love we have is because of our history, not because we belong together. You fuck Angel and anybody else you want and I don't say a word because were friends and it's who you are. It's who you've always been, Nick."

A dry laugh filtered through the receiver. "Funny you'd mention, Angel. Do a little research of your own into Lake's relationship with his manager and see what you uncover."

"Why?" He was planting seeds of doubt and even though she suspected there was something more to Angel and Lake than met the eye, she wasn't going to be prodded by Nick.

"Fuck! Fuck! Fuck!" Nick growled over and over into her ear.

"I've got go." Eliza was confused, hurt and pissed. The conversation was a runaway freight train on a path of total destruction. It was time to jump out of its way.

"No, please don't hang up. God, E…I'm sorry. I don't know what I'm saying and doing. I'm going crazy over this. You've always felt like mine and I feel like I'm losing you. Can we go to lunch this week…please…pretty please? I just want to see you."

It broke her heart that they'd come to this point. It was never easy for either of them when they were dating other people, because they were virtually inseparable and did everything together. They were best friends and while most people suspected they were more, it just wasn't in the cards for them. The fact that he wanted more now was just shitty. She didn't know if he wanted more from her, or if he just didn't want her with Lake.

"Sure. Call me later and we'll set something up."

Eliza let the steam engulf her like a thick cloud that could banish the stress from her overwrought mind. She felt her body loosen as the hot beads of water pelted her head and back, streaming across her flesh like waves of silk. She was zoned out, deep in thought, when the cold air lashed her warm skin like a harsh whip. Goosebumps surged upward and her nipples pebbled at the sight of her beautiful Adonis. She hoped he'd calmed down since she last saw him. She wasn't in the mood to comfort his ego. He didn't say a word. He advanced on her with determination and need, grabbing her hands, pushing them over her head and pressing the wall of lean muscular mass against her slick body. The misty glass at her back, trapped her against him. The water sluiced between them, coating them in heat. She took a deep breath and then another. He had her pinned and was looking at her like she was his salvation. Maybe he was hers. Her stomach knotted like a fist. Her heart was beating against her breastbone fitfully. She couldn't decide whether he looked better wet or dry, but didn't care when his hand left hers and his fingers parted the wet folds of her vagina. Her free hand pushed greedily into the dark locks of hair that laid wet and soft on his head.

"Hmmm," he moaned, in that deep sexy rumble that felt like an orgasm in her ears. "Is that for me?"

Eliza nodded. She didn't know if he was referring to the fact that she was wet with desire for him, or if he was asking if her pussy belonged to him. But with his fingers teasing her sensitive sex, the answer to both was – *yes*.

His mouth fell against hers and the familiar dance of yearning settled in the pit of her stomach. He released her other hand, kissed her damp neck and added another teasing finger. Eliza felt frantic. She pulled his mouth to hers and kissed him urgently.

"I need to be inside you." The words fell from his mouth like slow poured molasses, igniting a fire that burned so hot neither of them were safe.

"Need is a big word."

"I know," he breathed, tickling her lips. She nearly buckled when his fingers slid out of her.

Lake reached underneath her thighs and lifted her into the air. Eliza locked her ankles around his waist and her arms around his neck as the belled head of his penis slid into her needy, hot core. She let out a tight whimper when his dick plunged against her uterus. The fullness left her gasping for breath, but her body wanted more, so much more.

"You feel so fucking good," Lake moaned. His hips rocked her back and forth against the glass as he drove his dick into her melting body. He was beauty in motion. Tiny drops of water tickled his lashes, his lips were glossy and his body looked like it was covered in sheen of oil. She couldn't quit touching him – his face, his chest, the ripple of abs that tightened and loosened as he fucked her.

"Lake." His name came out uneven and sharp like broken glass. She was already starting to feel the pressure in her abdomen as he increased his pace into her shameless needy pussy. He was stretching her endlessly with every spear of his massive erection into the hilt of her core.

"I can't get enough of you," he moaned, then reached down between their slick bodies and circled her engorged nub. It was her undoing. Looking to brace herself to anything before her body split open and devoured him, she found the edge of the glass wall above. Lake pumped into her and she came around his cock in shuddering waves. The pulsing of her vagina and the pulsing of her heart were in direct competition. His mouth seized hers with incredible potency and claimed her tongue with the same fast thrusts of his hips. She felt him grow inside her and warm cum coated her channel, rich and creamy, branding it as his.

His face was buried in her neck, loving the sensitive skin with passionate lips, caressing her as their bodies fused into one. She needed to see him…needed his eyes to find her in the haze of lust. "Look at me…please…"

"I'm here." He dropped his forehead to hers. His voice coiling around her heart. "Right here." His wet nose circled hers, playfully teasing, as he captured her mouth in a telling kiss. The emotion of the moment hit her hard. She was falling in love with him, or…was already there.

Chapter Twenty

Eliza walked into the closet to get dressed. It felt odd to have clothes that were chosen for her, but none she picked out herself. It was like living at Saks Fifth Avenue and plucking new clothes off the rack, simply cutting the tags off and putting it on. She emerged from the closet in a tight-fitting navy pencil skirt, a white tuxedo blouse and neutral patent leather Prada pumps.

"Wow!" Lake radiated appreciation and let his eyes wander over her from head to foot. Her cheeks tightened and her heart warmed. She prowled across the room and kissed his cheek. She knew the outfit looked good, but his response was like a sprinkle of confidence. "Katherine did an excellent job with your money."

"I'll say. You look incredible – maybe a little too incredible. Go change."

"Absolutely not," she replied, smoothing her skirt.

"You need to find another line of work. It's unfair to your patients to look like that and talk to them about their sex lives. You're no cure for the common sexual ailment, I assure you. If they're there for infidelity issues or hyper-sexuality, seeing you, despite your brilliance, would make any man or woman abandon a cure. You should have been a Playboy Bunny, not a psychologist. You're too hot for your own good."

"Nice speech," she said, walking back into the closet to pick out earrings. Eliza rolled her eyes when she knew he could no longer see her. The validity of his conversation was ludicrous. "Who's driving me to work?"

Lake followed her into the closet and tipped the lid back on his collection of watches. "Me." He pulled out a buttery, solid gold Rolex with a diamond bezel that sparkled with the brilliance of a Tiffany chandelier all over the closet. He pulled it across his hand and secured it with a snap to his wrist. He was the picture of tailored elegance, dauntingly handsome in a dark gray suit, white French-cuffed shirt with monogrammed cufflinks and a dark navy tie. Her mouth watered at the sight of him. She licked her lips and walked away before she provoked the sexual beast.

"Me as in Sam, or me as in you?"

"Me. I want to drive you to work."

"Great, I'm going to go grab my purse."

"It's on the buffet in the entryway."

She walked into the hall and dug for her makeup bag, remembering that she needed to take her birth control. Hell, she needed it now more than ever and frankly couldn't remember the last time she took one. Definitely not the night Lake took her drunkenly home from the club or Saturday night either. One or two missed days wasn't a biggie, but three – four and five, wasn't good. She dug and dug, finally spilling the contents on top of the buffet. She always kept them in her purse…always. She looked in the bottom of her purse and still nothing. There was just no way she'd misplaced them. She rubbed her neck and contemplated the possibilities and only came up with one. The man who knew exactly where her purse was. The nosey man who wouldn't tolerate secrets from her, but probably had several of his himself.

"Lake Mitchell." Eliza marched to the end of the hall with her arms folded over one another and waited for the blue-eyed deviant to pop his head out. He walked out of the bedroom and sauntered towards her, nonchalant and unassuming.

"Eliza Swift," he retorted, delivering her full name, as she did his.

"Give them back." She flipped her arm out and held out an open palm.

"Give what back?" Lake was playing coy, but she could see the guilt in his grin and eyes.

"My birth control. It's not funny," she stammered, getting madder by the second.

"My swimmers are at an unfair advantage if you continue to take those pills."

"That's the point. Besides you were cocky enough to believe you could get me pregnant regardless. I laughed and blew it off, but that's a hell of a lot different than you actually trying to get me pregnant."

"Replace them if you want, but I'll keep throwing them away."

"Why would you do that?" she fumed. She could feel the blood throb in her head, like it was about to explode. She was gritting her teeth so hard she was sure to spit the porcelain digits across the hall like bullets. "You don't know me well enough to know if you want to have a future with me. A child binds us together for life. Even if we don't make it we will always share that life." She snatched her purse up and stomped towards the door. She really wished she had her car. She wasn't playing this game with him. Talking to him was like throwing herself against a brick wall and expecting to get through. "I'm not having this discussion. Take me to work!"

"Wrong way." She turned and glared at him. He was actually smiling. She wanted to slap the shit out of his smug ass and he had the nerve to be cavalier. "You done?"

"I have nothing more to say on this subject."

Lake walked up to her, smelling like sin and looking even better and leaned in to kiss her, but she turned her cheek, denying him that connection.

"Suit yourself." He smirked. The heat from her chest and neck pushed its way over her face. *Asshole!* "Follow me."

They walked in silence, Eliza following behind Lake, spearing daggers into his back with her eyes as they walked through the house to the garage.

Eliza was fuming. The grip she had on her purse would have killed the animal two times over. When the door opened to the garage it was a sight to behold. Despite her will to leave him in silence she was in awe and blurted out. "Holy hell!" There were no less than eight cars in a perfect line, each more luxurious and expensive than the next.

"I know. Aren't they all beautiful? Which one do you want to take?" He looked like a kid in a candy store, grinning at the proud sight before them.

"It doesn't matter." Eliza let her excitement fizzle.

"Come on, E…indulge me." His voice was soft, and pleading. He sighed and let his grin fall. "I know you're mad at me, but I won't back down. We can talk about it tonight."

"White." She pointed across the room to the sleek, low-profile car that was polished to perfection. "That one."

She wanted to tell him that she wasn't coming back tonight but wasn't interested in fighting. She hadn't been home since Sam picked her up for dinner and she needed the space and time to think about Lake. He was taking over her life and not with baby steps. He was a hulking force of nature, a tornado, cyclone and tsunami, threatening to dominate every facet of her world.

"Lamborghini. Excellent choice." He perked up and bounced in step to the car. She followed, dragging her feet the whole way.

Lake pulled up in front of her office building and she quickly reached for the door handle. The silence in the car was deafening. She was hurt – really hurt and needed to relieve the suffocation. Lake curled his fingers over her arm. She turned back to assess him, but his eyes were stoic and his emotions were under lock and key. Eliza didn't feel like hearing what he had to say anyway. "Quit being so smug. I'm mad damn it!"

"I know you are. I can't take it back. What's done is done. I'm sorry you feel that carrying my child would be such a hardship on your life."

"Don't you dare try and turn this around on me. This isn't about me carrying your child. It's about you trying to control my fucking life."

"Don't use the "f" word. I hate it."

"Whatever." She tugged her arm from his grasp like he'd scalded her and watched the door rise like a space ship. She grabbed her purse and started towards the building, almost to the stairs when the shuffle of pounding feet snapped hurriedly across the concrete. Lake threw his body in front of hers to stop her forward progress. Overwhelmed, she sighed and looked away.

"Look at me," Lake demanded.

She looked into his eyes and found his perfect brown imperfection. The smell of soap and rich sandalwood washed over her like the undertow of a current that threatened to pull her under. The ground beneath her feet felt shaky. She needed to be firm so he understood, but the more she stared into his challenging eyes, the more her heart betrayed her by igniting the flame within.

"Yes?" she said flatly.

"Kiss me."

"No!" She pulled her head back and looked at him wearily. His mind was with her pills – gone.

"No? I thought we had a talk about how much I didn't like the word *no*. Do you not remember me smearing cream cheese frosting over your mouth?" He donned a wolfish grin that did nothing to help his case. "I think it ended in you having the best orgasm of your life." He leaned into her ear. "I wore that one. It was the best ever."

He ran his smooth, freshly shaved cheek across hers, grazing his soft lips over her mouth in the process. Eliza wanted to be embarrassed, but she was used to his wicked mouth and knew he loved getting a rise out of her.

"Kiss me," he repeated.

"Everything can't be cured with a kiss." The smell of peppermint lingered on his breath. She wanted to believe her words were true, but his kisses were enchanted.

"Let's find out." His lips pressed against hers and his soft warm tongue rolled across the part, seeking entrance into the depths of her mouth. She wanted to be strong but fell into his kiss. She had likened him to kryptonite, but knew that when you were on the other side of that power it kept you locked in. Powerless to do any more than give in to desire and need. His kiss was like a slow, methodical dance, absorbed in weighted emotion. Her heart swelled with every lap of his tongue. He released her mouth and put his hand against her cheek. "I want you."

Three small words that gripped her every time they fell out of his mouth. Eliza had never known a *want* like Lake's. It grabbed her soul and left her withering. Her words were cold. "Maybe that want is too great."

He grabbed the nape of her neck and looked at her with unwavering resolve. "It's not too great. You have the power to give me *everything*, all of you."

Her heart and head were dueling. It was a flight or fight moment. "And why would I give you everything?"

"Well," he said, stroking a line down her cheek. "I'm successful, charming, rich, and passionate."

"Yeah, you're also deceitful, overbearing, and arrogant. I'm not concerned about rich and I'll never disregard your passion. You might be the most passionate person I've ever encountered. When I dream of sharing my life I…" She stopped speaking mid-sentence. His eyes were narrowed on her like she was about to reveal her soul to him. He waited eagerly for her words, but Eliza didn't release them. "I've gotta go."

She stepped around him and rushed up the stairs. Her head was swimming with unsaid words. She didn't know what her dreams were, but getting pregnant out of wedlock right before her thirtieth birthday wasn't one of them. "I have appointments."

"E." His voice was low…threaded with sandpaper…sad.

Her heart seized, but she couldn't relent. Trust was a two-way street and he'd taken a piece of hers today. "Let's talk later."

"Sam will be here at five to pick you up. I'll see you tonight?"

It was more of a question than a request. She just let it go with a nod. She didn't need to look back. She could still feel the heat of his eyes radiating into her skin. Eliza wondered as she walked away if Lake Mitchell had ever been left standing in the wake of a woman. She bet it was quite the opposite. Far more women had been left wilting as they watched him turn his back and leave, clinging tightly to the hope that they would regain his attention.

Molly was already at her desk when Eliza entered the office.

"Va-va-va-voom!" Molly chirped happily. "You look fantastic, Dr. Swift."

"Thank you, Mol." Eliza masked the angst she felt over Lake and accepted the compliment. She often criticized the immaturity of her youthful receptionist but had learned to embrace her quirky comments.

She managed to see all of her patients that day but not without the assistance of antacids and ibuprofen. Her acidic stomach was in competition with her throbbing headache to pull her body into the abyss of hell. Eliza was so preoccupied with her own thoughts, she didn't think she even heard the words of her patients. She probably needed to issue refunds. A few head nods and single word responses didn't amount to therapy on any level. She finished jotting down her scarce notes when she heard a squeal from the other room. Without thought or a knock, Molly burst into the room.

"O.M.G! The most beautiful long-stemmed, red roses, just arrived. Come see! Come see!" She flapped her hands so quickly, Eliza was sure she was about to take flight.

"Nice knock, by the way."

Molly's face fell.

Eliza sighed. She'd just stolen another person's happiness. "I'm sorry, Molly. In the future, please knock."

"Promise." The illumination swept over her face and the flapping started. Following her lead, Eliza walked from her office into the small reception space and watched her giddy receptionist present the bouquet like a prize on a game show. Even Eliza couldn't act unfazed. It was over-the-top exquisite. There was no less than three dozen red roses with bight verdant foliage and baby's breath.

"Wow!"

"Wow is right!" Molly jumped up and down, pointing to the miniature card that was spiked out of the vase on a plastic pitchfork. "Can I open it? Please…please…pretty, pretty please." The shrill of her voice resonated in Eliza's chest. As much as Eliza feared what could potentially be written on the card, she indulged Molly's excitement and let her open it.

I'm sorry. Love, Lake Molly looked from the card to Eliza. "Lake? *The* Lake Mitchell," she repeated, bouncing on her toes. "The eleven?"

"One in the same." Eliza plucked the card from Molly's fingers and looked at the words. He had every reason to be sorry, but she wouldn't deny his effort to fix it.

She walked back to her office and stared out the window. The warmth of the late afternoon sun stroked her face. She leaned her head against the window and shut her eyes. She wasn't ready to hear his voice. She knew hearing him would weaken her resolve. She needed to set some clear boundaries. She decided to text.

The roses are beautiful. I know you're sorry, but I'm still mad.

His response was quick. *I know you are, but you can't walk away from me when we're talking.*

We weren't talking. I was talking and you weren't listening.

I was listening, I just didn't want to hear what you had to say.

Eliza hated to admit the truth but pushed out the words anyway. *I can't concentrate today.*

I can help with your concentration issues.

I'm sure you can, but I don't know how I feel about you right now.

His reply was swift. *I'm absolutely sure of how I feel about you.*

She hesitated, still holding the tiny card in her hand. *I'm sorry. Love, Lake.* He was full of big words about "future's" and "love" and "*everything's*" and "want" and "need." Things were moving quick…too quick. Real emotions were coming into play. She needed a reprieve. She was lost in thought when her phone vibrated in her hand.

"Tell me what you want, Eliza?" he asked, impatient to stake his claim on her heart and life. "For someone who's a therapist you sure do have a hard time opening up."

"I won't deny it. You have my head spinning. At first I thought this was about desire and sex. I was your obsession and then you became mine. I feel like things are changing. I'm scared you're going to break my heart."

"I'm coming to pick you up. We need to talk."

"No! Lake, I need to go home."

"Okay, then I'll come pick you up and take you home. But you and I need to have an honest conversation about what we want."

The power he already held over her heart was daunting. He was pulling her into his life and taking over more and more of hers in the process. If he came and got her she wouldn't be able to hide from that truth. He would know she'd already succumbed to giving him more than she cared to admit. "I don't know. I just think…" Lake cut her off.

"I feel like you're punishing me."

"I'm not punishing you." If she was honest, she probably was, but it was punishing her too. "I have to protect myself."

"Protect yourself from what?" Lakes voice was strung tight with anguish. Eliza knew if he were standing in front of her, he'd be raking his fingers through his hair and she'd be gnawing the shit out of her lip.

Falling in love with you. "You…" she whispered.

"Please let me come get you, E. I need to see you. We need to talk. Please don't push me away."

"Okay." It was the worst possible scenario, but she didn't stop him. Deep down, she knew he already owned a piece of her.

"Thank you."

"Don't thank me yet. I'm angry."

She slid her finger over the screen, plopped down in her chair and laid her head on the desk. She closed her eyes and let the silence soothe her weary soul. The emotions bubbling inside her were like a threatening storm. Exhaustion crept in like a dark fog and the night was still young. Eliza was screwed. One mesmerizing glance from his transitive blue eyes and she would falter. She wouldn't be able to fight the desire and she would probably end up giving him the rest of her heart willingly.

She stepped from her desk and smoothed out her fitted skirt and shirt. It was partially hampered from sitting all day, but still laid beautifully against her lean frame. Despite her trying day, life breathed within. She didn't resemble the zombie she felt like. She rustled her fingers through her hair and pushed nude lip gloss over her lips.

The carpet in her office was going to be threadbare by the time Lake arrived, the path worn clean from Eliza's pacing. What did she want? Was he even capable of giving it to her? She heard the roar of the expensive engine growl outside the window. The door jetted into the air and Lake was out of the car walking towards her office building. Her heart galloped behind her ribs and her palms grew moist.

"Good afternoon, Mr. Mitchell," Molly chirped. Her voice was three octaves' higher than normal, sappy and sweet like raw sugar. Eliza wanted to roll her eyes but knew the effect he had on women – on her. Molly was no less enamored, and the display of ostentatious roses that centered the room didn't help.

"Where's my girl?"

"*Your girl* is right in there."

Eliza was leaning against the wall, grateful for the support. She tucked her hands behind her back to hide the nervous tremble, but it did nothing to curtail the frantic beat of her heart when he stepped into the room. He walked through the door – debonair and poised, straight to Eliza. No fear and no hesitation. She had to admire his confidence, hers had faltered and stalled. He put his hands on the wall behind her, caging her head and grazing her lips, but not fully kissing her. The constriction against her chest was immense. Lake was a magnet calling to her heart. He was there to take it…all of it. By force or will – he was making his claim on her.

"Stop fighting me." He pressed his body into her and kissed her gently. She could feel his hard length against her pelvis and swallowed hard. "What do you want, Eliza?"

"It's not that easy, Lake. I want a lot of things."

"I want a lot of things too, but the difference between you and me is that I'm not afraid to ask for them. I can't give you what you want if you don't tell me."

"I want honesty."

"Do you feel like I've been dishonest with you?"

"No, but you take liberties that I'm not always so thrilled about. I don't need to you to pay off my debts. I don't need an extra wardrobe, or your assumption that I'd willingly just stay with you every night. I have a home and career of my own. I have my own money. You can't buy my affection." Lake was grinning, and it was just fueling her to push on. He was so fucking smug. "I'm nervous about what I don't know. You've lived a pretty big life and I'm worried about that."

"I have lived a pretty big life, but it's one I'm willing to share. I've told you about my father, my mother and my uncle. That's something I've not shared with many people. Sometimes those scars run deep, but I'm trying to be more open to giving you my past because I trust you not to use it against me and I know it's important to you. It's crazy for you to say or even think I'm trying to buy your affection. I have more money than I will ever spend in a lifetime. Buying you nice things makes me happy. You having clothes in my home is practical because I want you to be with me. I didn't assume you'd stay, but I was hopeful you would want to. What else?"

"I need to know I can trust you. Sometimes you make me feel fragile." She turned her head to the side, hiding, teetering on an emotional breakdown. She couldn't face his intensity anymore. He placed a warm, delicate finger on her jaw and brought her face and eyes back to his. "I think you could really hurt me, Lake."

"God, Eliza…" Lake said it like she'd just stabbed him in the heart, but she was the one bleeding before him. She felt the sting of tears and knew she was about to cry. His lips settled onto hers and she knew she was going to crumble under the emotion of his mouth. She was sure her heart was beating heavy enough for him to feel against his chest. Her last comment was the realest statement and her greatest fear.

"If you think I could hurt you it's because you think you could fall in love with me." His eyes roamed hers for the answer to his comment. She couldn't hide that it was as accurate of a statement as hers.

"Yes," she whispered honestly.

His sigh tickled her lips with damp heat, affection softened his eyes. She gave him what he came for, the words, the chance, and her acceptance. She admitted that she could fall in love with him. It was the only thing he needed to hear. That there was a chance for her to be his – completely, fully, no holding back – real love. The kind she'd never really known and was petrified to offer. He brushed his thumb across her cheek to catch the lone tear that had escaped. "Please say you want me, Eliza. Trust me with your heart."

She brought her hands to his cheeks and spoke softly against his lips. "I want you."

"Please come home with me." His lips pressed softly at her neck, igniting her desire like a match. "Please don't make me beg. Let me have *everything* – let me have *you*."

She didn't want Lake to beg. Somewhere deep inside Eliza knew she already belonged to him. With every stroke of his tender lips against her sensitive skin, her want was morphing into need. "Yes, to your *everything*."

"*Everything*?" He wanted her confirmation. He used the word in a manner that was so all encompassing she knew it was not only figurative, but literal.

Eliza tilted her head and offered him a nervous grin. "Some things."

"We'll see."

Chapter Twenty-One

The house was eerily quiet when they arrived home. Lake had given Katherine and Sam the night off. The smooth crooning of Sam Smith filtered through the house. Eliza set her feet free from her designer pumps and peeled her skirt down her thighs. She was unbuttoning the front of her blouse when the shock of warm hands smoothed over her stomach, leaving a trail of goosebumps across her skin.

"I see you like Sam Smith. I don't know whose voice is better, his or yours." She knitted her fingers through his, grounding herself in his love. "Dance with me, E." He spun her around and wrapped her against his chest. The sway of his body against hers was fluid and sexually charged. His hips kissed hers and his eyes pulled her under his spell. When he looked at her she felt like a rare diamond, brilliant for him and only him. Eliza wondered if Lake could feel it when he touched her. She was already in love with him.

"Let me take over, baby. This isn't something you can control…let me love you." Eliza nodded, her cheek was pressed to his chest, the smooth cotton a soft caress against her skin. The remnants of sandalwood and soap were already wreaking havoc on her sensitive nose. He could take over. Eliza would let him. She didn't want to overthink or overshadow what was happening between them. "Come with me."

He walked her from the closet and brought her to the foot of the bed. With a delicate touch he finished unbuttoning her blouse and pushed it over her shoulders, letting it pool at her feet. Her nipples peaked hard against her modest bra as he stared at her with unmatched longing. He ran his index finger from the hollow of her throat, down between her breasts and stomach, gliding it beneath the band of lace that covered her sex. He unclasped the bra that decorated her supple tits in fine white lace then dropped to his knees and slid the G-string down her hips. His lips found her abdomen and she drew in a ragged breath. "You're exquisite in every way."

He stood up and brushed his lips over hers. "Do you trust me?"

Without hesitation, she offered two words. "I do."

Pillows were scattered across the floor and the comforter was rolled down, leaving only the fitted sheet below. Lake scooped her up and centered her in the middle. He slid his arms from beneath her and kissed her deeply. His tongue rolled over hers like a tidal wave, washing her fears away.

"Spread your arms and legs for me, E. I want to tie you up." Her stomach dropped against her spine and her lip found its way between her teeth. "I won't hurt you or do anything you don't want. I'll make it good."

Eliza did what he asked and moved her body into a perfect "x." She tried to settle into the nervousness, but felt so exposed, emotionally and physically. Four expensive silk ties stroked her ankles and wrists, binding her to the heavy four-post bed. She wiggled her hands and feet to see how much give was in the sensual trusses, but found herself helpless under the ties. She was in complete trust of her paramour.

"I'm going to blindfold you, Eliza. Your mind will work out what's happening and you'll have my voice, but you won't have the use of sight or touch. It's going to make you nervous. You'll have to trust me."

"I do." Her voice didn't breed as much confidence as her heart and mind offered. Her nerves were ricocheting wildly inside her tightly coiled body, boomeranging against heart and head. Inky darkness claimed her vision and her breathing kicked into high gear.

She could feel the weight of his body push off the mattress next to her. She waited for what felt like hours, only the sound of faint music could be heard overhead. The rhythm soothed her, but trust or not, her anxiety was bubbling to the surface. She heard the clink of things being placed on the nightstand to the right of her head. Holy fuck, she was edgy. The unknown weaved images through her mind

– sexual and sensual, but sadistic and painful. She prayed her heart hadn't led her astray. Her skin crawled with raw untamed fear.

She could hear the rustling of his clothes being removed from his body and hated not relishing in the first sight of his smooth muscled flesh. She rolled her head to the side of the bed where she heard his movements and prayed silently for him to touch her. She needed the grounding…she needed him, his voice, his touch. The bed dipped next to her and she let out a hitched sigh.

"I missed you," she whispered, barely able to find her voice.

"I missed you too. Listen to my voice and feel…"

Eliza nodded, then something cool and wet tickled the side of her mouth. She teased the tip of her tongue nervously in its path and smiled when it was sweet. More drops cascaded between the open seam of her mouth to tickle her sense of taste. Savoring the juice, she took a stab at discovery. "Cherry juice?"

"Good girl." She was garnered with a kiss so sensual it left her breathless and dripping between her legs. His pleasure was palpable, bathing her in warmth like a million hot rays of the radiant sun kissing her flesh. "Open up." His voice was so lusty and sensual. She didn't know if he meant her mouth or legs, so she opened her mouth and let the slack of her binding tighten as she spread her legs impossibly wide. Cold air attacked the wet flesh of her pussy and she heard Lake moan above her. The cherry rolled across her lips and she thrust her tongue out to make sure her guess was right.

Hadn't something like this happened in 9½ Weeks? Kim Bassinger was fed a jalapeno when she had been teased with something deliciously sweet. Lake wasn't cruel, but he was deviant. He rolled it back over her lips and she pulled it into her mouth.

Cold liquid trickled in heavy drops over her breasts. Her nipples pebbled tightly against the assault and the chill electrified the hairs on her skin to stand tall. She retreated into the mattress but it didn't stop the cool sensation. The sting of teeth and pinching fingers over the peaks of hard flesh ushered a whimper from her throat, but it was quickly followed with the pleasure of wet heat. Lake was masterful at knowing her thresholds and Eliza was learning to love it when he brought her to that edge.

Something thicker, still liquid, streamed between her tits, gliding down the line of her quivering stomach. It pooled in the tiny crevasse that centered her then followed a path to the top of her sex. She inhaled, drawing in her shaky abdomen. Her back arched off the mattress and her core shuddered with need.

"Breathe, E. Your body's shaking."

"I know." Her voice was a pant…a cry for help. She was so hyperaware of him that she felt like she could fuck the air and get off. "I can't stop it." She could barely manage breathing let alone being still. She was clinging tightly to her body's threshold. She knew it wouldn't take much to make her come apart. He reached between her legs and stroked his fingers over her wetness, dragging it up to her tight swollen clit.

"I love how you want me…your desire is like honey against my tongue." He slid his fingers into her core and her hips reached out like a vise, begging for more, always more. His fingers skimmed the sap and then made purchase between her lips. Eliza lapped at his fingers like a greedy whore, dying to cum and taking anything he'd give her. It was her unmistakable nectar and honey – real honey. He pulled his fingers from her greedy mouth and sunk his tongue into the recesses, tasting her and kissing her with as much desperation as she felt. When his fingers dove into her hot core, the need escalated. She pulled at the bindings, stretching her legs open so he'd finish her off. She bucked into his hand like a cowboy strapped to a fierce bull, praying the seven second ride was enough to win her a prized belt buckle in rodeo glory.

"Please…," she cried out, begging. "Please, baby…oh, god…yes!" The need for release pulled at her stomach making her sick – the pressure between her legs was immense. The orgasm that he pulled from her was powerful and split up her body, cracking her wide open, revealing her soul and her desire for him like a bright light. The pulsing wouldn't stop and neither would he. She came again and again. "Fuuuccckkkk!"

He swallowed her filthy word with his mouth and stole the last of her breath. The world melted. The darkness that blinded her suddenly felt like her savior. She was happy to hide the truth behind her eyes. She loved him.

"God…Eliza…" She didn't know who was more affected by her orgasm, him or her. The rise and fall of his chest crashed into hers. His breath was hot and labored over her mouth and the yearning in his voice was unmistakable. "I've never encountered anything like you. I knew it would be good, but never like this."

"My want is *need.* Lake, please."

Lake told her she would one-day beg and she couldn't remember a day since he'd walked into her world, that she didn't want to beg him for one thing or another. His magical mouth, his pristine body or the slice of heaven that hung between his muscled thighs.

"Shhh…" The rattle of ice against glass echoed next to her. The icy drops pelted her lips, one after the other until she opened her mouth and accepted the onslaught. When the cold, sharp edge of the ice grazed across her areola, she flattened into the mattress to escape the frigid torment. She pulled her lower lip between her teeth, trying to suppress the shallow whimper that was an inevitable reaction to the new sensation. Her body pulsed with desire as drops of the melting ice followed the contour of her chest and pooled into the hollow of her throat.

She courageously found her voice. "More."

"Shhh…let your body react, but stay still."

He continued to tease her burning skin. Her composure was slipping away, an ebb to his flow. She pulled on the ties that imprisoned her hands and legs. She wanted to touch him, claim him. Every fiber, hungry to possess him. He was between her legs…edging closer to her weeping pussy. She moved her hips, fucking the air with desperation. Praying the scent and sight of her would consume him and he'd give her what she needed – him, only him. She cried out, as the first beaded drop slid coolly from the top of her sex, down to the waiting pool of warmth between her shaking thighs. One drop, and then another, hit her heated mound, causing her tensely threaded legs to instinctively want to shut. But his strong, steady hand on her knee let her know she was fighting an internal battle with self-control, and she'd win it, or be held accountable. The firm tip of the ice hit her core and she was powerless not to react. She willed him, without words to stop the cold torture of her most sensitive skin, but suddenly the warmth of his mouth was on her and she was the one melting. Sucking and lavishing her with his skilled tongue. No longer able to suppress her voice, she moaned out his name. "Lake…"

That was it…finally. His body come down over hers in a heated rush, his cock at her greedy opening. She arched into him. "Take me…"

"Are you mine?" His breath was stroking her lips like a feather.
"Yes."

"Tell me, baby."

"Yes…yes…I'm yours. Please…Lake."

He drove into hard, filling her, stretching her. She was unable to contain every ounce of emotion that was bottled up inside her. It was too much – too fucking much. Tears dampened the blindfold. She needed to touch him, kiss him. He must have read her thoughts. He was thrusting into her harder and harder, moaning into her neck as he reached up and removed the black mask that covered her eyes. A golden haze set him aglow in the dim room as the darkness fell from her vision. His eyes settled over hers and the depth of everything between them swept over her, showering her heart and soul like a lightning storm on a beautiful day. She kissed a claim of love across his mouth and accepted her fate.

Lake kissed her over and over, threading the words together. "Please…be…mine. I want you to be…mine."

The world seemed to fade around them and she came with a thundering cry, milking the emotions from his cock. He expanded and throbbed in her heat and came undone. "Fucking hell..." Warm jets of hot cum coated her womb.

"Tell me you're mine." She needed the words as much as he did.

"I'm yours." He stroked her hair away from her face and kissed her tenderly.

"Tell me you want me."

"I don't want you, baby. I need you. I want your love, Eliza."

Emotions were high. She was afraid to give him those words, but knew everything about this was different...extraordinary.

"I've never given any woman those words, but this is different. I'm genuinely happy. I yearn to touch you, kiss you and hold you. I've never wanted someone the way I want you. It's unlike anything I've ever felt. I want you to want me."

"Lake..." Eliza whispered. She didn't know what to say. They were dancing around it.

"Tell me what you're thinking?" He was beautiful and full of hope above her.

Her voice trembled. "My heart has never felt fuller. I'm glad you're mine."

A full toothy grin stretched across his gorgeous face and the sparkle of sheer happiness glinted his eyes. It was a moment of pure understanding and magic. Words...without words, a tiptoe into the deep end of the ocean. "I'm glad you're mine too."

Lake framed her face and fucked her mouth with the sensual familiar dance of his tongue – sealing their moment forever. The night was the beginning of something else between Lake and Eliza. Something neither of them could deny nor hide from. He no longer had to beg her to stay, and she no longer wanted to run.

Chapter Twenty-Two

Three weeks came and went. Eliza had more than utilized her wardrobe at Lake's and supplemented it with pieces of her own. Days were devoted to work, but Eliza's nights were devoted to Lake. They occasionally stayed in her downtown loft when she demanded it, but nine times out of ten she relented to his will and found herself at his house. It no longer felt like a mansion she admired as a child, but a home with a family she was growing fonder of daily. Lake continued to call her feisty and difficult when he wasn't getting his way, but Eliza stayed true to form. Only giving in after he'd gone to ridiculous lengths to prove his demands were valid. She was falling more and more in love with him every day, but still hadn't given him the one word he was so desperate to hear.

Monday morning came early, the familiar nudge of Lake's hand against her back let her know it was time to unravel herself from the warm sheets and his body to get moving. She didn't tell Lake, but she had made an appointment with her gynecologist early that morning. She needed to find another form of birth control because hers kept disappearing. It was a bone of contention – a not so funny game that she wasn't willing to play anymore. Two days on, a day off, two days on, two days off. She'd been on birth control since she was sixteen and had never been as careless with contraceptive as she was right now, at the peak of her sexual run with the most animalistic, dominant male ever. She was a walking, talking sperm depository, but she wasn't complaining. She'd never felt as loved and cherished in her whole life.

Eliza didn't have time for big hair and makeup, so she swept her long chestnut waves into a loose knot on her head, stroked mascara over her lashes and circled her cheeks with a touch of blush – simple and modest. She chose white linen dress slacks and paired them with Lake's favorite emerald green silk shirt, nude Gucci's and diamond studs. Lake was still in the shower when she finished. She was going to catch hell for breaking his goodbye kiss rule, but she didn't want to be late. She grabbed her keys from the buffet and was about to leave when she felt a claiming arm circle her waist.

"I know you weren't about to leave without kissing me?" She turned in his arms and ruffled her hand through his wet hair. Her heart warmed at the sight of him.

"No...well...maybe?" she stuttered. "I have an early appointment and you were still in the shower. I'm sorry, baby." Her lips found the corner of his mouth and he tackled her with a demanding kiss. "I'd never purposely walk out on you. I love you."

"What?" Lake pulled his face back like her lips seared him. With wide eyes and a knowing smile, he stared her down. Her heart clamored in her chest and her stomach flopped nervously.

"What?" Eliza diverted her gaze, the heat of his challenging stare was about to burn a hole in her skin. She'd given up the words so nonchalantly, like it was natural to say – it wasn't. She'd hidden them for so long. Too scared to reveal how much he really meant to her.

"Eliza..." Lake growled, moving his head back into her line of vision. He was chasing her attention.

"I can't believe how scared I am." The carotid artery thumped at her neck, blood surged frantically through her body. She had never fainted a day in her life, but her knees felt weak beneath her.

"Please...please...repeat yourself." Lake's hands warmed her cheeks as he framed her face and stared into her eyes. "I've been waiting and waiting. I'm madly in love with you, Eliza Swift. I want those words...I need them."

"Why didn't you just tell me?" she swallowed hard, then swallowed again. Saliva kept pooling in her mouth like a threat to vomit. Her whole body was trembling. The desperation in his eyes imprisoned the words in her throat. She was afraid to offer them again, knowing if she did they'd be real.

"I needed you to decide that I was worth investing your heart in. I knew giving it away would be the hardest thing you had ever done.

I wanted it to mean so much to you that you wouldn't hold it from me. I've been in love with you for weeks. I didn't want to scare you or push you too hard." He kissed the side of her mouth and she sunk into his hands…his adoration. Overwhelmed, her eyes fluttered shut. She was melting. The emotions were too much. She was lightheaded. Her small world was spinning off axis and she knew it was rotating towards the sun. Lake was her sunshine, her warmth, her desire, and her understanding. Everything she'd ever wanted in a man, packaged in a super nova of love and unstoppable passion. "Eliza, look at me." She found the unique bourbon defect in the sea of sparkling blue and let it warm her soul. "I love you."

Tears burned her eyes and swelled at her eyelids. A shuddering whimper found its way between her quivering lips. "You're going to make me cry."

"No, E…you're going to make me cry if you don't tell me you love me back."

"I love you."

"Say it again." The broad smile that overtook his face was a gift, packaged up tight with a perfect bow. Eliza didn't know who was glowing more, as he swallowed her tears with gentle heartfelt kisses over her cheeks.

"I love you." Her heart grew and grew with each monumental word.

"I love you too." His teeth clinked against hers as he pelted her lips with a million kisses. "Now you may leave."

She turned to walk out the door on rubbery legs and didn't look back. She could feel the heaviness of his gaze burning her back, but knew she'd never leave his arms if she turned around. Lake wanted *everything* Eliza had to offer – her love and her life, her compassion and her desires. With those last three words, she had finally given the final piece of the puzzle. And he had given her back so much more. He loved her.

She pulled up to the doctor's office and was ushered back without having to wait in the lobby A perk of being a doctor herself, even if it was a Ph.D. The fact that Dr. Joyce Spellman was an old friend of hers didn't hurt either.

"Hey you," Joyce greeted her when she walked into the exam room. "I didn't think you were due to see me for another two months?"

"It's an early visit. I wanted to talk about other forms of birth control. I've been on the pill forever, but their kind of an issue for me right now. Or, maybe, it's me that's the issue." Eliza shrugged impishly. "I've been careless." *I've been sabotaged!*

"Say what," she jabbed. "Eliza Swift, the most uncompromising, well-put-together woman I know has been skipping her pills?"

Eliza knotted her hands together. She could feel them heating at the center. "Crazy boyfriend and stupidity. I should have come sooner."

"Crazy boyfriend?" Joyce lit up from the rolling stool and pushed forward, peddling her feet like a toddler on a tricycle until she was at Eliza's knees, salivating for information.

"I've been seeing someone for almost a month…I'm happy." The pickle of heat swept over her skin and slid down her spine. "Really happy."

Joyce gently touched her knee. "I'm happy for you, E. You deserve it."

"Thanks, Joy," said Eliza, reverting back to the playful name she called her as a teenager.

"So…sex…really good sex, I hope."

"The best," Eliza blushed.

"Protected sex?" Joyce wrinkled her nose and bunched her shoulders to her ears.

Eliza sighed. "God, Joy. I'm shrinking into a sixteen-year-old-girl again. The answer's no." She moved her hand to her forehead and placed her elbow on her knee.

"Okay." Joyce patted her knee and Eliza found the courage to look at her. "You're a big girl, E. And one of the most responsible people I know. I am not here to beat you up about it. However, you can't start any form of birth control again until you have your next menstrual cycle. When are you due?"

Eliza looked up at the ceiling, trying to work the dates in her head. "This week maybe…yeah…this week."

"What will you do if you don't have a period?" Joyce asked, head tilted with a questioning curl of her lips.

"Don't be ridiculous," Eliza harrumphed, whisking the air in front of her friends face with the brush of her hand. "I'll have my period. I've been on the pill for thirteen years."

Joyce crossed her arms over her chest and looked at Eliza. "And…what will you do if you don't have a period?"

"I'll shit my fucking pants!" Eliza spewed like vomit into the air.

"And?" Joyce slid closer and circled her palm around her ear, urging Eliza for more.

"And…I'll call you immediately."

"Good girl." She reached into her pocket and retrieved her prescription pad. "You know Eliza, you're no spring chicken. Your birthday's right around the corner if I recall. Thirty isn't old, but maybe it's time to consider things like babies and, cover your ears…marriage. Eeekkkk!" Joyce shrilled loudly, laughing. "Marriage is good, E – kids are good. I don't know who this guy is, but if he's got your attention he's worth something."

"I think I love him." Eliza was glowing, radiant like the sun. "In fact, I know I love him."

Joyce tore the prescription from her pad and held it in front of Eliza. "Don't start these unless you have your period, and if by chance you don't, then I guess we'll be talking."

"I'll start. I always do."

Chapter Twenty-Three

"Good morning, Dr. Swift," Molly bubbled from behind her desk when Eliza walked into the office. "I don't know what you've done, but today the flowers are more magnificent than ever. It's a fairytale." She weaved her fingers happily together and looked at the sky like the dream was within reach. "Most of them are in your office, but look." Molly pointed to a beautiful spray at the corner of her desk, plucked the tiny card and sighed. "They're for me!" She bounced over to Eliza and thrust the miniature card into her face. Eliza had to move her head back to read the familiar script.

Molly, Take care of the most important thing in my life. Lake.

"Oh my god, Dr. Swift, it's the most romantic thing ever!"

Eliza had to admit it was a really cool gesture. Molly loved Lake on looks alone and now he had her heart bottled up tight. She tucked the card back on the plastic tine and beamed giddily.

"Yes, Moll, it is the most romantic thing ever." She pushed past her and headed towards her office. "Please tell me you made coffee?"

"I did, but you have to see your flowers first."

Molly threaded her arm around Eliza's elbow and pulled her into the room. Eliza's jaw fell to the floor and her breath left in one fail swoop. "Oh my God!" Eliza cupped her hand over her mouth. Molly wasn't exaggerating. It was like being at a wedding. She'd never seen anything like it. The fragrance of lilies and gardenia, lilac and rose blossomed against her nose – fragrant and savory, dozens and dozens of flowers were everywhere.

"I know, right?" Molly jumped wildly, grabbing her heart and jostling Eliza from her stupor. "Oh, god…tell me you love him. If you don't I'll totally take him off your hands."

"Molly!" Eliza gave her a playful bump of her hip.

"It was kind of a joke," she giggled. "But Dr. Swift, he's so gorgeous and totally into you."

"I do love him." Eliza looked at Molly and felt her age drop by ten years as she radiated with delight and the two of them jumped up and down in unbridled elation. "I absolutely love him."

"Oh, thank god!"

Eliza took a deep breath and tried to regain some semblance of professionalism. It felt like she had already put in one hell of a day and it wasn't even 9:45. She gave Lake the final piece of her heart with the words *I love you*, and she earned it in return. Everything felt right with the world. She pulled her phone from her purse and sent him a text.

Unbelievable display of flowers. Molly is overjoyed – super cool of you and I'm pretty happy too! Thank you.

Keeping you two happy is my new priority. We need to talk about your birthday tonight?

What birthday?

Your 30th birthday, next Saturday.

Eliza wasn't big on birthdays. Her mother had always made such a big deal about them. She hated being paraded around and on display to open gifts. It was tacky. It always felt like someone else's party – her mother's, but never hers. *Dinner with my favorite guy is fine. An orgasm or two…even better.*

You're on! I love you, baby. See you tonight.

I love you too.

Eliza turned her phone to silent, placed it on the desk and clamored towards the mug of coffee in Molly's hand.

"You've got a full day today and a couple of newbies."

"Great!" She brought the heated ceramic cup to her lips and practically inhaled the dark liquid into her impatient mouth. It was the first familiar part of her extraordinary day. She walked over to one of the vases and buried her nose into the fully open bloom of a white rose. Even if you weren't big on flowers, the sheer magnitude and beauty was undeniable.

Her morning patients proved easy, each was long-standing and making real progress in recovery. One of her male patients who struggled with infidelity, finally honed in on what was failing in his marriage and what the reasons were for his "grass is greener" theory. It was time for him to move to couple's therapy. It was the pinnacle moment when private sessions moved to couple sessions. Openness and honesty were usually better achieved in single patient sessions, but if she could break through the barriers of anger and animosity, patients had a real chance to heal.

"Dr. Swift, Ms. Lott is here. Shall I send her back?"

"Sure." Eliza pulled out her compact and swiped nude gloss over her lips then stood up and brushed the creases out of her linen pants. She was vaguely aware that someone had entered the room, but the voice that echoed out almost knocked her on her ass.

"Gorgeous as usual, Dr. Swift." Eliza stared, hoping her eyes were playing tricks on her. They weren't. The flirtation wasn't surprising.

She walked around the desk and offered her hand. "I don't believe I've ever caught your last name."

"I never gave it to you," she challenged. "Angel Lott."

The stunning blonde clasped a cold hand against Eliza's. Angel scanned Eliza overtly and shook her head. Heat set her flesh on fire and her stomach churned like a brewing sea. What the fuck was she doing here?

Eliza wouldn't be played in her own office, nor would she show any signs of weakness or comfortability. She had to admit, Angel was just as beautiful out of the dim light of the club. Her long platinum hair was braided to the side and she had on minimal makeup. She was casually dressed in white skinny jeans, a white sheer shirt and a thin cardigan that laid smoothly over her shoulders. Casual, yet preppy. It was a stark contrast from the skintight dresses and leather skirts and bodices she wore to manage The Raven's Nest. Eliza thought the word "manage" was a little loose, but it was her title. Clearly not her only one. Angel didn't just shuffle paperwork. She was the main attraction.

"So to what do I owe this honor?"

"I wanted to talk. It's what you do, isn't it?" Angel smiled mischievously.

"It is," Eliza replied. "Is this a social talk or a professional talk?"

She watched Angel carefully. She still hadn't responded to her question, but was smirking as she took in the obscene display of flowers.

"Well, let's put it this way. I paid for your time, so today we'll go with professional." Eliza refrained from rolling her eyes and turned around to get her portfolio from her desk. With a wave of her hand she invited Angel to sit.

"Please have a seat."

Angel looked at the sofas and chairs then grabbed Eliza by the hand. Eliza froze in her tracks and looked at the offending clutch of fingers over hers. She quickly pulled her hand away.

"This isn't the club, Angel. This is my office."

She tipped her head back and giggled. "My bad." Angel was brazen and forward. Her flirtation could be predicted, but Eliza wasn't feeding her ego or her insubordination. Angel was pretty, there was no denying it, but what happened at the club was undisclosed, private and confined to members. What happened in this office had her bound by patient-doctor confidentiality. It was a very slippery slope to have her here. Everything in Eliza's head told her to refuse to see her, but honestly she was interested in a little intel of her own. There was more to Angel than met the eye.

Eliza followed Angel to the couch and Angel looked to her for confirmation of where to sit. "Here okay?"

"Of course." Eliza's skin prickled and the hair on her arms stood on end.

Angel sat casually with her knee propped up on the cushion, tucking her heel behind her opposite leg. She draped her arm over the back and shimmied into the pillows. She settled in and mocked being at ease, but Eliza knew different. She could play at being confident, but it was a façade.

"Can I get you anything to drink?"

"Sure. What do you have?"

"Coke, Diet Coke, Sprite…" Angel cut her off.

"Diet Coke, is great."

"Sure." Eliza didn't keep alcohol in the office, but today seemed like a good day to have a hidden bottle. Not for Angel, but for herself. "With ice or without?"

"With, please." Angel cleared her throat. "I can't help but notice the unbelievable amount of flowers. Shall I guess who they're from?"

"If you'd like. Or, I could just tell you." *Let the games begin.* She walked the glass of ice and the unopened can to the coffee table. Angel grabbed the can, the familiar crack of the top sounded out and she poured it steadily into the glass. Eliza grabbed her notepad and made her way to one of the rich leather chairs on the opposite side. "I think you and I can avoid the games. The flowers are from Lake."

Angel looked across the table at Eliza, her eyes tight – assessing. Eliza met her stare head on. Angel could pretend this was something other than a social call, but she knew better. "Sure you don't want to change your mind about making this social instead of professional. I'd be happy to refund your money."

"Not at all. Where shall we start?"

"Let's begin with some preliminary information and then we'll go from there." She wrote Angel's name on the top of the paper. "Age?"

"Thirty-two"

"Married? Single? Or Divorced?"

"I think we both know the answer to that."

"What makes you think I'd know your social status? The only place I've ever seen you is at The Raven's Nest. I assure you plenty of the members there are married. They pay handsomely for the ability to not worry about the details of their personal lives."

"Touché," she countered. "I'm single."

"Children?"

"No children."

"Do you want children?"

"I do, but it may never happen for me. The only man I've ever loved moved on quite some time ago, and my current on-again, off-again lover…if that's what you want to call him, has his eyes on someone else."

Eliza felt like she'd been dangled a carrot, but refused to bite down. "Parents?"

"Happily married for thirty-seven years."

"Siblings?"

"One sister, but we're not close."

"Is that something you'd like to discuss?"

"She doesn't agree with the way I live my life. We don't speak. She's a prude."

"Okay. I guess that brings us to profession?"

"I manage The Raven's Nest for your florist," she teased, with a twirl of her finger.

"Funny." Eliza looked around the room with a lazy grin across her face, never happier with the overt display. "How long have you been working there?"

"Three years."

"You like it?"

"It's fun."

"Interesting. I would think that at some point, you'd grow tired and want something more. It's not exactly the kind of job that promotes a family life or children."

"I don't know. Most of the people that come there have children and families."

"But it's a playground for the members. They can live out their fantasies and go home. For you, it's a profession. It must get lonely."

Angel laughed heartily. "You think I'm lonely? I have my pick of the wealthiest men who'd do anything for a chance to be with me. I'm hardly lonely, Dr. Swift."

"Yet the two men you want don't share your affection."

An icy glaze filtered across Angel's smug smile. "I guess it can be lonely…or at least it seems to be lately."

"Let's talk about that," said Eliza. "Obviously things have changed in some way."

"Things have changed a great deal. Lake was never one to hang around the club. It's always been just a business for him, but now he's non-existent. It does require his attention, but he's preoccupied."

"I'm sure Lake would never let a company he owned falter. Isn't that why you're there? To see that his interests are secure and that business runs smoothly. You seem to have the pulse of the club from what I can see. I'm sure you're very capable."

"Oh, Lake hasn't told you? I'm more than capable. He knows firsthand." The smirk that pushed against her cheeks glared at Eliza tauntingly.

"Funny? We've been inseparable. I guess he's never thought enough about you or your capabilities to mention it," she stated matter-of-factly. "I'm sure it's an oversight. He has been very preoccupied." Anger simmered beneath her skin, causing her muscles to tighten and her hands to grow clammy with damp heat.

"I guessed as much." Angel took a long slow sip of her Diet Coke and stared over the glass. Eliza wanted to water-board her with it. "But he's not my only issue. Nick Slade is my other issue."

"Damn it, Angel!" Eliza slammed her portfolio shut. The crack of leather snapped in the air. "This is bullshit – not therapy. We aren't girlfriends."

"Call it what you want. We may not be girlfriends…as you so keenly put it, but you do interest me."

"In what way?" Eliza crossed her legs with a sigh and pushed her tense muscled back into the rich cool leather. Angel was prodding, toying with her, teasing her with innuendo and cryptic leading conversation. Lake, then Nick. She was more than the manager of The Raven's Nest.

"Where shall I start?" Her voice was like a sweet tart. All sugary on the outside, but tart in the middle. Eliza should have been done listening to the toxic babel, but she was captive to know the depth of the involvement with both men.

"Don't start. What do you want Angel?"

"I want to know what it is that you have that I don't." She looked at Eliza with less bravado, genuinely curious. "I get you're beautiful. Hell, even I'm attracted to you."

"We're not competing, Angel." At least Eliza sure hoped not. Doubt was already seeping into her bones like cancer, slow moving, but sure to kill. "I don't know the history between you and Lake, and I don't care. Lake sought me out, not the other way around."

"He might have sought you out, but it didn't take long to latch on. You don't need to explain the power of Lake Mitchell. I know firsthand."

Eliza's stomach roiled. Hearing Angel mention her familiarity with the man she was in love with made her nauseous. Angel was the ex-girlfriend that was also his employee. He never said it was her, but Eliza should have put the pieces together sooner. The blatant move to hold his hand when she knew Eliza was looking, the over-protective behavior at the club, the way Lake talked about Angel with such contempt. It all made sense. He wasn't just protecting her. He was keeping his interests close at hand. She wasn't oblivious to his past but didn't want to hear about his relationship from a former fuck of his either. Bile crawled up her throat, clawing its way like a green monster. She swallowed it back and looked at the wolf in sheep's clothing in front of her.

"I hope you didn't come here to talk about Lake because that's not going to happen." Angel squared her eyes on Eliza, stunted to speak further on the matter. "What else do you have Angel? I won't talk about my relationship with Lake."

"Wow!" She scooted to the edge of the couch and a slow grin curled her cheeks. "You're in love with him." She nodded her head, thoughtfully…slowly, rubbing her chin. "You don't have to answer. It's all over you."

"I don't plan to answer."

"Let me just give you a little piece of advice. Don't get pregnant. He'll bolt."

She stared at Angel, confusion masking her face. What Angel said, made no sense. The biggest quarrel she and Lake ever had was over his getting rid of her pills. Had Lake gotten Angel pregnant? Worse yet…did he run from his responsibilities? Eliza quickly did the math in her head and fought the urge to look at her taut belly. She swallowed the tight lump in her throat.

"I can't imagine Lake bolting from anything." She couldn't and wouldn't believe it. He was the most honorable man she knew outside of her own father.

"Well let's just say my experience was different and leave it at that."

"This conversation is going nowhere." Eliza moved to the edge of her seat. She needed to get up and end this torture.

"Let's talk about Nick?"

"Let's not." Eliza threw her hands into the air, but Angel wouldn't relent and continued pelting her with acidic tales.

"Nick and I have been lovers for quite some time." Eliza suspected as much, but to hear it made her skin crawl. She rubbed her arm instinctively like ants were marching up her flesh. "Not exclusively – obviously." She eyed Eliza with contempt. Nick and Eliza's relationship was hard to define and was under more strain than ever, but she and Nick weren't lovers. Some small part of Eliza took gratification in Angel thinking so. "He's all but closed me out. He seems to be distraught over you. Or, rather the loss of you, it would appear."

"Nick and I are friends, Angel."

"And lovers," she retorted.

"I won't answer that. It's none of your business." Eliza got up from the chair and so did Angel. The Mexican standoff ensued.

"That's where you're wrong. Lake and Nick are my business. The reason they hate each other is because of me. Nick stepped up to the plate when Lake decided he didn't want to be a father."

Eliza burst out with the most awkwardly timed cackle. "Nick Slade, the man I've known since I was six years old, agreed to accept the paternity of a child that wasn't his when Lake didn't want to be a father? That's a joke, right?" She continued laughing as she walked to her desk. "Lake was either trapped or lied to. I don't know which. He would never walk away otherwise. He is the most genuine man I know. He doesn't take anything lightly – including pregnancy."

"What are you insinuating?"

Eliza was insinuating a lot, but couldn't prove anything. "Don't come here and plant seeds of doubt and innuendo, because I'm not buying it. Lake's a great man, and if Nick could ever get out of his own way he would be a wonderful husband and father…to the right woman." She knew it was a dagger straight into Angel's armor, but she no longer felt the need to protect her. She was no angel. She was the devil.

"Apparently he believes that *you* are the right woman." Angel cast her eyes to the floor, her shoulders fell. Eliza couldn't feel bad for her, even if she'd been rejected by both men. "Nick told me last night that you were the most important woman in his life. He'd made a mistake not following his heart and that he wanted you back. I've never seen him so jealous or mad. He sure never acted like that with me."

"I'm sorry he said that. It was very insensitive." Even Eliza couldn't help saying so. Angel was clearly wounded. Her feelings for Nick ran deeper than maybe she even knew and he was rejecting her for a chance with Eliza. A chance that would never come.

"I didn't cry in front of him, but I wondered what it was that you had that I didn't. Lake, Nick and me, we were all really close at one time. Nick used to talk about his best friend. We never knew that friend was you. When he brought you to the club it was like lightning struck."

"That's ridiculous." Eliza shook her head. "Nick didn't want to take me there. I had to beg him."

"I bet he didn't." Angel sighed. "Lake would have gone after you no matter what. He hates Nick. But then you walked through the door like a sparkler on the Fourth of July, stunning us all. A beautiful brunette with captivating hazel eyes, a body made for the runway with a smile that lit up the room. Hell, we all lost it. Lake has to have you, I can't quit trying to seduce you and Nick understands after twenty-three-years of friendship that you're the only woman he's ever wanted. It's pretty powerful shit…wouldn't you agree? You're the femme fatale of all of our lives – the girl with all the cards."

"Wow! Femme fatale? All the cards?" Eliza brushed the loose tendril of hair from her forehead and threaded her hand around her damp neck. "I think you've got the wrong girl."

"I can't decide if you're really that modest or don't see yourself as others see you." Angel glared across Eliza's desk with her head tilted, questioning her with heated blue eyes. "You're right about Lake. He doesn't take anything lightly. If you're in love with him, it's because he wants you to be – he's relentless in his pursuits. And despite being a playboy, Nick's a pretty great catch."

"I'm done talking about this."

Angel adjusted the cross-body pouch at her hip and pulled out her keys. Just the rattle of the metal made Eliza feel more relieved. The end was near. "There is one last thing I think you should know."

Eliza sighed as she walked towards the door. How many times did she have to say she was done talking? This bitch wouldn't shut the fuck up. "What's that?"

"Lake always comes back to me. For one thing or *another*." She smirked. The innuendo wasn't lost on Eliza. "Always."

"Awesome!" Eliza opened the door of her office, strangling the brass handle and rolled her arm out with a flick of the wrist for

Angel to get the hell out. Molly, stared wide-eyed from her desk as Angel sashayed across the room. "Molly will you return Ms. Lott's money. It would appear that I'm not going to be able to treat her after all."

Molly looked from Eliza to Angel curiously, and then reached into her desk drawer to retrieve Angel's check. She handed it back and Angel proceeded to shred it into confetti over her desk. Eliza was too pissed to care and Molly was too stunned to utter anything.

"Well, I guess I should be going. I have a meeting with Lake in fifteen minutes. Shall I tell him you said *hi*?"

Eliza's blood seeped like molten lava through her veins. Her heart was erratic beneath her ribs and her stomach was knotted tight with disdain. She wanted to lunge across the room and grab the knifing, blonde porn star by the throat, but with complete composure, she replied, "Just tell him I love him and I'll see him at home."

"What?" Angel went slack-jawed and then snapped her mouth shut.

"You heard me," said Eliza, with a false smile. Tears were forming in the back of her eyes.

Angel stormed out of the office and Eliza stood dumbfounded, trying to take everything in. What the fuck just happened? This was bad…so, so bad. She could feel the walls of her heart being bricked up, one after the other.

"Who the hell was that?"

"That was Lake Mitchell's ex-girlfriend and Nick Slade's lover. She came here to weave a thread of doubt though my heart. I'm so fucked!" Eliza realized her use of the "f" word and instantly slapped her hand over her mouth. "I'm so sorry."

"You're not fucked." Molly pushed back from her desk and stood up, pointing towards the door where Angel had just exited. "She is."

Eliza grunted and let her body fall forward, grabbing her knees as she fought to breathe. She swallowed the stream of saliva that was a precursor to vomiting, and circled her arm around her waist, willing her body to calm. Tears pooled in her eyes. Oddly, a low rolling chuckle slipped from her lips as she shook her head in disbelief. She knew with that visit everything had changed, in her heart and in her head.

Molly's small hand warmed Eliza's back as she stroked her nervously. She had to be shocked at the sight of her boss losing it in the middle of the office. Laughing and crying in complete hysteria…completely…utterly…fucked!

"Are you okay, Dr. Swift?"

"I'm not sure, Molly." Eliza straightened, wiped her cheeks with her hands then turned, walked back into her office and promptly threw her full body onto the couch. She bounced like a rag doll before settling in, lifeless and sad.

"What a mess," Eliza mumbled into the cushion.

"That was Lake's ex-girlfriend?" Molly's voice questioned from above. Eliza barely knew what to say or where to start, the tangled web felt binding.

"Yes. She's also the madam and manager of an exclusive sex club." Molly looked at her in bewilderment. Eliza didn't elaborate that the club also belonged to Lake. It was a secret she'd cling to. "Oh…and don't forget. She also fucking my best friend – Nick Slade."

"What did she say? Why was she here?" Molly sat on the edge of the coffee table staring at Eliza…waiting for a big reveal. Needing more…just like Eliza had been when Angel was laying out the Reese's Pieces for her to gobble up.

"Planting seeds of doubt. Looking for the chinks in my armor and basically screwing with my head…my heart," she finished in a whisper.

"She can plant whatever she wants, Dr. Swift. There are no chinks in your armor."

Eliza rolled over, then sat up. Molly stared at her, eyes drawn tight. She was trying to bolster Eliza's confidence, but she didn't know if it was going to be enough to overshadow the damage. Some days she found Molly so juvenile, but she found the role reversal refreshing. She was grateful for her friendship, even if her reassurance wasn't actually penetrating below the surface. "You've been working here too long. You're starting to sound like a therapist."

"It's what I'm going to school for dumb-dumb. Why do you think I work here all day and go to school all night? So I can get experience from someone I admire…who others admire. Someone who's damn good at her job. So quit moping and get up and go get your man. Lake loves you and you love him. Angel has every reason to be jealous of you. That girl couldn't hold your lunch."

Eliza stood up and pulled her quirky receptionist into a grateful embrace. "Thank you, Mol. I really appreciate it."

"Appreciate it?" She pushed Eliza back and gripped her shoulders jerking them with her fingers buried in her flesh. "Are you kidding? Lake Mitchell may be an eleven, but you're at least a twelve or better. Don't let the over-processed bimbo make you believe less."

She nodded, not really feeling it, but pushed a false grin across her cheeks. "Please tell me I don't have any more patients today?"

"No, but your mother called."

The last of Eliza's air rushed out and she felt her shoulders slump at the news of her mother's call. "Stupendous! The hits just keep coming. You can go ahead and go home. I'll finish up here and lock up."

"Are you sure?"

"Enjoy the rest of the afternoon. I'll see you tomorrow."

Molly walked out and rifled through her desk, and then popped her head back through the door frame. "See you in the morning, Dr. Swift."

"Have a good evening."

"You too." The night couldn't possibly be as bad as her afternoon, but she wouldn't say as much. Things could always get worse.

Chapter Twenty-Four

Eliza heard the door shut and her office went silent – she was alone and man did she feel alone. She crossed her arms over her desk and buried her head in the squared crevasse. Closing her eyes, she let the heat of her breath caress her face.

Angel's words were etched in Eliza's head, engraved for eternity. Pregnancy. Abandonment. Nick and Angel – Lake and Angel. What was the truth and what were lies? It just didn't make sense. Lake was pulling out all the stops to win her heart and playing with their lives by stealing her birth control. She never thought it would come to fruition, but the more he toyed with her ovaries, the more she gave the idea validity. Maybe not now, but she wanted kids and she wanted them with Lake. Her heart was cracking in her chest, tears – hot and heavy slid down her nose and puddled onto her desk with no end in sight. She was more anxious the ever to start her period. There was a potential for tragedy on the horizon. She weakly overlapped two fingers in a twisted, hopeful cross. Eliza wasn't one to believe in such trivial things, but she had nothing and everything to lose.

Where did Nick fit into all this? They needed to talk, face-to-face and clear their hearts and heads. He may not want Angel, thank goodness, but he couldn't have her. Her heart belonged to someone else and even if it didn't work out for her and Lake, Eliza and Nick were never going to be more than friends. The weight of that thought…no Lake…no Nick, hit her so hard her chest was cracking open. She was fully exposed, tormented by the thought of losing everyone she loved. It was a punishing possibility.

He always comes back to me. One way or another…always. Eliza wondered in what capacity. She didn't think Angel meant emotionally, but even the thought of him running to her sexually made her stomach lurch. She was in love with him – madly, truly in love with him. Now it felt tarnished by ex-lovers, doubt, and deceit.

She wanted to talk to Lake, but couldn't. Even though she returned Angel's money the boundaries of confidentiality were clad tight. Losing Lake would be nothing compared to losing her career. She was screwed to carry the burden of a heavy heart and insecurities around like a slow tightening noose. Coming in as a patient was a well-played hand.

Eliza wiped her face and reached for the phone. Only one person could ease her soul. He wouldn't betray her confidence or judge her for the outcome.

Her dad answered immediately. "How's my favorite girl?"

"This morning I was on top of the world, but now I'm not so sure. I could really use a calming voice and some well thought-out words. You up for the job?"

"I'm your father, honey. I'm always up for the job. Plus, there's something I wanted to talk to you about anyway." Eliza already felt a degree of angst and sadness lift with his adoration. "You want to meet for a dinner?"

She gazed out the window down to the Plaza shops and restaurants. "That would be wonderful. Shall I ask or is it a given," she teased. It was always Plaza III, his favorite steakhouse.

"It's a given. I'll meet you there in thirty minutes."

Eliza slid her finger across the end button, then reluctantly called her mother.

"Good evening." Sylvia picked up on the first ring.

"Good evening, Mother." Eliza's nerves constricted under her skin. She prayed for kindness. She couldn't handle her mother's ridicule. "How are you?"

"Well, I've been better." Eliza cringed. "Why do I have to find out from Johnathan Mitchell that my daughter is dating the most eligible bachelor in Kansas City? No wonder you seemed a bit evasive at the Classic Cup. You were already seeing him."

"I had just started seeing him. I didn't want to get your hopes up."

"He's hardly anyone, Eliza," she prodded.

"You're right, he's definitely someone, but we're just dating. There's no engagement rings or kids in sight so you can continue your prayers on my behalf." *The first part was true, and she prayed the second part was just as true.*

"I don't need to pray for you. He might be the most eligible bachelor in Kansas City, Eliza, but you'd be one hell of a catch for any man. Don't discredit your worth. You are intelligent and beautiful."

It was probably the nicest thing her mother had ever said and couldn't have been timelier. "Thank you, Mom. I appreciate that." Eliza warmed like she'd been hit with the full beam of the sun, but knew it was reflected from a glacier.

"Where the hell is your confidence, Eliza?"

She chuckled. "That's what I love about you, Mother. You always stay true to who you are."

"Grow up, Eliza. Be the woman I know you are. The one we raised you to be. Go after what you want and don't let anything stand in your way." Sylvia brushed past the conversation like it was a simple matter of will. Eliza agreed it probably was, but still felt a little hurt by Angel's accusations. "Now, your birthday is next Saturday. Your father and I want to take you out to dinner."

"Oh god." Eliza groaned into the receiver. Surely her mother wasn't serious. "Together? You and Dad? Who's coming? You always act like an idiot when Daddy brings Candice around. And she always pours on the flirtation, just to get under your skin. It's not how I want to spend my thirtieth birthday."

"Well then you'll be pleased to know that you won't have to be subjected to any of that. Apparently things aren't so rosy for Candice and your father. He's not bringing her." Glee threaded her voice even if she would never admit it. "We will expect your boyfriend to be there."

"He may have plans." His plans were to take her out for a quiet dinner and fulfil her request for orgasms, but she wasn't so sure that was what she wanted anymore. "No big to-do's, please."

"Whatever." Her mother groaned.

"Simple, Mother. I'm turning thirty, not thirteen. No ponies, no parades, no cakes and streamers, or any of that other crap…please."

"No cake…you've gone too far. There will be cake by god. Thirty is a big deal, E."

Her mom was playing at her heartstrings by dropping her name to an acronym, but Eliza wasn't fooled. "You heard me. No big overplayed birthday extravaganza. Dinner, that's it…and cake."

"Yeah, yeah." Sylvia sighed in exasperation.

"Listen, I have to run. I have a dinner date with Dad and I haven't even told Lake I won't be home for dinner."

"*Home* for dinner?" she chirped happily. "That is hardly casual."

"I guess," she replied. "I'll talk to you later this week."

"Give your father my best," she sapped, like slow poured syrup down rough tree bark.

"Sure," Eliza lied. She and her father made it a habit not to discuss her. "Bye."

She stared at the weighted phone. She didn't want to call Lake. Was he still with the Angel of death? *Damn that bitch for coming to her office.* She didn't have to worry long. Her screen lit up with his mega-watt smile. It was the moment of truth. She skimmed the screen with a trembling finger.

"Hey you." Eliza greeted with as much cheer as she could pour into her voice.

"How's my girl?"

"I'm good." Thank God they were separated by a phone. If Lake could see her eyes, she would never be able to pass those words off as anything more than the lie they were.

"I want to see you. I've done nothing but think about you all day. Come to my office?"

"I can't. Besides, I'm sure you're busy." She knew it was a crap move, but wondered if he'd mention his meeting with Angel.

"I'm always busy, E. But I'm never too busy for you. I was hoping to talk to you about a few things." Her stomach soured with the thought. She wasn't up for anymore heavy discussions. That ship sailed with Malibu Barbie.

"I'm meeting my father for dinner at Plaza III. It will have to wait."

"Sure." His voice deflated. "When will you be home?"

"Your home or mine?" she offered sadly. She didn't want to face him.

"Eliza…" Lake growled into the receiver. "Since when is it yours or mine? You and I haven't been apart in weeks. You finally tell me you love me, I give you those words back, and now I have to wonder where you're sleeping. Don't do this?"

"Do what?" She sighed. "It's been an unusual day. I'll be at your house after dinner, and we'll talk then, I promise."

"I love you, Eliza," Lake said matter-of-factly. "Don't you dare let that bitch come between us!"

"What?" She dropped her head to the desk. She couldn't discuss it with Lake. It was the worst possible scenario, already playing out like a horror story. She was shocked Angel mentioned coming, but the thought of them together made her feel worse.

"Why didn't you tell me she came to your office?"

"It's patient-physician confidentiality, Lake. I can't discuss it, so please drop it."

"You told her you love me?"

"I did…I do…I…" she stuttered. "The things she said…"

"What the fuck did she say? God damn it! Don't you dare leave that office! I'm on my way."

"No!" she yelled, angry about the whole fucking mess. "Lake I have to leave. I won't keep my father waiting."

"Then I'll join you."

"No!" Eliza yelled again. Her voice was so tight and strained with sadness and anger she thought her vocal chords were going to snap. "I can't talk about you if you're there."

"That was a joke, right? Maybe you should just talk *to* me, Eliza."

"I've really got to go. We'll talk later."

"Eliza!" The screech of her name resonated in her ears and chest like a wrecking ball as she hit the end button. There was nothing more to say.

Chapter Twenty-Five

Eliza pulled up to the restaurant and the young valet hurried from his stand to take her car. The popular steakhouse was packed as usual when she pushed through the heavy glass turnstile. She saw the silhouette of the man who gave her life seated at the bar and practically ran across the room to get to him.

"Hey, Daddy." She came up behind him and swept her arms around his shoulders, warming her cheek to his. He smelled familiar of cedar and soap. "Sorry, I'm late."

"You're right on time." He reached around her slim waist and pulled her into his arms. "Are you okay? You look tired. Beautiful as ever, but tired."

"I guess I am a little tired," she conceded. Drained was more like it, but she wasn't here for the pity. She was here for the advice.

"Want to get a drink or go ahead and be seated?"

Eliza felt her heart constrict. Her gynecology appointment hit a collision course with Angel's words of woe and she felt fucked. Two wrongs didn't make a right. She prayed she wasn't pregnant, but drinking her way through it until it came to fruition or went away didn't seem prudent. "Let's get our table."

Her father threw a twenty on the bar and walked Eliza to the hostess stand. "Two, Cindy. My usual table with Jeremiah, please." Halston Swift didn't own the restaurant, but sometimes Eliza thought he should have. He practically lived there. It was his power lunch venue and where he entertained his clients. They accommodated his every wish. He was a big tipper with deep pockets.

"Make that three, Cindy." Eliza's heart stalled in her chest. Lake was at her back. His voice melted her. His scent filtered her senses and the heat of his body in such close proximity felt like fire against her skin. She didn't turn around.

Eliza's father turned with a broad gleaming smile and stepped over to welcome the intruder behind her. Eliza looked over her shoulder to a lukewarm Lake, drilling holes in her flesh with his piercing blue eyes.

"Well, all be damned, Lake Mitchell." Her father thrust his hand in Lake's and embraced his shoulder like they were the best of friends. Eliza sighed. They knew each other. She didn't know why she was surprised. Lake was a billionaire businessman and her father was probably the most recognizable attorney in the state, if not the country. Anyone who was anyone knew her dad. "It's been too long."

"Far too long," Lake agreed with a sincere grin. He looked at Eliza then back to her father. "Halston, I'm deeply in love with your daughter, and she's angry with me. If you would grant me a moment of her time I sure would appreciate it."

Eliza's mouth was agape and her heart was beating rapidly. Her own father was clueless about her personal life. She'd gone from having no one to being in love and he didn't even know she was dating. Her father gave her a wicked grin and offered her over on a silver platter. "Of course, you two take your time. You'll be joining us for dinner?"

"If you don't mind. I'd love to." The awkwardness was like an electrical current between them. If he thought she was mad before, Lake hadn't seen anything yet.

"Eliza and I would love to have you join us." Her father smiled happily and rubbed Eliza's shoulder for approval. "Wouldn't we?"

Eliza gave her father a half-smile and a tip of her head. "Of course."

"Great," Lake beamed, a clear win in his book. "Tell Jeremiah I'll have a scotch and water."

"Of course." Her father nodded, all smiles. He reached over and kissed Eliza on the cheek then whispered. "I guess we do have a lot to talk about."

"Maybe I'll have that glass of wine, after all." She turned and walked out the door with Lake hot on her heels, rounding the corner until she felt like she was out of earshot of the valet. When she spun around Lake halted in his tracks. "What are you doing here?"

"I'm in love with you, Eliza. When you're upset, it makes me upset. You hung up on me then wouldn't answer my calls. I had no choice."

"I didn't mean to hang up on you, but you weren't listening." Eliza stupidly stomped her foot. No tantrum was going to work with Lake. "You're so stubborn! I didn't want to be late."

"I'm stubborn." Lake ran his fingers through his hair and looked into the air like he was begging for some kind of divine intervention. He stepped into her and gently caressed both sides of her waist. "I just told your dad that I'm deeply in love with you." The smile that pushed his cheeks to his eyes was brilliant. It was hard to look away. He was so gorgeous and clearly proud of his statement.

"I know." She looked away, but he wasn't letting her free. He cupped her cheek and recaptured her gaze.

"I'm not afraid to live up to those words, Eliza. I am deeply in love with you." She didn't doubt it and loved him more for the reassurance.

"I know you aren't. I'm just trying to make sure that I can live up to them too."

"Angel means nothing to me, Eliza. I know you feel bound to keep whatever she said confidential, but she is a liar and an instigator who'd do anything to hurt you or me."

"I can't get into it." Her voice fell. It was an impasse she couldn't deny.

"Don't let her lies ruin us, Eliza. I'm begging you."

"That's the problem, Lake. I don't know the lies from the truth."

Lake groaned, frustrated. His eyes were squared on her, hopeful for answers he'd never get. Nothing good could come out of her talking *around* her worries, without being able to voice them. She was basically screwed into holding the details of Angel's accusations secret.

"You'll only know the truth if you give me a chance to answer the questions."

"I'm sorry." She rested her hands over his forearms and urged them from her waist. They needed to get inside and let this topic go. Lake tightened his arms around her, desperately trying to fix the unknown.

"Do you love me?"

"More than anything," she said honestly.

Lake put his hand over Eliza's heart. The warmth radiated through the verdant green silk. People were walking by, but she barely noticed. The power of his presence washed the rest of the world away. "This is as real as it gets. Nothing and no one can come between us unless we let them. The Angels and Nicks of the world can go fuck themselves." The slow glide of his tongue parting her lips was decadent and sensual. She was powerless against his kisses and he knew it. They muddled her brain and settled desperately between her legs. They held more meaning than his words and right now she needed every bit of the power they held to bring her back from doubt and fear.

"I love you, Eliza."

Lake fingered a lock of hair around her ear and dropped his forehead against hers. She wanted to crawl beneath his skin and adhere herself to his heart. She wanted to claim his imperfect eye so it only saw her. She wanted his lips to only know her kiss and the taste of her skin. She wanted his hands to only know the feel of her body. She wanted his laughter and his anger, his compassion and understanding. He said he would never share her and she was desperate to say the same. Lake had lived two lives to hers. It felt unfair that Angel had him first. She didn't have a right to feel jealous, but she did.

"I guess I need to go sit at the defendant's table and sell myself to the most powerful attorney in the state. I hope he ordered that scotch." He pressed a warm kiss to the top of her head and tucked her under his chin.

"I didn't realize you two knew each other."

"Your father's widely known. Those who can, pay richly to know him. He's on retainer at Synergy. We don't usually need anyone of his caliber, but he's a good man to have on your side."

"Indeed." Eliza didn't need confirmation of her father's power. She had lived in the wake of that power all her life.

"Let's go. I'm sure he's waiting to size me up."

Lake grabbed Eliza's hand and walked back in with her clutched tightly to his side. She could feel the dominance blossom like radiant heat and wondered how he was going to interact with her father. Like Lake, he was a force all his own. They sat down and her father pushed Lake's scotch across the table. Eliza strangled her wine glass like it had somehow offended her and let the burgundy fluid warm her throat and stomach. She wanted to sigh with relief as the alcohol washed over her but refrained. Her father smirked at her side and Lake beamed at her other. It was going to be a long night.

"Okay, Dad…enough." Eliza chided, out loud.

Her father sat back farther in his chair and prodded her with a tip of his head and a deep chuckle. "You tell me, honey. The most influential businessman in Kansas City, if not the country, just walked in and professed to be in love with you. I guess I'm just waiting to hear your response to that. I didn't even know you were dating and you're my only child." He twirled his wine expectantly, looking at Eliza then to Lake, who was also anxious to hear her response.

"Dad, I'd like to introduce you to my boyfriend, Lake Mitchell. Lake and I've been dating for almost a month now. This morning I told him I loved him and he gave those words back."

Lake cleared his throat. "Truth be known. I've been in love with her for weeks now."

Suck up. "He wasn't invited to dinner this evening because I wanted to talk about him incessantly. It looks like that won't be possible." She grinned at Lake and playfully grabbed his thigh. He quickly covered her hand and wove his fingers in between hers like loving vines. He beamed across the table, clearly thrilled with her response. She tipped her head to the left. "Lake, this is my father, Halston Swift."

"I'd shake your hand again, son, but I fear your hands are full." Lake burst out into a full belly laugh, set his drink on the table, and gripped Eliza's hand tighter.

"I fear you're right." Lake laughed. "But I'm in love with her. She's beautiful and intelligent, loving and compassionate. She makes me want to be a better man so I can live in her light." Butterflies tickled her belly and heat warmed her cheeks. Charm slid off him in waves, covering the table in awe. "She might be a handful, but I think I can take her." Lake flashed his panty-dropping smile and Eliza melted. She didn't retreat from his comments or the look of love that blanketed his eyes. She'd bask in his rays and soak it all in. Each look and word renewed her confidence. She wasn't wrong about Lake. That bitch could go straight to hell.

"I think from the way she looks at you, you've already taken her. She's special, Lake. You're a lucky man."

"I couldn't agree more."

Eliza was starting to feel like an eavesdropping bystander. The heat of embarrassment clung to her neck and her hand grew clammy against Lake's. "Okay, okay, you two. Let's eat for goodness sake."

Dinner went off without a hitch. They spent the rest of the night talking about business, the city, politics, sports and everything else under the sun. Eliza was happy to see the two most important men in her life fall into step with one another.

Eliza covered her mouth to hide her yawn, but always observant, Lake gave her a wink and put his hand in the air for the server to come to the table. "Please put it on my tab, Jeremiah."

"Lake, you came as my guest. I'll pay."

"Save your money, Halston. You might need it soon." Lake winked at Halston and Eliza's stomach dropped to her feet with the insinuation. Lake pulled her chair out and reached for her father's hand. "I apologize for forcing my way into your dinner with Eliza, but it's been a real pleasure."

"The pleasure was all mine. I look forward to spending more time with you. As a matter of fact, my daughter turns thirty this coming weekend."

"I mentioned it this morning." Lake pulled their intertwined hands to his mouth and kissed it. "She wanted to do quiet with me." Lake winked. "But dinner would be lovely. I look forward to meeting her mother. I've heard so much about her."

Her father let out a slow sigh and shook his head. "She's a force all her own."

"That's for sure," said Eliza under her breath.

"Eliza and I will be in touch with you and Sylvia this week and we can firm up some plans."

Eliza let go of Lake's hand and wrapped her father up tight. She really wanted to talk to him alone, but knew he treasured being included in her personal life. "I love you, Dad."

"I love you too, honey."

She pulled back from his arms and grabbed his shoulders. "Oh my god, Dad. You wanted to tell me something. We've been rattling on all night. I'm so sorry."

"Well, I guess you'll find out soon enough." Her father looked pensive and sad. It was a rare sight. "Candice moved out."

"Oh, dad. I'm sorry."

"Don't be." He shook his head. "She wasn't interested in me. She was only interested in what I could give her. Honestly, Eliza, I'm too old to play games with someone half my age. I don't know what the hell I was thinking. It was short-lived and I had an iron-clad prenuptial agreement."

"Are you okay?" The therapist was coming out.

"Funny enough, I'm actually relieved." Eliza was happy to see his face brighten. "I have been avoiding your mother's calls because I don't want to hear her gloat. Other than that, I'm good." He looked past Eliza to Lake. "You think Eliza can be difficult. Her mother can bring a man to his knees."

"Dad!"

"I'm sorry. That wasn't meant to hurt you, but your mother is the most infuriating woman I've ever met. I can't believe I was married to her for thirty years. I also can't believe I ever let her go."

"Wow!" Lake and Eliza said in unison and looked at each other.

"Jinx!" said Lake, jabbing her in the arm.

Eliza rolled her eyes. "Really? Are you ten years old?"

"You're not supposed to talk until someone says your name three times." She dropped her shoulders in mock frustration and looked over at her dad.

"Sorry Lake, but she's my girl." He looked at her with adoration and repeated her name three times.

"I'm out of here." Eliza was exhausted and weary from the day. The wine didn't help. "I'm on information overload." She gave her dad a loving smile, and then turned and kissed the side of his jaw. "I'll see you at home."

They exited the building and waited for the valet to retrieve Eliza's car. Lake leaned into her back and wrapped his hands around her waist. "I think that went rather well."

"I agree."

Her car hadn't come when Sam pulled up with the limo and rushed to open the door.

"You go with Sam, and I'll drive your car home."

"Or, I can wait for the car and you can ride with Sam."

Lake had well over a million dollars tied up in exotic sports cars and luxury sedans in his garage. The thought of watching him get in her white Camry made her want to laugh.

"Get in the car. Eliza," Lake demanded.

"Okay already. Don't get your panties in a wad."

"Who says I have panties on?" The corners of his mouth curled. He'd never go commando at his office, but she loved it when he was lighthearted and playful.

Eliza walked back over and cupped his face with her hands. "Don't tease me, it's been a really long day."

"I don't intend to tease you," He whispered hotly into the shell of her ear. Chills negotiated each knot of her spine. "I'm in love with you. I intend to make sure you know how much."

Chapter Twenty-Six

Sam pulled the limo around the circle drive in front of the massive double doors of Lake's home. Eliza stepped from the car and looked up at the substantial manor. The house was starting to feel like hers. The smells, the sounds and the people that made up Lake's life felt like hers too.

Sam touched her shoulder and brought her out of her trance. "What are you waiting for?"

She looked at Sam timidly. It seemed odd to admit, but Lake had always preceded her, or she'd arrived with him. "I was waiting for Lake to get home. I was just admiring the house. It never ceases to take my breath away." She looked back at the architectural beauty and offered an appreciative smile. "Or estate rather," she corrected.

"Or home," Sam amended with a grin that warmed her heart. "Your home, Eliza."

She circled her arms around his shoulders and gave him a grateful hug. She couldn't have used his words more. His acceptance and genuine kindness helped seal the crack of uncertainty.

The door opened and Katherine stood in the entryway with her hands on her hips. "What in the world are you two waiting for?"

"I don't have a key?" Eliza twisted a strand of hair around her index finger and drew her bottom lip between her teeth.

Katherine shook her head with a bewildered grin and walked slowly out onto the steps, curling a finger towards her. Eliza uncoiled her hair and stepped towards Katherine. "You've always had a key, Eliza. I know because I put it there."

Eliza looked at Sam and shrugged. Apparently, Eliza was the last to know.

"My keys are in the car with Lake," she disclosed.

"Well that would pose a dilemma, but since I've opened the door and Sam has a key, why don't you come on inside? I've made Lake's favorite cake."

"Carrot?" It probably went without saying. Eliza hated to admit it, but today felt like a day that her favorite cake should be waiting.

"Is there any other?"

Katherine's demure grin could be seen by the light of the large gas lanterns that lined the house and driveway. Eliza walked shyly into the open arms of the woman, who'd for all intents and purposes, cared for her like a mother. Her soft features and silver hair glistened in the glow of the full moon. She was like an amazing fairy godmother. Living in the shadows of the house, taking care of its needs and the needs of its owner. She admired Katherine and Sam. No two people cared more for Lake and she loved them for it.

"This is *your* home, Eliza." Katherine was soft and warm and smelled of cream cheese frosting. Eliza looked up at the beautiful house and wondered if those words were true. They both turned and watched the headlights of her Camry scale the gray driveway. "Come on before he devours that cake and you don't even get a slice." Eliza covered her mouth and giggled, she knew firsthand the power that cake held over Lake.

"The house smells like heaven," said Lake, inhaling the air like it had healing powers. "I can't decide what to do first. Steal a kiss from the most beautiful woman on earth or eat my cake?"

"I think if it were me, I'd go for the girl." Katherine gave Lake a playful whack on his arm. "You are incorrigible."

Lake played the hurt victim, grabbing his arm and rubbing it up and down in a show of cowering defeat. Then with the swiftness of a cat, he picked her up and kissed her quickly on the cheek. "Put me down for crying out loud, or I will really punch you."

"You wouldn't."

"I would, but I don't want to embarrass you. So let me down before you get hurt."

"Thank you for the cake." Lake eased her to her feet and pawed at the sleeves of her sweater, righting his playful mistake.

"You're welcome." Katherine looked to Eliza with an inquiring eye. Eliza sat taller on the kitchen stool. "What's your favorite cake?"

"Strawberry," she said definitively. Katherine and Lake looked at one another with a knowledge she didn't share. Curiosity got the better of her. "What?"

"It was my mother's favorite cake too."

"Oh." She didn't know if that was a good or bad thing, but stood by her response. "It always reminds me of summer and the sun, and the tiny pieces of strawberry in the cream cheese icing seem to melt in your mouth. Plus, it's pink and what girl doesn't love pink?"

"I think we'll keep her." Katherine gave her a loving smile and walked out the door. It warmed her heart to know that the most important people in Lake's world were pulling for her…for them.

"I agree." Lake walked determinedly across the expansive kitchen and settled between Eliza's legs. "They like you."

"I like them too." Heat swept over her face and a grin warmed her cheeks.

"I more than like you. I love you." Her breath escaped with a sigh. Lake ran his thumb along her jaw and her face fell into his gentle touch. She needed him and his love now more than ever.

"I love you too, Lake." She ran her hands over his dress slacks and felt the lean muscular definition of his thighs under the smooth expensive fabric. She could already see the bulge of his thickened arousal protruding from his zippered seam. She looked up at him and grazed her hand across the material that was keeping him from her. "Your cake is waiting."

"It can wait a little longer."

"Oh, but the smell of that cream cheese has to be toying with your nose and stomach," she teased.

"It is, but the thought of eating you for dessert sounds better than that cake." He grabbed her around the hips and lifted her up onto the kitchen counter like a weightless child. She buckled into the death grip he had on the most sensitive spot on her body. "Something wrong?" He drove his thumb into her sides and she wiggled to move from his accosting hand. It was useless, she was trapped. The more she moved the more he claimed the delicate skin. He released her and the fun turned into quiet sensual need.

Lake removed her shoes and clothes methodically slow, taking time to savor each tantalizing inch of her flesh, kissing and caressing her delicately. Goosebumps scored her hot flesh as he touched masterfully like a well-read road map. Desire charged the air like an electrical current.

Eliza leaned up and unbuttoned Lake's shirt, pulling it from his slacks and pushing it over his shoulders until it pooled at the floor with hers. She leaned over and pulled one of his pert brown nipples between her lips, sucking and licking it into tight submission. One, then the other, like they could feed her.

Lake moaned into her hair and pulled her face up to his, needing her eyes. His held the same desperation. His kissed her gently, slowly…meaningfully. "God, I love you. You take my breath away, Eliza."

Her blood ran hot on the inside, but her nervous energy made her flesh cold. Her nipples peaked and tightened with the heat of his gaze. He ran the back of two fingers beneath her chin, slowly down her chest and between her breasts. With one palm on her stomach and one on her back he gently eased her down onto the cold slab. She yearned for his touch so much she didn't fight the icy stone, but gasped when his thumb circled her swollen bud and found the dip of her wet sex. She was saturated with desire, slick with need for her beautiful lover. The man who held her heart despite the day's events.

"I'm dying inside." It didn't feel like a lie – or an exaggeration. She wilted a little today and she needed his love to bring her back to life. "I need you."

"Where do you need me?" He withdrew his thumb and leaned over her body, skimming the wet digit over her lips. The scent of her damp heat lingered at her nose like a rich bouquet. Her stomach quivered with anticipation. Eliza nodded submissively and pulled his fingers into her impatient mouth. She lavished it with her warm tongue, sucking it like she would his hard length. She could feel him grow more rigid between her legs.

"Do you need me here?" He brought his wet finger from her mouth to her chest. Both of his palm seized the swells of flesh that covered her beating heart then made pinching claims of her erect nipples. She arched into his hands, begging for more. Tonight she'd ride the line for pleasure or pain. Eliza clasped her legs around his waist and pulled her hips to his, needing to feel the strength of his tight waist against her heated skin. Her hands rose to touch his perfectly chiseled face. Liquid heat sparked the blue in his eyes and the brown defect called out in subtle perfection.

"Yes. I need you there."

Lake ran his tongue over the crease of her mouth teasingly, tasting her. His thick fingers slipped between the swollen folds of her pussy, dipping and teasing her drenched core. Her spread legs opened farther in invitation. "Oh, sweet, sweet, Eliza," Lake purred, drinking her in. His eyes were like dark pools of desire, casting the azure she loved away, leaving raw lust in its wake. He licked his lips and she chased his tongue with her mouth, seizing it playfully.

"Lake…please."

"E…do you need me there?" He stroked her juice over her clit in methodical circles and she felt the knot of anticipation grip her core with a deep seated pull. Her pussy pulsed in demand.

"Fuck…fuck…fuck…" She no longer cared if she was reprimanded for the word. There was nothing else. Desperation had a hold of her mind and body. Her stomach tightened as the unease of an intense climbing throb settled in her abdomen like the slow roll of thunder. A harsh bolt of lightning couldn't suppress how badly she wanted him to take her. The truth he sought didn't need answering. She needed everything…all of it…all of him.

"I need all of it too, baby. Your mouth, your heart and your pussy. I need *you*, Eliza."

She was slipping into a lustful coma with every sweet stroke. "Please! Oh god...yes, yes, yes." She begged. "No edging, baby. I need to cum."

"I'll give you what you need. No edging…just love."

Lake spread her wide. Wet heat lapped at her clit, circling and sucking greedily, winding her up like a frantic spinning top. When he filled her full with three claiming fingers, she cried out in ecstasy. The friction of each deep thrust and his lavishing tongue split Eliza in two.

"Oh, Lake…!"

"That's it, my beautiful girl." Lake's hand and mouth continued the onslaught of passionate torture. "Let go, baby…give me more…" With his words, she came again. Her thighs cramped and she arched off the hard granite into the stabbing pleasure of his fingers as they drained her.

Lake's voice was muffled behind her own labored pants. Blood filtered through her ears like the ocean crashing against the surf, drowning him out. Her stomach felt like it was on fire. Her body was his to wield – edging, multiple orgasms, female ejaculation and the seduction of her forbidden hole. The verboten place that she would never have given to another. She had never known such pleasure.

Needless to say, Eliza no longer identified herself as vanilla. Lake had expanded her sexual world so much she'd long forgotten her inhibitions and craved the way he'd fuck her senseless one minute then make love to her the next. If she was honest, he owned her body from the very night he bestowed her with such a powerful orgasm that she actually came on his Brioni shirt. He promised her a climax so profound that she would cry…she had. She'd yearn for his cock so badly she'd beg…she had, desperately, nightly. He said he'd fuck her so good she'd fall in love with him. She did love him. No one had ever penetrated her heart with such overwhelming intensity. But what he didn't understand was that it was never the fucking. It was his heart and soul that claimed her more and more every day. The way his liquid blue eyes seduced her, mesmerized her and stripped her bare. She didn't just crave Lake Mitchell, she wanted to devour his soul, imprison his heart and seize the silken flesh of his exquisite cock as hers and only hers. He wanted control of her will and she'd gladly submit it because she needed his love to sustain her like the air she breathed and the food that nourished her.

"Every one of those belongs to me…you belong to me." Lake kissed the top of her sex then laid his cheek against her trembling abdomen. She buried her fingers in the silky brown locks that laid as limp and damp as her used flesh, weaving her nails through his scalp. His moan settled in her stomach and his arms circled her waist.

"Yes, I belong to you." No truer words were ever spoken.

Lake pulled her limp body from the hard surface, nestling her against his muscled chest as he carried her towards their room. She teased the smattering of hair that sprinkled Lake's chest. His lips trailed down the tight chord of her neck and protruding clavicle, sweeping heat against them to the thrilled delight of her pebbled skin. The smooth brush of rich velvet teased her back and legs as he lowered to the bed. Their eyes never faltered as he removed the rest of his clothes. Eliza's stomach felt warm and edgy as the last effects of her orgasms dissolved like fulfilled dreams. She gazed at the sight before her, refined flesh, over striated muscles and the thick rod of manhood she felt finally belonged to her. She was shrouded in the rapture, fueled to want more. He said he wouldn't settle for less than everything. At the time, she found his statement devastating and unattainable. In the end, she wasn't giving him *everything*, she was giving more. Surrender. Complete submission.

Lake wide hands settled around her ribs as he climbed over her as a predator and a lover, spreading her legs farther open with his knees. Yearning simmered from his eyes like a striking match, blazing hot. He angled his head and captured her mouth with the most hedonistic kiss she'd ever known. She could taste the scotch intermingled with the musk of her sex as his tongue swept through her mouth like a tidal wave of pent up lust.

"I need you to know how much I love you, Eliza."

"I know," she resolved in words. "I love you just as much…maybe more. I should have said it sooner. I was scared." Her heart swelled with a flood of emotions and tears pooled at the corner of her eyes.

"Shhhh…" Lake seized her mouth once more, swallowing each soft whimper.

"Make love to me." Her heart and soul were encapsulated, wrapped up tight in another's. Lake's power over her was like nothing she'd ever known. She could see her entire life in the rolling sea of his eyes. He didn't reply aloud to her request but brought his hands up, using one to steady the weight of his body, and the other to grab his rock hard erection. He stroked the silky flesh then teased the head with the sweet nectar of her impatient pussy.

"Open your legs…wide, baby," Lake purred over her.

Her legs spread with his demand and touch. His blue eyes glinted fervently above her, feral and determined. He moved into her painstakingly slow, making sure she felt every erotic inch of his cock as it stretched and filled her body.

"Lake…" His name rolled over her tongue like the slow sip from a rich, dark bourbon – sweet and savory, succulent and smooth.

"Tell me this is what you want…what you need." He pulled out of her slowly then drove back in with the same measured pace. The sexual dance jostled her hips and breasts beneath his immodest eyes. Her body was begging again for its freedom as his thrusts charged quicker and deeper into her sucking core. The pulsing throb held her prisoner beneath him.

"I'll never surrender you to anyone, ever. You belong to me and I'll do everything and anything in my power to cherish what I've been given." The passion filled words and the urgent rock into her hips pushed her past the breaking point of her emotions. Overwrought, hot tears spilled down her temples. She could no longer hold his tender gaze. People killed for this emotion and now she knew why. "Give me your beautiful eyes, sweet girl."

She let the wet flutter of her damp lashes peel back from her cheeks and found the perfect brown stain in the sea of blues that set her body and heart free. He was so stunning it took her breath away. Slow and easy, rough and hard he pumped in and out of her slick channel, his thumb over her pouting clit. The emotional rush that came with the soul branding sent her mind and body reeling. "I'm close," Eliza mumbled against his soft lips. "Please don't stop…please."

"I can feel you claiming me." His words were a strained groan, murmurs of pleasure as he devoured her mouth, sucking and licking with the pace of each forceful stroke. "Take me baby…come with me."

Lake's cock swelled with each slamming thrust into her greedy pussy and they both came undone. Jets of hot cum burst into her pulsing cunt like hot lava, searing and demanding the rest of her. The powerful climax shattered them, body over body, a tangle of hot, damp flesh…panting…moaning.

Eliza cradled him into her arms, caressing his face and showering him with a thousand gentle kisses, unending love and emotion. His lips, his eyes, his chin, his hot moist neck. She couldn't get enough of him. She sighed and continued.

"You're like a dream, sweet and gentle, nurturing and caring. I love it when you kiss me like that." Lake breathed into her hair. "You'll be an excellent mother."

Her body tensed against his. He quickly brought his head up to see her face, gaging her eyes. Her stomach flipped and twisted nervously. "Eliza?"

"Yes," she said, trying to regain her easy post-coital demeanor.

"What about that comment would cause you to tense up? You would absolutely be a great mother. You're extremely loving and kind. Maybe it's an idea you just haven't put too much thought into, which is surprising. I thought it was every girl's dream to be a mother."

Eliza fumbled around for the words, searching for a sentence – anything that wouldn't incriminate her knowledge of a jilted Angel and the fact that she still hadn't started her own period, which now seemed daunting. The Lake above her had all but expressed how he'd love nothing more than to plant his seed in her womb every time they had sex, but she couldn't hide her fears. She just needed to evade and redirect the conversation. "I do think about it. My dreams are bigger than just kids though. I want an honest friendship and love. I want marriage, a career and a family. I've been holding out for all of it…the best."

"As you should…" Lake looked at her, questioning, like he was missing something. He cupped her cheek, circling her ear with his fingers. His caress was so tender she wanted to melt. "You deserve the best, Eliza."

She kissed him softly and circled her nose around his. She needed to escape his eyes. She couldn't breathe. "I need to go potty."

"No." Lake stilled her with the weight of his body. "What you need to do is tell me what *is* going on in that beautiful head of yours."

"Nothing," she lied. "I'm happy. Everything's great." Her smile was genuine. She loved him wholeheartedly.

"What if *I'm* the best?" Lake questioned.

"You *are* the best, Lake." Eliza framed Lake's face with her hands. Her chest was warm and her heart felt full. "I love everything about you. I love that you're demanding. I love that you're gentle and kind. You worship me and make me feel special. I've never loved anyone like I love you. You're incredible. I'm just having a moment."

"Don't take those moments from me. I want to know what you're thinking. How you're feeling. If I've done or said something that makes you uncomfortable, you need to tell me." Lake reached for both of her hands, locking them to his and bringing them over her head to pin her down. She was captured and he was going to make sure she paid attention to every word from his mouth. Her domineering man was never one to back down. "You will be an amazing wife, and a wonderful mother, Eliza. Your friendship knows no bounds. You are an incredible lover that's giving and selfless. I yearn to be with you. I think about you all day long. I can't wait to see you at night and feel sad when you leave in the morning. You can have all the things you want from this life."

"I love you."

His rubbed his nose to hers and kissed her mouth passionately. "Okay, I'll let you go to the bathroom on that, but I think we need to talk more about this 'best' and 'kids' and 'future' thing." He released her hands and moved to let her roll from underneath his body, and slapped her ass as she turned over.

"Ouch!" Eliza shook her head and made a beeline for the bathroom. She had barely escaped with a few choice words and wondered what the hell Angel was talking about. Her stomach soured at the thought of her callous claims. She was anxious to start her menstrual cycle. She didn't want to have to fear his reaction, though it didn't seem plausible. Lake's retreat would crush her soul. She looked up at the ceiling as if she were looking through it to the heavens above. She didn't want to spend her thirtieth birthday pregnant and scared. *Please God!*

Eliza took the opportunity to wash up and brought a warm washcloth out for Lake. He was the master of tender post-coital care. She wanted to reciprocate the gesture. She walked back into the bedroom more composed and stood amazed by the naked Adonis in the bed. He was perfection personified, leaning against the headboard, sexy as fuck, devouring a piece of carrot cake the size of his head. She was fraught with uneasiness and he was clueless and happy. Her heart skipped as he grinned lovingly at her and held out an enormous bite of his beloved dessert. She approached with the steamy hot washcloth. He winked and spread his legs so she could tend to his gorgeous flaccid penis. She shook her head playfully and took the huge bite of cake in her mouth.

"See how good you are at caring for little things…mothering me."

"There's nothing little about the size of your penis," she mumbled around the cake. "Taking care of you makes me happy. You've made your point about being a good candidate for motherhood. I'm flattered by your confidence. When, and if, it ever happens for me, I hope I live up to your cherished words."

"I like everything that you just said. Come here and kiss me."

Eliza dipped her tongue against his and captured the sugary sweetness that coated his mouth. She pulled back and Lake pushed another bite of the succulent dessert into her mouth. "Ummy," she garbled around the forced bite.

"Me or the cake."

"Both." Eliza eased from the side of the bed and turned to walk back to the bathroom.

"Unless I'm crazy, maybe my swimmers are every bit as good as I hoped they'd be."

Eliza's stomach flipped and her heart all but stalled in her chest. She turned around, almost gagging on the cake, and put her hand over her mouth. "I guess we'll know soon." Saliva pooled around the spongy cake, she was going to be sick. She turned with poise and walked back into the bathroom. Gripping the marble vanity, she tipped her head and shut her eyes. She didn't realize she was holding her breath until she couldn't get enough air in her lungs. She was going to hyperventilate if she didn't calm down. Turning her body to the side, she ran her hand over her lean, taut stomach. Could it be possible? Tears pricked the back of her eyes. She looked up at the ceiling to halt the flow.

"Let's talk about it." said Lake. The baritone of Lake's voice made her jump.

"There's nothing to talk about." Her words came out so fast and clipped it sounded dishonest even to her.

"You have an unfilled prescription for birth control in your purse, thank the Lord, and we've been together almost every day for more than a month. I'm not an expert, but I'd say if you don't start your period any day now, we'll absolutely have something to talk about."

"Do you purposely go through my purse? What the hell?"

"I wanted to put money in your wallet and the prescription isn't exactly hidden."

Eliza pushed past him, irritated – out of sorts. Her composure now depleted. "What makes you think I need any money?"

"You may not *need* anything, but I don't ever want you to not have the things you want. I thought about taking a deposit slip out of your checkbook, but I didn't want to make you mad."

Eliza crossed her arms over her naked breasts and glared at Lake. Her jaw was tight and her stomach was in knots. "Do you think your behavior doesn't make me mad?" She held her hands in the air and started shoving at the digits with accusations. "Throwing away my pills in the first place, always going through my things, giving me money, and…and…shit! Now my prescription. Damn it, Lake." She looked down to her nakedness, dejected and apprehensive. "And why are we standing here naked, arguing? This is a ridiculous conversation."

"E." Lake's voice was gentle and calm, a complete contrast to her own.

"Just stop, please." She held up her hands in defeat. She let her shoulders fall and bent over and reached for her knees. This time she might actually be sick. "This day started overwhelming and it appears it will end the same way."

"It started with you telling me that you loved me, finally, which makes it the best day of my life. I am not overwhelmed by anything that's been said since the day I walked into your office. I knew I wanted you then, and I am absolutely sure I want you now. Quit freaking out and get over here."

Eliza didn't move from the proverbial quicksand beneath her feet. The warmth of Lake's flesh sloped over her back and his arms circled her waist. "Just be in love with me."

The heat of Lake's breath tickled her back as he laid his head between her shoulder blades, bringing her back from the self-inflicted despair. "I am in love with you." She reached her arm behind her and buried her hand in his hair. "The cake was good."

"Deflection." Lake moaned, sending vibrations through her back. "Amazing, Dr. Swift."

"It's the best I can do right now. Just hold me and be quiet for a minute."

Lake pulled her impossibly tight, cupping and molding himself to her lean frame as she overcame the emotions that had gripped her in a way that she was no longer willing to talk, and even less willing to listen. She could feel the rise and fall of his chest against her back, soothing and easing her from the anxious state she'd worked herself into. "Do you believe in fate?"

It was a valid, philosophical question, but one that went against the *be quiet* approach she was looking for. It wasn't in him to drop it and she understood from their short history, he'd never relent and never back down from anything he felt strongly about. "Yes."

"Me too." He rested his chin over her shoulder and teased the words into her ear. "I knew the minute I laid eyes on you that you would be mine."

"Even when I rejected you?"

"Then and now. Stand up and look at me." Straightening, she turned into his arms. Lake was radiating with love. It was palpable –

tangible. "You are an incredible gift. I promise I won't take it for granted."

Eliza's chest blossomed. It was like every word from his mouth held some intense meaning. She'd never met a man so extreme in every way. Lake was a balls-to-the-wall dominant man, who knew what he wanted, and never backed down from it.

"Me either." She grabbed his chin and brought his face to hers. "Everything, right?"

"From me, and you…all in." He grazed his lips over hers and placed the soft words *I love you* over her lips. Eliza puddled against him, moaning with joy, at the depth of his emotion.

She was in love, about to be thirty and hadn't started her period. The earth was shattering brightly beneath her. She didn't know the outcome, but it was unstoppable either way.

Chapter Twenty-Seven

Tuesday flew by in a rush…no period! Wednesday the same – still no fucking period! Neither she nor Lake mentioned it. Eliza was days away from thirty and life had become a whirlwind of love, lust, and unknowns.

"Don't work today," said Lake, standing in front of her as she sat on the edge of the bed slipping on her heels. He was halfway dressed for work himself, but looking as forlorn as she felt.

"I wish I didn't have to, but I'm already late. Making love to you is wreaking havoc on my mornings." He smiled and she laughed.

"You keep accosting me. You're insatiable," he chuckled and kneeled down in front of her. "Stay home and I'll make love to you all day."

"Tempting offer, but it's too late to cancel on my patients." She caressed his chin. She hated to let him down, when he'd never asked her to play hooky before. She had more to do today then just work, but she didn't need to get his panties in a wad over it, so she didn't mention it.

"Work-a-holic." He kissed her tenderly and set her free.

Eliza pulled up to her office and sat in the car, staring at the building. She regretted not just calling in and spending the day with Lake. She grabbed her purse from the passenger seat and trudged up the stairs when her phone vibrated from inside her purse. She was surprised to see a text from Nick, asking her to meet for lunch. She didn't know how to respond. She hadn't spoken to Nick for over a week and only occasionally replied to his texts. She grew tired of defending her love for Lake and his jealousy had taken a toll. After Angel's visit, she avoided seeing him altogether.

She knew half the shit that spewed from Angel's lips was bullshit. Half her claims seemed fraudulent at best. She wondered if she and Nick were still seeing each other or if Nick had really cut her off in hopes of securing a future with her. She'd been avoiding her best friend for too long. It was time to clear the air. He could be a part of her life or he could live in the shadows of their friendship. The time for game playing was over. Angel could go fuck herself.

Okay

Plaza III at 12:30

Hell no. Of all the places, he could pick, she knew that would be like walking into the lion's den. Lake, her father, and every successful business person in town ate lunch there. *No. How about Kona?* It was big and discreet. She didn't need the assuming eyes of others making her lunch with Nick something it wasn't. Lake was going to lose his mind when he found out. This was a thin-ice lunch as it was, she didn't need to fuel the flames of the dragon.

See you there. I miss you.

It felt odd to be so cryptic with Nick. Their history was long and loving. They'd been through everything together. *Okay.*

The thought of Nick wanting to make some sort of commitment to her after years and years of friendship saddened her. She had loved him in one sense of the word or another since they were kids. People always assumed they were lovers, not friends. They were inseparable. Even their parents assumed that they'd one day make it a reality. They'd tried on several occasions to be more, but it just never worked and they always fell back into friendship. She hated that he was turning the tables again. She may no longer be an intimate part of his life, but hoped they could still remain friends.

It seemed like the morning came and went. She saw four patients and finished all her charts when she looked up at the clock and realized it was a quarter 'til twelve. Guilt and nervousness overcame her as she grabbed her purse to leave. She decided to text Lake.

I should have taken you up on the offer to bask in your love.

Yes, you should have. No regrets. Many mornings ahead. I'll take a raincheck.

I'll never turn you down again...promise.

I hope that applies to everything and anything!
Scary...it does☺ I love you sooooooo much!
I love you toooooooooo! (Extra o's)

Eliza walked to the hostess stand at the restaurant and spotted Nick waving from the bar. He walked over all smiles and kissed her on the cheek. "Hey, beautiful." They were always affectionate with one another, his kiss wasn't uncommon, but it made her feel edgy. She let it roll off her without saying anything. They were friends that hugged and god forbid kissed, but she knew Lake would lose his mind.

"Hey, you." She smiled.

The familiar scent of Nick's cologne swam across her nose and she fell in-step with him to the table. She slid into the booth and he slid in across from her, grinning mischievously. She was instantly reminded of just how lethal his beauty was. Nick had always been devilishly handsome and whether they were with him as a date or as a friend, women swooned foolishly over him. Eliza had always been no different. Friends or not, she never minded accompanying him anywhere. He was a sight to behold.

"What?" asked Eliza, impatient with his ogling.

"You look sexy as hell." He winked. "It's really nice to see you, E."

"You too. How are you?" His smile fell and the sting of nerves tickled her skin.

"Lonely," he replied.

"You've never been lonely a day in your life, Nick Slade. So don't give me that shit." Eliza tilted her head, let out an exasperated sigh and rolled her eyes. Of all the things Nick might be, that was probably not one of them.

"I want you back." He reached across the table and folded his hand over hers. Sadness caressed her heart and she felt her chest grow tight.

"Why?"

"You belong to me. I love you. I'm such an idiot."

"I wonder if you know what love is." Eliza gave his hand a squeeze and then pulled her hand from the table. "I don't belong to you any more than you belong to me, Nick. There was a time I thought I wanted that love. I would have begged for those words, but we're friends. We've been down this path. It never works. It breaks my heart to hear you say that you love me."

"I'm trying to figure how to navigate without you. We've been a *thing* for so long, it's weird not to be able to see you or talk to you. Despite what you think, I've always loved you. You've been a part of my life forever. I wanted to see if you were happy."

"Listen, Nick…"

He cut her off.

"You don't have to explain anything to me. I can see from the look on your face, how happy you are. You're radiating brighter than the sun. It's blinding to see…it hurts, but I'd never ruin that for you. Lake and I will probably never be friends, but I won't stand in the way of your happiness. I have to admit, I feel incredibly sad and extremely jealous. Since we were kids, you've always felt like *mine*. I guess I just expected that you'd always be there and now that you aren't, it stings."

"Nick…" Her heart was breaking for him. She would always love him…always. She'd be there for him even if it meant having a "come to Jesus" with the love of her life. "I've always been there for you, but I'm not the girl for you." *Either is that bitch Angel!*

"I really wish I could prove to you that I am that guy."

"You and I both know that that train has come and gone. We've been going through this since we were teenagers, trying to make it more than what it was. If it was meant to be, it would have already happened for us. I'm not sad about it anymore. It used to tear me up inside to see you with other women, but I had to let it go. I hope that one day you find someone that makes you quit looking."

"I fucked up taking you to the stupid club. I can hardly wrap my head around you and Lake. I threatened him with his life if he hurt you."

"You did what?"

"If he hurts you or breaks your heart, he'll pay dearly. This isn't some business deal he thinks he can fuck me out of. I know he's backing his dad. He all but told me when we argued about you on the phone. But I love you, Eliza. Maybe not the way you always wanted, and certainly not the way I should have, but no less valid than a lifetime of friendship."

"I don't want to lose you as my friend." Her voice shook and her eyes stung as tears pooled at the edge of her lids. His love was no less valid, and history would keep him in her life. She needed his friendship and would have to find a way to keep it, despite the hatred between Nick and Lake.

"You won't, Eliza. I promise." Nick reached for her hand and this time she gladly handed it over, cradling it in his. "Don't cry, E. I'll fix this. I don't plan on hiding when I want to see my friend. Lake's fiercely protective. If he's half as in love with you as I have been all these years, then he'll lose his mind over us being together. I'll make sure our friendship doesn't hurt your life."

"You don't have to fix anything. I am in love with Lake, but he's not going to keep me from my friends. I'll talk to him."

Chapter Twenty-Eight

Eliza left the restaurant and drove through the plaza to get back to her office. As she turned the corner, she spotted Lake's Lamborghini in front of Hall's Department store. It was as unique and unmistakable as him, both worth staring endlessly at. Lake was running across the street towards the doors of the finest jewelry store in the city. She thought to honk her horn, but was behind two other cars a half block down the road, so she let it go. She watched as he walked into the store. He looked as handsome as she'd left him this morning, tall, dark and sexy as fuck. Her heart warmed at the mere sight of him. A grin spread over her cheeks – he belonged to her and she loved him.

Eliza finished her afternoon on a high note. The patient that challenged her as being sexually educated but socially naïve sat grinning across from her. The one who tipped her off on the existence of The Raven's Nest in the first place. His words had virtually changed her life and without saying as much, she'd grown mentally and physically from the experience. She and Lake snuck in a few times after hours just so she could experience the things that piqued her curiosity, but the real lessons happened at home. Eliza didn't need to be strung up, or tethered to a cross to learn about sex. She was being seduced by the master.

"You seem pleased with yourself today." Eliza jotted down the last of her notes with a subtle knowing grin.

"As do you, Dr. Swift. You seem different."

"Do I?" A genuine warmth settled in her chest. She wouldn't explain that difference, but she knew it was evident. It wasn't just the fact that she being fucked silly, it was because she was in love. "Maybe I am." She set her pen down and offered him a compliment. "You've made some strides yourself."

"I'm trying. I'm still a little deviant." He chuckled and pumped his fingers with air quotes. "But I'm not fucking everything in sight."

"There's something to be said about monogamy. And for the record your behavior wasn't as deviant as it was reckless. I'm glad you're investing in getting to know more of the women you encounter. I assume it's enriching to be able to share more of yourself. You're very successful and attractive."

"Thank you." He leaned forward and looked at her mischievously. "What does a man have to do to get into the good graces of a woman like you?"

"I don't date patients, but I'm flattered." That was the first lie. That was how Lake had come into her life. He may have seen her in his club, but until he walked through her doors, she'd never laid eyes on him. "Besides, I'm taken."

"The good ones always are."

Eliza didn't know who had gotten more out of their session, but was grateful to have the day come to a close. She was eager to get home. She wanted a cold glass of wine and a hot bath, and if she could have both with Lake, even better. She called his phone, but it rolled to voicemail. Within seconds, she got a text.

I'm in a very dull meeting, surround by uptight suited men. Almost done. How's my girl?

Misses her guy! I'm done and headed home.

Our home? He questioned.

Ours as in yours? Yes! She hadn't been back to her loft in days, and that was only to get some things to take back to Lake's

Ours as in ours! She'd been there so often it did feel like hers.

I need a hot bath and wine.

Yes, to the bath, but no alcohol for you.

She didn't reply.

It's time to face the music sweet girl. I love you!!!!!!

She understood the jest of his text. She swallowed hard and looked at her slender frame and flat stomach. She wondered if it was really true. Was she pregnant or not? Still no period. She had already stopped at the drugstore on the way back from lunch and bought not one, but four different brands of home pregnancy tests. It was time to quit dancing around the subject. She was praying for four negatives, but the reality of four positives didn't seem so unbelievable anymore. She smoothed her hand across her abdomen and the warmth seeped beneath her dress.

I love you too.

She pulled up to Lake's house and watched a cheerful Katherine wave from the back door. She had really come to love Katherine and Sam. They were family. She grabbed her purse and bag of pregnancy kits and greeted Kathrine in the kitchen. "Good evening." She tucked the bag under her arm. "I'll be right back."

"Sure, honey. Take your time."

She knew she needed to hide the boxes from Lake, nothing was sacred or off limits to him. He was the master of discovery. She didn't want to take any chances and dug down to the bottom of her panty drawer, tucking them away under the mound of fine lace and satin. She'd find out first and then deal with the fallout one way or the other. She shut the drawer and sighed. Her hands trembled. She rubbed them together, warming them before heading back to the kitchen.

The smell of garlic filled the air making her stomach grumble loudly. At the stove, Eliza leaned over Katherine's should and watched as the older woman stirred the thick red tomato sauce. "Wow! What are you cooking?"

"Lasagna, Caesar salad, garlic bread, and tiramisu."

Eliza wrapped Katherine into a warm embrace. "You're the best. I feel so spoiled."

"I'm glad. It makes me happy to spoil you. Lake is like my son and you feel like a daughter to me. You're good for him, Eliza." A rosy flush warmed Katherine's features. "I've worked for Lake and his family for a very long time. His mother would have adored you. Lake's never been more settled or happy in his whole life. He's usually busy, gone and stressed out. Now he's under this roof more and we all know it's because of you." Katherine grabbed Eliza's hand and pulled it to her warm, soft cheek. Eliza's own mother wasn't as compassionate. She smiled tenderly at the mother figure who'd shown her such kindness and care. "Lake's excited about your birthday."

Eliza let out a chuckling-groan. "I know. A little too excited." Katherine dropped her hand from her cheek, but still held onto her by the fingers.

"Let him fawn over you a bit. It's good for him."

"Maybe a little fawning won't hurt." Anticipation swirled in her belly. She was up for a little spoiling. "Thank you for being so kind to me. I feel lucky to be a part of Lake's life. I adore you and Sam just as much."

"We both feel the same." Her genuine smile warmed Eliza's heart. Katherine needed to spend time with Sylvia Swift. The softening of her hardened shell would be a welcomed change.

"I am dying for a hot bath," said Eliza with an exhausted sigh. "I think I'll escape and do that before dinner. When Lake gets home please let him know where I'm hiding."

"Sure, honey."

Eliza made her way back down the corridor to the master suite. As the water filled she lit the candles around the sunk-in tub that resembled a small pool. It looked so inviting her skin sizzled with eagerness. The scent of vanilla from the candles and the floral of bath salts tickled her nose, easing the tension in her tight muscles. Nothing would complement the moment like a full-bodied glass of wine. She sighed. Four white plastic sticks and hot urine stood between her and a full-bodied Chardonnay. Her fate awaited.

Eliza had to admit how scared she was to know the results. She watched the tub fill with steamy hot water and undressed. She looked at her lean naked body in the mirror and shook her head as she turned to view her side reflection. Her stomach had never looked flatter. As a matter of fact, she looked thinner than she had in a long time. "No fucking way I'm pregnant," she said under her breath. Five weeks with Lake. Five weeks of him coming inside her almost daily. What started as playful banter was now the possible reality awaiting her…awaiting him. "Fuck it!"

Eliza walked back into the bedroom to retrieve the pregnancy tests. It was like walking down a long, cold plank. She'd either sink or swim when she jumped off the end. The idea of being pregnant made her nauseas – petrified. Oddly, she felt a little melancholy about the prospect of delivering the news that she wasn't. She knew, despite Angel's warnings, Lake was excited. There would be no inconclusive results.

The clock read 4:02 as she passed back to the bathroom. She didn't know how much time she had, but ripped through the packaging on all four boxes, extracting each stick and lining them up on the counter like tiny soldiers, each going to war with her mind and body. Her hands were as shaky as a rock skipping over murky water. She grabbed them all at once and bolted to the toilet. When she finished, she wiped them off and rushed over and tossed them beneath her towel. She was going to enjoy her bath before the world came crashing down around her.

Eliza eased her shaky, nerve-riddled body into the warm water. Her stomach was queasy and tight. She swallowed the saliva that pooled in her mouth, threatening to cast the contents of her lunch from her belly. She hit the button on the remote next to the tub, and the bluesy melodic voice of Amy Winehouse echoed through the large marble room. Eliza took a slow languid breath, shut her eyes and slid beneath the water. The world around her became muffled and faint, the music, no more than a ghostly rhythm above her. A million thoughts trampled her mind. She was on the cusp of thirty, she was in love and right outside the tub were four plastic sticks that could potentially change her life forever. She opened her eyes. Lake stood above her looking down into the tub at her submerged figure. She flew up to the top with lightning speed and gasped for breath, sucking in water like she'd been water-boarded, gagging uncontrollably. "Holy shit!"

Lake jumped back as the water splashed over the side of the tub, laughing nervously while she floundered in the water like an idiot. "I'm sorry. I didn't mean to scare you."

She tried to hide her panic, but she was panting and coughing. Her skin heated. The tests were under her towel and four ripped open boxes were hidden under her dress on the vanity across the room. *Think. Think. Think.*

"You okay, babe?" Lake asked.

"I'm good." The water settled back around her and she worked to regain her breath. "Sorry, I just didn't expect to see you above me when I opened my eyes."

Lake leaned down and put his hand on the back of her wet head, pulling her into a sweet, affectionate kiss. "I missed you. Do you have room in there for me?

"I absolutely do. Would you go get me a glass of water first? I'm thirsty."

"Sure." Lake gave her another kiss then shook his fingers playfully in her wet hair before releasing her. "Sorry I startled you," he repeated. She listened as his footsteps grew distant and he left the room.

She looked at the ceiling in silent prayer, it was the second time today. This praying thing was becoming a habit. She'd never needed as much divine help in her whole life. With the quickness of a leopard on the hunt, Eliza hurdled out of the bathtub, slopping more water onto the floor. Time was critical. She threw her dress aside and wrestled the boxes sloppily into her arms, pamphlet's and fragments of cardboard spilled to the floor. "Fuck! Fuck! Fuck!" She frantically scrambled and picked everything up. She turned in circles. Where…where…where? Her eyes jetted haphazardly around the room. Without another thought she opened the vanity doors and tossed the boxes in one after the other. Shit flew this way and that, but she didn't give a shit. She raced across the marble, skidding to an abrupt halt at her towel. With her head turned, purposefully, she threw them in with the boxes.

She knew her behavior was ridiculous, but it didn't keep her from acting, and acting fast. She couldn't know the truth…not right now…her emotions would be a screenplay, dramatic and readable. The heavy steps of Lake's gait echoed loudly. Panicked, she twisted around to get back to the tub, but slipped, legs and limbs flying out from under her. With a thud she was on her back, blinking at the ceiling. She couldn't breathe. The air ripped from her lungs. "Shhhiii...," she gurgled, gasping.

Her pulse revved up as footsteps raced towards her. She wanted to slither away across the floor or curl into a ball, but she couldn't do either. It was taking all her effort to get her lungs to work. She was surely dying. Embarrassment and fear gripped her like the grim reaper calling her home as Lake fell to his knees and scooped up her wet body onto his fabulous, custom suit. "Oh, my god, Eliza. Jesus Christ! What the hell happened? Are you alright?"

His beautiful blue eyes washed over her body frantically then found her face. And finally she was able to take a breath. Tears sprang to her eyes. She was an utter fucking mess. Her back hurt from the impact with the floor. But worse, the agony of what she was hiding made her heart hurt too. She drew her body closer against his and buried her head into his neck, inhaling the rich remnants of lingering soap, cologne, and pure masculinity. "Answer me, Eliza. Are you hurt anywhere?"

"I…" She took in another shuddering breath. "I think I'm okay. My back smarts a little."

The tension in his muscles eased at her admission. He was frightened.

"Baby girl, what were you doing?"

Her throat tightened. She couldn't answer. She just shook her head, spilling more of her dampness over him. She leaned over and kissed the side of his jaw.

"You're back, huh? Warm water should help that." He shook his head at her and sighed. His body shifted as he toed off his shoes. He adjusted her in his arms. She was waiting for him to ease her back into the water when she felt him lift up onto one leg and step into the water fully dressed.

"Oh my God! What are you doing?"

"Taking a bath with the love of my life."

That set her off to crying again. Her emotions seemed to have jumped off a cliff, leaving her a husked out shell. "I've. Gotten. You. Wet…" She whimpered between each word.

"You think I give a shit about this stupid suit?" He kissed her cheek and let her legs down into the warm water so she was standing against him. He held onto her, hugging her tight. Her nipples were tender little buds from the slice of cold air that caressed her frigid skin. They rubbed painfully across the smooth, rich fabric of his jacket. "It's a crime to look so beautiful. I can't think straight. You're like a stamp on my brain and heart. There's no way around my feelings. I love you." He lifted a wet strand of hair from her face. "God…please tell me you feel the same way I do."

She started to nod, started to speak, but he sealed her into a hypnotic kiss. His hands were buried in her hair, threading and weaving like his tongue. The passionate, tantalizing dance of a claiming kiss. "Yes," she whispered against his sensual lips. "I'm lost in you."

Was it even possible to love someone like this? Neither of them moved. They just stared at one another, seeking each other's understanding that this was bigger than the both of them – intense, real. Like the air, food and water it took to merely exist…it was *everything*. Eliza was the first to move, never breaking eye contact with him. She wanted to remove his half-soaked clothes. What lied beneath was so much better.

She pushed his jacket off his shoulders and arms, and tossed it aside, then she slowly unbuttoned his damp dress shirt. The wet fabric pressed tantalizingly over his physique. She fingered the faint soft hair that sprinkled the dip between his breasts. This sight of pert tan nipples made her mouth water. She pushed his shirt over his shoulders and tossed onto the damp pile of mixed fabric. Her heart was beating in tempo with her breathing, calm and unhurried.

"May I roam?" Eliza ran her fingers over the knotted flesh that secured his tight abdominal muscles like a glove. She skimmed the waist band of his slacks and an easy moan perched from his throat. A playful echo that delighted her ears.

"Please do." Lake's full toothy smile hit her like a blinding ray of sun. She happily soaked it up. This beautiful man loved her. *This beautiful man could have gotten her pregnant.*

She finally had him completely naked. It always took her breath away just seeing his exquisite male form. He was a chiseled god, sexy and potent in every way. His cock sloping left, hard and ready – glorious. "Beautiful."

"Now what?" Lake teased.

Eliza didn't answer with words. She ran her fingers through the dark prairie of curls that hugged his pubic bone, teasing, but not touching his rigid staff. Lake giggled and threw his head back. It was beautiful to hear him laugh. She feathered the patch again and got the same response.

"Was that a giggle?"

"Oddly enough, I think it was." His smile was infectious. "That tickles."

He ran his finger over her forehead and pushed her hair behind her ear. Her head followed, leaning into his hand, kissing his wrist. Every touch by him felt sensual. She wondered if he could see her melting.

His thumb slowly slid under her chin, down her neck and chest. Running a smooth line down her torso. Her stomach drew in as he circled her belly button. He was watching her eyes as he rested his palm on her abdomen. The message wasn't lost on her.

"I love you, Eliza Swift."

"I love you too, Lake Mitchell."

His words felt like a decree. He was telling her, without words, he thought she was pregnant and he wasn't scared of it. It was a "no matter what" statement. This man wasn't a runner.

Eliza eased down into the hot water, to her knees and ran her tongue along the full belly of his erection. Sucking the tip and collecting the sweet nectar of his pre-cum. Her want for him was like a hunger she had never known. She watched his eyes roam over her as she grabbed him tightly with her hand and took him fully between her lips.

"Baby..." Lake moaned.

He ran his fingers through her hair and watched as she worked his tight, silky flesh with her hands and mouth, drawing him out and feeling him grow with every stroke. She worked every solid inch of him until his legs grew stiff. She knew his body like her own. He was about to come undone.

"Jesus, E...I'm there, baby." She slid him out of her mouth and with the plunge of her circled fist, white hot cum scored her breasts. His breathing was dense. His stomach tight as he pumped out every last drop. Lake dropped to his knees and met her in the fragrant water. His hands framed her face, his eyes an unmoving gaze, reaching for her soul. It shattered her senses and the rush of a million butterflies attacked her belly. There wasn't a woman alive who didn't want a man to hold her face in just that way. He kissed her, over and over, and she melted into him like warm chocolate.

"You're mine."

"In every way," she whispered.

Lake leaned over and grabbed the towel from the side of the tub and drug it over her chest, wiping the slick stain from her breasts. Eliza sighed, grateful for the bruising she was sure already knotted her back, that the four fateful tests didn't go skidding across the floor.

Eliza leaned back against the slope of the tub and pulled him down between her legs. His body felt soft and silky against her stomach and legs. The buoyancy of the water held his weight. She laced her arms beneath his and pulled him closer. He rested his chin below her breasts and smiled happily.

"So tell me why you were out of the tub. It scared the shit out of me when I heard you come crashing down in here. You could have cracked your head open on the marble floor, silly."

"I…" she hesitated. "I had to pee."

"Next time just pee in the tub."

"Ewwww." She grimaced and teased his hair playfully. "Absolutely not."

"Okay, maybe not, but next time it might be a good idea to wipe your feet and wrap yourself in a towel."

"You got it." Eliza smiled, knowing she'd just dodged a bullet.

They both took turns bathing one another, talking about their day and simply sharing in each other's lives. It was easy and comfortable to be in the presence of one another. One minute it was serious and the next Lake was making her laugh deliriously. He was the perfect mix of all things male, but with surprising sensitivity.

Eliza dried off and got into a satin and lace nightgown that Lake had laid on the bed. It was beautiful and skimmed her flesh. She was more of a tee shirt kind of girl but understood how much he loved to wallow in the sight of her. This luxurious nighty amped that vision up tenfold. She was smoothing on her favorite perfumed lotion when Lake walked in with a huge tray of food, all the fare that Katherine had cooked earlier.

"Let's hang out and eat in bed."

"Sounds wonderful." Her belly grumbled and her mouth watered at the smell and display of food. She was famished. She hadn't eaten since meeting Nick for lunch and didn't have much there because of the emotional angst. She needed to tell Lake about meeting Nick, but tonight wasn't the night to bring it up. Tonight she needed the warmth of his love, not an argument. She had four sticks to worry about and that was enough to deal with for one night. Her destiny awaited.

The night finished with Lake devouring an enormous piece of tiramisu while Eliza dozed off with her head in his lap. The petting stroke of his hand took her under. Before she knew it the lights were out and Lake was curled against her back, his arm over her waist and his hand smoothing the silk against her tummy. She fell asleep to the gentle rhythm of his breathing.

Eliza rolled over. The inky blackness of the room was taunted by the red glow of numbers on Lake's nightstand. It was a little after three. She stared at the ceiling and contemplated whether to move from the warmth of Lake or ease from his arm and go look at the stupid tests. Curiosity won, and she slowly slid from the bed. Lake's arm dropped from her waist, but he didn't wake. She held her breath and moved stealthily into the dark bathroom. She eased the door shut and decided to turn on the light farthest away.

She crouched down and quietly peeled back the vanity door. The subtle screech of the hinge caused her as much panic as the contents inside. Her stomach fisted like a vice and her heart rate soared. She'd have a heart attack before she even got to the big reveal. Holy hell she was scared to death. She reached into the darkened space and fought with box after box trying to get to the four tests interwoven with the mess she created. She finally found the first small plastic stick and pulled it out. Eliza looked up to the ceiling nervously, hoping for another miracle, and then looked down at a very stark plus sign.

Panic seared her entire body. Her eyes went wide. She clamped her hand over her mouth and dropped the stick to the floor, letting it rattle on floor. Heart pounding, she grabbed stick two – positive, stick three and four the same. Tears spilled like flashes of heat against her cheeks, sluicing between her hands, salting her quivering lips. A whimper escaped her throat like the desperate croak of someone's last breath. She looked up and closed her eyes as tears poured down her temples at an unstoppable rate. She felt guilty for hoping for different results, when being pregnant was the miracle. Woman all over the world wanted this very thing and couldn't have it, and here she was kneeling on the cold marble floor crying her ass off.

She loved Lake and knew he'd make a wonderful father. She'd already put to bed the idea of him being a runner, but she was scared – truly scared. She wanted this baby, but it was just too soon, too much pressure for such a new relationship. Eliza was scared that despite their love that it would tear them apart. Lake wanting it and getting it were two totally different things. The idea of telling him made her chest feel like it was going to cave in.

She gathered the sticks and shoved them back into the cabinet. So overwhelmed, she crumbled onto the floor, lifeless, weeping between secured lips. She was losing it, her body heaving beneath her as she cried, alone. Her nose was running sloppily down her cheek, but she didn't remove her hand from her mouth to wipe it. She tried to steady her breathing, but it was one of those times, she just wanted to let it all out and sob the angst from her heart and head. She'd never felt more worried, or stunned. The cold marble cradled her frail body for what seemed like forever until mental exhaustion claimed her and the darkness took over.

"Babe…Eliza." His voice…the vibrations of his feet padding across the floor and the beam of light caused her eyes to flutter open. Her hair was matted to the side of her face and her skin felt as chilled as meat hanging from a hook in a frozen locker. She didn't know what time it was or how long she'd been on the floor, but was afraid of what Lake would see if he looked deep enough into her eyes.

He stroked a warm hand over her pebbled flesh and she didn't even move, dead from the exhaustion of her reality. "What the hell are you doing on the freezing floor?"

Eliza rolled onto her back and looked into his concerned blue eyes. She desperately wanted to voice the truth, but the words were like lead in her throat. "I felt sick. I thought if I just laid down for a second, it would go away. I didn't mean to fall asleep."

"Come here. You are worrying me sick with this evasive shit. This ends tomorrow." Lake pulled her up into his arms and carried her back to the bed. "We need to find out if you're pregnant."

It was her window…her opening and she didn't utter a word. She already knew the answer to his question, but didn't have the guts to give him that knowledge.

"Tomorrow, E. No more waiting, no more denying." He took her to his side of the bed and tucked her under the covers, sliding behind her and cradling his warmth over her like a heated blanket. "I love you."

"I love you too."

Chapter Twenty-Nine

Eliza woke like a cat cocooned in the warmth of the billowy covers, stretching her achy limbs. As if the slip on the marble wasn't enough, sleeping on it was one more taste of hell. She pulled Lake's pillow over her head and buried her face into the cotton, inhaling all the scents she loved, laundry detergent, shampoo and aftershave. All things Lake Mitchell. She eased from the darkness to the bright sun, fighting to get through the crack of the heavy lined drapes that puddled beneath the window sill. She rolled over and gasped at the clock. It was nine-forty. She threw the covers back and lept from the bed. As quickly as she did, she flopped back onto the mattress, bouncing lifelessly. A million emotions imprisoned her. Being late for work didn't even seem to matter. She needed a moment to take it all in. She laid there a good ten minutes and decided that everyone deserved to play hooky at least once in their life. Today was her day. She wondered if Molly had called in a panic. Eliza never missed work. Her phone was in the foyer. She needed to call her and tell her to cancel all her appointments for the day. Every one deserved an emergency reprieve from work and today was hers. There was no bigger emergency than finding out you were pregnant and holding that secret dormant like a festering zit that needed to be expelled.

She put her forearms over her head and thought about the four positive pregnancy tests in the bathroom. When was she going to tell Lake? How was she going to tell him? "Shit...," she whispered through woven arms. Nausea loomed like a breaching storm. Nerves...more than likely. Pregnancy...a strong possibility.

She put her feet on the floor, nestling her brightly painted toes in the long hairy rug. Lake's voice was barely audible outside the room, but it was him. She knew his voice like her own. She went to the closet to get the silk robe that matched her beautiful nightgown. She cinched it around her waist and started for the door when she heard the rise of his baritone reverberate from down the hall, then to her surprise it was followed by the shrilling growl of a female. The voice was unmistakable. Eliza's heart dropped to her stomach and she stopped dead in her tracks. It was Angel and Lake in a very heated argument. Why the fuck was she at their house…on a Friday morning, a work day? Her house – sacred ground. Eliza didn't want to eavesdrop, but the anger burned and sizzled like oil spitting in a pan. She tiptoed into the hall.

"I'm warning you. Don't you ever go to her office again! It was out of line and borders on stalking," Lake seethed.

"Stalking?" Angel yelled back. "Our history is bigger than these little flings of yours."

"Flings?" Lake growled. "You're fucking delusional. Our history was brief and it was over years ago. You and I only have one thing in common, The Raven's Nest. You're my employee, nothing more and nothing less."

"She's just a passing fancy just like the rest."

Eliza rose up her neck with the accusation that she was expendable.

"She's ten times the woman you are, and she doesn't need to manipulate me for my attention. Don't make assumptions about her or presume to know me. You are walking a very thin line, Angel. It's time you get back to Nick or whatever new guy you're fucking."

"I could be fucking you," Angel reached for Lake, but he batted her hand down.

"Don't you fucking touch me. Who do you think you are?"

Absolutely, thought Eliza, never more proud of Lake for not allowing her garish advances.

"You weren't saying that eight weeks ago when I was sucking your dick," she chided. Eliza's stomach lurched. She was going to throw up, right there in the hall while they fought. Neither of them knew that she was glued to the wall at the end of the corridor.

"Nick's still hung up on *your* girl. He claims he's in love with her. As a matter of fact, I believe he tried to sell his love to her just yesterday when they were at lunch together."

Sarcasm dripped from her voice, cutting the air like a knife. Eliza didn't tell Lake about meeting Nick and could see the steam roll over him like a tidal wave. She was going to pay dearly for that discretion. Lake raked his hands through his hair. What a clusterfuck. She felt like a pawn in a triangle of scorned lovers. She wanted to flee back to the bedroom, but decided to face it head on, and walked up the hall, to a pissed Lake and smirking Angel.

"If I'm the topic of the conversation, maybe one of you should have included me." Eliza used a little sarcasm of her own.

"Did you see Nick yesterday?" Lake barked at her like she was a child.

Eliza didn't answer but stared Angel down with hatred and contempt. She was hell-bent on destroying her life by any means possible. It started in her office, planting seeds of doubt and fear and now she was bringing it to her home. She was a threat of the worst kind.

"Answer me!" Lake yelled.

Her fists curled at her sides and her pulse rocketed through the deep vein of her neck. "Are you still fucking her?" Eliza seethed, using his tone against him. "Or is it just her mouth you use?"

Angel cackled at her side, but Eliza didn't even acknowledge her.

Lake's mouth fell then he sighed. "I haven't had sex with her in years. Two months ago, when I was drunk as hell, I woke up in my office at the club with her sucking my dick. I was barely aware of what was happening. I regretted it then and I regret it now."

"Yeah, well I was drunk when you took me home from that fucking club…maybe, I regret that too." Eliza heart cracked. She didn't even mean those words but couldn't fight the bubbling need to hurt Lake. "I need my purse. I have to go to work."

"You aren't going anywhere, Eliza." Though his voice rumbled, the look of fear laced Lake's eyes. She knew it well. She'd been wearing it for days.

"Maybe Nick can soothe your broken heart," Angel hissed with a wicked grin.

Lake's entire body coiled like it took the utmost restraint to remain still. "Angel, I swear to God, one more word out of your fucking mouth and I promise you the wrath of my anger."

Angel didn't stop. "Who do you think is a better lover, Nick or Lake? I'm going with Nick."

On a loud exhale, Lake stalked to the door and flung it open, glaring at Angel. "Get the fuck out!"

"Yeah, it's time for me to leave as well!" Eliza took two steps forward then stopped when Lake's anger took another lash.

"Don't you move another foot god damn it!" Lake's voice cracked and split like shattered glass.

It was complete chaos. No one said a word. It was an emotional time bomb and the fuse was running out on all of them. Eliza tried to contain her anger, but it was bubbling up in her like a volcano. "Enough, Lake." She walked past the scene before her and headed towards her purse.

"Eliza, please!"

Lake's voice was imposing but trimmed with sadness. She was so used to bending to his demands, but the fight was gone. She was broken. A day from turning thirty, and pregnant. She continued moving forward until she heard the crow from Angel at her back. She turned quickly and stepped into her face. "Laugh all you want you stupid whore. The jokes on you! Lake doesn't want you and from what I can tell, neither does Nick. Isn't it funny that you knew of my existence and I knew nothing of yours? It's because I mean something. You're the one who's a passing fancy, I assure you. Nick still doesn't mention you. When Lake told me an ex-lover worked for him, he didn't see fit to say it was you. Maybe you're not worth declaring, but I don't really give a shit. I don't know how I got pulled into this cluster-fuck, but you, Nick and Lake can work it out without me."

"Don't you worry, I intend to," Angel replied.

"Coming to our home was the biggest mistake you've ever made." Lake stepped out of the doorway and waited for Angel to leave. His jaw was impossibly tight.

"*Our* home," Angel sauntered past him onto the front step then pointed at him. "No asshole! You were the biggest mistake I ever made."

"Great." Lake stepped back from the door. "I told you that I was putting the club up for sale a week ago, that still holds true. But effective immediately you're fired. I don't want to be associated with you on any level. The Raven's Nest holds no value to me. I got the only thing from it I want. She's my future not that club."

Lake was pointing at Eliza, but she didn't care. He could keep his words. She was numb to anything he had to say. They were all past the point of no return.

"Fuck you, Lake!"

"Bye, Angel." Lake slammed the door and groaned.

Eliza snatched her purse up and turned around to a wall of muscled flesh. The instant invasion of Lake's beautiful scent fanned over her nose. She was shattering into a zillion pieces under his cerulean eyes. "Get out of my way!" She tried to push him aside, but he was like a brick wall, large and unmovable.

"No!" He held her shoulders and stared her down. "What the hell is going on?"

"What the hell is going on?" she repeated. Her voice was unrecognizable – a shrill of fire on her lips and tongue, ready to sear her opponent. "You tell me, Lake." Eliza shrugged Lake's hands off her shoulders like they were embers incinerating her flesh. She tried to side step him, but he moved into her path, blocking her way. Anger flared and like slow moving serpent as harsh words poured from her mouth. "I guess it wasn't an obsession, after all. Maybe you were just getting back at Nick for fucking your ex-girlfriend and apparently fucking her mouth is a favorite pastime of yours. So don't let me stand in the way of progress."

"Now you are really starting to piss me off," Lake stammered between gritted teeth. "Angel and I haven't been together in over two years. I was passed out and woke up to her giving me head. I shouldn't have let it happen, but it did. It was before I ever laid eyes on you, but I'm still sorry. I wish I could take it back. She and Nick can have each other. I don't give a shit about either one of them. But I do give a fuck if my girlfriend is going to lunch with another man behind my back. That I do care about." He took a step back and circled his hand around the nape of his neck stroking it hard. She hated his anger. She hated hers. The earth was dividing, splitting them into two halves when they used to be one. "Maybe Nick's the one who brought you to the club. I thank God every single day for that. Wanting you has nothing to do with a vendetta against him. I don't give a shit who he's screwing. I wanted you from the moment you walked into the room. Nick uses women and that's why I don't like him."

"That's rich coming from a man who owns a virtual brothel," Eliza snapped. She felt like she just kept hitting him with sucker punches, but she was the one being pummeled. She had nothing left but anger.

"I'm in love with you, Eliza. I've never used you and I haven't been dishonest with you since the day we met."

"Maybe these little omissions are just as hurtful." Eliza felt her throat tighten and looked to the ground. "I did see Nick yesterday."

"Why? And why am I hearing about it from that bitch?"

"Yesterday was a whirlwind. Seeing him was insignificant in the grand scheme of things. I needed him to know I was in love with you and that my friendship was all I could ever offer him. I had planned to tell you, I just didn't." Sadness was creeping through the crimson anger that threatened to strangle her. "I'm sorry."

"I don't want you to see Nick anymore."

Eliza stared at Lake and contemplated her next words. She had nothing, and everything left to lose. "Did you get Angel pregnant and then walk away?"

"What?" Lake's eyes narrowed on Eliza like she'd spoken in a foreign language. He shook his head.

"She warned me not to get pregnant because you'd run. It sounded so unlike the man I loved it was hard to swallow. I've been distraught thinking about it. Angel said you walked out on her when she got pregnant."

"Angel said what?" Lake ran his hands through his hair. Utter bafflement settled into his features. "I never got Angel pregnant. That's a fucking lie. Nick got her pregnant. "Honestly, I don't ever think she was pregnant. She wanted to trap someone, anyone. But, I always wore a condom with her and everyone else…"

Eliza cut him off. "But you didn't with me." Her voice cracked and bled. "Why? Why? Why?"

"I don't know, Eliza. I was so into you." Lake's voice sounded pained as he pled his case. Every word more desperate than the last. "I wanted you *so* much, like I've never wanted anyone. When it came down to it, I made a conscious decision not to use one. I wanted it to be real and special with nothing between us. It was pure magic and I don't regret it, but I'm sorry I didn't talk to you about it first. It was selfish." Lake took a step towards her, but she took a step back. Hurt marred his face like a heavy mask.

"Know this," he demanded. "I never walked out on anyone. I wouldn't do that. Oh, my God, that's why you won't find out if you're pregnant. She lied to you and you've been scared ever since. I know you're pregnant. I can feel it in my bones. Eliza I'm madly in love with you. Don't let her fill you with doubt."

"I'm trying, Lake, but it hurts to hear her say that I'm a passing fancy in your life and that you always go back to her. The thought of her touching you…tasting you…having any piece of you, makes me sick. A physical pain that's tearing me up inside. I know it was before you met me, but it doesn't ease the pain. I'm confused and hurt, let down by this whole confusing mess. I told you not to break me. I begged. I feel like a piece of me is dying."

She stepped around Lake, sagging on the inside and out. Tears were coming hard and fast. With a burst of fear and anger Eliza took off running down the hall with Lake chasing after her. She flew into the bedroom, but before she could shut the door he was there, grabbing the back of her robe and pulling her back into his chest. He wrapped his arms around her waist and trembled against her back. The emotional anguish coming off of him was overwhelming.

"I'm so sorry."

"Let go, Lake," she sobbed.

"I'm so, so sorry." He buried his head in between her shoulder blades. The heat of his breath singed her back. The weight of his head was as heavy as her heart. They were both panting under the labored weight of emotions that exposed them like an unfolding nightmare.

"Let go, Lake," she repeated. Her voice was barely audible. Blood was filtering through her ears and throbbing at her temples.

"No," he beseeched. "Please, no."

"Please. Let me go." The threat of puking or passing out was within range. She was weak and washed out, defeated. He pulled her in tighter, afraid to let her go, then undid his arms from the binding cocoon he'd worked to cover her in. She turned around and looked into his desperate eyes. "I need to go."

Eliza rushed into the closet and threw the robe off, letting it pool to the floor like a black shiny oil spill. She pulled on a pair of jeans that hung loose over her hips and waist. She might be pregnant but she was shrinking from the stress. The tee shirt she donned slid smoothly over the silk nighty that still encapsulated her enflamed flesh. She didn't have the wherewithal to take it off. She was suffocating under his stare, his sadness. Her appearance no longer mattered, she just needed to get out of there so she could fall apart. She pushed her feet into her tennis shoes then scrambled for something, anything. She didn't know what she needed. Everything was hers – her life was here. She pushed past Lake to grab her purse. He stood, pale and diminished by the turn of events that were threatening to destroy his life, but Eliza couldn't save him. She needed to save herself.

He reached for her hand, but she denied him that touch. His moan was a cry, like a scared caged animal. "Where are you going?"

"I'm not sure, probably home." She looked away from his eyes because she knew those words would slice him more than all the words before it.

"*This* is your home, Eliza. Don't you fucking run on me. I love you."

His words shrouded her like a leaded net, meant to weigh her down. She went to him and dropped her head against his chest for the barest of moments before she pulled away and walked out the door.

Eliza barely made it out of the driveway when she threw her car into park and had a full-body break down. What a tangled web of lies and deceit? Theirs and now hers. She'd had no less than two openings to tell Lake she was carrying his child and she remained silent on both occasions. She was a coward. Her life was in the house behind her. She said she was going home, but like Lake, she knew it wasn't her home anymore. Going there felt foreign, but she was too distraught to contemplate anything more. She slammed her car into drive and headed towards downtown. She was halfway there when her phone rang. She didn't want to answer it, but had to know if it was Lake. To her disbelief, it was Nick.

She thumbed the screen. "Perfect timing." Eliza couldn't mask the crying and didn't want to. She was distraught.

"What the hell? Eliza…what's going on?" Nick yelled into the receiver.

"Don't yell at me, Nick. I'm so fucking fragile I'm about to fold in on myself." She wept loudly, sadness claimed her heart and soul.

"I fucking hate Lake Mitchell," Nick spat. "I swear to God. I'm going to kill that mother fucker."

"Stop it, Nick!" Her voice quivered and broke.

"Angel called me right after she left Lake's. She said that she told Lake that you and I went to lunch yesterday, that Lake flipped. I can't believe how vindictive and mean she's become. I'm sorry that I told her, E."

"She's a bitch, but her telling Lake isn't something I'm worried about. He was pissed to hear it from her, but you and I are friends. I should have told him, but other shit came up yesterday and I never got to it." The realization of her worst fears were lingering before her. She was losing everything. "Angel said Lake's using me to punish you for fucking her."

"Oh…" Nick's voice dropped an octave. "I've got to admit, at one time I thought that too. But as much as I hate Lake I know it's not true. Angel and I aren't seeing each other anymore. It was never more than casual and mostly sex. The fact that I didn't want to have anything more to do with her, and her knowledge of my love for you, made her insane. When you and Lake started seeing one another, she turned into a jealous lunatic."

"Good god, Nick," she said through tears clogging her throat. "I'm madly in love with him and…" She hesitated then blurted it out. "I. Am. Pregnant." It wasn't even *I'm pregnant*, like a statement. It was *I am pregnant* like it was an unbelievable fact, an unanswered question.

"Fuuccccckkkk nooooooooooo!"

The screech of Nick's voice through the receiver made Eliza shutter and pull over to the side of the street, screeching to a halt before she killed herself, or worse, someone else. "Nick," she breathed with a shattered voice. "Did you get Angel pregnant?"

"What?" The phone went silent. "Hell no!"

"I swear to God. I don't know fact from fiction anymore. Was it Lake? Was it you? Who ran out on her?" questioned Eliza.

"No one ran out on her. She lied to Lake and me. I don't think she ever was pregnant. It was a plot to try and keep two men who didn't want to have anything to do with her anymore. Lake and I have hated each other ever since because we both believed something I don't think was ever true. Did he say he didn't want *your* baby?"

"Leave it alone, Nick." Eliza didn't want to tell Nick that Lake still didn't even know, and felt worse that Nick was the one that knew first. "We'll work it out."

"I'm going to murder that son-of-a-bitch!" Nick's voice was harsh gravel over smooth vocal chords, thick with hatred and contempt.

"Nick, I'm begging you. As my friend, please leave it alone. I'll figure this out. Angel has been planting seeds of doubt and now I know most of the crap she said is nothing more than lies. I promise you, Lake and I will work it out."

"Can I tell you something?"

"Anything," she whimpered. Eliza put the car in park and dropped her forehead against the steering wheel.

"I wish it was mine, Eliza...ours... you and me."

"Oh, Nick..." Her voice faltered and cracked once more and tears rolled down her cheeks. She'd never known such pain and heartache. "I'll always love you. You know that, right? We've shared a million moments and I won't ever forget one of them. No matter what happens, promise me we'll always be there for each other?"

"God, E, you're breaking my heart."

"I know," she replied honestly. The anguish was tangible. "Call me later and check on me. I'm headed downtown to my place. I need to be alone."

"I don't want you to be alone. Tomorrow's your birthday."

"I know, yippee." Eliza grunt snorted into the phone like an idiot. She was on the verge of a psyche crisis. "I'll be fine, just call me later and make sure I didn't drown in my own tears."

"I love you, E. You know I'm here for you. I'll always be here. I'll never quit loving you."

"I know."

Eliza swiped her thumb across the screen and turned her phone to silent. With a spin of her steering wheel, she put it in drive and pulled back onto the road. She pulled into her unused parking spot and sat in the car. There was a time when she couldn't imagine roaming around Lake's palatial estate, and now her own home seemed unfamiliar. She grabbed her purse and made her way to the door. The keys rattled against the lock as she pushed through. No longer familiar, these were her things. Every definitive piece was chosen by her. It was a shell that once housed her life and now she was a shell in it. She shut the door, dropped her purse and keys to the floor and like a zombie walked across the room and sank onto couch.

The flow of tears seemed never ending. The weight of the world had gotten the better of her. It wasn't long before she cried herself to sleep for the second night in a row. She was living her fears…pregnant, a day from thirty and alone.

Chapter Thirty

Lake stared at the red taillights of Eliza's Camry as it pulled out of the driveway. He wanted to run after her, but didn't. Was it better to give her the space or cage her in? He never wavered on his decisions, but Eliza was different. The more he forced his will on her, the more she retreated. He loved her stubbornness, her will to fight for her beliefs and what she wanted. He prayed with every ounce of his being that it was still him.

Lake slammed the door shut and walked into the bedroom. He was walking past the bed then turned back and fisted the pillow that caressed her beautiful head every night, lifting it to his nose and burying his face in the soft cotton. The scent of her flowery shampoo and perfumed body lotion covered the luxurious linen. It was official, he was losing it. He threw the pillow down and started for the bathroom when his phone rang. He grabbed it urgently, hoping for a miracle and instead found himself staring at the second most hated person on his list – Nick Slade.

"What the fuck do you want?"

"We need to talk, you prick!" Nick yelled.

"Yeah, we do. Stay the fuck away from my fucking girlfriend you asshole!"

"Asshole?" Nick chided. "From the way she was bawling her fucking head off when I just hung up from talking with her, I'd say you're the asshole. I warned you not to hurt her."

"I didn't try to hurt her. Your stupid whore of a girlfriend…"

Nick cut him off. "Cut the shit, Lake. Angel's no more my girlfriend than she is yours."

"Regardless, she's…" Lake stopped his conversation mid-sentence because he heard a knock on the door. He bolted from the bedroom, down the hall and threw open the door, only to feel the crushing blow of a fist ignite his face. He stumbled back, threw his phone down and charged Nick who'd made an unwelcomed appearance at his door. "You made a mistake coming here you piece of shit." Lake hit Nick on the jaw and watched his head fly to the side. Then as he raised his fist again, Nick blocked his punch and pushed him back. Lake fell to the ground and Nick flew on top of him like a steamroller, pushing his back into the hard concrete.

"The only mistake I ever made was bringing her to that goddamn club." Nick and Lake were a tangle of arms and limbs. Lake had his collar fisted at his neck and he had Lake pinned to the driveway. "I knew you would hurt her. I just never thought you'd get her pregnant, and then rip her fucking heart out."

The air in Lake's lungs siphoned out in one fell swoop. His eyes constricted then gaped at his adversary. His stomach dropped into an acidic pool against his spine. He released both hands from Nick's shirt and with the heave of his chest and hips threw him off. He sat up and stared wide-eyed. "What did you just say?" Lake looked at Nick shaking with anger and panic. His stomach lurched and twisted. Sweat dripped down his spine.

"I have never hated anyone as much as I hate you. You're a fucking jerk. You don't deserve Eliza. You never did. I have never heard her cry like that and I've known her all my life." Nick and Lake rolled up from the ground and stood face-to-face. Daggers bled from Nick's eyes. I'll never forgive you if you don't make this right."

Lake held up his hands in surrender. "Did you say pregnant?"

Lake threw his hands to his face and let his head fall back to stare at the heaven's, but his eyes were closed and his heart was hammering in his chest. The idea of fatherhood and the reality that Eliza was actually pregnant snapped at him like a cracking whip. Destiny had come calling. Eliza was pregnant.

"Yeah, dumb-fuck…pregnant." Nick's anger scorched Lake, but they were nothing compared to his words. "Are you stupid?"

Lake dropped his hands to his knees and looked at the ground. It felt like the earth was shaking beneath his feet, a virtual earthquake threatening his life and the life of the woman he loved. His jaw hurt, his shirt and pants were stretched and torn, but all he could do was picture Eliza, crying…broken, hurt and pregnant with his child. "I knew it was true." Lake straightened. "But she didn't tell me."

"Oh…shit!" Nick looked at the sky with his hands buried in his hair and groaned. Anguish covered his face. "I thought you knew."

"Oh my god…" Lake's feet seemed to fly forward on their own accord and without stopping he ran into the house. He barreled down the hall, through the bedroom and into the master bathroom. He stared at the room frenziedly. He didn't know where to start, but it was all coming together. She already knew. "Where god damn it…where?" he yelled. He went to the vanity and pulled out each drawer, pushing and prodding everything, but came up empty handed. He looked in the trash, but still nothing. Then he dropped to his knees and started opening the cabinets. He combed each one thoroughly until he got to the last one. He reached in and found the remnants of two empty boxes and knew he'd hit the mark. He heard Nick walk into the bathroom but didn't acknowledge his presence. He put the two empty boxes on the floor and started pulling out everything, like his life, depended on it, and it did. He grabbed at the first stick and looked at the sign – plus. Then he reached in and gathered up the rest – all positives. Lake fell back onto his calves and stared down at the four life changing pregnancy tests, each one a step closer to the dream of a life he wanted more than anything, with the most perfect woman on earth. He looked over at Nick, who was staring dumbfounded and quiet.

"She didn't tell me," Lake ushered out sadly. "We talked about it last night. I knew she was pregnant. I found her in here lying on the cold marble floor at three o'clock in the morning. She said she was sick."

"Yeah, sick of you," Nick retorted, angrily. "She obviously didn't want it to be true. Four tests seems a bit excessive don't you think? Maybe she didn't tell you because she doesn't want it."

Lake's heart plummeted to his stomach and the flame of ire climbed up his spine. Lake jumped up from the floor and pushed

Nick so hard he fell back against the wall and sank to the floor. "If you say that again I swear I will kill you."

Nick held his hands up in front of Lake. "She loves you," Nick said, getting up. "She's in love with you. That's what she came to tell me yesterday."

"I know." Lake gathered the four tests in his hand and started down the hall. Nick could find his way out. "I've got to find her. I need to bring her home."

"Lake!" Nick yelled after him. Lake turned and stared at him with disapproval. "Give her some time. She didn't tell you...I did."

"Which makes it doubly worse. Why would she tell you and not me? That pisses me off to no end."

"Because she's scared. We're best friends and she needed to tell someone. Can you imagine the heaviness of holding that secret." Nick's shoulder sagged and he sighed. "I know this is hard for you to wrap that tiny brain of yours around, but Eliza and I have pretty much been together in some capacity since we were kids. I don't ever plan to be out of her life. You may have won her heart, but she'll always be my girl."

"The hell she is." Lake leaned back against the hall wall and stared Nick down. "She may have been yours at one time, but she belongs to me. I'm so in love with her it's consuming me. It's you and Angel and all this crap that's fucking her up. I knew she was pregnant, but she just wouldn't discuss it. I wanted her to be pregnant. Hell, I threw her pills away."

"You did what?" Nick started down the hall towards Lake, fury threading his brow. Lake stood ready to kill him if he dared faceoff with him again. "You really are a piece of shit."

Lake looked at the floor and clutched the four sticks to his heart and closed his eyes, guilt replaced his anger.

"I'm in love with her. It was stupid. She was so mad at me. It's one of the few fights we've ever had. Things just moved so quick for us and I think she wasn't able to get back on them until she had her next period, which five and half weeks later, never came. I knew she was pregnant, she did too. But she obviously confirmed it yesterday. That's why I found her on the floor in the middle of the night with swollen eyes and matted hair."

"This is a fucking tragedy."

Lake groaned and angst marred his face. "She was afraid to tell me because Angel filled her head with lies about me running out of her when she was pregnant." Lake slid down the corridor wall into a crouch. Emotions were high. The morning was spiraling out of control. His heart was pounding desperately against his ribcage. The heat of Nick's glare stabbed him. "I never got Angel pregnant." He pointed at Nick. "You did."

"The hell I did," he fumed, defensively. "I used a condom with her every single time."

"So did I." Lake confessed, looking at his fate curled tightly in his fist. "I don't think Angel was ever pregnant."

"I don't think she was either. She manipulated both of us with a lie. Angel is jealous and mean spirited, and gunning for Eliza."

"She better not breathe near Eliza or I'll ruin her." Nick rubbed his chin wearily, staring holes in Lake's flesh. The situation between them was precarious at best. "I put the club up for sale."

"What? Why?"

"For Eliza. I want a life with her, Nick." Lake knew it was the right decision a week ago and more so now. "I don't want it to interfere with her career or our lives together." He held the sticks in the air in front of Nick. "I don't want it to interfere with the lives of my children."

"I know it's extremely profitable, but I totally get it." Nick nodded his silent approval. "You know Eliza would never make you sell it. Her love has no boundaries or limitations. She's fierce when it comes to protecting the people she loves."

"I know, but she means everything to me. Wait here," Lake walked into the master bedroom, then came back with a small leather embossed ring box, *Tivol* was inscribed in gold on the top. He pressed it into Nick's warm palm and watched his fingers curl around it with a sullen face. The knowledge of what rested inside was a heavy pull between them.

"Wow, I'm going to have to say 'no' but I'm flattered." Nick mocked him with a growling-chuckle and a shake of his head.

"Ha, ha, asshole! I was going to ask her to marry me tomorrow night at her birthday dinner. I already asked Halston for her hand in marriage and got his blessing. Now, I'm totally screwed."

Nick eased back the hinged box. His eyes widened in amazement. "Wow! Even I have to admit it's impressive."

"Five carats. She's worth it. I'd give her the world if she let me." The pain in Lake's chest was like a sledgehammer over his heart, chipping away a piece at a time.

"She is worth it." Nick snapped the lid shut and stared at the floor. The air was dense with frustration, sadness and understanding. They both loved Eliza. "What are you going to do?"

"I'm not sure. I'm not supposed to know she's pregnant, but I do." He looked directly at Nick. "I don't offer you much praise, but I admire your chivalry. Thank you for defending her honor. I'm glad you came to kick my ass, or I wouldn't know."

"I would have never betrayed her trust. I thought you knew. She was just so broken. It crushed me."

The word *broken* sliced through Lake like a razor. "I'm fucked either way." Lake tipped his head back and looked up at the ceiling. He needed a miracle. "I don't want her to think I'm asking her to marry me just because she's pregnant. I wanted her the minute I met her. No woman has ever made me feel the way she does. She's the best thing that's ever happened to me. I was going to ask her regardless of her being pregnant or not. I didn't care either way." He looked at Nick who was shifting his feet impatiently. "I just wanted her to be mine."

"Do we really have to talk about this?"

"No. You can and leave."

Nick walked over to Lake and handed him the small black box. "Listen, I'm sorry for hitting you."

"You were fighting for Eliza. I won't fault you for it. I know you're important to her and I'm okay with it. I won't deny her your friendship." Nick looked weary, but it wasn't a trick. If his friendship was true, which Lake believed, he wouldn't make her give it up. They had history. One Lake didn't particularly understand or like, but no less valid. Nick's hand was extended. A peace offering – Lake accepted. "Will you do me a favor?"

"Maybe," Nick said, cautiously.

"Don't tell her you told me. I think it would hurt her. It's possible that I could have stumbled onto those tests, but doubtful. Either way, I'm going to wait for her give me the words."

"Sure."

Lake watched Nick walk down the hall towards the door and his good sense got the better of him. "The American Restaurant tomorrow night at 7:00. I'm sure she'd love to have you there."

"Wonderful," Nick groaned. "As if it couldn't get worse, I have to watch you propose as well."

"Quit being a dick. Do you know how hard it is for me to even invite your stupid ass?"

"You know how hard it is for me to even be here? You're in love with my childhood sweetheart, my best friend. She's carrying your child and you and your father are trying to fuck me out of a company with an undisclosed bid. Now we're supposed to be friends. I know it must be torturous for you to extend the olive branch, but I assure you, it's even harder for me to take it. Eliza's our common thread. I'd do just about anything for her. So ask me again."

"Just be there, asshole."

"You do have a way with words, prick," Nick countered.

"Yeah, well…let's just hope I find the words to save my life before then."

"I can see how much she means to you. You'll find a way."

Lake followed Nick to the door and watched him walk towards his car. So much of his life had been turned over that morning.

Angel, Eliza and now Nick, each a role in the upheaval. One Satan. One the love of his life and the mother of his child. And the other an adversary he suddenly had more understanding and respect for. It was an awkward moment for Lake, but the olive branch was about to grow. "Nick."

Nick turned with his hands in his pockets. "Yeah."

"I'll sell you the club for cheap if you and your dad back out of Star Incorporated. It's my father's deal to get. I was just the financial backing. It's a dinosaur, but he wants it."

"You've always hated your dad."

Lake jiggled the four white sticks in the air. "He adores my soon-to-be bride and he's about to be a grandfather. It's time I make amends."

"You really do want to be a father, don't you?"

Molten lava couldn't have warmed Lake's heart more. "More than you'll ever know."

"I'm glad." Nick smiled. "They want too much for The Star."

"I agree. But if you quit countering we'll have them by the balls. Clubs yours if you want it."

"I'll think about it."

"See you tomorrow night?" Lake questioned.

"Yeah. I'd never miss my girl's birthday party." Nick smirked.

"Cut the shit and get out of my driveway." Lake chided and walked back into the house.

He strolled out onto the patio, inhaling the fresh air like it held magic. The sun warmed his skin. He set the ring and his phone on the table and took a seat. He wanted to jump in his car and defy the laws of traffic to bring Eliza home. He steepled his fingers under his chin and sighed. Would she let him in? Her love for him was true, but she was angry – hurt. Everything felt so tragic. His heart was breaking as precious seconds ticked by. The thought of her all alone, crying and pregnant with his child was the hardest burden he had ever borne.

Yet through the gloom and despair a niggle of happiness encased his heart, grounding him. He was going to be a father.

Lake spent the next several hours on the internet learning anything and everything he could about pregnancy. By the time he was done he felt scared of everything. He wanted to cocoon her for nine months, but he knew he was in for the fight of his life. Eliza was fiercely independent.

Every minute that ticked by without her made Lake's heart ache. For once in his life, he didn't have all the answers. He didn't know what to do or how to fix it. She held his life in her hands…in her uterus. He grabbed his phone and sent one simple message. *I'm yours forever.*

Chapter Thirty-One

Eliza woke up to the corals of pink and orange against the Missouri River. The sunset met the inky water in the distance. She had done more than take a nap, she'd slept. She didn't know too much about pregnancy, but she was sure the side effects included being tired, hungry and emotional. She was covered in spades.

She flattened her hand over her stomach and tried to picture the life that probably resembled little more than an oval seed. Never in a million years would she have dreamed on the eve of her thirtieth birthday that her life would be in such turmoil, messy and out-of-sorts.

Yet…was it really so bad? A baby. Hers and Lake's. She pictured a little boy with Lake's blue eyes or a girl with his thick dark hair and her heart tugged with an emotion so sudden and large, her throat clogged with tears. She pressed down on her stomach as though she could sense the new life inside her, a life suddenly more precious than her own or her own worries.

She rolled onto her side and reached over to the coffee table for her phone. She missed several calls from Nick, Molly and both her parents. She opened the single text from Lake, forgoing all others. *I'm yours forever.*

Eliza's heart shuttered in her chest and her lungs constricted. She was surprised he wasn't beating the door down like a Neanderthal, kick and screaming to be heard, bullying his way into her house and demand his *"everything."* She wanted to run back into his arms and stay engulfed in the safety and security he sheltered her in. The sadness on his face when she walked out the door almost crippled her. She barely made it to her car.

Angel had succeeded in fracturing everyone. Lake, Nick and herself. They were all broken hearts and torn up shards of shattered emotions. Yet Angel had destroyed herself in the process. Lies always surface. No one hides from the truth forever. Angel's tangled web of lies cost her everything. The thought of Lake and Nick investing any emotion or energy into such a wretched woman made her stomach roil and pitch like a tsunami. She might be attractive on the outside, but on the inside there wasn't a redeeming quality. If she ever saw her again, it would be too soon.

She needed to tell Lake she was pregnant. He believed when she was doubtful. No matter what, he deserved the truth. She placed her hand back on her stomach, suddenly feeling very protective. Come what may she was having a baby...Lake's baby. She was almost thirty. It was time. God's plan for her was set and she wouldn't alter it. Without hesitation she sent him a text.

I accept. How long is forever?

His response was immediate. *A lifetime. I'm lost without you. I'm so sorry, Eliza.*

I'm in love with you.

I'm in love with you too. I want to spend the rest of my life living in the wake of your smile, your compassion and love.

You're going to make me cry. Tears slid over the bridge of her nose and dampened the linen fabric of the couch. She and Lake were so profoundly connected in every way, no beginning and no ending, infinite. He was her air, her nourishment. His love fed her soul.

I can't bear to think of you all alone. I miss you.

I don't have any food here. I feel like I'm starving to death.

Come home, E. There's food here. I can take you to dinner?

Eliza hesitated. Spoonful's of extra crunchy peanut butter, while appetizing, wasn't going to cut it. She was scared to face Lake and even more scared not to. *Thinking.*

About food or me?

I'm always thinking about you...you are my nourishment.

My heart is swelling. Please call me. I need to hear your voice.

Eliza didn't respond. She hit his contact and the phone rang, an eager shrill that settled in her chest like a heavy rock. Lake's voice resonated in her ears, familiar and deep. "I love you."

"I know you do. I'm sorry I walked out on you this morning. I was so overwhelmed, Lake. My heart was breaking…for me…for you…for us."

"I know. That's why I didn't force you to stay." Lake's voice seemed so distant, fragile.

"We need to talk." Eliza was walking in the shadow of an unknown fear. She laid her hand over her stomach and scored her lip with her teeth. Fear and anxiety was consuming her. She couldn't go on like this. The secret was too much to endure.

"Yes, we do," Lake replied. "Let me take you to dinner."

"I'm so exhausted." Her head felt like a lead ball and heart felt heavier. "I want pizza and I want you."

"You already have me. My love for you will never waiver. I'd love to eat pizza. My home or yours?" She could hear the sadness in his voice. The idea of her not being there was probably an awful reality. They'd never spent a night apart since the very first night they made love. Five weeks, one day and eighteen hours, together – inseparable. This wasn't her home anymore.

"You know what?"

"What?" His voice was soft and low, unstrained and unhurried.

"This place doesn't feel the same to me as it used to. I've been at your house so much lately that everything seems new and different. It's kind of weird to be sitting among my things and feel out of place."

"I'm sorry. I've been selfish with you. I'll be wherever you want to be, Eliza. I never meant to take you from your things. I just want you to be happy." Lake was one again pleading for forgiveness when he didn't need to. Eliza hated that she'd weakened him in any way.

"I am happy, Lake. I won't deny how heartbroken I was this morning, watching Angel reach out to touch you split me in two. Then acting like you belonged to her in some way was the final blow to my heart. I just couldn't bear it." Fresh tears spilled and her voice cracked. She couldn't suppress the whimpers. "I know you can't change the past. I was wrong for punishing you for it. I didn't mean the things I said."

"Please don't cry…this is killing me, Eliza. I'm so in love with you. I'm sorry I let her into our home. It was the worst mistake of my life. She said she wanted to make an offer to buy the club. Regardless, I should have given you and our home more respect. I'm sorry I was so careless with your heart."

Tears continued pouring down her temples. She couldn't even bring her body to sit up, she lay there lifeless, glued to the couch. "I hate Angel, but I don't want you to sell the club for me." Sobbing ensued and she covered her mouth. She was imploding on herself.

"God, it breaks my heart to hear you cry like that." Lake's voice was pained. "Angel is history. I've already called Robert and he's had the locks changed. Neither of us will ever see that bitch again. I promise. I know I don't have to sell it, but I want to. I'd never let that place hurt your career. It gave me the only thing I'll ever need. It's a part of my past. You're my future, Eliza."

"Come…" It was one simple word. She couldn't give more. Her voice was trapped somewhere behind her flooding heart. She needed his rescuing. She needed his love.

Lake sighed. "I've been sitting in my car this whole time, waiting for you to say that you were coming home or letting me come there. I'm hopeless without you."

"Come give me my *everything*."

"Absolutely." His voice lifted from the pits of the hell they were in. "Pizza?"

"Yes." She sat up and let the dead weight of her legs fall to the floor. "We'll just have to go on one of your hellacious runs tomorrow."

"Sure." His masculine chuckle reverberated through the receiver.

Chapter Thirty-Two

Eliza took a quick shower, hoping to throw some life back into her tired limbs, but failed to do more than get clean. She tossed on loose sweat pants and a tee shirt, let her brightly painted toes rule her feet and left her damp hair loose down her neck and back to dry.

She stepped out onto the balcony and let the darkness of the night take away her fears, but it couldn't alleviate her quaking stomach and trembling hands. She sat down on the lounge chair with her arms clasped tightly around her waist. Her head fell back and eyes closed as the moist breeze skimmed over her exposed skin, leaving a trail of goose bumps. Exhaustion still had a hold on her. Her world had spun off axis, but she was ready to accept the miracle.

She was lucid when the faint roar of a high powered engine grew louder and louder. She didn't have to guess. She could feel him in her bones like a sixth sense. Her eyes fluttered open as the shiny red Ferrari came to a halt in front of her building. She uncurled her knees, pushed off the chair and peered over the rail with her lip tucked tightly between her teeth. Lake stepped out, regal and tall, perfect dark hair, rare eyes and an even more exquisite physique. She wondered if he knew the power he had over her. He said he'd never relinquish her to another and she felt the same. He was hers…only hers. Her heart unfurrowed and bloomed like a beautiful rose. He was simply gorgeous. And the father of her child. A rush of warmth shot straight to her heart. Girl or boy, the life growing inside her had scored an ace in the genetic pool. She gave him a faint wave of her hand and a sincere smile. It was now or never.

Lake stood on the sidewalk, his head tilted back and his arms spread wide in complete surrender. His gaze settled on her like a smoldering flame licking her skin. She cupped her hands over her mouth and stared wide-eyed at the love of her life. Her chest constricted and her eyes started burning with fresh tears. "I love you, Eliza Swift. You are my whole world."

She ran through her condo, threw back the door and shuffled back and forth anxiously on her bare feet as the ding of the elevator chimed like a dinner bell in her ear. Her nourishment was here to feed her heart and soul. He had on dark jeans and a plain white tee shirt. The growth of dark stubble peppered his cheeks and chin, only adding to his incredible sex appeal – as if it could get higher, but it did. Eliza's stomach fluttered with anticipation and when he gave her the full-beam of his smile she literally swooned, pressing her back against the frame of the door for support.

The unstoppable force of nature that made Lake the dominating force in her life swooped over her like a gale of love and adoration. His arms were open, reaching for her. It was her turn to take a leap of faith. She jumped into his arms and wrapped her legs around him. The familiar scent of soap and sandalwood seized her nose. She wove her fingers through the thick silk of his dark hair, tipping his face to hers. His blue eyes were glassy, liquid with tears that made her melt. She claimed his mouth with fervent lips, taking him with a passionate kiss she hoped would show him what words would never say. This was no ordinary love, it was *everything*.

Eliza kissed the tears from Lake's cheek, absorbing the salty moisture like she did his love. They were messy, sniffling and whimpering against one another, but they were one.

"I'm so in love with you, Eliza." Her breath took flight on a cloud of hope.

"I'm crazy in love with you too." She ran her cheek over his and enjoyed the familiar friction. "I missed you."

"Tell me about it. I've been frantic." He kissed her forehead and let her legs drop back down to the floor. His thumbs brushed over her cheeks, and then held her face steady, captivating her with unwavering determination. "No more tears unless they're tears of joy."

She nodded, then went up on her toes to steal another kiss. "I'm sorry I left."

"I'm sorry you felt you had to. Watching you leave almost killed me. I've never felt so distraught in all my life. I will move heaven and earth to make sure that it never happens again."

The chime of the elevator caught their attention and the smell of pizza filtered through the hall. "Oh my god." Eliza inhaled the scent and brushed her hand over her stomach which was growling so loudly it could be heard by both of them.

"Jesus, baby," Lake said, on an exasperated sigh. "Please tell me you've eaten something today…Eliza."

She looked to the floor. "I've literally been asleep since I left your house. I didn't wake up until you got my text. I'm sorry." She didn't know why she was apologizing, but she felt like she needed to.

"No more…you've got eat." He kissed her cheek and handed the deliveryman forty dollars, almost seventeen more than it was worth, but she wasn't arguing.

She grabbed the enormous cardboard box like it was a life preserver, and oddly it felt like one. She wasn't just hungry, she was famished. Her mouth watered with the savory scent. "Let's pig out!"

Lake grinned and waved his hand towards the door. "After you."

Eliza walked hurriedly though the entryway, bypassing the kitchen altogether for the living room. She set the heavy box in the middle of the floor then stood up and brushed a kiss over Lake's cheek. "Have a seat. I'll get us some plates and napkins, and something to drink."

He nodded, toeing off his shoes before kneeling down on the plush rug next to her coffee table. She opened the refrigerator and called across the room. "What do you want to drink? I have beer, water, wine and Coke Zero."

"I'll have a beer"

"Me too," she whispered, wondering how far she could poke the lion. Apparently her hushed tone wasn't soft enough.

"Eliza...!" Lake snapped, with a groan. She peered from behind the refrigerator door and gave him a playful wink.

"Just teasing." She set the drinks on the counter, tossed Lake the roll of paper towels, foregoing the plates, and walked across the room with his beer and her water. It was going to be a long nine months. He was extremely protective of her already, she imagined it was going to get worse.

"Not funny." Eliza knew it must be an act of sheer will that kept him from the discussion of her being pregnant. She wondered how long she'd let her anxiety get the best of her before she blurted it out.

She pushed open the lid on the pizza and the room instantly filled with the delicious smell of Italian meats and vegetables. Her wonderful man had called in the most decadent pizza ever, piled high with everything she loved, savory and big. And she thought she couldn't love him any more than she already did. Her stomach growled with anticipation. She'd never felt so hungry. She breathed in the sent. "Yummy!"

"You're funny."

"It's totally making me happy."

"Ouch! Now I have to compete with pizza."

Eliza leaned over, grabbed Lake by the nape of his neck and pulled his face to hers. "You don't have to compete for me, baby. You said you were mine forever and I accepted."

"Yes, you did." Lake was rubbing his palms over his thighs excitedly, fidgeting and licking his lips. He was staring holes through her, amping up her anxiety. Eliza wondered why his nerves were so out of whack when she was the one with the secret. Heat singed her stomach and a flourish of butterflies fluttered wildly. She needed to eat before she threw up. She reached down and eased a sloppy wedge to her mouth taking a less than classy bite that oozed grease and blood red tomato sauce out of the corner of her mouth. The bite she inhaled kept her from tending to it with her tongue.

Lake rose up on his knees beside her, and with a shaky hand, pulled a small black box from his front pocket. "I know we have a lot to talk about, but I want to go first."

Eliza stopped mid-chew, looked at the box clutched tightly in his hand and then up to his resolute face. He was grinning nervously, eyes soft, staring into hers like they held the world. He had expressed as much…outside. *Oh shit…!* She couldn't believe he was holding his shit together, when she was about to implode. *Holy fucking hell!* She was utterly frozen in the moment. "Lake…" she mumbled around the doughy bite. Tears were already searing the back of her eyes. With trembling hands, she tossed the slice back into the box and covered her mouth. She was trying desperately to swallow, but her throat was tight.

"I love you, Eliza." Lake reached over and gently pulled her hand from her mouth. "I wanted to ask you to marry me tomorrow night at your birthday party, but I don't need to make some huge display of it. Besides, if you turned me down, I'd fall apart in front of everyone." Lake edged closer and laced his fingers into hers.

Eliza coughed as she finally managed to push the food past her esophagus.

"Don't you dare choke on me." He chuckled.

She grabbed her water and took a heaping swallow. "I might choke anyway." She laughed through her tears. Lake leaned over and kissed her gently, thumbing the sauce off the side of her mouth and licking his finger. It was surreal. This…all of it…seemed surreal to Eliza. She wanted to pinch herself, but Lake's touch grounded her to the moment.

"I asked your father for your hand in marriage and I got his blessing, but the only person who can give me the answer I want, is you. You mean the world to me, Eliza. I know it's been a whirlwind love affair, but I've never been surer of anything in my life. You make me want to be a better man. The *forever* I offered you this morning, is something I want more than anything. I want the permanency of knowing that every day I'll get to kiss you when I wake up and again before I go to sleep. Loving you is the greatest thing I've ever done."

Lake opened the box, revealing the most exquisite ring Eliza had ever seen. Her hand instinctively covered her mouth when the emotions became too much and the threat of a whimper scaled her throat. He moved up onto one knee and smiled so brightly she could have basked in the glow for eternity.

"Eliza, will you marry me? I promise to love and cherish you, honor and respect you for the rest of our lives. Spending a lifetime loving you will be the greatest gift I've ever been given. Please…please, say, yes."

Eliza dropped her hand from her mouth and with a smile, nodded her head up and down.

"Is that a yes?"

"Yes," she whispered.

"Oh my god," Lake squealed like a girl, flinging his body over hers. She went down on her back and wrapped him up with her arms and legs. He smothered her with his love and she accepted his weight willingly. She could feel his labored breath, hot and steamy against her cheek, and the hammering of his heart over hers. "Is that a yes?" he repeated, begging her to say it again.

"Yes." She framed his beautiful face with her palms and kissed him over and over, repeating the word for him as well as her. Her future was unfolding before her eyes. "Yes, I'll marry you."

She traced his face with her finger, the slope of his nose, the crease in his forehead that only came out when he was angry or worried, his supple lips that made a perfect heart at the top. He was really hers…only hers…forever hers.

"That was the scariest thing I've ever done." Lake, sighed. He looked at her with profound love in his eyes, glowing warm above her. "I'm so happy you said, yes. I promise you won't regret it. I'm crazy in love with you." He started kissing her wildly, pecking her cheeks, her eyes, her nose, and mouth.

Eliza wrapped her herself tighter to him, like a child clinging on to a parent for security. He wanted to marry her and he didn't even know that she was pregnant. She was more scared than ever to reveal the last bombshell of the day. She didn't even know if she'd be able to find her voice. The last several days had been so tumultuous, and now it was her turn to be scared shitless. She looked into his steady eyes. "I'm crazy in love with you too. I will absolutely be your wife."

Lake took the ring from the box, unwrapped her arm from his waist and slid the platinum and diamond encrusted ring onto her finger. "It looks beautiful on you."

Eliza looked at her finger, completely flabbergasted. The ring was remarkable in every way. The center stone was a large emerald-cut diamond, flanked on each side by triangle diamonds. It had to be five carats or more and sparkled brilliantly in the dim lights of her living room. "It's amazing, baby."

"You're amazing, Eliza. I'm the luckiest man on earth." He brushed his thumb over her bottom lip and her heart skipped a beat. She arched into his mouth, begging for more of the magic she'd come to know and love. His tongue slid across the crease of her lips and she readily gave way to his tender advance. He buried his hand in her hair and pulled her into the sensual familiar dance she'd come to cherish. His kisses were like making love – passionate and sensual.

"It's my turn." She eased out of his kiss and they both sat up. He was staring at her with the anticipation of a child on Christmas morning. She had a feeling he knew what was coming, but regardless she needed to own up to the words. Eliza couldn't let another minute pass without letting him know the real depth of his future. He wasn't just gaining a wife. He was gaining a life.

"Come here." Lake pulled her onto his lap so that she was straddling his thighs, facing him. His blue eyes were tender, compassionate. He was like a calming storm over her fears. Her stomach was gurgling wildly, tight and nervous and her heart was waltzing against her ribs. She felt like she was on the brink of a heart attack. He reached down and grabbed her trembling hands.

"I love you," he said, reassuringly.

"I hope so, because what I have to say may trump you asking me to marry you, if there's such a thing." Her eyes fell to his chest. Lake unclasped his hand from hers and lifted her chin so he could see her eyes, which were once again pooling with tears. She'd never cried so much in all her life.

"Eliza, I'm desperate for these words." He brought her hand to his mouth, kissing her palm then placing it over his beating heart. "Please quit torturing me, baby."

"I'm pregnant." Eliza couldn't hold back the tears in her eyes or the emotions behind those two words. She brought her newly adorned hand over her mouth and let the feelings she'd bottled up finally spill out.

"Oh my god." He tipped his head back and took a deep cathartic breath. "I knew it. I could feel it in my bones…in my heart of hearts. And then…" He glanced away like he was debating how to frame what he said next. "Nick came over to wipe my ass on the floor. It kind of came out."

"What?" Eliza jerked back.

"He didn't mean to." Lake shook his head. "God, I'm defending Nick Slade. It wasn't the ideal way to find out for sure, but the moment I heard, I've never felt such a rush of happiness." He pulled her to him and kissed her sloppy wet lips. "This is the single greatest day of my life. I'm so in love with you. Please don't cry, baby. I couldn't be happier."

"It's not the way we should be starting our lives together. I think it was meant to be a joke when you said your sperm could penetrate my birth control." Eliza giggle-snorted through messy, snotty tears. Even she knew how ridiculous it sounded coming out of her mouth. "I feel like a careless youth and that's not who I am.

I'm sorry." Eliza was pleading for understanding, but Lake put his finger against her mouth to keep her from saying more.

"Stop, Eliza." He wiped the onslaught of tears. "Shhhhh…maybe the first night it was kind of a joke. I'd never been that careless about sex before, but I made a conscious decision not to use a condom. I wanted it to be real. I shouldn't have thrown your pills away. That was wrong of me, so very wrong Eliza. I should never have taken your choices away and I'll never do anything like that again. But after the conversation we had that night, I just couldn't quit thinking how incredible it would be for you to be pregnant with my child. If you would have told me you weren't pregnant, I still would have asked you to marry me. I know you were scared to find out, and even more scared to tell me, but I love you and I'm thrilled at the prospect of being a husband and a father. I'll do my best to be both of those men. You just need to give me the chance to prove it."

"I have no doubt you'll live up to being both of those men. I hope I can do the same."

"I'm confident you'll excel at being my wife and the mother to our child."

"Lake?" Eliza wiped her nose with the back of her sleeve like a child and grinned innocently.

"Yes?"

"I'm so hungry I could eat *you.*" She giggled, laying her forehead on his chest and her hand over the tight bulge of his penis.

His fingers circled the nape of her neck, rubbing and kneading the tight chorded skin. "You might be too ravenous to eat me. I think we'll forgo your favorite cut of meat and just stick to the pizza."

Eliza hugged Lake and their chests bounced playfully against one another as they laughed stupidly. Emotions were high, but she knew his attempt at respite from the seriousness of the night was a relief for both of them. Eliza moved off his legs and Lake pulled the pizza box between them. She collected the half-eaten slice and devoured it, moaning with pleasure as the cheese strung from her mouth. Contentment was the only word she could think of to describe the moment. She was wearing his ring and carrying his child. She couldn't imagine being more fulfilled than she was at that moment. Looks like he was getting his *everything* after all...and then some.

Epilogue

Lake watched as the second love of his life toddled into the closet. One precious little hand clutched her favorite teddy bear while the other reached up in invitation. It wasn't one he'd miss taking.

"Daddeee," she squealed, stomping her little shoes that squeaked like a dog toy over and over to his amusement. Eliza and Lake hated them after the first hour of tortured noise, but she loved them so they tolerated the annoying shrill as she ran through the house.

Lake's heart jerked in his chest and a smile spread across his face. The word never grew old. He reached down and picked up the labor of his love. She was the spitting image of her mother. Today was her first birthday and she couldn't have looked frillier in pink and lace. The sole dark curl on her head was pinned back with a beautiful silk and crystal embellished flower.

"Happy birthday, Gracie-poo." He dipped down and kissed her forehead. She clasped two little pudgy palms on his cheeks and pulled his face down to hers then brushed her little nose around his. His favorite kind of kiss. Lake melted. She puckered her tiny pink lips and he obliged her with a delicate peck. "You look beautiful, baby girl."

"Doesn't she?" Eliza beamed from the doorway, dazzling him with a mega-watt smile. She sauntered over and wrapped her arms around him and Grace. It was the perfect Mitchell sandwich. Lake draped his hand around her back and seized her mouth. She was a knockout in a sweeping black strapless sundress.

"You look beautiful too, momma."

"Beu-ti-ful," Grace uttered between them.

"That's right. You and Mom are the best looking chicks I know."

"Like ticken." Grace smiled and so did Lake.

Eliza giggled and bounced her finger off Grace's nose. "That would be chicken, my love." Lake could see his daughter trying to work the missing consonant out in her head. When she couldn't quite get it, she reached out for Eliza.

"Pay Daddy no attention. He meant to say girls." She took Grace from Lake's arms. "Almost ready?"

He lifted the glass lid on his watch case and plucked a simple gold Cartier from his collection, clasping it on his wrist. "I am now. Who's here?"

It was Grace's big day. The invitations said one o'clock, but it was twelve and already people were making their way into their home. Since his marriage to Eliza and the birth of their daughter, Grace Ellen Mitchell, his mother's namesake, his door seemed to live on its hinges. Life was quiet no more and he couldn't have been more pleased about it.

"Katherine's in her domain putting the finishing touches on the cake and Sam's manning the grill." Eliza poked Lake in the side. "Your job. And your father just arrived. Looking dapper as usual."

"Alone?" Lake questioned.

"No. He brought Sarah." Eliza smiled and kissed his jaw. "That's six months now. Might be something to it."

"Maybe." Lake tilted his head and grinned at his hopeful wife. He didn't want to feed the fire on the personal affairs of his dad, but Eliza was a hopeless romantic. Lake had to agree that it would be nice to see his father settle down and find happiness. Their relationship was on the mend and he'd actually started to enjoy his father's presence in their lives. He'd turned out to be a much better grandfather than dad. Lake was grateful. He'd always hold him accountable for his mistakes, but he'd quit punishing him for them when his father finally broke down and offered him an honest, heartfelt apology for his betrayal and shortcomings.

Lake, Eliza and Grace left the confines of the closet and went to attend to their guests. The house was dripping in pink birthday paraphernalia, signs and streamers, presents stacked upon presents.

Lake had caught hell over the gifts, but he didn't care. It was his daughter's first birthday and he went all out. He'd even gone as far as buying her a little Tiffany bracelet that he had engraved. *Daddy's girl.* Eliza was going to lose her shit over it, but Lake would fuck her back to happy later on. There was more than one way to skin a cat. He spoiled her and he spoiled Grace. It was his favorite past time.

Stepping momentarily away from his girls, Lake crossed the room to shake his father's hand. "Dad." He reached over and gave Sarah a kiss on the cheek. "Sarah. Thank you for coming. Beautiful day for a party. Don't you think?"

"It is." Johnathan Mitchell clutched Lake's shoulder, gave it a squeeze and offered a smile. "You've done good son."

"Yes I have." The glow of genuine pride warmed Lake's chest.

The sun was shining brightly. It was a beautiful spring day. Sam was donning an apron next to the grill, beer in hand, poking at the meat. Lake knew duty was calling. The spread of food was minus the addition of steaks. Lake and Eliza had cut the baby food short when Grace had started grabbing for the real thing. They quickly discovered she was quite the carnivore. Lake couldn't deny how happy it made him to watch her gnaw on tiny cuts of steak with the two tiny rows of sharp teeth – eight in all. So steak it was for her big day.

Lake was about to walk outside when he heard the door open behind him and the tiny squeak of his daughter's shoes padding across the floor.

"Uncul Nickie, Syvi, Paw-paw," Grace cajoled, arms wide.

Nick pushed a giant present into Eliza's hands and rushed Grace, scooping her up and throwing her into the air. She giggled wildly as he did it over and over. "Hey, pretty girl." She wrapped her arms around his neck and gave him a big smooch.

Nick was always a staple in Eliza's life and now his and Grace's too. He'd made good on his word when Nick and his father backed out of Star Incorporated and Lake sold him The Raven's

Nest. At Nick's request, Lake remained a silent partner. They weren't adversaries anymore. They were really good friends, partners in business, and they both loved the same women. In the end Lake couldn't deny he'd misjudged Nick. Which probably had more to do with the conniving of Angel than anything else. Angel had gone MIA after Lake fired her. Not seeing her ever again was no hardship on any of their lives.

Nick reached over and kissed Eliza on the cheek. Lake's chest constricted. He always had to suppress his jealousy where Eliza was concerned, but he knew their love for one another was platonic, based on history and friendship. Lake crossed the room and proffered his hand. "Nick."

"Hey, buddy." Nick set Grace down and shook his hand. "The house smells great. Like cake and steaks."

"Steak," Grace offered the word up with a smile and tugged at Nick's slacks. "Up."

"That's right, baby girl. You're favorite." Nick picked her back up and tickled her under the chin. She went wild, laughing into his teasing finger. Her little diamond encrusted flower danced on her head like a bouncing corsage.

"Yes, Nick, you can help my husband man the grill." Eliza reached up, nestled her hand into the back of Lake's hair and pulled him down by the neck for a kiss. "You'll be rewarded later," she whispered, tickling his ear with the heat of her breath.

His heart bounced greedily and his stomach warmed at the thought. Lake tugged her at the waist and whispered back. "I'm counting on it." She smelled so good and looked so sexy it was all he could do not to escape with her to the bedroom, leaving his beautiful girl and her guests to fend for themselves. "I love you, baby."

"I love you too."

"Umm hum. That's quite enough you two," Sylvia walked around Nick and presented herself. She wasn't missed by either of them, but was long overdue for their attention. Nick took off with Grace and Lake and Eliza edged closer to her parents.

"Sylvia. Always a pleasure." Lake grinned then kissed her on the cheek.

"I know you love her, but you must share her, dear." Sylvia gave him a loving smile and wrapped her daughter up in an amazing display of affection. She'd grown rather warm since rekindling her relationship with Eliza's father. Even surprising them with an impromptu Vegas wedding. Eliza and Lake attended just to see if perhaps they were being punk'd. Ever the snob, Sylvia admitted defeat, but recovered quickly. "Hey mom. Thanks for coming." She let her mother go and swept in to embrace he dad. "Daddy."

"Hey, baby girl. Where do you want us to put the pony your mother bought?"

"What?" Eliza groaned.

His cheeks were brandished red and a smirk pushed at his cheeks when Sylvia playfully palmed his chest. "Good god, Halston. Don't tell her that. I'll never hear the end of it. Besides it's not a pony. It's much smaller."

"Mother…" Eliza warned.

Lake grabbed Eliza's hand in an attempt to diffuse her angst. Sylvia was the queen of everything big. Today would be no different and Lake had a few surprises of his own. He kissed the back of her hand and recognized the glow that reignited her face. "I'm sure whatever it is Grace will love it."

"Yes, she will." Sylvia took flight and Halston shrugged his shoulders and laughed.

"She's your mother, E. You know there's nothing I can do to control her." He held up his palms. "Besides what home can't use a puppy?"

Eliza slapped her hand on her forehead and sighed.

Lake chuckled despite Eliza's clear aversion. "She'll love it."

Lake pulled her into his chest as Halston left to join the others. "It's okay, baby."

"Is it? It's so like my mother to make decisions about our household without asking. She's so…" Eliza was shaking her head, hands on her hips with her bottom lip tucked in between her teeth.

"…Sylvia." Lake used his thumb to gently pull her lip from its tortured imprisonment. "She's always true to herself I'll give her that."

Eliza circled her arms around Lake and pressed her cheek against his chest. He kissed the top of her head, inhaling the floral scent of her shampoo. She'd been a little out of sorts for days. He tipped her head back and gazed at her. "What's up, beautiful?"

She smiled, licking her lips and kissed his chin. "Nothing." She tried to bury her forehead in his shoulder, but he wouldn't let her off the hook. Something was up with his beautiful wife and he was going to get to the bottom of it.

"This isn't about a puppy, E. Give it up, baby."

Eliza laced her fingers between his and pulled him over to the massive pile of gifts, plucking a slender box from the middle. It was oddly wrapped with blue paper instead of the customary pink. She turned and presented it to him.

"For me?" Lake's heart started racing rapidly and his pulse took flight.

"I had to wrap in blue or else I'd never be able to find it in all the others. I was going to wait and give it to you later, but now is as good a time as any." She was blushing and her eyes looked glassy. He wanted to save her, but he didn't know what he was saving her from.

He plucked the gift and unwrapped it. It was a long velvety black jewelry box. He stared at Eliza and gave her a lopsided grin. She was a jumpy ball of nerves in front of him, rubbing her hands over one another. "Bracelet?" he teased.

"Nope," she grinned. "Quit the torture, my love and unhinge the box."

Goose bumps crept over Lake's skin and excitement scaled his spine. "I love you."

"I know you do."

Lake didn't need to open the box. He knew what was inside. He knew Eliza like the back of his hand. She was glowing more than normal, burning bright before him. He could barely keep up with her sex drive and she was fidgety. But to appease his curiosity and to taunt his bride a little more he pushed the top back. His lungs seized and his breath escaped. The smile that spread across his face was so broad it hurt. He held the plastic stick in the air. "Yes?"

"Congratulations Daddy."

And just like that the Mitchell's were four. He swept Eliza into his arms and kissed her with every ounce of love in his body. His heart had never felt fuller. His beautiful wife was pregnant and his family was whole. Lake always thought he would be the one expanding her world, but in the end, the lessons were his. Eliza Swift was his miracle…his teacher…his love.

The End.

Author Biography

Heather Miles has three published books in the Merger Series. MERGER, MERGER UNDONE and MERGER COMPLETE. The complete box set is available on all platforms.

Heather, originally from Kansas City, lives in Cleveland, Mississippi. The heart of the Mississippi Delta and home of the blues. She is married, has two children and two unruly dogs that keep her constantly on the move.

She is a full-time author of contemporary romance. You can follow her by signing up on her website www.heathermiles.net

She is a member of Romance Writers of America, River City Romance Writers, From The Heart Romance Writers, Passionate Ink, Contemporary Romance Writers, and The Independent Author Network.